WITH ONE HAND WAVING FREE

A NOVEL

KEN FULLER

Copyright © 2024 Ken Fuller

All rights reserved

ISBN: 9798878175180

By Ken Fuller

Non-Fiction

Radical Aristocrats: London Busworkers from the 1880s to the 1980s (1985)

Forcing the Pace: The Partido Komunista ng Pilipinas. From Foundation to Armed Struggle (2007)

A Movement Divided: Philippine Communism, 1957-1986 (2011)

The Lost Vision: The Philippine Left: 1986-2010 (2015)

The Long Crisis: Gloria Macapagal Arroyo and Philippine Underdevelopment (2013)

Hardboiled Activist: The Work and Politics of Dashiell Hammett (2017)

Raymond Chandler: The Man Behind the Mask (2020)

Fiction

Foreigners: A Philippine Satire (2019)

Red Button Years trilogy:

Love and Labour (2019)

Romance and Revolution (2020)

Red Button Men (2021)

Journalism

A Mad Desire to Read: Books and Their Authors (2020)

Memoir

Restricted Horizons: Candid Memoirs: Volume 1 (2022)

PART ONE

1

"With the departure of the Portuguese from Mozambique," Joseph Thornton was telling the assembled export staff, "our market there was cut off—or so we assumed at the time. The fact is, however, that our equipment is far superior to anything they might be able to obtain from the Eastern bloc, although hardly as cheap. With the continuing raids into the country by Rhodesia, it is obvious that the market there is quite buoyant—a perusal of the casualty figures is enough to tell us that. I suggest that you, Mr Logan, contact their embassy here and put out some feelers. Our aim should be to have Creighton fly into Lourenco Marques from Dar. And soon."

Formally, he was Joseph Thornton, export manager of Merritt & Thwaite, providers of medical equipment, but it was Major Thornton, former defender of Burma, who was speaking now, directing his small but elite corps of warriors into the various zones of action in his clipped military tone. He thrust out his chin pugnaciously and clasped his hands behind his back. If the army of British industry was on the retreat, he had said a couple of Mondays ago, that was no reason why M & T should conform to the general pattern. We should show the way, blazing a trail into new territories, reconquering old ones taken by the Japanese, the Americans and our erstwhile allies the Europeans. If we must be part of this joint European operation (meaning the European Common Market), he had said as an aside, we should ensure that Britain becomes the HQ. One did not, when all was said and done, assign a leadership role to defeated nations such as France and Germany.

Thornton lowered his noble head with its shock of thick, undulating grey hair as he glanced at his notes, then looked around the boardroom table to locate the Latin American section.

"With the renewed fighting in Central America, it looks as if the rebels might this time be successful. While not communist, they are known to dislike the Americans. Mister Ronald and I think that this situation is not without its positive aspect. They have, after all, promised to develop a health service once they achieve power and, given that such a service is almost non-existent at present, the opportunities for us are both obvious and almost without limit. Perhaps you could see to that, Mr Diego? They have a representative in London, I believe."

"They do indeed, Mr Thornton. A close personal friend of mine, as it happens," replied Patricio Diego, a small lean man of fifty or so rumoured to be of Cuban origin. "And you are perfectly correct: the leadership levels of the rebel forces do not contain any communists, although they are active at the grassroots level, and it would be wrong to write them off. Even if they were to gain the leadership of the movement, though, it would be worthwhile negotiating with them. They, after all, would develop the health service you mention, and probably more extensively that the more moderate elements."

Roger Drummond began to lose interest. Tall and lean with a crop of tightly curled dark brown hair, he eased his chair sideways and stretched his long legs, gazing at the large windows lining the east side of the room. When he had worked at the Acton factory, his workmates had remarked that he bore more than a passing likeness to the actor George Cole, then best-known for his portrayal of Flash Harry in the St Trinian's comedies and therefore earning Drummond his nickname: "Flash." There was, he admitted, a resemblance, particularly when he drew his lips, which were perhaps a little full for his lean face, into a sneer; so he tried not to sneer too often, claiming to new entrants at the factory that he had acquired the sobriquet because of his flashing smile.

Outside, the July sun on this late Monday morning fell upon a panoramic view of the City, the windows of steel and glass office blocks winking through the smoky blue haze. Down in the streets office girls would be scurrying to and fro in their summer frocks with a smile for everyone. Men back from their Mediterranean holidays would sport a healthy bronzed glow above their white collars. He sighed and felt the prison walls of the M & T building close in on him. Why couldn't he be out there, free? Such a day was designed for looking at the girls, not for listening to Yoni (his own nickname for Joseph Thornton) drone on and on. He felt like reaching forward, slapping Diego about the head and telling him not to be so bloody sycophantic.

It was on such a day, some years earlier, that he had met Hilary.

At the time, he had been living in a bedsit in Ladbroke Grove and was on the dole, having been made redundant due to the closure of the factory in Acton where he had worked for the previous three years. Since leaving school with eight O levels and As in English and History, he had gone through a succession of jobs for which he was over-qualified. Being on the dole was, at the age of twenty-four, no great trauma, for the free time enabled him to catch up on his reading and even to write a little, and he was confident of gaining employment as soon as he started seriously looking for it. He had no ties, his parents having moved to Bristol, and no responsibilities.

Then along came Hilary.

Every morning, apart from Mondays, when he had to sign on the dole, he would go to Kensington Gardens to read, sunbathe and look at the girls. It was the first time he had been out of work for more than a few days and he basked in the freedom. He remembered how, when he had been nineteen, he had developed a deep resentment of getting up to go to work, especially in the summer months. Nevertheless, he *had* tried to wake up on time; but the resentment had been so deep as to be psychological, and he quite simply had not heard the alarm clock (which he increased to two after a while) on at least two mornings out of five. As he had been working as a postman at the time, his late arrival had not endeared him to his superiors. And even when he did manage to wake up on time the walk to work had been painful. With the sun just peering over the horizon and the air still fresh and cool, unsullied by too concentrated a dose of petrol fumes, he had felt as if he were dragging himself to prison. He often wondered what it would be like just to sit in one spot and watch the day begin; despite resolutions to do just that on his day off, however, he had always been too tired to make it. Now, with all this time at his disposal, he was able to do exactly that, and several mornings he had taken one of the first 52s from Middle Row garage and travelled to Hyde Park Corner, where he sat on a bench and watched the sky behind the charioteer on Constitution Arch turn first to peach, then to milky blue. At around nine, he would take a bus to Victoria for breakfast in one of the cafes beside the bus station, then return to Hyde Park Corner and walk across into Kensington Gardens, where he would resume his reading.

On the day that Hilary entered his life, he had been reading Dreiser's *An American Tragedy*. While on other days he had divided his time between reading and watching the girls in the hope that one would return his glances, on this day he had given them a miss, having just reached the part where Clyde Griffiths murders Roberta Alden.

He no more than glanced in her direction as she sat down just yards from him. It wasn't until he was getting ready to leave (it was 12.30 and he thought he might slip away for a pint and a ham roll at one of the pubs in Notting Hill Gate, returning, maybe, to fall asleep with the sun on his face) that he noticed her in any real sense. She was of medium height, blond and, he thought at the time, reasonably attractive (in the months to come he would begin to wonder if the adjective "beautiful" might be applied to her; after a few years of marriage, "reasonably attractive" would seem about right). She smiled at him as they exchanged glances. There seemed to be only one thing to do, so he smiled back. But once this was done its inadequacy became immediately apparent, for to walk away would have been taken as a snub. So, pausing at her bench, he had to speak.

"Hello. I've been coming here all week—how come I haven't seen you before?"

She looked up at him and he noticed the trace of down on the side of her face. "It's my day off. I work at Whiteley's, down Queensway." Her smile was really quite pleasant, her teeth strong and white. She wore, as far as he could tell, no makeup apart from eyeliner. "I saw you here last week, though. I was sitting over there, beneath the trees."

It made sense for her to sit in the shade, for today the sun had begun to turn her face pink.

"You seem to like thick books."

He grinned. "Yes. Last week it was *The Titan*. It's the second part of a trilogy by this bloke." He held up *An American Tragedy*. "The whole work's called *A Trilogy of Desire*."

"Sounds spicy."

"It was considered to be at the time it was written. Not now, though. Do you read much?"

"A fair bit. Nothing too heavy though. Are you a student, then?"

"No." He held back on disclosing his employment status. "No, I'm just catching up on my reading."

"Do you hope to get something out of so much reading—apart from just entertainment, I mean?"

"Do you always ask complete strangers what they want out of life?"

She almost blushed and he immediately gained confidence from this, feeling—foolishly, he would later realise—that the situation was completely within his control.

"I actually asked what you wanted out of your reading, but since you mention it, what *do* you want out of life?"

"That's the sort of question," he said, not wanting to prolong her embarrassment, "that a person of twenty would ask—you know, as soon as they realise that life has great possibilities, but before their illusions have been shattered." He offered her his profile in the hope that he looked suitably worldly and philosophical.

"You still haven't answered the question," she said. "Besides, how did you know I was twenty?"

He shrugged. "Wild guess. And to answer your question, I want to 'dance beneath the diamond sky with one hand waving free.'"

"Is that a Beatles song?"

"Dylan."

"Oh."

"Listen, I was just going for a light lunch before the pubs close. Why don't you come?

"I'm not really much of a drinker..."

"You won't have to be—like I say, they'll soon be closing for the afternoon."

"Alright, then."

As she rose to her feet, he saw that her legs, clad in loose-fitting flared denims, promised to be a little on the thick side. Her breasts, however, looked large and firm beneath her checked shirt.

*

It took him three weeks to get her into bed, and it would occur to him in later years, as he began to see the pattern of their relationship more clearly, that this had happened shortly after he had yielded to her advice that he get a job. In fact, it was on the very day that he went to Chiswick to enroll in the London Transport training school that she offered up her virginity.

"I wouldn't do this for anyone, you know," she said afterwards, as he lay with his head cradled in the curve of her neck. "You're special to me, Roger. You know that, don't you?"

To prove just how special he was to her, there was a little patch of blood on the sheet. Yes, she did succeed in making him feel special. He could, after all, do a lot worse than Hilary: she was presentable, knew how to speak without dropping her aitches, could cook, and if she seemed overly eager to conform to social norms he was sure that he would be able to introduce her to a more open-minded approach, given time.

"You know the day we met in the park?" she said slowly, her brow pinched as if she were troubled by a nagging worry.

"Mm."

"What did you mean when you said you wanted to dance beneath the clear blue sky with both hands waving free?"

"*Diamond* sky. *One* hand waving free."

"Alright, but what did you mean by it?"

He sighed, rolling onto his back and reaching for a cigarette. "Oh, it's just that since leaving school five years ago I've held a few jobs that seemed okay at first. They paid the rent and the people were interesting for a while. But after a time they all began to put me to sleep. For instance, the longest I worked in any one place was at that factory in Acton. We used to solder tiny electrical components into some form of apparatus—after three years at the place, that's all I ever understood about the work. Every morning, especially in the summer, I walked down to catch the bus at Ladbroke Grove station and for those few minutes I was glad to be alive. You know how everything smells fresh and alive early on a summer morning? As the bus drove down Cambridge Gardens the trees would scratch at the upstairs windows, weighed down with all that green; and if we stopped at the lights and the windows were open, I might catch a whiff from someone's flowerbed. It felt so good at those moments, but at the same time I knew that I was saying goodbye to it all. The bus was taking me to Acton, where I would be locked up in that bloody factory for the rest of the day.

"And I soon realised that something happened to me inside the factory. I switched off. It was if I were reduced to semi-consciousness as soon as I clocked in. It was the same with everyone else—I could see it, even if some of them couldn't. With the older workers it was even worse because they were asleep even outside of work. You would see them on the bus, reading the *Sun* or the *Mirror* and they were like sleepwalkers. The crappy newspapers they read just reinforced the attitudes that were necessary if they were to spend all day at the bench, their minds switched off. Their attempts at conversation mainly reflected what they had read on the bus: immigration, of course, the too-powerful unions (even though they were all members of one), sex. It was as if they didn't consider what was happening to them worthy of mention. The truth was, of course, that they didn't *know* what was happening to them. There were some exceptions, but they mostly had labels stuck on them: 'crackpot,' 'communist' or whatever.

"Well, I realised what was happening to me. Every day I spent in the factory I was being robbed of my consciousness. As I could see from the size of the cars in the directors' carpark, I was also being robbed of the wealth I produced, although that didn't worry me too much as I could get along on the little they let me keep. But I wasn't going to be a zombie."

"But you stayed there for three years. If the place hadn't closed, you'd probably still be there now."

She was smarter than he thought. "You're right," he admitted, grinding his cigarette out in the ashtray on the bedside table. "But how can you escape? If you want to live, you have to work, and for most people loss of consciousness seems to be a precondition. Anyway, the 'one hand waving free' bit was, I suppose, my romantic way of saying that I wanted to escape all that but didn't know how. If the chance does come, that hand will be both waving goodbye and saying, 'Look, here I am! Over here! I've escaped! I'm free!'"

Her amused smile bore just a tinge of concern. "You are silly," she said softly, in an almost motherly manner she had not shown him before. "Don't you think all those other men were dreaming of escape too? I bet they all did the football pools every week, didn't they?"

"Yes," he agreed amiably. "There was a syndicate at work and some of them filled in their own coupons as well."

"And that was their main hope of escaping. In a way, they were a bit more realistic than you. You just hoped. At least they stood a chance, however small, of coming up on the pools."

"But they were all older than me. When they were my age, they may have just hoped like me. Perhaps they started doing the pools as a desperate *last* hope, when hope alone proved not enough. That's the difference between them and me: I haven't given up hope yet."

"Why is it only one hand waving free? Why not both, if you're really free? What's the other one doing?"

"That's a very good question, Hils." He looked down at her and smiled. "I don't have a clue. Maybe it means we can never be *totally* free. Remind me to ask Mr Dylan next time I see him."

"And another thing: why do you leave me out of this? Don't you think it's the same for me? Do you think I want to spend every day on my feet, dealing with old ladies with their blue rinses and rich Arabs with more money than I can dream of? I felt exactly the same as you just after I started work and the novelty had worn off. Can you honestly believe that I look forward to a lifetime of what I'm doing now? But you have to be realistic, don't you? Like you say, the rent has to be paid. You have to go on doing it while you keep your eyes open for something better."

"That may be fine for you and me," he argued, "but someone, meanwhile, has to do the jobs we want to escape from. The things we want to escape *to*, on the other hand, may be out of reach for most people. Do we leave them there, forget about them, write them off?"

She smiled a tight little smile and, propping herself on one elbow, her generous breasts swinging with her movement, leaned over to kiss him lightly. He noticed a hard glint in her eyes as she said, "Yes, we think about us." That may have given him pause, had he not found his hands on her breasts and his penis stiffening.

*

So, for the next few years they thought about themselves.

At the time, he gave hardly a thought to what was happening to him—that he was allowing Hilary to turn him inwards, to erect a wall between him and the rest of the world. He might have had a fleeting sense of doubt at one point, but this was quickly dismissed. He was like a businessman who suspects that the line of territory into which his partners are leading him is on the wrong side of the legal boundary but who thinks of the glittering material rewards and plunges on, only fully realising the consequences of his action when he faces the judge.

Hilary did provide rewards, material and otherwise.

"Men like this, don't they?" she said when, quite early on, she first gave him a non-material reward.

"I don't know about anyone else," he said, "but it's something I could grow to like."

To earn this particular reward, he had promised that he would stick at his job on the buses. She seemed for some reason to suspect that, given half the chance, he would be back on the dole, although this had never been his way. He did not tell her that he actually liked the job. It was a challenge to take on a busload of commuters at Victoria in the morning and have all the fares collected by the time the bus reached Knightsbridge. As Middle Row garage was one of the oldest in the fleet and lacked the sports and other facilities, even a canteen, enjoyed by others, the manager was canny enough to turn a blind eye to most of the minor breaches of discipline. Had he not done so, attendance at union meetings would have soared and he would have had trouble on his hands. The crews came in all shapes and sizes: drinkers, gamblers, weekend hippies, cricket-playing West Indians, one King Street communist, one Gerry Healey Trotskyite (the apolitical majority could never understand why these two always disagreed at union meetings), a few grey men whose lives revolved around the job, and even one bushy-haired young Irishman with a degree in English.

Yes, he liked the life of the garage even more than the job itself. It may have been when, having initially urged him to stick it out rather than revert to indolence, Hilary began to insist that he give it up that he had the first flash of doubt. Nevertheless, she convinced him that it must be done.

"You can't be serious! Can you honestly see yourself as a bus conductor when you're forty?"

"But the money's not bad. I thought you wanted to save for the deposit on a house. Then there's the free travel pass—if I give up the job, I give that up too. This job at Merritt & Thwaite means a damn long—and expensive—journey every day."

"We've got enough to build on. You'll be making an investment if you move to Merritt & Thwaite now. The money may not be brilliant to start with, but you must look at the potential. With your intelligence, you're bound to move up in no time. Besides, you have to make the move while you're still young. They're not going to take you when you're thirty, are they?"

She had a point. He thought of himself as a bus conductor at forty, fifty, sixty, and shuddered.

"Look, Roger, we'll get the house, start a family and then we'll have everything we need. By that time, you'll have a good position at M & T. You'll have all the time in the world for your books. I'll stay at home and look after the house. We'll go abroad for our holidays. We'll have a good life. It will be *our* life, which no one will be able to touch or take away from us."

In fact, one of the attractions of his current job was that, especially when he was working a late turn, it provided almost as much leisure time as when he'd been on the dole; in addition, every few weeks he would have four consecutive rest-days if he chose to take them rather than working two of them at the overtime rate. But the prospect she portrayed was a warm one: he and Hilary comfortably before the fireside, he reading, she turning the pages of a magazine before coming over to give him his reward for providing all this.

He agreed to give it a try.

"You like this, don't you?" she said later.

This meant a trip down the M4 in a hired car to Reading, where what remained of Hilary's family was located.

Joseph Thornton was a tall man inclined to stoutness and pomposity who chose dark blue suits and ties to complement the grey wavy hair that, he seemed convinced, gave him the aura of the wise, dependable statesman. In his ten years as head of exports he had expanded the firm's business with the former colonial countries, mainly in East and West Africa. He came from Hilary's father's side of the family, fighting for a hold as it slid from the not particularly dizzy heights (in colonial administration before the "winds of change") it had once occupied.

"Roger and I are going to be married, Uncle Joseph," Hilary announced when she succeeded in dragging the lanky bus conductor to the baronial semi-detached along the Burghfield Road on the south-western fringe of the town, "and he really needs a better job. I think he needs something with a future."

Uncle Joe peered over the top of his glasses as he stuffed his pipe. "And you thought that medical equipment might have a future."

"Well, I *was* sort of wondering if there might be something at your firm, yes."

"And what about you, Roger?"

He could see that Uncle Joseph, before he had been called home from Kenya by the Colonial Office, would not have bothered with someone like him. But he could also discern that Joseph had seen the need to adapt to a changing world, so that now he was forcing himself to be polite to him, although he was not conscious of the effort and believed that he was merely treating Drummond as an equal.

"What Hilary says is right, Mr Thornton. I'm looking for something with a future," he said, modifying her statement, although he smiled inwardly as he did so, knowing that her formulation was nearer the truth. This was almost a game as far as he was concerned, after all. Left to his own devices, he would never have dreamed of aiming for such a job, and he had laughed at the idea when Hilary had first raised it. She had been so generous to him later that night, however, that he had agreed to come along to see Uncle Joseph and now he was enjoying it, prepared to bluff and lie and not too worried about the outcome. There was also, he was forced to admit, the fact that he had, over the past few days, caught himself considering the consequences of a favourable result and half-relishing the prospect of the life it might bring after a few years' hard work.

"I realise that I've wasted a good few years since I left school," he continued reflectively. "But, on the other hand, maybe that hasn't been such a bad thing, because at least I *know* that they've been wasted and feel, really *feel*, at last, that I have to do something with my life."

"Don't quite follow you, old son," said Uncle Joseph, puffing his pipe into life.

"Well, I think many people who go straight into a career from school or university feel they're on a treadmill. They've never known anything else, and they begin to get restless, wondering what it's like out there in the big wide world. It's rather like a man who gets married without having first…"

"Yes, quite. With you now, old son. At least I think so." Far from having the amused twinkle that Roger had expected his analogy to produce in them, Uncle Joseph's eyes were as dead as those of a fish.

"Well, I'm *in* that big wide world now and I can tell you that it's pretty meaningless. I want something to aim at." This, being not entirely untrue, was delivered with some conviction.

"And why do you feel that M & T can give you this meaningful life?"

"I don't know that it can. I want to find out." He sensed Hilary stiffen beside him, but he had chosen his words quite carefully, believing that a little honesty would not go amiss with Uncle Joseph; he seemed to have judged the situation correctly, for Uncle Joseph nodded.

"But why M & T?"

Drummond took a deep breath and brushed a non-existent hair from his only suit. He looked up and, catching Uncle Joseph's eye, took honesty almost to its limit. "Because Hilary is your niece."

Hilary's knees bounced together as if she were about to wet herself. Very calmly, Drummond watched Uncle Joseph's reaction. During the interview, the securing of this job had become a challenge. No, that was not quite true, for although he had allowed himself to become somewhat attracted to the potential fruits of success, he was still undismayed by the prospects of failure. It was more the fact that he wanted to succeed on his own terms, not Hilary's, but to do this he had at least to *try* to succeed. Hilary's present discomfort amused him so much that he had great difficulty in repressing a smile, and so he was greatly relieved when Uncle Joseph chuckled, allowing him to relax his own facial muscles.

"You're an honest young man, Roger. But M & T would expect something in return for this opportunity for you to realise your own possibilities. What can you offer?"

An almost arrogant grin now flickered at the corner of Drummond's mouth. He had the job, of that he was sure. "I like to do a job well. I have the ability to absorb new ideas very quickly. I have a quick and lively intelligence. I..."

"What do you feel about the Commonwealth countries?" Uncle Joseph spoke with his chin thrust forward, one arm draped along the top of the mantelpiece, as if he were making a speech.

Roger's quick intelligence did its work, centering on the fact that Uncle Joseph had, apparently quite deliberately, used the word "feel" instead of "think." "We have a responsibility toward them. They don't have the resources or the expertise that we have at our disposal, and although all members of the Commonwealth, Britain included, are nominally equal, some must shoulder a greater burden than others..."

"That, in a nutshell Roger, is the philosophy of M & T. We have been in many of these countries since long before independence, and we have been able to build up a unique relationship with them, one of trust and understanding. Some of these American and Japanese firms now..." He shook his head in distaste. "You know the only thing they're interested in, Roger?"

"Profit?"

"Right again, Roger," he said, smiling at Hilary, as if approving her choice of fiancé. "Profit! Do anything to flog their stuff. Bribes, price-cutting, sales campaigns—anything. And they don't even care *what* they sell. They go into a country where the biggest single problem is malaria and they'll go all out to sell kidney dialysis machines, if that's where the profit is. They understand neither the countries nor the peoples, and they aren't willing to try to. That's the difference between them and us, Roger. We *do* understand, and we do our best to help these countries develop their health services, meagre though these must be compared to our own."

Yes, thought Roger, but even M & T wouldn't be quite so ready to help if there was no profit in it.

"I'll do my best to get you into exports, Roger, because it seems to me that you understand. We're going to need all the help we can get, keeping the bloody Yanks out of our markets. On top of that, you'll soon be one of the family, and that could do with a little help too. I'll speak to Ronald on Monday morning, although it would be quite improper for me to sit on the panel when you take the formal interview."

*

On the drive to Hilary's mother's house in Shinfield, they excitedly discussed the prospects now opening before them. Hilary again calculated that within a short time they could, if she continued with her job, have enough saved for a deposit on a house. Then a little car—followed, of course, by children. Drummond shared her enthusiasm, adding a frill here and there, thinking, in the part of his mind that remained detached from the conversation, that it was one thing to scorn the material comforts of life when they were nowhere in sight and quite another when you were confronted with them.

Hilary's mother, when they broke the news, shook her *Observer*, peering over the top of its pages at them. "It's your funeral, lovey," she said to Roger.

"Mother!" Hilary shrieked, all but stamping her foot. "Why must you always be so negative? What's so wrong with Roger wanting to make something of his life?"

"Nothing, if that's what *he* wants," she said evenly. "Is that what you want, Roger?"

Drummond grinned sheepishly. "Come on, Mary, don't be awkward."

She fished out a cigarette and placed it between her lips, her cheap lighter poised as, narrowing her eyes, she sought the words in which to clothe her thoughts. "People seem to think that to 'make something of their lives' they have to *get on*, acquire things—and very often things that have little bearing on those lives. Making something out of their *lives* is so much more important to them than making something of *themselves*."

The lighter snapped and she sucked at the flame with her cigarette. "Hilary's father was like that, you know. His family had come down rather sharply in the world by the time he met me. Their fortune—and it was *never* a fortune in the monetary sense—vanished with the Empire and the two sons, Joseph and Harold, saw their mission in life as restoring the family name in some sense. It could never be in quite the *same* sense, of course, because the world had moved on. No, they were reduced to seeking money." She chuckled dryly, perhaps a little cruelly. "But the ideas they were equipped with belonged to their parents' generation: Joseph joined this antiquated firm which is bound to go under before we're much older and Harold, poor love..." She blew a cloud of smoke at the ceiling, her eyes glinting with malicious satisfaction. "He always resented me a little, you know, because I came from what he would call the lower middle class. Forced to marry beneath himself, you see. God, the life he led me! You would have thought that I was Eliza Doolittle, the way he insisted on me behaving when his bloody boring guests were at the house. I hated every minute of it."

Drummond appraised his future mother-in-law, a still attractive woman not long into her forties, and for a fleeting moment wondered how their relationship would have developed if he had met her, rather than her daughter, in Kensington Gardens.

*

Hilary disappointed him that night, for having almost landed the job he expected the reward to be commensurate. It was, however, almost half-hearted.

After it was over, he rolled onto his side and lay silently, listening to the sound of Hilary's uneven breathing. After a while, she sighed and leaned towards him, kissing him lightly on the shoulder.

"Why were you so horrible at Uncle Joseph's?" she asked, her tone wounded.

"How was I horrible, for God's sake?"

"Fancy telling him that the only reason you were interested in M & T was because I was his niece! What must he have thought?"

He rolled his head away from her and smiled into the darkness. Hilary, he knew, was both dismayed that he had abandoned the plan that she had formulated before their visit and confused that his way had worked.

"He thought I was honest, Hils," he said. "What's more, *I* thought I was honest, too."

2

After the first few months at M & T, there was a rough patch when the old reluctance to drag himself to work returned and, despite Hilary's increasingly shrill entreaties, he found himself turning up late. On a few occasions, even when he left the flat on time, he would deliberately linger in one of the sandwich bars round the corner from the office. Then there was the horseplay.

"Morning, Mr Thornton."

He stepped into the lift beside Uncle Joseph, casting an eye over the dark suit, the grey tie, the carnation. In public, Uncle Joseph was always "Mr Thornton." Even in private, it was never "Joe," but "Uncle Joseph."

"Morning, Drummond." Now, a few weeks after Roger Drummond had begun arriving at the office an hour late and, never by intention, sharing the lift with him, Thornton no longer bothered to look first at his watch, then at his order clerk. Instead, he issued his greeting, making it sound as if he were clearing his throat, and promptly turned his eyes to the door as it sighed to a close. They would remain like this, silently shoulder to shoulder, until they gained the fourth floor, like a couple whose marriage was being swept by the icy blasts of indifference, Drummond often thought. Then the lift door would sigh open, and Thornton would spring into the corridor and march to his office, leaving Drummond to slouch to his.

Given the character of the firm, there was little that Thornton could say, Drummond knew. M & T was run as it always had been: paternalism from the top, with an expectation of unquestioning loyalty from below. The phrase "industrial relations" was as foreign and, in the eyes of management, as irrelevant to M & T as it would have been to the primitive clan. Hence, Drummond had realised, their seeming inability to discipline him for the odd late arrival. So far, at least, the furthest they had gone was to give him disapproving looks; and Thornton had ceased to do even this. Sooner or later, he supposed, he would be called to the bridge for an interview with the ship's master. Mister Ronald, a former naval officer of considerable rank, would treat him like a wayward son and politely suggest that he was letting down the rest of the crew. As long as he got the work done, though, he knew that he had nothing more to fear. And, once he arrived, he did indeed get the work done.

He watched Thornton march jauntily down the corridor in front of him and wondered what kind of mentality was necessary to enable the man to face each day's work as if it were fresh and exciting. Perhaps the body snatchers had invaded, for surely no human could turn up each morning and cheerfully chain himself to a desk for eight or nine hours, happily sifting and coordinating orders which, without a scientific understanding of the equipment involved or, in some cases, a fair knowledge of those parts of the world to which they were shipped, could only have the most abstract significance.

"Morning, Roger."

"Hi, Jerry. How's tricks?"

This, weeks earlier, had been enough to cause a turning of heads in his direction. "Hi?" Surely that was some kind of Americanism, wasn't it? "How's tricks?" Now what did *that* mean? The other four occupants of the Exports (Marketing) office, although not quite as arthritic as Joseph Thornton, had been at M & T long enough to know that such expressions were not used. Mr Smart was just as bad for calling Mr Drummond "Roger." Jerry Smart could not, being black, be expected to observe all the traditional norms, but there had been signs lately that he was quite deliberately setting out to follow in Mr Drummond's footsteps.

"Fine, my man, fine." Jerry slapped Roger's outstretched palm as they both struggled to suppress grins. Although they had never spoken about it, each week they seemed to raise their outrageous behaviour a further notch. As one expression became acceptable to their fellow clerks, they quite spontaneously found new ones to shock and dismay.

The Exports (Marketing) office was large, spacious and light. Placing M & T in offices like this was a bit like dropping a tiny piece of Victorian England into the late twentieth century, but the company, contrary to the opinion of Hilary's mother, knew what it was about: M & T's reputation and the bedside manner which, since 1857, it had cultivated with clients throughout first the Empire and then the Commonwealth, had the effect, once coupled with new technology and just a smidgeon more efficiency, of increasing the number of noughts at the foot of the annual profit column.

Joseph Thornton would soon gather the department heads and their deputies into the boardroom for his Monday morning briefing, detailing the sectors needing concentrated effort this week, stock which was teetering on the brink of obsolescence and thus must be shifted fast (although, of course, he would cloak this in euphemisms) and loose ends to be tied up. As rebellion had begun to stir in his breast, Drummond had decided to give Thornton a nickname. For days he had searched and searched for one which, while deeply offensive and guaranteed to puncture that certainty about his destiny to lead (which, Drummond was sure, he had inherited from the days of Empire) would yet be as refined and, ideally, as obscure, as possible. Finally, it had come to him: Yoni. He had not, of course, used it to his face, but the office had become quite familiar with it.

"Yoni?" Norman Trant, the goateed senior clerk had repeated. "Whom do you mean, Mr Drummond?"

"Joseph, of course. Everyone calls him Yoni, even Mister Ronald."

Norman's eyelids had fluttered nervously. "Maybe so, Mr Drummond, but I don't think that we...that you should...Why, if he ever overheard, I'm sure that he would not...Anyway, what does it mean?"

"Not quite sure. I believe it's an Indian delicacy, in which case he may have earned it as a term of endearment while he was in Burma after the war."

"Oh, and *during* the war, Mr Drummond," the loyal Norman had corrected him. "Mr Thornton, or Major Thornton as he was then, defended Burma against the Japanese. I thought you knew that."

"Yes, then after the war he defended it against the Burmese, didn't he?"

Norman had dropped his eyes. "Really, Mr Drummond, I think you go too far at times."

The use of the nickname had been discontinued, however, because one day Jerry Smart had noticed that Miss Evans, the one woman in the office, blushed every time she heard it. Upon hearing of this Drummond, determined to see for himself, had strolled casually over to her desk.

"Excuse me, Miss Evans, do you know if Yoni will be in his office this afternoon?"

Miss Evans, a trim, dark-haired woman in her late twenties who could easily have been attractive (had she not worked at M & T, Drummond thought), swallowed hard and looked down at her hands as they rested on the keyboard of her typewriter. Then she dropped them into her lap and bit her lip. "I think," she said softly in her Welsh lilt, "that Mr Thornton has a luncheon appointment, so he may be back rather late this afternoon, Mr Drummond."

"Our Miss Evans has read the *Karma Sutra* quite recently," Drummond had reported back to Jerry.

"How do you know that for Christ's sake?"

Drummond had laughed. "So you don't know what it means either!"

He obviously did not, because it was not until two days later that he had heatedly protested, "Do you realise that you've been calling Joseph Thornton a cunt for the past three weeks?"

"Why should that worry you?"

"Because if they fire you, I'll be stuck here on my own."

"Not quite true, Jerry: you'll still have Miss Evans."

Jerry's eyes had widened. "There's a thought, Roger."

As Drummond was soon to discover, however, Miss Evans's knowledge of the *Karma Sutra*, may have been second-hand.

*

That Drummond's childish behaviour did not persist beyond a few months seemed to Hilary to be firmly linked with the marital reward system she had developed. It was true that during this period, which her husband would later think of as Drummond's First Rebellion, the rewards were first reduced, then withdrawn, but this played no part in his reform.

He was in fact somewhat indifferent to the reduction in his rations, as by this time he had begun to find their sex-life disappointing. While Hilary had somewhat expanded her repertoire in order to provide rewards commensurate with his conformity to the life-plan she had so meticulously mapped out, adding little grace-notes to routines established earlier, these performances were, he came to realise, purely physical in nature. Carefully planned to provide him with carnal pleasure, they succeeded in this, but he had no clear idea whether that pleasure was shared by their designer. There was little emotion involved, and certainly no passion. It was almost as if she were masturbating him: there was sex, but no sexual love.

It was perhaps not surprising, therefore that, this early in his marriage, he (after a fashion) strayed—with, of all people, Miss Evans. The incident probably would not have happened had they not both consumed emboldening but not disabling quantities of alcohol at the Christmas party held in the boardroom that year. Drummond was on his way back to the boardroom from the toilets when he saw Miss Evans making her way down the corridor towards him. Normally, this might have been uncomfortable, with either one or both averting their eyes in mild embarrassment as the distance between them narrowed, but now their gazes were unwavering; indeed, Drummond did not even think of workaday normality, noticing as she approached how her dark grey trouser suit clung to her body and, as her face came into focus, that she was wearing a smile he had never seen before. And then they stood, wishing each other a Merry Christmas in perfectly polite tones, he bending to implant a chaste kiss on her lips, which she presented in an upturned pout. But when their lips touched chastity took flight and their mouths opened, arms enfolding each other in a burst of mindless passion that had fireworks exploding in Drummond's head. This, he knew instantly, was what his domestic sex-life so sadly lacked. As they fell against an office door, Drummond reached for the handle and admitted them into the darkened interior, smoothly closing it behind them with his foot. The buttons of her blouse unfastened without hitch or fumble, he lifted her bra and cupped her breasts in both hands, noting that the nipples were not only hard and erect but unusually long. As Drummond wondered how far Miss Evans might wish to take this exploration, she solved the dilemma by issuing a series of encouraging entreaties. "Bite them, Mr Drummond," she breathed, gripping his curly hair with the fingers of one hand. As he complied, she used her free hand to unzip the trousers of her suit, whispering in a playful tone that sounded as if she were smiling, "You won't neglect my yoni, will you Mr Drummond?" As she leaned against the office wall, Drummond reached into her trousers and inserted a hand into her panties, travelling over the lightest of bushes until his fingers encountered the moistness below and entered, causing her to gasp and force her open mouth onto his. As his hand worked away, he felt one of her own pull down his zip and, slipping into his underpants, grip his aroused penis, where it laboured until, some fevered minutes later, the inevitable but uncommonly powerful emission.

For a while, they stood panting in each other's arms, Miss Evans's head on his shoulder. It was difficult to discern what might be on her mind as she whispered, "Thank you, Mr Drummond. That was perfectly lovely." Drummond's own mind was not entirely unoccupied, having turned to a typically male question regarding the long-term implications of the act just performed. Helpful as ever, Miss Evans also resolved this question by, after he had sincerely reciprocated her thanks and inanely suggested that, in the absence of tights, her feet must be cold in the December weather, assuring him that they were perfectly warm in a pair of her boyfriend's socks.

"Oh, you have a boyfriend, Miss Evans?" he said, trying to keep the note of relief from his voice.

"Mm. You must know him. Mr Sharma, in accounts. At home with a cold since yesterday."

Thus did they, quietly chuckling as the source of her knowledge of Indian erotica was revealed, silently agree that this would probably never occur again. In any case, he reasoned, they had merely masturbated each other, although he knew that Miss Evans—he had never called her Shirley—had established a standard of passionate engagement that Hilary would be hard put to match.

That was almost not the end of the day's excitement for, having arranged their clothing and stepped back into the corridor, they heard, as Drummond quietly closed the door, the buzzing of an alarm. Drummond waved Miss Evans ahead of him and, fearing that a security device had been activated, reopened the door and saw, on the far side of the capacious office, the hand of Mister Ronald lifting from a leather couch and falling onto the coffee table, where it stifled an electric alarm clock. M & T's commander, having exceeded his normal rum ration, had been sleeping it off while passion raged.

*

Drummond's reform stemmed from the interest he began to take in the firm—or, rather, its clients, real and potential. In particular, he was fascinated to have it confirmed, by at first casual and then painstaking study (he read and re-read books like Kwame Nkrumah's *Neocolonialism: The Last Stage of Imperialism* and Walter Rodney's *How Europe Underdeveloped Africa*), that the roots of underdevelopment lay in colonialism itself, and that its continuation after "independence" was explained by the fact that the economies of the new nations were subject to dictation by the major Western countries, their banks and corporations, and the multilateral agencies like the International Monetary Fund that represented their interests.

From there, it was but a small step to developing an interest in the Third World leaders and personalities who had in the recent past attempted, or were now attempting, to steer their nations out of the dependent backwaters and into more sovereign seas. He read of Julius Nyrere's modest socialist experiment in Tanzania, of Cheddi Jagan's battles against imperialism and its local servants in Guyana, and somewhat later, of Michael Manley's attempt to give meaning to the word "independence" in Jamaica.

    He now saw more clearly than ever that the fortunes of Merritt & Thwaite rested upon the inability of its clients to manufacture their own medical equipment, and that Uncle Joseph's talk of the "responsibility" owed to the less fortunate Commonwealth countries could be viewed as little more than a cynical exploitation of this fact. Not that he believed that Joseph Thornton's platitudes amounted to a conscious attempt to construct a falsely benign image: the old boy was really not that intelligent. Despite his new clarity of view, Drummond at this stage had no thought of rebelling against his employer on its account, possibly because he had no developed political outlook and his views were often of a romantic turn, emotional rather than intellectual. Instead, his heightened understanding brought the curtain down on the immature form of rebellion he had followed during his early months at the firm. Perhaps his reading induced a sense of shame or guilt regarding his asinine antics at M & T. So he began turning up on time and taking a real interest in what the company was doing, prompted by a vague feeling that the day would come when his understanding and sympathy might serve the interests of the Third World clients in a more substantial manner than did the firm's official mythology.

*

With this new approach to his work, Roger Drummond's star began to rise, and within another two years he was appointed at Uncle Joseph's assistant. With his rehabilitation, he and Hilary took a mortgage on a house in Acton. It was not as grand as the house in Hilary's dreams, but it was large enough and situated in the right kind of area to provide the foundation upon which that dream of a life together could be made real. Its three bedrooms, lounge and dining room meant that there was enough room for his books and for the children when they came.

During this period, Hilary, who had reinstated the reward system, watched over him as a probation officer might supervise one of her charges, anxious that he should not fall into recidivism. It was almost as if she doubted his commitment to her.

"Oh no, Roger," she would say when he suggested an evening out with an acquaintance who was in her opinion not "dependable" or "responsible." "He's so superficial. And from what other girls have told me, Janet has good cause to worry about what he does on those evenings when he comes home late from the office."

He knew that she was really afraid that such a person might "contaminate" him, that he might, under suitably alcoholic conditions, be persuaded to be unfaithful to her, but at the time this merely caused him to smile: he was almost glad that she cared enough to stop him from going out to have a good time. Besides, she would reward him each time he surrendered. Sometimes, he only pretended to disagree so that he could be rewarded at the end of the dispute, in the hope that this time she would allow the reins to slip from her hands; but the process remained carefully regulated.

As time passed, he turned more and more to the private world of books, perhaps not realising that the world they formed was not *really* private but a means of reaching the real world that lay beyond Hilary's wall. One day he was among striking tin-miners in Bolivia, the next he might be at the barricades in the Paris of 1871. Although he did not see that his reading offered an escape from the situation imposed on him by Hilary, he was conscious of the fact that, in choosing situations far removed in time or distance from himself he was doing so because the immediate world outside of Hilary's domain appeared to constitute no real alternative at all: his experience in manual jobs had shown him that the members of his class were quite content to remain under the tutelage of their masters as long as they were fed well; and his time at M & T persuaded him that the salariat might even be prepared to allow the status quo to remain intact whatever happened to the wages/cost of living ratio. So he read of peoples to whom the urge to rebel against injustice did not seem like the imposition by an elite leadership of an alien ideology; they rebelled, and even made revolutions, because they had little choice.

The only time he put his foot down in those years was when Hilary had tried to direct his reading.

"You seem to read a lot of books about revolutions and uprisings, darling," she said.

Before meeting Hilary, he had always shunned the word "darling" as being something that middle-class couples with false accents said to each other. Anyone from the streets of his childhood caught using such a soft word would have been laughed at. But he had come to accept it and even to like it from Hilary. He did not stop to analyse his original objection to it and so failed to see that they were fast becoming the kind of middle-class couple he had once despised. He did not at first admit that the kind of life that Hilary had mapped out depended on the assumption of the values which would inevitably, unless he checked the process in time, turn him into his own opposite.

"Yes, love," he replied, and there was more to his use of this word than a casual choice of endearment.

Hilary realised this as well. She had coaxed him, although never prompting him directly, into the unabashed use of "darling" and now here he was, using the more working-class "love"; and there was an edge to his voice that was distinctly defensive. Nevertheless, she convinced herself that she must be imagining things. She smiled on regardless.

"I don't think that's such a good idea, do you? You could end up agreeing with them, after all. Those sorts of people must have some points in their favour, and we can all sympathise with their *situation* to a certain extent, but you mustn't make yourself unhappy by taking their ideas too seriously. Why don't you read a good thriller?"

He placed the book he was reading at the time—John Reed's *Insurgent Mexico*—on his knees and looked up.

"Do you consider yourself fortunate, Hilary?"

She shrank. "Hilary" was worse than "love." She felt a flutter in her chest.

"What do you mean, darling?" she asked with some trepidation.

He saw her fear: he was about to be independent.

"Do you feel fortunate to live in a country that for centuries has lived on the sweat of slaves and the colonised?

"No. darling, of course I don't—if you mean am I glad that these things happened."

"Happened? They're still happening. How much do you think a Ford worker at Dagenham gets compared to a Ford worker anywhere in the Third World?"

"I don't think Whiteley's have branches in Africa, darling." She smiled. "You're so silly, really."

"Put it this way: would you like to live in the same sort of conditions that poor people in, say, Uganda have to put up with?"

"Of course not. I still say you're being silly."

"Would you like this country to be socialist?"

"If you mean communist, you know the answer to that."

"In other words, you like things the way they are."

"Yes, darling," she said in a humouring tone.

"Then you should feel fortunate, because this country *does* live off the backs of people in the Third World."

"I don't see what this has to do with my original question."

"Because we all benefit, whether we like it or not—and I gather that some of us like it better than others—from this situation, the life we lead is unreal in a certain sense. I once lived with a friend for six months, rent-free. I felt I was cheating, Hilary, although my friend was losing nothing by my being there. I wasn't paying my way. Well, it's the same in this case. The whole bloody country isn't paying its way. Our lives are unreal. You never get the real thing unless you pay the full price. I read about the Third World to remind myself that in those places people are living *real* lives. It may be harder, but it's also a damn sight more genuine. Don't you see?"

She dropped into a chair opposite him, crossed her legs and opened a magazine.

"Mm. I can see you feel strongly about it, anyway."

As he returned to his book, he felt her watchful eyes upon him and he would not have been surprised if, in the next few days, she had searched the house for signs of his departure to take up a gun in a land of palms and peasants. That night, he was given not a reward but an incentive to stay.

3

Life at M & T provided both rewards and frustration, tradition contributing much to the production of both.

It was tradition that ensured continuity of the almost paternalistic attitude to the Commonwealth countries that Uncle Joseph had mentioned, and there was some satisfaction to be had in dealing with people who looked upon you as a trustworthy friend, as happened whenever representatives of the various governments were in London. (Uncle Joseph met them, taking Drummond with him; later, when Roger had proven his

Bit wordy / archaic

worth, he was trusted to go alone.) The company, Drummond saw, looked upon these clients almost as younger members of the family that M & T headed. They were trusting sons and nephews who, it seemed, would no sooner turn to another supplier than they would withdraw allegiance from their parents. He was realistic enough to suspect that part of the attraction of this outlook lay in the fact that while such a relationship could be preserved (these were the days when the multilateral lending institutions were not quite so stringent in imposing conditions on the procurement processes of Third World governments in receipt of their loans) M & T would have a market that was as secure as any. There was no need to sell or compete and give oneself ulcers in the process; one merely pointed out the alternatives and made a recommendation. It was like advising one's children on a choice of career, or choice of subject at university, whereas the employees of other companies in the same field seemed, when Drummond came across them from time to time at conferences and exhibitions, to be more like unrequited lovers, pursuing their quarry with an energy and ruthlessness that was both undignified and exhausting.

Tradition was, though, also a barrier. With his fresh outlook, Drummond was able to make immediate improvements in the running of the office. For example, they carried an immense amount of stock given the size of the firm, some of it outdated and virtually unmarketable. With virtually no opposition from Uncle Joseph, he was able to reduce the volume of equipment in the stores by cutting back on new orders until stocks shrank to more manageable proportions, thus increasing profitability. For this he received a generous and unexpected bonus. To his proposals for outdated stock that obstinately refused to move, however, there was rather more resistance.

"We should donate it," he suggested to Uncle Joseph.

"*Donate* it, Roger?" Uncle Joseph echoed sceptically. "You mean give it away?"

"Invest it," Drummond said slowly, "would be a better way of putting it. Within the next few months there will be a disaster—flood, earthquake or volcano—in a country where we have no toehold. We donate the equipment and receive payment in the form of an order at some time in the future."

"I can't see Ronald agreeing to wipe off thousands of pounds' worth of stock, Roger. Not just like that."

"But it's been there for years, Uncle Joseph. There's no prospect of selling it because it's virtually obsolete and, in fact, it's costing us money simply to have it hanging around."

Uncle Joseph fell into a respectful silence. He obviously knew that Drummond was right; in fact, when Roger had first joined the firm, he had been almost apologetic about some of the inefficient business practices of M & T.

"I think it would go down rather better with Ronald if it went to one of our regulars, you know, Roger."

"But what would be the point of that, Uncle Joseph? We don't need to win them. Besides, if they're our regulars they'll already have more contemporary equipment than we would be giving them. That *would* be throwing the stuff away."

"Very well, leave it to me. I'll mention it to Ronald."

Several days later, Drummond was called into Ronald's office. Ronald Mathews, managing director and major shareholder, was known to all staff as Mister Ronald. His office, like all the offices at M & T's new premises, was large and furnished with heavy, gloomy pieces; these had obviously come from the firm's previous offices and were, Drummond thought wryly, in much the same category as the obsolete equipment they were to discuss.

"If we make a donation of this equipment to some deserving nation, Mr Drummond," Mister Ronald said when Roger was seated opposite him, "that nation should be one in which the Americans have yet to set foot. You see my point?" He was a lean and fit-looking man who always discarded his jacket in the office, his crisp white shirt no doubt serving to remind him of the tropical whites he had worn while serving in the southern hemisphere. His full head of white hair was combed into a quiff and his eyes as they engaged Drummond were startlingly blue and clear. But then he swung his chair and gazed out of the window to where the City went about its business, averting his gaze in much the same way as one does when the doctor is about to do something painful to one.

"Well, Mister Ronald, I take you to mean that the presence of the Americans could complicate matters when this nation is ready to place an order. They might persuade the beneficiaries of our magnanimity that gratitude was out of place in the world of dollars and cents."

Ronald nodded with satisfaction as if, having been unable to find the words himself, he had called Drummond in just to have him strike this euphemistic formulation. "Yes, that's exactly what I mean, Mr Drummond. Precisely."

"But I think that would be a mistake, Mister Ronald." Another member of the staff would have ended this sentence with "if you'll forgive me for saying so," but Drummond never bothered with this kind of sycophancy, partly because he knew that it would strike a false note. He knew that the management was amused by what they saw as his brashness, but that they were also impressed by his refusal to keep his opinions to himself when they clashed with their own. They were realistic enough, he knew, to see that their own values were no longer dominant and that someone like him was needed to put this realism into business practice, something from which most of them appeared to shrink.

"Why do you think that, Mr Drummond?" Ronald said quietly, half-turning, a finger touching his chin as he looked sideways at Drummond.

"If the Americans see no reason to go into a Third World country it can only be because that country has little or no natural resources. If a country has no natural resources, it's doubtful whether it will have the wherewithal to place an order big enough to justify our initial gift."

Ronald thought for a moment and nodded, and there seemed to be a little sadness, a touch of resignation, in the gesture. "Your reasoning has something of an American flavour to it, Mr Drummond."

Drummond smiled wryly. "Not through choice, I can assure you, Mister Ronald. If we want to play their game, we unfortunately must accept their rules until we are in a position to change them."

"Quite so, Mr Drummond, quite so." Mister Ronald stood up and walked around the desk, hands clasped behind him, leading Drummond to the door. "Let me know when you hear of a suitably deserving case and we'll see what can be done. I think we all accept now that what you say is perfectly true: that stock is of no use to us whatsoever. If it can be used to help one of the poorer nations after a disaster, so much the better."

Drummond's victory in this matter had, however, been preceded by his meeting Lemay.

*

Often, Drummond found his Third World reading material in the Grassroots Bookshop on Golborne Road, just off Ladbroke Grove; this was run by the Black Liberation Front, and although he sometimes received inquisitive looks from customers and staff, he encountered no hostility. It was here that, one Saturday afternoon in 1976, he ran across Eddie Collins, whom he had first known as a busworker at Middle Row garage. When Drummond expressed surprise at meeting him in the bookshop, Collins, short and tanned, explained that that he was currently on leave from his merchant ship, which made monthly trips to the Caribbean; he had a lively interest in the region and so usually visited Grassroots when he was in the area. Drummond had got on well with Collins at the bus garage, noting his presence at every union branch meeting, and so, having made their purchases, he suggested they go in search of a coffee. When Collins remarked that there was nowhere particularly close, Drummond told him his car was outside.

"So what about you, mate?" Collins asked as they sat in a small Turkish Cypriot café on the Harrow Road. Collins was in his late twenties, a few years younger than Drummond, and wore an earring. "With a fairly new model car, I guess you're no longer on the buses."

Drummond grinned. "You guess right, not that I would have minded a few more years on the back."

"Nah, you're too tall, Rog. You would have ended up with a stoop. The ideal conductor is about my height." He laughed. "But I was a driver. So why d'you leave—you get the push?"

"No, nothing like that. My missis decided I needed a career—you know, the sort of job where you can afford a car and a mortgage. So I'm an assistant exports manager in a firm that flogs medical equipment." He shrugged apologetically.

"Fuck." Collins leaned across and took a paper napkin from the holder and dabbed at his chin. "Sorry, mate, I didn't mean to choke on me coffee. It's just that you never looked like the manager type."

"I'm still not sure I *am* the manager type, Ed."

"Then why do you stick it? Apart from the car and the mortgage, that is."

"Those are of more concern to my wife." He began to trace a pattern on the table-top with his forefinger. He glanced up at Collins. "The fact is that, leaving aside all the bullshit that goes with it, it's interesting. See, virtually all our clients are Third World governments, and I've become very interested in their problems. That's why I was in Grassroots—I pop in there around once every couple of months to stock up on books."

"Well, what do you know!" He grinned at Drummond. "Any interest in the Caribbean?"

"Oh, very much so."

"Well, listen. I'm in touch with a group called the Arawak Support Group—the ship I'm on sails to Arawak every month. There's a lot of interesting things happening there. In fact, I live in Southampton these days, and the only reason I'm in London now is to make a bit of a report to the support group at its monthly meeting tomorrow morning. You're welcome to come along if you think you'd find it interesting."

That was how Drummond first met Lemay.

*

"Hi, this is Alex Preston," Collins said the next morning when Drummond picked him up at a flat in Chepstow Road, just off Westbourne Grove. "Alex is assistant secretary of the support group. We used to be in the merch together." Preston, a large white man in his late thirties clutching a bulging cardboard folder held closed with elastic bands, gave Drummond a tight, fleeting grin and slid into the back seat of the Ford Granada, where he alternately rubbed his forehead and glanced at his watch.

Drummond drove up to the Harrow Road and Collins guided him to Chippenham Mews, where the meeting was to be held at a small community centre. Inside, Collins introduced him to the chairman and suggested that the meeting be asked if there was any objection to his attendance. When the chairman, a light-skinned Arawakian man in late middle age, opened the meeting at 10.15, there were around fifteen present, with the black members roughly equally divided between Arawakians and Jamaicans. He introduced Drummond as "a comrade of our longstanding member Eddie Collins," causing the two former busworkers to exchange amused glances, and, having ascertained that there were no objections, formally welcomed Drummond to this meeting of "our modest but sincere little group."

Much of the early proceedings were lost on Drummond, as there was considerable discussion arising from the minutes of the previous month's meeting, during which a short white woman with a crucifix at her throat and light hair parted in the middle, giving her the appearance of a nun, persistently but politely complained to the chairman that a number of tasks assigned to the secretary, a very dark pipe-smoking Arawakian who from his smart sports jacket seemed to be a veteran of the

1950s, had simply not been completed. She was assisted by an Arawakian man with a grey-streaked beard who in his soft, lisping voice pursued the matter when the chairman attempted to move on after the secretary had delivered a not particularly satisfactory explanation. Drummond noticed that people began to fidget uncomfortably, and he suspected that they found this criticism of the group's shortcomings embarrassing in the presence of a stranger.

"Mr Chairman," came a strong, confident voice from the row behind Drummond, "while I am sure our guest is extremely impressed by this demonstration of the democratic character of our organization,"—whatever tension had existed was instantly dispelled in a chorus of good-natured laughter—"could I suggest that the matter under discussion be remitted to a meeting of the committee, to take place immediately following the conclusion of the general meeting?"

Drummond looked over his shoulder and saw a bespectacled man somewhere in his mid-thirties, of medium height with light brown skin, a close-cropped beard and receding hairline. The man grinned at Drummond and resumed his seat.

The chairman nodded sagely and looked to the men on either side of him—the besieged secretary and Alex Preston, who was scribbling minutes—before declaring, "An excellent suggestion, Brother Lemay. Is that agreed?"

It was, with one voice chuckling, "Lemay to the rescue—as usual" and causing another wave of laughter.

The chairman now asked the reprieved secretary to give a brief account of correspondence received since the last meeting, and this turned out to be mainly notices of meetings and appeals for assistance, either moral or financial, from other London-based solidarity organisations. Somewhat to his surprise, Drummond found himself jotting down details of one or two of the meetings, including one at Friends House, Euston Road where Philip Agee, the CIA-officer-turned-whistleblower would be speaking.

A coffee-break was then declared before the main item on the agenda—reports on the situation in Arawak by Garry Lemay and Eddie Collins, followed by discussion. As he finished his coffee, Drummond was approached by the amiable chairman, who asked if he would like to say a few words about himself at the close of the meeting. Drummond felt his heart flutter, but nevertheless agreed, and when he resumed his seat began to make a rough note of what he might say.

Unusually, it was Collins, the Englishman, who gave a first-hand report on the situation on the ground in Arawak, while the Arawakian Lemay, being London-based, made a more analytical speech. During his last two trips to Arawak, which had fallen either side of the general election won by the left-of-centre Arawak National Party led by Lester Robinson, Collins had met with leaders of the left— most notably Daniel Morgan of the Arawak Workers' Party. The AWP had given Robinson cautious support during the election and at the time of Collins's most recent meeting with Morgan had been considering whether it should propose a formal alliance based on "critical support." At street level, however, the response to Robinson's win had been tumultuous, so much so that it seemed probable that the right-wing Arawak Democratic Party, which had formed the previous government, would be isolated for some time.

When Lemay strode to the front of the hall with just a single sheet of paper in his hand, Drummond assumed that his speech would be fairly brief. Instead, it lasted for forty-five minutes, and Drummond could not remember the last time he had been so impressed by another human being; absorbed by the content of Lemay's speech and his authoritative delivery, he abandoned his attempt to make notes for his own remarks and simply listened.

Lemay began by sketching in the colonial background, during which time the British had allowed neither democracy (apart from concessions to the white plantocracy and, later, the mulatto ruling class that had emerged) nor development, confining the economy to sugar and bananas, the proceeds from which went to fund the purchase of British manufactured goods. This, and the legacy of slavery, had led to a form of consciousness—a lack of self-confidence and a slavish worship of things foreign—that was rightly termed colonial, dependent. Thus, although there had been slave rebellions aplenty in the past, there had been no really sustained or united push for independence from below. Thus, independence when it came in 1966 was not won by Arawakians but "granted" by London. This was what the Jamaican scholar and left leader Trevor Munroe had called "constitutional decolonization," and was soon discovered to be no independence at all, because the same economic regime was maintained, with the additional factor that US capital arrived on the scene, keen to install the "Puerto Rican" model in Arawak, relying on labour that was kept cheap by a state that discouraged organising efforts and persecuted labour leaders who attempted them. While workers were subject to super-exploitation and the denial of their rights, the peasantry entered long-term decline as agriculture failed to modernise.

This was the reality of the last decade of so-called "independence." But in recent years the Arawak National Party, formerly little better than the Arawak Democratic Party, having purged its socialist wing in the 1950s, had undergone a rebirth. Workers seeking a more just labour regime, peasants who could see no future unless the countryside was dragged into the twentieth century, even small and medium capitalists whose own future was blighted by the lack of real economic development, and members of the intelligentsia with links to their counterparts in other parts of the region where the signs of progressive change were already evident—representatives of all these classes and strata had begun the task of transforming the ANP into a party that would put the interests of the country first, casting off the influence of London and Washington and charting a course for real independence.

At the same time, some labour leaders and intellectuals had insufficient faith in the ability of the ANP to transform society to the extent that was required. For example, the ANP might issue what, objectively speaking, were anti-imperialist slogans, but would it be up to the job of mobilising the working class? Then again, the capitalists and some of the middle-class forces in the ANP might well waver and seek compromise at the first sign of pressure from Washington. Those concerned by such questions, deciding that a party more firmly committed to the working class (which would provide its base) and more forthrightly anti-imperialist, would be required, had therefore founded the Arawak Workers' Party.

The ANP victory at the recent general election was, said Lemay, truly overwhelming. But it would be a mistake to place too much confidence in a large parliamentary majority: the colonial consciousness and dependent outlook still formed a powerful current in Arawakian life, and popular support for the government could decline quite quickly once the ADP, urged on by Washington, recovered from its humiliation and commenced its dirty tricks and misleading propaganda; furthermore, the very fact that the parliamentary majority was so large meant that there were several Assembly members who were, at best, lukewarm anti-imperialists who could be expected to defect if offered generous incentives to do so. Moreover, it should be clearly understood that the ANP was not a socialist party, although there was now once again a socialist tendency within it. Nor was Prime Minister Lester Robinson a socialist, although he was fond of the word, and it would be a mistake to rule out the possibility of him becoming one. It was not even a consistently anti-imperialist party, although there were consistent anti-imperialists within it and there was now a possibility that the ANP could, given sufficient pressure from within and without by the working-class forces, become such a party.

As mentioned by Eddie Collins, the AWP had offered only cautious support to Robinson's party during the election campaign. There were two main reasons for this. First, it was obvious that the ANP was going to win handsomely, with or without AWP support. Second, there had been a fear by some in the party that it would be a mistake to tie the AWP too closely to the ANP this early in the day. Should the new government promptly renege on its electoral promises where would that leave the AWP in the eyes of the Arawakian people? Eddie had also mentioned the process underway in the AWP. As a result of recent telephone calls and a lengthy document sent via the diplomatic pouch, Lemay was able to advise the meeting that this process had been completed. The AWP had self-critically examined its electoral stance and decided that it had been not only incorrect but opportunist.

The election of the ANP, Lemay declared, represented the first chance in ten years for Arawak to break out of the cycle of underdevelopment and dependency, and that chance must be grasped with both hands. The role of the AWP must, therefore, be one of firm, consistent support for each of the government's progressive measures and criticism—bold but fraternal, unafraid but never arrogant—whenever it faltered. Moreover, support of those progressive measures must not be confined to slogans but must take the form of mass mobilisation and, moreover, of the participation of the masses in all government programmes intended for their benefit. The party having arrived at this decision, a mass rally would later today be held outside Government House, to be addressed not just by the AWP's Daniel Morgan but by Lester Robinson also. The proposal of a de facto alliance between the two parties had been discussed with Robinson and he had agreed to it. Today's rally should effectively silence any backsliders in his own party.

Finally, Lemay paused and looked around the hall. "My dear friends and comrades," he said, removing his glasses, "the current situation in Arawak today is one this support group has campaigned for since its formation two years ago. I hope and believe that your support will be just as firm in the months and years to come—bedeviled by problems as they will undoubtedly be. The alliance between the Arawak National Party and the Arawak Workers' Party will have several consequences, one of which will be that good, honest, hard-working, patriotic left-wingers whose abilities have for years been denied an outlet will now be appointed to positions where they can make a difference. Indeed, this would have occurred to a certain extent even without the alliance." He turned to the chairman and smiled. "Even some people who may not deserve all of those adjectives may be offered posts. In this regard, my own role in the support group will have to change, as the government wishes me to occupy a position in the High Commission." He grinned as the applause began and held up his palms. "I will still be available to address your meetings, and I daresay we will also see each other when you come to demonstrate outside the High Commission whenever the government takes a wrong step. But let's never forget that we are all on the side of the people of Arawak."

*

After an exhaustive discussion came the moment that Drummond had been dreading, as the chairman thanked those in attendance for a very successful meeting (latecomers had swelled the numbers in attendance to around thirty) and, just as he was about to declare it closed, remembered that he had asked the newcomer to say a few words about himself. Drummond got warily to his feet, glancing at the few notes he had been able to make.

"I'm...I'm no public speaker," he began warily. He waved the single sheet of notes. "Ask me to speak about myself and I still need notes." This was greeted with sympathetic amusement. "Then you put on a speaker like Garry Lemay and expect me to follow him." Laughter. He screwed up the single sheet of paper and let it fall to the floor. "I come from a working-class family. Did well at school, got a few A levels, but then had no idea what to do with them. So I did a number of jobs. The longest—three years—was as a machine-minder in Acton. When the factory closed, I went on the buses, which is where Eddie and I met. After that, I joined a company that supplies medical equipment, mainly to Third World countries. I'm still there, as assistant exports manager."

He paused to let this sink in. "But you're not really interested in my job-history, are you? Politics? I'm not a member of any political party, but over the years I've evolved towards what I suppose is a left-wing position. That's come mainly from my experience at work. I've seen what working within the profit-system does to most people, how it sucks them dry and prevents them from being fully human. Believe it or not, it was not until my current job that I began to think seriously about politics. Yes, and me an assistant manager! I've come to see that my company preys on the fact that the countries it sells to are unable to manufacture their own medical equipment. Why? Underdevelopment. So I've been reading—Walter Rodney, Nkrumah, Cheddi Jagan—in order to understand more." He snorted in self-deprecation. "I suppose I've become an anti-imperialist."

He cleared his throat and, looking around, was surprised to see that he had their attention. "You know, I've never talked about this to anyone before. If there's a reason for that, it's probably because I've never fully realised what was happening to me. I came to this meeting because Eddie invited me. We hadn't seen each other for several years until we bumped into each other yesterday afternoon." He grinned. "In Grassroots Bookshop, of all places." A smattering of laughter. "I'm glad that happened, because it wasn't until I came here and heard Garry Lemay speak that I understood the road I had travelled and the place I had arrived at. Everything he said made sense to me because, I realised, it was what I believe. Even though I know nothing about Arawak, its situation is repeated all over the Third World. So I guess we're on the same side. Thank you."

If the applause had been friendly before, it was now affectionate. As Drummond resumed his seat, he felt a hand on his shoulder and, turning, saw Lemay's hand extended.

"Let's meet for a coffee sometime soon," said Lemay as he handed Drummond his card.

4

Within the next few months, there were several natural calamities—floods in the Indian sub-continent, an earthquake in the Middle East and a phenomenon in Africa so frequent that it had come to appear natural: a local war. One after the other, the management ruled them out. M & T's contribution would become lost in the flood (Mister Ronald's lips had twisted in discomfort at the pun) of assistance to Bangladesh, and the Middle Eastern and African countries were thought to be too unstable. Exasperating as these refusals were at first, Drummond came to see that they were, in fact, quite justified. Having accepted his proposal in principle, these knock-backs were made on sound business grounds. He found it remarkable that the managers adjusted so swiftly to the thinking involved.

Then came the floods in Arawak.

The Caribbean Island had a population of less than two million, although this made it one of the more populous former British possessions in the region, after Jamaica and Trinidad. Its sugar industry had been allowed to run down, mainly through lack of investment due to competition from European beet, long before independence and bananas were now its main foreign-exchange earner.

"You say that it depends on bananas for its livelihood, Roger?" Uncle Joseph asked the day after he suggested Arawak as the recipient country.

"Yes, Uncle Joseph. And a bit of tourism."

"And yet you admit that the banana-growing areas have been worst-affected by the floods?"

"Also true." Drummond sat with his hands folded on his lap, the suggestion of a smile playing at the corners of his mouth.

"Might this not affect the ability of the government to place the kind of order we have in mind?"

"In the short term, yes. Taxes, both from the cultivators and the wage-labourers on the large plantations will fall this year. Tourism will drop off for a while, although the coastal areas are quite unaffected. In addition, the government will have to plough money into relief work."

"Not exactly a recipe for success by the sound of it, Roger." Uncle Joseph paused and looked across at him ruefully. "But you're acting like a man who knows more than he's letting on. Come on, tell all."

Drummond opened the folder on the desk before him and took out a newspaper. As he opened it, he looked up at Uncle Joseph and smiled. "This is a recent copy of the *Arawak Weekly Chronicle*, which is published in London for the benefit of the Arawakian community in this country. The story I've marked concerns a bauxite survey carried out by a Canadian company.

They've identified considerable deposits and are recommending that the government allow them to begin mining immediately. Bauxite is an essential ingredient in the production of aluminium, which in turn is essential for the US motor and arms industries. The deal the Canadian company has proposed envisages a fixed levy per ton of bauxite exported. The US bauxite companies are now interested and will try to conclude deals as well. Within the agreed limits of competition between companies such as these, they will try to outbid each other, as a result of which the final levy figure will probably be half as much again as that mentioned in the newspaper story."

"Still not very much, though, is it?" Uncle Joe said, stroking his chin as he bent over the newspaper.

"Per ton, no. But when you consider the global figure, it comes out at a tidy sum. Now, a country like Arawak will most likely plough a great deal of that money into the infrastructure, as they find industrial development on all but the smallest scale to be beyond their capabilities. This, given the recent change of government, will almost certainly mean the expansion of their rather rudimentary health service."

Uncle Joseph smiled up from the newspaper. "You've obviously done some research, Roger. How do you know so much about a place I've no more than heard about?"

Drummond returned his smile. "I read a lot, Uncle Joseph."

*

It was decided that someone from the office should fly to Arawak in time to meet the equipment when it arrived on the Arawak City docks and, once there, both hand it over publicly and spend a few days establishing contacts and identifying areas in which a relationship with M & T might prove helpful to the government.

"Oh, they *must* send you, darling," said Hilary when Roger told her. "It was your idea, after all, and you know so much about the place."

The suggestion startled him, for he had quite honestly not considered the possibility of being sent himself. He hoped that Hilary was not going to insist that he put himself forward or lobby Uncle Joseph behind his back.

"No, Hils," he said coolly. "I've been with the company for such a comparatively short time that the question simply doesn't arise. And I wouldn't like to be accused of ambition."

She smiled. "I don't think anyone could accuse you of that, darling. I wouldn't have believed your concern for the future of the firm if I hadn't seen it for myself."

"It's not so much that, more a question of wanting to do the job well and get some satisfaction from it."

"Mm. Well, it seems to me that Uncle Joseph and the others need reminding from time to time that the improvements that you've made haven't fallen from the sky."

Uncle Joseph thought it best that he go himself. There would be people in government, he confided to Roger, who knew the family name and who would associate it with dependability and straight-dealing. A cousin, after all, had been governor of Bermuda for a time. Meanwhile, he said with a broad consoling smile, Drummond would oversee the sales office.

He laid a hand on Drummond's shoulder. "I've told Hilary that she's quite right: you do deserve to go, but we have to let you notch up a few more years before we start moving you too far ahead of the field, if you see what I mean."

"But I..." Drummond began to protest.

"No, I know you didn't want to go yourself," Uncle Joseph cut in, raising a restraining hand. "All I'm saying is that Hilary is right. There's nothing wrong with being a little ambitious, Roger. Do you see what I mean? You're part of the family, after all. We can help each other, you and I."

Drummond averted his eyes, not wanting to reply affirmatively to this proposed pact to further his career, even if it was designed to benefit the name of the Thornton family. It had its attractions, though.

"Yes, I see what you mean, Uncle Joseph," he said. "But I want to deserve that help."

"Of course, Roger, of course. And you do, believe me, you do." Now, you'd better brief me about whom I should see in Arawak."

Drummond breathed a sigh of relief, glad to return to ground that was both more familiar and requiring no opportunistic declarations from himself.

"Certainly, Uncle Joseph. The newly-elected Arawak National Party—ANP—is, like the opposition Arawak Democratic Party, committed to the Westminster model and is financed by one of the major trade union federations, with which it has strong links, and the more liberal sections of local business."

"Is the National Party to the left of the Democratic Party?"

"There are the remnants of a Marxist wing that was purged in the early fifties, which has now been joined by a new generation of socialists. But perhaps more important than that is the fact that the party is much more prone to nationalism than the ADP. It's also committed to improving the social services, of going as far as it can afford to along the road to a welfare state."

"Where will this leave us, Roger?"

"The ANP's nationalism shouldn't affect us at all as this, if it develops into the dominant ideological strain, will be turned against foreign control of the economy. We don't quite fall into that category, Uncle Joseph. If they decide to limit imports, this will affect luxuries more than any other class of goods. We are suppliers of medical equipment. The new government will need such a supplier if it is to develop its health service in line with its promises."

"They don't have the capability of manufacturing their own equipment?"

Drummond shook his head. "Out of the question. The economy doesn't generate the kind of surplus required for that level of investment. If they decide to channel some of their future bauxite income into industry, it will undoubtedly be into the export sector: over half of Arawak's food is imported, and that needs to be paid for. Their main objective is to get away from the one-crop economy and so medium-level manufactured goods, using local raw materials, would fit the bill."

"Are the communists a force?"

"Their party is of moderate size but quite influential. But don't worry: their line is one of support for the ANP government."

"Is there anything else?"

"I'll provide you with a briefing note on the leading personalities, but that's about everything you should know about the broad picture."

*

But not quite everything.

Shortly after Uncle Joseph arrived in Arawak, Drummond received a visit from Garry Lemay. Lemay removed his glasses, threw his document case onto Drummond's desk and fell into a chair, where he buried his face in his hands in a comic display of exasperation. A small gold ring glinted from a little finger.

"Amazing," Lemay said, taking his hands from his face and tapping his fingertips together as he looked around the office.

"What is?" Drummond asked, on his guard.

"How well you appear to have slotted yourself in here. And in such a short time, too. I noticed it as soon as I walked in the door."

Drummond relaxed. "Must be the new suit."

"And the way you sit behind that desk. It's almost disconcerting. For me especially, because in our discussions over the past month you've led me to believe that you were acting in the best interests of my country. Now, seeing you in what has obviously become your natural setting, I'm forced to wonder."

Drummond sighed impatiently, irritated that someone he considered a friend seemed to be questioning his commitment. "Listen, Garry, I know perfectly well that I appear to fit behind this desk. If that weren't the case, I wouldn't be able to hold down the job. Your interests, it seems to me, are best served if that continues to be the case. I think you're becoming a little paranoid. But something has obviously happened to bring this on, so why don't you tell me what it is?"

Lemay stood up and walked to the window, standing at Drummond's side, hands in pockets, as he gazed thoughtfully down into the street. After a full minute, he eased himself down onto the desk, a sad smile cancelling the irritation from his face.

"Then why did you allow a man like Thornton to represent your company in Arawak? His family history runs parallel to that of the Empire, you know. Not only that, but they had a reputation, it seems, for dealing with their subjects in a particularly callous and brutal manner. They were never the stars of the Colonial Office circuit, but maybe that's why they excelled themselves when it came to putting down rebellions and punishing those disloyal enough to form trade unions. Not being the top dogs, they could afford to do so, and no doubt they felt that they were increasing their chances of promotion."

"Oh, Garry!" Drummond cried, relieved that Uncle Joseph was the target. "He's the exports manager, whereas I'm merely his assistant, and so I had no say in whether he was sent to Arawak. Regarding his family history, all I have is his own account of the Thorntons' imperial role—and he appears to believe that they were paternalists. Besides, all this was years ago, and I doubt, since you haven't pinned his name to any particular misdeed, that he was involved. Isn't that so?"

"Yes, Roger, that is so. But he's one of them, and makes no secret of the fact, is even proud of it. There are people in the ANP who were around before the winds of change. They used to meet their counterparts from Africa, India and so on at colonial gatherings in London. You forget, Roger, that what we now call the Commonwealth was once run almost as if it were one country, albeit with some powers delegated to the local level. If a Thornton had the soldiers shoot down demonstrators somewhere in Africa, people in the Caribbean looked upon the incident as relevant because they were also part of the bloody Empire. More than that, there were Thorntons in Trinidad, Barbados and Bermuda. And this fool who is visiting Arawak now is, when asked if he's related to *the* Thorntons, crowing about it!"

Drummond felt the perspiration break from his forehead. "Oh Christ."

"Exactly. Oh Christ. However, he's not a bit like his brood."

Hope, like a delicate flower, raised its head. "He isn't?"

"No, you would be hard put to imagine him having people shot. He goes around dripping sympathy on everyone and treating them as if they were children. And that, in this day and age," he added, looking Drummond straight in the eye, "is almost as bad!"

"Oh no."

"Is that all you can say?"

"What else *can* I say, Garry, except that I'm sorry? If I'd had any idea that he was going to behave like that I would have tried to find a way to prevent him going."

Lemay picked up his document case from the desk and straightened his jacket. "Well, I suggest you do something about him, Roger. Get him retired and take over his job."

Seeing Lemay preparing to leave, Drummond almost started from his seat. "Wait a little, Garry. Where does this leave us?" He hoped the question did not sound like a pitiful appeal to Lemay's friendship.

Lemay smiled and shook his head. "Believe it or not, Roger, it leaves us halfway there. The gift of the equipment went down well, very well. And with luck, the memory of Thornton's behaviour will soon fade."

Drummond shook his head. "Sorry, but I'm not sure exactly where that *does* leave us."

"It means that pretty soon M & T will be able to add Arawak to its list of paying clients—if those figures you mentioned still apply. But Thornton must not be seen or heard of again. Get him grounded—or ditched." He paused at the door, turning back into the room with a smile betokening a confirmation of their friendship. "Sorry I frightened you. Let's have a drink sometime next week, eh?"

Drummond took a scrap of paper from his wastebasket and threw it at him playfully.

*

Since that Sunday-morning meeting of the Arawak Support Group, Drummond had developed his friendship with Garry Lemay. Lemay had followed a similar path to Drummond, having drifted from job to job until he found his footing. Apart from visits, first with his parents and then alone, he had not lived in Arawak since the age of ten, but he had always identified with the land of his birth. This seemed to have intensified in the past five years or so, and as a result he no longer exhibited the shrill intensity that had so characterised him as a younger man, when he had been drawn to black nationalism. Commitment had allowed him to relax and see things as they really were, and hostility had been worn down by an increasing understanding.

After their first encounter, Drummond and Lemay met regularly. Lemay kept suggesting an evening together with their wives, but Drummond usually had a ready excuse. The picture Lemay had, over several meetings, painted of Marie made her a fairly intimidating figure when compared to Hilary. Drummond found himself feeling just a little ashamed of his wife. But then he supposed that Lemay's obvious pride in Marie would have that effect on most married men.

Garry Lemay's pride in and fidelity to his wife had remarkable echoes of his attitude to his country. Sometimes, when he was talking about Arawak, he might equally have been talking about Marie. When he used the word "we" it came so naturally that it was quite obvious that he really felt a part of Arawak and that his future and that of his country were in his eyes inextricably bound together. Neither was this a starry-eyed patriotism of the my-country-right-or-wrong type. He had felt that the previous government was wrong for the country in that it was selling off his birthright to foreign investors. He supported the ANP but seemed to be a member of the AWP. For several years, he had gone home every year and it seemed that he had become a party member during one of his most recent visits, and he now appeared to be well connected at the leadership level. Drummond's admiration for Lemay developed apace with their friendship. This admiration, though, was tinged with envy, for when he compared himself to Lemay he felt distinctly incomplete. They both took their careers seriously, and yet Lemay's, although admittedly new, was more a part of his life; there was no sharp dividing line between his working life and his private life. Indeed, the very concept of a "private" life seemed anomalous when applied to him. His life was all of a piece. Drummond, on the other hand, was still the dilettante: he had attended neither of the public meetings of which he had taken details at the support group meeting and, indeed, he had not returned to Chippenham Mews since that meeting.

They were two men with distinct careers, but as their friendship became more relaxed and trusting it occurred to them that there could be a point at which they touched: Lemay wanted to see his country develop, the poverty and want of his people relieved, and Drummond's firm dealt in merchandise which could assist that process. Drummond allowed the other man to lead, his own career to take second place to Lemay's ambitions for his country. Gradually, they had arrived at a plan whereby M & T would supply medical equipment to the ANP government on terms more generous than any of its competitors or, for that matter, than M & T usually considered wise. Drummond supplied the idea of the gift himself, and the floods provided the opportunity.

After Lemay's visit to the office, however, Drummond found himself pondering his true motives. Had he been drawn into Lemay's dream in much the same way as he had been lured into Hilary's? Was there no more to it than that? If this were the case, then his motives must be considered noble, because he would gain nothing from it, unlike his participation in Hilary's scheme. But was there more? Did he see this as his chance to make an impression on Ronald? Was there, at the back of his mind, the idea that, notwithstanding the fact that M & T's profit margin in any deal with an ANP government would be much tighter than usual, he could use the conclusion of the deal (and it might prove larger than anything they had handled for several years) as a springboard to Uncle Joseph's job?

He would have preferred a situation in which he could have chosen to either confirm or confound his self-doubt. It was ironic that it was Lemay himself who was denying him that opportunity, for in his insistence that Uncle Joseph be ditched he was giving Drummond the excuse (the instruction, almost) that he use the deal to further his own career.

5

Children did not come.

It was a long time before their dream (even he thought of it as *their* dream) became reality. He had been naïve enough, when the enthusiasm that Hilary had communicated to him was still fresh, to hope that they would simply step into it, if not upon leaving the registry office, at least upon moving to their semi-detached in Acton. But of course, it did not come that easily. There were things to be bought for the house, and jobs to be done on it before it was in a fit condition to hold a dream within its walls. And then there were things external to the house. To communicate with the outside world (his job, Hilary having given up hers three years after they were married, the cinema and occasionally the theatre) without having to make more than the briefest contact with its inhabitants, a car was necessary. Then there were holidays; after a few years of experimenting, they went regularly to Crete in the off season, the absence of British tourists at that time of the year bolstering the illusion that the island was *their* holiday haunt.

Children during these years of building the dream would have delayed its completion, and so there was agreement between them that their arrival should be postponed. But then the dream arrived. They found that the house was as they wanted it, the car had several years' life in it, and there was enough money in the bank for holidays and unforeseen emergencies. The question of children, were they serious about having them, should now have come onto the agenda. But Roger Drummond found himself shying away from the subject. Whenever he thought that Hilary was about to introduce it, he would raise a problem needing an immediate solution, however trivial, such as emptying the rubbish bin in the kitchen, washing the car, or arranging the evening's television viewing. Then, as the months passed and she did not insist on discussing it, he began to wonder if she too was content to give children a miss. So, whenever she looked as if she were about to raise an important matter, he said nothing, testing her. Not once did she mention children.

He could not be sure why she did not raise the matter, but he suspected that she thought that children would shatter the peace of their life, their dream made real. It took him a few months to identify his own motives. For the moment, he allowed himself a sense of relief; the cancellation of children meant that everything in his life was known.

Slowly, this conception turned into the slightly more disturbing one that his life was made. The dream was built and his remaining years, more than half his life, would be spent living in it. Nothing would change. Of course, there would be minor adjustments and modifications, but no real *changes*. Then it came to him that he was glad that they were not going to have children as he knew at heart that this life was not enough and children, rather than changing it, would have anchored him in it. Not only was this life not enough but, he finally realised with a jolt, Hilary was not enough for him either.

*

The rewards stopped. This is not to say that they no longer had a sex-life. They did, but their lovemaking (was it *really* that, he now began to ask himself; had it ever *really* been that?) became so infrequent that it could not be described as reward. Thus, he became convinced that in deciding not to have children Hilary was, as he had suspected, ensuring the continuity of their tranquil philistine existence.

Perhaps unconsciously, she had tricked him. She had continued the reward system while their dream was a-building and then, upon its completion, dropped it, leaving him aground on this barren rock of middle-class philistinism and sexlessness. He noticed that he was changing. His movements were becoming slower, his step less vigorous, his expression more morose. He no longer hurried home. He often thought back to their first serious discussion, when he had explained his "one hand waving free" line, and it seemed to him now that while Hilary had mentioned her own perfectly meaningless working life she had not, as he had suspected at the time, merely been trying to keep him company, even to display some form of ideological kinship; no, she had been deadly serious, and all along she had seen him as the means of her escape into another form of life, equally meaningless though it might seem to him.

It had been part of the mythology of his working-class youth that the middle class, especially the men, were no good in bed. Women from that class, the myth ran, were merely waiting for a lusty proletarian to awaken their full sexuality. Middle-class couples led empty lives built around a shallow materialism, on the things they had accumulated. The acquisition of a new car and the flaunting of some new gee-gaw were substitutes for blinding orgasms. Middle-class wives, seeking the best of both worlds, took working-class lovers.

Once, after the car had broken down during a trip to the cinema, he noticed a youth staring at them as they rode on the tube. In his early twenties and wearing the compulsory faded jeans (had he not married Hilary, Roger Drummond might still, at the age of thirty, have been wearing them), his gaze was, when directed at Hilary, frankly lecherous; at twenty-seven, she was just the right side of over-ripe, her breasts swelling tantalisingly beneath her thin summer blouse. When his eyes shifted to Drummond, the young man's expression visibly soured into something approaching contempt. It was at this moment that Drummond knew that he had really arrived: those with nothing but their ability to do a day's work only made insinuations, albeit unspoken ones, about one's ability to satisfy one's partner when one had acquired the persona of stability and self-assurance associated with the employing class and its managers. The irony was that Roger Drummond had never felt less assured of himself than at that moment. It was as if he were looking at his own reflection in that young man's eyes; and he did not like what he saw. Hilary had done this to him. He began to resent his wife.

*

"Why don't you take off your nightdress?" he would ask.

"No, darling, it's far too chilly," she would reply, even though the house was centrally heated.

And he would grope for her breasts beneath the nightdress, later lifting the hem above her knees, all the while remembering how her body had once felt, pressed to his. On one occasion, his low grunt as he thrust forward had been a disguised sob.

"Yes! Push! Now!" she would command him, much too early, wanting to get it over with as soon as possible. And as she pulled him further into her, he would be unable to hold back, his emission occurring almost lazily, like an arrow from a half-drawn bow. Once, remembering how years earlier she had expressed the wish to have him "come over me," he had withdrawn and ejaculated across her stomach with the idea of re-entering her immediately and beginning afresh.

"Oh, you *haven't!*" she cried. "*Why,* darling? Ugh! Look at the mess you've made. Get me a towel, quick."

And she had closed her legs, keeping him out. When she had cleaned herself, he switched off the light and turned his back to her, teeth clenched.

On Sunday mornings, she would invariably arise before him, baring, as she had always done, her body before him upon her departure to the bathroom. As she turned her back to the window and peeled her nightdress from her, her breasts thrust out, she appeared to be deliberately flaunting herself before him, ensuring that he saw the body she no longer allowed him to feel next to his own. He ached to make love to her on those mornings; but even though it had been she who had coaxed him into making love in the mornings, something he had never been able to do with anything like enthusiasm before he had met her, when the reward system stopped this ceased also. "I don't feel the same about doing it in the morning anymore," she said. "It's much nicer at night." And yet still she stripped before him.

One Sunday morning, the inevitable happened. Unable to contain himself, his penis thickening, he reached out and took her wrist, pulling her to the bed. She lost balance and fell against him, her breasts brushing his face.

"No, darling," she said. But she giggled, a good sign.

He persisted, tugging at his pajama-cord and climbing astride her, pressing his lips to hers to stifle her protests. His heart lifted as he felt her body relax. Taking his mouth from hers, he drew back and smiled down at her, expecting a consenting smile in return.

But she was gazing up at him almost distantly, as if she were not really there, beneath his anxiously quivering body but, say, by the window, looking on in mild distaste as he attempted to force himself onto some reluctant stranger. Her eyes closed and opened again, just once. "No, darling," she repeated.

The wish to make love to her evaporated and his penis softened almost immediately. Stifling a groan, he lifted himself from her and threw himself face-downwards onto the bed. He began to hate his wife.

*

"To dance beneath the diamond sky with one hand waving free." The words of the song came back to him frequently now. But where could he find that sky? What were the alternatives to life with Hilary? He had few friends—she had seen to that. She had seen to it that as this life of theirs was built, so his old life—

friends, his interests apart from reading, his very inclinations (to change jobs with ease, for example)—was dismantled. He could see no way of getting back to it.

Of course, that previous existence had not really been a life at all. Hilary had caught him before he had had time to develop any real interests, any real direction. There had been the reading, and the half-hearted attempts at doing some writing himself, but even his reading had been eclectic. This, he realised, was because he had lacked direction. His subsequent reading suggested that he might have developed into some form of socialist, but surely if that *had* been his road he would have taken it—there had been no lack of opportunity, after all. There had been a lack of inspiration, however: he had made the point of attending, at least once, a meeting of every union branch of which he had been a member and each time he had come away dispirited. In his experience, the typical union branch consisted mostly of unread men (and the occasional woman) who, persuaded that in negotiating for better ventilation or a few more bars of soap in the washroom they were engaged in a mission of lasting importance to their class, twisted their mouths around the most pompous and jaw-breaking of words. If the government of the day had an incomes policy, they would accept the legal maximum, even though they knew that this meant that the employer gained at their expense, rather than fight for a more just settlement. There was usually one individual in each branch who regularly raised matters of more than local importance—support for a strike elsewhere, for example, or, some years earlier, for a demonstration against the war in Vietnam; such members were often ridiculed and sometimes shown hostility, the majority displaying such insularity and poverty of thought that Drummond found himself simultaneously sickened by them and, in a curious way, sorry for them.

A life among people such as these would, it appeared in retrospect, have been the most likely alternative to participation in Hilary's dream and so it was small wonder, he saw now, that he had chosen Hilary.

*

After lunch one Saturday, he persuaded Hilary to make love. That persuasion came close to force. She had never liked doing it in the afternoon, but today he felt the need to do so, to subdue the forces churning inside him. At first she protested, reminding him that he had promised to go for a walk in the park with her. They were in the sitting room, she on the sofa with the newspaper opened across her knees, he in one of the matching chairs, his loins stirring as he fixed her with a gaze that was purely sexual, devoid of all affection.

"But you did promise, darling."

The slight whine he detected in her voice merely increased his desire, and he realised that he wanted to screw her rather than make love to her, to hear that whine without words attached to it. For once he wanted to lead the way, to inflict his sex upon her and then to have her acknowledge the change in roles by some vain protest.

He walked across to where she sat, dropping to his knees in front of her and pulling the newspaper from her lap. "Plans can always be changed, Hilary," he said, his voice soft yet commanding. "Let's stop living our lives as if we had to conform to some kind of blueprint, shall we? Let's do things on impulse from time to time." He ran his hand along her leg until his fingers touched her panties.

She giggled nervously. "What are you doing, darling?"

"The impulse I feel right now is to make love to you right here," he said, hooking a finger in either side of her panties.

"Oh, you're mad, Roger," she said, as if he had suggested the impossible. "Quite mad."

He resolved to argue no more, knowing that if she were encouraged to debate the issue Hilary would succeed in extinguishing his desire, with the result that it might smolder for days, never bursting into flame and causing him to feel that he was being strangled by a sense of frustration. No, it had to be fought out.

"Lift up your behind," he said, rejecting the use of "arse" as it occurred to him. His hands at her sides now, he tugged at the top of her panties.

Her face registered the shocked realisation that he was serious. "Oh Roger," she protested weakly as she shifted her behind further onto the sofa.

Forcing her knees apart, he jiggled one hand into position between her legs and, supporting her back with the other, half crotch-lifted her, half pulled her onto the floor. She tumbled across him and rolled onto her back. Before she had time to gather her wits and struggle to her feet, he twisted onto his knees and threw himself onto her, kissing her hard on the mouth and forcing his legs between hers. One hand clutched her hair while the other squeezed her left breast hard. Feeling her nipple harden, he pressed his rigid groin between her legs. He tore his mouth from hers and released both hands, letting her head roll back, briefly noting the mixture of confusion and excitement on her face. His hands flew under her dress, lifting her buttocks and pulling down her panties in a swift movement. The hem of her dress fell about her waist, revealing the whiteness of her legs and the brush of light brown pubic hair. At last she spoke.

"Not in here, Roger," she murmured, knowing now that she would have to participate.

He pulled her to her feet without a word, pushing her through to the bedroom, unfastening her dress and slipping it from her shoulders as he went. As they reached the bed, he turned her and eased her dress down with both hands. He unbuckled his jeans and stepped back, pulling them from his legs. Then he practically flew at her, covering her warm mouth with his own and feeling his penis press into her stomach as he pushed her down onto the bed. He looked into her eyes as he tore his mouth away, then bit her throat, moving down her body, ripping away her brassiere and taking her pink nipple into his mouth, sucking hard. And then further down, to where she had never allowed his mouth to travel before, objecting that the practice was "dirty," flicking her clitoris with his tongue before plunging it into her vagina—which, he noted, was wet. Presumably knowing that it was useless—and, anyway, far too late—to protest, Hilary moaned, and he had no way of knowing whether this was pleasure or complaint; but she did not try to close her legs, and so, emboldened by this advance, he briefly disengaged while arranging his body over hers and, when his straining penis hovered over her face, his tongue re-entered her. After a brief hesitation, he felt her mouth close over his penis as another taboo fell. Now he no longer wanted to simply screw her but to please her, to have her body respond in a way that made it plain that she was experiencing carnal pleasure, and so he concentrated for a while on her clitoris, sucking it, lightly biting it, while sliding two fingers into her vagina. She began to buck and tremble, and her mouth tightened around his penis. He patted her leg (like, he realised later, a professional wrestler indicating to his opponent that they might disengage from their current holds without disadvantage to either) and crawled around to face her. She whimpered as he sailed into her. He threw his left leg over her right, moving further into her and feeling her pubic hair rubbing against his own. Then he struggled to a kneeling position and lifted her onto her right side, enabling him to travel further into her. She issued a little cry, and it was not clear to him whether this was intended to register alarm. He guided her into a kneeling position. Now he was ready.

He crushed her large white breasts together with one hand, squeezing each of the nipples hard in turn, while he cupped his other arm under her body and pulled her hard onto him. He plunged in and out of her, squeezing her breasts even harder. Hilary had never been very demonstrative in lovemaking, but now she cried and whined aloud, and it seemed possible that she was crying. He looked down at her soft white body almost as a detached observer as he screwed her, her aspirations, and the class from which she had sprung. He screwed her for all that she was and for all that she could never be, out of revenge and disappointment.

Then, to his surprise, she lifted herself onto her elbows and began to move her hindquarters backwards with each thrust. He caught a glimpse of her large breasts as they hung vertically, their tips brushing the duvet with each movement. "Yes, Roger, yes!" she panted as they moved together. She glanced at him over her shoulder and seeing her face, a curl of hair glued to her forehead with perspiration, he felt the love of the early years wash over him again with all its old force, strengthened now by the sense of her vulnerability. Such a person could not be screwed.

Withdrawing, he turned her over. She half came up to meet him as he came on top of her, seeking his lips and holding them in a kiss as warm and loving, and as charged with passion, as she had ever given him. She reached down and brought him back into her, squeezing his penis between her thumb and finger. Then their bodies melted into one, his hands travelling urgently up and down the sides of her body as their excitement mounted, pressing the sides of her breasts. Her body began to buck as she came, and her legs swung about his waist, imprisoning him inside her. He lifted her, a hand beneath each buttock, his breath coming in short gasps. Looking down at her, he saw that her face was more open and honest now, more beautiful, than he had ever seen it. Her mouth lay open, her eyes tightly closed as she whimpered lightly. Then, as if she did not want him to come unless his body was within her reach, she released her legs and, placing a hand behind his neck, pulled him back down onto her. He felt her whole body stiffen, her swollen breasts thrusting into his chest as she began to come again. The top of his penis felt a wave broke over it and his movement accelerated, all his actions free of conscious direction now and responding to the dictates of the two bodies become one. His hand slid under her buttocks and he felt her buck as it brushed her anus. His penis swelled to bursting point and the waves of orgasm began to lap at his mind, bursting open its private vaults and secret chambers.

"I want you to love me," he found himself whispering urgently. "I want you to be all there is to live for!"

They came together in a prolonged orgasm that took them both by surprise in its length and intensity, each clutching desperately at the other's body. Afterwards, they lay panting, rocking in each other's arms. After a while he slept, astonished that he had found the possibility of such passion and intensity in his marriage and yet, blinded by this, forgetting that his original aim had been thwarted, that the contempt with which he had set out had been transformed into something like love. It did not occur to him that Hilary had strengthened her hold over him, having been provided with the means to commence the reward system anew.

6

"Yes, a most satisfactory trip, when all is said and done," Uncle Joseph said as he and Drummond sat opposite Ronald on the Monday morning after his return. He glanced down at his hands as they lay on the desk, stretching his fingers and subjecting the nails to some scrutiny. "Our gift was received with...well, gratitude would really be putting it far too mildly. They were quite overwhelmed."

"And how did your discussions with the government go?"

Uncle Joseph pursed his lips. "Frankly, Ronald, they're a tricky lot. Think they know all the answers, brimming with confidence. Bloody health minister tried to give me a list of their requirements. Told her that when the time came we'd see if we agreed with her ideas of what was needed."

"How much of the country did you see, Uncle Joseph?" Drummond asked, embarrassed by the older man's patronising attitude.

"Enough to know that a lot needs to be done, Roger. Their health service, if it can be called a service, is practically non-existent, especially in the rural areas. Not so bad in Arawak City, the capital, but even there the hospital is hopelessly overcrowded."

"And what does this mean for us—in straight commercial terms, that is?"

"If the bauxite thing goes ahead—and everyone there is confident that it will—I don't see why they shouldn't have a new hospital in the capital and a series of clinics and health centres in the countryside. A smaller hospital on the north coast, perhaps, directed to the needs of the expatriate community and tourists. Could be a very big order, Ronald, as big as we've handled in a few years."

"And you're confident that the new government will choose us to fill it?"

Uncle Joseph shrugged nonchalantly. "We may have to do some bidding when the time comes, but I'm confident that the contract will come our way. It's been money well spent."

Ronald smiled and issued a satisfied sigh. "Good. This is not the sort of thing we've done before, but it looks as if the idea of the gift was well worth pursuing. Well done, Joseph, you've done us proud."

Drummond started. He caught Uncle Joseph's eye, and a sheepish, timid creature it was, darting shiftily like that of a cat caught at the fishbowl.

*

"I know what you're thinking, Roger," Joseph said when they gained the privacy of his office, his arm thrown across Drummond's shoulders, "but you're wrong. Ronald is well aware that the credit for this venture should go to you. Don't worry, your contribution won't go unrecognised. Let's wait until we have the contract signed, eh? Besides, it's all in the family and that's all that really matters, isn't it?"

*

"If you don't move on Thornton soon, you'll miss your chance," said Garry Lemay.

It was Sunday morning and Drummond had, having given Hilary an excuse, slipped across to Lemay's flat, a modest two bedrooms and lounge just a few minutes from Notting Hill Gate. Drummond slouched on the large brown-leather sofa, pulling fretfully at the front of his sweater while Garry perched on the edge of a chair at the table, watching him with some concern.

"Did I ever tell you that Thornton was Hilary's uncle?"

Lemay stood up and slapped his forehead. His shirt was open at the front and a gold charm bounced upon his hairless chest.

"Shit! Her *uncle*? You mean he was the one that got you the job?"

Drummond nodded.

Marie's light musical voice floated through from the kitchen: "Anybody use some coffee?"

Lemay affected a glare at Drummond as he called back over his shoulder: "Good idea, sweetheart, because Roger's conversation is a little intoxicating."

"Come on, it's not that bad. He's not *my* uncle, after all."

"You mean you're still willing to put the knife into him—your own wife's uncle?"

Drummond placed his hands on his knees and pushed himself to his feet. He walked over to the window and looked out. The landlord of the Artesian was just opening the doors. He recalled now that when he had attended the meeting of the Arawak Support Group, he and Eddie Collins had visited this street to pick up Alex Preston, who must live a few doors away.

"Yes," he said. "If nothing else occurs to me, I'll simply go to Ronald and tell him that the deal will be off if Joseph remains." He turned and looked at Lemay. "There's no need to look quite so shocked. You're making the mistake of thinking what it would be like for you to put the knife, as you so charmingly phrase it, into Marie's uncle. Marie's uncle, I daresay, isn't a pompous old windbag like Uncle Joseph. A pompous, colonially minded windbag at that."

"What about Hilary? Won't she be upset? Come to think of it, is there any way you can keep her from knowing?"

Drummond shrugged. "She may find out, I suppose. It's really of no importance."

Lemay tilted his head and closed one eye, as if to get a clearer picture of Drummond. "You're talking about your *wife*, man." He said it as if it hurt him.

"Exactly. *My* wife. See, you're making the same mistake again, thinking of *your* wife."

"Coffee!" Marie's bell-like announcement almost startled them, shattering the uneasy silence that had sprung up between them. As if to illustrate the truth of Drummond's argument, she entered the lounge with the coffee, a substantial figure in jeans and a jumper several sizes too large for her, her dark face transformed by a wide-eyed, questioning glance that she switched from one to the other. "Not arguing, I hope," she said, and it was evident to them that genuine concern lay beneath her light-hearted manner. When they had first met, having been subjected to Lemay's litany of wife-worship for weeks, Drummond had been startled by Marie's plumpness, but within a short while he had seen that she was beautiful.

"No," Lemay assured her, "not in any real way."

Drummond grinned involuntarily, seeing in the other man's statement his implicit agreement with his own estimate of Hilary. He realised now that he had never told another person what he thought of Hilary. It was curious how the truth, choked down and smothered within oneself by various forms of self-protection, could fly out of one's mouth, almost independently of will, when talking to a friend. It was no accident that he should confess to Garry, however, for his marriage was the success against which the failure of his own was judged. Was there a pathetic appeal for advice contained in his blurting out of his hitherto concealed feelings? He was unsure, and yet he knew there was something more to it than a mere desire to bare his soul.

His eyes followed Marie as, having placed a coffee at his elbow, she crossed the room to Garry. Her light, perfect movements evoked in him the sting of knowing that she was forever Garry's. As she straightened up and turned back into the room, she caught his gaze and he forced himself to look away.

"Okay, I get the picture," she smiled. "I'll leave you to your man-talk. Lunch will be ready in an hour or so. Sure you won't stay, Roger?"

"No, I really must get back, Marie. Thanks all the same."

"How is Hilary, by the way?" She paused at the doorway, running a slim hand through her prolific Afro.

The question caught him off-balance, pitching him into a whirlpool of conflicting emotions. "Oh," he said finally, with a glance at Garry, "she's fine."

"Well," she said, pretending not to have noticed his hesitation, "look in and say goodbye before you go." Then she was gone.

Garry sipped his coffee meditatively, peering at Drummond from beneath lowered brows. "What I really meant," he said, replacing the cup in its saucer, "was that...Well, I suppose I was surprised by the fact that you were being so open—brutally honest, in fact—about someone you'd committed yourself to..."

Drummond sucked his teeth in irritation, a gesture he had picked up from Garry.

"I guess you drifted into marriage," Garry advanced speculatively, "without..."

Drummond stood up. "Okay, don't lecture me! The last thing I want is a lecture. If I'd known I was going to get one I never would have mentioned it." He stalked to the window and looked out, dragging a hand through his hair. "You know, you really are a smug bugger, Garry. You don't realise how lucky you are, that's your trouble. You've not only got a marriage, you've got a cause as well. Well, some of us are not so fortunate. Hilary is as much tied to England as Marie is to Arawak. I have to make my life here. You used to think that you had problems as a black man in this country, didn't you? Anyone can have problems in this country, Garry, anyone. Its whole history has been one of lies and falsity. The same process that enslaved your forefathers made intellectual slaves of the rest of the population. Yes, Hilary is one, but so are other people." He paused and waved a hand at the window, a gesture of exasperation. "I don't have a cause, Garry. If I had, I wouldn't drift into things like marriage, or this job of mine..."

Slowly, Garry raised his hands and placed them over his ears.

"That's right, make a joke of it!" Drummond chided, but even so he felt himself relax. "You bastard."

Garry grinned. "Sorry I started lecturing you. And yes, I'm a smug bugger. But tell me how I can help, Roger. I do want to, you know."

Drummond nodded. He looked at Lemay and smiled. "Just listen from time to time, I suppose. That's all I want, really—just to pour it all out to someone occasionally. It's dangerous to store it up for too long. Things tend not to seem so bad after I've had a good moan about them. Is that a deal?"

"You know who you remind me of? The old me." He winked. "Deal."

"And don't worry about Thornton. I'll think of something."

*

In the days following their rather rough afternoon rutting session, Hilary seemed to treat him warily, as if she were circling him with a mixture of apprehension and anticipation, both fearful and hopeful that he would suddenly pounce again. One evening, noting that look glittering in her eye as they passed each other in the living room, he turned back and seized her aggressively, whereupon she swiftly dispelled any notion of sexual fear by committing to the ballet with an urgency previously absent.

Afterwards, as they lay dazed and sated on the floor, Hilary suddenly giggled.

He rolled toward her and placed a hand on her perspiring breasts. "What's so amusing?"

"I was just wondering what the neighbours would have thought if we'd accidentally left the curtains open."

They giggled together like two pot-smokers sharing an esoteric joke. Drummond's mirth was heightened by the fact that this kind of witticism was fresh territory for Hilary, although if he had given it more thought he might have seen that, deriving from the curtain she liked to draw between their small unit and the outside world, it hardly contradicted her mindset. He was, therefore, ill-prepared for what came next.

"You know, Roger," she murmured, "I'm not happy that Uncle Joseph stole your thunder over the Arawak thing."

Arriving home after Joe's debriefing, he had, he recalled, given Hilary a terse, ill-tempered account of the meeting.

"But as Joseph himself said, it's all in the family, so I'm surprised that you're concerned by it, Hils."

She turned her flushed face to him. "Family, indeed! It's not as if," she laughed, "I call myself Hilary Thornton-Drummond in an attempt to preserve the name. Is it, now?

"But surely Joseph himself wants to do that, doesn't he? And what about Mary?"

"Why should my mother be bothered about it? She was merely married to a Thornton, and to be perfectly honest she can't stand Uncle Joseph."

"And Uncle Joseph himself?"

Hilary smiled ruefully and shook her head. "It's an act, darling. He may be a silly old man, but he can be quite ruthless. He has no family, and he knows it."

Tempted to sarcastically thank her for the warning she had failed to give him all those years ago, all he could manage was, "And-and-and...*you*, Hilary?"

She kissed him lightly on the lips and ran a hand lightly over his curls. "You're my family, Roger." A sigh, then a very level gaze. "And I think you should persuade Ronald to make sure that you rather than Uncle Joseph negotiate the Arawak contract."

Dimly at first, he began to perceive the lair into which his horniness had led him.

*

The incident in Mister Ronald's office had both fired Drummond's determination to carry out Lemay's recommendation regarding Uncle Joseph and dulled his desire to act immediately. Yes, he had been angry, but he had also felt crushed and dispirited. But now? He felt used. Joseph Thornton had used him, and now the old man's niece was using him—not to shore up the prestige of some mythical family, but to improve the quality of her own life and to enhance the cachet of their own two-person unit. If that were not enough, Hilary had, in effectively cutting her ties with the Thorntons, placed the sole responsibility for her future happiness on Drummond's shoulders. All we have is each other, darling: that was her message. But that was not *enough*, goddamn it! How many times in the last few years had he thought of leaving Hilary and their vacuous existence? And now, as a result of his harebrained attempt to "rearrange the sexual furniture," as an acquaintance had once described his own method of prolonging his and his wife's satisfaction with their own marriage, she had him trapped once more.

Oh yes, he had little doubt that this was what she was about. Within days of their romp in the living room, it had all become very clear to him. He could see how Hilary must have planned every stage of their life together. First, he had to get a job, any job, although this was, admittedly, a step he would have taken anyway. Then the move to M & T, followed by progress through the ranks, accumulating on the way the house, the car, and the bank balance that allowed Hilary to become a hausfrau. But, it turned out, not children. And throughout those years she had kept the truth of her feelings about Joseph Thornton and "the family" to herself, only releasing this information when she felt the time was right, when his new knowledge would release him to make further progress within M & T at the old man's expense.

But he could, surely, walk away from it all, couldn't he? Easier said than done. First there was the threat implicit in Hilary's unspoken "Leave me and I have nothing, darling. The responsibility for what happens then will be entirely yours." And walk away to what? Then again, while it was easy to see that Hilary had, not particularly expertly at first, used sex to control and guide him throughout their marriage, it was quite another thing to abandon what they had now. The level of intensity of the passion he had enjoyed with Shirley Evans was now surpassed. After each of their two recent adventures in sheer sexual abandon he had for several days afterward had flashbacks. Not particularly pornographic, these usually consisted of images of Hilary bathed in sweat and looking both vulnerable and sexually aggressive, of her face melting into an expression of deep sexual love. Even knowing what she was and how she was manipulating him, Drummond was not sure that he would be able to walk away from the sexual athlete into which Hilary had been transformed.

*

One Friday afternoon, just as Drummond was about to leave the office for the weekend, he received a call from an American named Philip Streeter.

"I was wondering if we could meet sometime, Mr Drummond."

"You realize that I'm not the exports manager, don't you?" Drummond responded cautiously. "You probably want to speak to Mr Thornton."

"Oh, no, Mr Drummond, it's you I'd like to speak to. Do you have time for a drink before you go home?"

"Are you in the same line of business as us?"

"Not at the moment." Streeter chuckled. "I'll explain everything when we meet."

"Alright. Which hotel are you at?"

"I live in London, Mr Drummond. I could meet you in twenty minutes if that's okay with you. There's a pub just around the corner from your office called The Crown."

Streeter turned out to be an earnest technocrat in his early thirties with a short haircut, steel-rimmed glasses and a sober black suit. Drummond thought he looked like a cross between a Mormon proselyte and a CIA man. He had, however, an easy smile and a slow Midwestern drawl that belied his appearance.

"Well, Mr Street, what's your business?" Drummond asked when they were seated with their drinks.

"I see you're a man who likes to get down to business, Mr Drummond. And it's Streeter. But call me Phil. Here's my card."

Drummond took the card and glanced down at it. "International Enterprises?"

"That's right. One of our subsidiaries supplies you with surgical instruments."

"Yes, Crawford's. Not in any trouble, are they?"

Streeter laughed. "They're fine, Roger, just fine. May I call you Roger?"

"Of course," Drummond responded, although his slight hesitation probably betrayed his discomfort at this enforced intimacy. "I must say, though, that when you describe them as one of our suppliers you make it sound as if we're the multinational and you're the small company."

Streeter's smile spread like a wave across his face. "You may be small, Roger, but you've been doing some pretty impressive things lately."

"Oh?"

"Sure. Like the gift to Arawak. You did your homework on that one, Roger, and that's what IE likes to see."

"As I said earlier, Phil, I'm not the exports manager."

Streeter studied him silently for a moment, then winked.

Drummond looked down into his whisky and rattled the ice-cubes against the glass. "Not going to offer me a job are you, Mr Streeter?"

Streeter laughed again. "Phil. No, Roger, a little more than that."

Drummond felt his eyebrows lift.

"We'd like your opinion on the possibilities of us buying out M & T."

"Why come to me?" he asked, masking his surprise.

"Because, apart from Ronald Mathews, whom we'd use as a figurehead—you know, respected father-figure kind of thing—you're about the only person we'd like to keep. You'd be in charge of the export market for us; and it would be a much bigger operation than you have now, needless to say."

Streeter shook a cigarette from his packet and offered it to Drummond. "We know that you were behind the Arawak operation, and we also know what the locals thought of Thornton when he was there. Relax, Roger: it's natural that we should know. We have people there—we own a cement company and pretty soon we'll be involved in the proposed bauxite operation. Thornton even stayed in one of our hotels, dammit." He blew a long stream of smoke at the table and pointed his cigarette at Drummond. "You're the man we want, Roger, no doubt about it. Now what do you think our chances are?"

It was Drummond's turn to smile. "Not very good, I'm afraid. M & T has a tradition of not liking Americans. But frankly I'm at a loss to see why people like you should be interested in a company like ours anyway."

"Believe it or not, Roger, it's partly because of your tradition of not liking Americans. Yes, that's a bit of an exaggeration, I agree. But you do *have* a reputation in the field. You're both trusted and respected. We would protect that image. In fact, it would be one of our selling-points. The M & T persona plus IE's resources could really go places, Roger. Of course, there are other considerations. It would be far more profitable for the group to own a company that sold Crawford's products than to have you sell them for us. We have links to a furniture company that could supply hospital fittings, and to a pharmaceutical company that could broaden its involvement in drugs without too much of a strain. M & T would be handling all of that. More, in the long run. It's worth thinking about, Roger. Will you let me know if the situation changes? My number's on the card."

Drummond drained his glass. "I'll think about it, Phil, but that's all I can promise you. For the moment."

7

At his most paranoid, Drummond even doubted his friendship with Lemay and suspected that he was using him also. Of course, this was true to an extent, but was surely noble in intent. Besides, Lemay was of the opinion—understandably, since Drummond had declared as much at the meeting of the support group—that M & T's assistant manager for exports shared his hopes for Arawak. But then the pressure from Lemay suddenly ceased, and he told Drummond that Arawak, as it sought to recover both physically and financially from the devastating floods of 1976, would be in no position to talk seriously of a contract for medical equipment for some time, and even then it would be on nothing like the scale that Joseph had spoken of upon his return to London. It would become clear later that this lengthy hiatus had started Hilary on the path leading to separation.

The voracious carnal encounters were not, of course, sustainable. Had Hilary felt the need to goad him into self-advancement, the reward system would have come back into play, but as it seemed that the Arawak contract would provide him with the only real opportunity, there was currently nothing to reward; and, besides, Drummond suspected that Hilary must be running low on new ideas. Their sexual encounters, therefore, diminished first in intensity, then in frequency, until both partners frankly began to lose interest without either realising at the time that these moist exertions had come to represent the only real bond between them. Sexually and emotionally, they were back in territory they had occupied a few years ago, but it would not be the same this time, for Hilary had come to share Drummond's indifference.

These days, they rarely went out together. Their most recent outing was to a buffet and booze-up in the M & T boardroom held to celebrate the 120th anniversary of the foundation of the company. Even here, they were not really together. Drummond, with no intention of ignoring her, had spent some time sitting next to Shirley and Lal Sharma, and before he knew it Hilary had drifted off on her own. By the time he spotted her, she was standing next to Ronald, her eyes gazing almost worshipfully across her champagne glass at the company patriarch as he imparted his wisdom. Watching them, Drummond wondered how he would describe Ronald's own expression, and decided that it appeared to be...appreciative. As Hilary left him to walk across to the buffet table, Ronald's eyes followed her, his gaze now even more openly appreciative.

"There was a time," he said to Hilary as they lay in bed one night, "when I thought I would never want to die." To make this brief declaration he had rolled over from his now-normal position huddled away from her, onto his back. "Now, with every passing year, I feel that when the time comes I won't be too sorry to go after all. Possibilities get exhausted, hopes are unrealised. People get exhausted and unrealised, too. I'm unrealised and I'm becoming exhausted. And I'm only thirty-two."

"Mm," Hilary acknowledged from her side of the bed.

For several seconds, silence reigned in the darkness, broken only by their breathing, hers light and easy, his heavier and more exasperated.

"Hilary?"

"Mm?"

"Make me never want to die."

"Yes, darling." She paused and he thought that she had fallen asleep, unmoved by his desperation. But, obviously having given some thought to his request, she continued: "I'll make you chicken fricassee tomorrow—no, Thursday, because tomorrow I've an appointment at the hairdresser."

After another silence, during which he blinked several times in stunned disbelief, he said, "I think it's going to take a little more than that, Hilary."

And she did not answer. Yet again the silence descended, and for the next two years, until she left their two-unit dream in Acton for a more promising one, it was never again to lift.

*

Apart from the prospect of the Arawak contract, the work of the company had hit a prolonged monotonous stretch in which existing contracts were serviced and renewed rather than new ones clinched. Creighton never had flown into Lourenco Marques from Dar, and the Central American market remained closed to M & T. The sole exception was a new departure that Joseph had managed to embark upon with a small, obscure former French colony in West Africa. Drummond's working life was, therefore, once more coming to assume a grey, lifeless aspect. As this now mirrored his domestic life, he found himself from time to time casting an evaluating glance in the direction of Shirley, only to be brought up sharp by the realisation that she was now Mrs Shirley Sharma, and had been so for some years. A pity, he thought, because Shirley might have been reason enough to come to the office every morning. Jerry Smart, of course, had resigned long ago, having found the company's patronising approach too much to bear.

/But then there was Arawak, which had come to symbolise for Drummond the downtrodden/Fanon's wretched of the earth. As the memory of the support group meeting and the warmth he had encountered there receded, Drummond tended to lose sight of what, unknown to Hilary, this was supposed to be all about, and so, if only in order to give the pretence of purpose to his increasingly meaningless life, he periodically reminded himself that he had no business dwelling on his marital problems or the treadmill of office life while his pledge to Arawak remained unfulfilled. Sometimes he groaned with embarrassment when he recalled the short speech he had made at Chippenham Mews, for what was he doing to carry through its implicit promise? He was a fraud—wasn't he? True, he could not be held responsible for the stalled contract, but he had never attended another meeting of the support group and had not even turned up at the Philip Agee public meeting as he had intended. His only contact with Arawak was via Lemay and even that relationship was in danger of lapsing into mere acquaintanceship as Lemay, with Washington now attempting to destabilise the Robinson government, found his duties at the High Commission far too pressing to spare much time for personal friendship.

Inspired by no nobility of purpose, or even by ambition, his first attempt to unseat Joseph Thornton sprang from boredom, as had the horseplay of his immature early period with the company. Even so, it was hardly a spur-of-the-moment affair, as he had, while covering Thornton's job during the old man's annual leave periods, done more than a little homework before approaching Mister Ronald in March 1978 while Thornton was once again in sunnier climes.

"Yes, Roger, come in, dear boy. I haven't had the opportunity of telling you how much I appreciate your running of the office while Joseph is away." Mister Ronald smiled. "You have a bright future here—you know that, don't you? Joseph himself speaks very highly of you."

"That's very kind of him, Mister Ronald. I do my best."

"Quite obviously so, Roger, quite obviously so. Now, what can I do for you?"

"Well, actually I've come to see you on a rather delicate matter." He could feel his heart pound and was aware that he sounded breathless.

"Not thinking of leaving us I hope, Roger?" The old man smiled understandingly, and Drummond knew that he had recognised the growth of ambition within him.

"Not at all, Mister Ronald. It concerns Benue."

*

During his periods behind Thornton's desk, Drummond had gone through the African contracts with an eye to discovering possible weaknesses in Uncle Joseph's research. What he discovered in the case of Benue, a small West African state sandwiched between Nigeria and Cameroon, indicated that research of an economic and political nature had been, in fact, barely conducted. If M & T tended to deal mainly with territories over which the British flag had once flown, this in itself guaranteed, in many cases, both allegiance to the West and economic dependence on (not to mention domination by) Britain and, to an increasing extent, the USA. Political and economic stability were, Drummond was convinced, accidental to a certain extent, as Uncle Joseph chose his markets using the traditional link with Britain as a yardstick.

One of Joseph's few gambles outside the Commonwealth, Benue was very much the exception that proved the rule. Once a French possession, it had been ruled by an alarmingly rapid succession of governments since independence in 1963. The French had been ousted, in effect (although they had decamped some time before the moment of truth, not willing to risk a mini-Algeria), by a militantly nationalist group led by a Benuegan captain in the French Army. The French had taken everything with them—tractors, personnel, supplies, right down to office equipment, apart from obsolete typewriters, which the departing French governor ordered thrown into the sea. This revanchist act had soon led to the downfall of the captain's government, as the discontent caused by the shortages was unrelieved by the prospect of better days to come for the numerous petty bourgeoisie concentrated in the country's one major city and the small but influential rural landlord class. The peasantry would have endured the hardships in return for land reform, but they were neither powerful enough nor sufficiently organised to prevent the government's overthrow.

Since then, a coalition of the first two classes had been formed to prevent the third from coming to power. In fact, however, they came to office, if not quite to power, with every other government, being preceded and succeeded by the reactionary coalition. This situation (twelve governments in nine years) looked now to have been finally ended by the intervention of Libya, which, with its oil wealth and its appeals for the unity of the Muslim people, had succeeded in getting all three warring factions around the table. Qadhafi himself had presided at the final conference, at which it was agreed that Benue would be ruled by a coalition representing all the various interests. It was rumoured that this undertaking had cost Qadhafi several million dollars in military assistance (the arms themselves came from the Soviet Union) and agricultural equipment.

It was on the basis of this settlement, Drummond surmised, that Uncle Joseph had concluded that Benue was now a relatively safe market—and it was true that until now it had been fairly prompt in paying its bills. But Uncle Joseph had reckoned without the fears and intentions of Washington.

Libya, Washington thought, would have extracted some ideological concessions out of Benue—the promise of active participation in the shaky anti-Israel front, perhaps, or, of more immediate concern to them, conversion to a more active anti-Americanism (as there were no US investments in the country, there were few domestic grounds for anti-Americanism, but the State Department, as US involvement in Vietnam had recently reached its humiliating conclusion, now tended to bring a global view to the most insignificant problems; Benue as part of a larger anti-American grouping and with Soviet arms was a different kettle of fish from Benue making shrill noises on its own).

Thus, Washington was ready to devote a certain amount of non-military resources to keep Benue if not on its own side of the fence, then at least astride it. The Qadhafi-inspired coalition facilitated this to a certain extent, for now both foe and ally were together in one government, and the contradictions of that government were there to be utilised. A deal had just been signed with the US Agency for International Development under which Benue would receive $45 million over the next two years on condition that the money was used to purchase US goods transported in US vessels. As the health service had never recovered from the French withdrawal, Drummond thought it likely that some of this money would be used to buy medical equipment. Then he discovered that the contract that Uncle Joseph had signed with the Benuegan government was renewable on an annual basis.

The present contract had just a few months to run, and it would obviously not be renewed. That might not have been quite so bad, had it not been for the fact that, in another new departure, M & T had commissioned research into a new drug to be used in treating an illness induced by an insect peculiar to Benue and a few surrounding countries. To recoup the costs of this research, given the kind of profit margins enjoyed by the big pharmaceutical companies, would have taken several years. Now that the contract looked like being cancelled, it would knock a hole in M & T's finances through which Joseph Thornton would, if Drummond had his way, disappear.

*

Ronald's face brightened with a mixture of amusement and something curiously akin to pride. "Ah yes, the Benue contract!"

he said, almost as if he had been expecting Drummond to raise the subject for some time. "Quite a departure for us, eh Roger?"

"Why yes, Mister Ronald, it's certainly that. Unfortunately, it has several drawbacks that I believe have been overlooked."

Ronald leaned back in his chair, still with that amused expression on his face, so that Drummond began to wonder if he were the unsuspecting victim of a practical joke. "Really? Well, if that's the case they've certainly been overlooked by Joseph, haven't they? But go on, Roger—which drawbacks do you mean?"

Drummond cleared his throat, a hand straying to the knot of his tie as he felt his face redden. "There is a strong possibility that the contract will be discontinued after this year. Benue has negotiated a USAID package with which they'll probably buy medical supplies and equipment. If this happens, not only will our own contract not be renewed, but the money we've advanced for the development of the new drug will be lost..."

"Oh, not *completely*, Roger, surely. Drugs are developed to treat diseases, after all."

Drummond knew by now that Ronald was playing with him; all the same, he was grateful for his reminder that the balance-sheet mentality was one that he had sworn to avoid. "That's quite true, Mister Ronald, but if we're not going to market it we'll incur a tidy loss—or at least it will take us years to recoup the investment. Ours is becoming a most competitive business, after all, and cash-flow must assume an important place in our calculations."

"But simply because the Americans will be supplying the non-drug needs of Benue for a few years there's no reason to assume that the Benuegans won't purchase our drug. It's something they desperately need. Apart from capital, they need manpower to develop, and men debilitated by that wretched disease have very little power indeed, Roger."

"But part of the costs of the research on the drug were to have been offset by the very volume of our non-drug sales, Mister Ronald. If that volume is nil, my reservations are surely justified."

Ronald chuckled, having obviously enjoyed the game. "You're a bright lad, Roger, a damn sight brighter than your uncle if I may say so. And you're right, of course. If the factors you've enumerated were all the equation consisted of, we'd be up the creek. But there's more."

Exhausted, Drummond slumped in his chair. It was clear that the downfall of Uncle Joseph had been postponed.

"Your Uncle Joseph had little to do with this contract. Oh, I let him think that he had negotiated it—had even thought of it—himself, but in fact most of the work was done behind his back. Now, you're obviously a man who does a lot of research. You probably spend a great deal of time at the library. Well, I'm afraid I've never been a stickler for that kind of work myself. Lazy, I suppose. Never had to work when we had the Empire, of course, and I suppose that's one of the legacies that is bringing this country down at present. But I'm just as guilty as the trade unionist who thinks he can have two tea-breaks in the morning and three in the afternoon.

"No, Roger, the research for the Benue contract was brought to me by a friend of mine. A member of the House. Shan't say which party. We owed each other a few favours and he thought we could pay each other back by collaborating on this contract. He's quite pally with the Arabs, belongs to one of those associations that promote trade with them. Anyway, he wanted to draw Libyan money into this country, and he thought that our little firm would give them a favourable idea of what British business was like."

"Libyan money, Mister Ronald?"

"Precisely. As you no doubt know, Libya has quite a strong influence in Benue these days. Wants to keep the Americans out. There is a faction in the Benuegan government, however, that wants 'em in. In Libyan eyes, that places us on the side of the government faction that wants 'em out. Here we are, quite small compared to some of these American companies, doing our best to help Benue and even financing some original research into a drug that will quite revolutionise the place. Then the pro-Americans cancel our contract."

"You expect Libya to step in and take up the order?"

Ronald smiled. "A much-expanded order, I might add. Libya is swimming in oil money and we're going to get rather a lot of it, Roger."

*

Trying another tack, Drummond now suggested to Uncle Joseph that what the firm badly needed was a product it could call its own. Since they were not in manufacturing themselves, they would have to commission the design and manufacture from one of their suppliers.

"Oh, I doubt whether Ronald would sanction anything of that magnitude right now," Uncle Joseph said at the time. "Bit of a new departure, that."

"We'll say that it's your idea, Uncle Joseph," Drummond had suggested. "As you say, it's all in the family."

"Mm. The idea has a certain attraction, I suppose, and Ronald *could* be made to recognise its merits. But what sort of product had you in mind?"

"An electro-cardiograph, perhaps. I see also that there's an amplified stethoscope on the market. Cheapest place to buy that is Germany, I believe."

"A *what*?"

Drummond smiled. "An amplified stethoscope, Uncle Joseph. Useful for doctors who are a little hard of hearing."

"You're not serious, Roger. Next, you'll be suggesting a respirator that whistles the *Stars and Stripes*. Hmph! This gadget is...American in origin, I take it?"

"It may well be, but that's the competition we're up against; it may be a bit gimmicky, but it has a very useful practical application where the heartbeat is very weak. A patient could be declared dead with such a heartbeat, especially in a country with no more sophisticated equipment than the normal stethoscope, which is really what we're talking about, isn't it?"

"Mm. Yes, I see. Well, leave it with me and I'll see what can be done." He raised an eyebrow at Drummond. "And I'm to put this forward as my own idea, you say. All in the family?"

"Absolutely, Uncle Joseph. All in the family."

A week later, Ronald summoned them both to his office.

"Joseph has come up with rather a good idea, Roger," the old man announced, a knowing glint in his eye as he watched for Drummond's reaction.

"Really, Mister Ronald?"

"Yes. Says it's about time we began putting our own name on things."

"Ah yes, Mister Ronald, Uncle Joseph did mention it to me. As you say, it's rather a good idea, especially the amplified stethoscope," he said with a straight face. "As a matter of fact, I've made a few enquiries, and the manufacturers are certainly able to supply us. It would simply be a question of agreeing on quantity and price."

"I see." Ronald tapped on his blotter with a gold paperknife. "Well, alright, but I want to see the figures before you go ahead with it."

The only real obstacle was encountered over the size of the order: the manufacturers would not countenance an order of less than a thousand amplified stethoscopes. This entailed, then, a considerable outlay by M & T. Drummond convinced Uncle Joseph that the equipment would be delivered within a fairly short space of time and advised him, in the interests of "the family," to continue presenting the argument as his own. With some reservations, Ronald finally acquiesced. After this, it was simply a matter of sitting back to let market forces, helped along by the actions of at least two governments, do the rest.

8

It was some months after this that Drummond received a call from Lemay, suggesting that he drop around to the High Commission in Earl's Court after work.

He drove past the building shared by the high commissions of Dominica and St. Lucia and knew that he was close. He had feared that the most frustrating part of his journey would come now, as he searched for a vacant parking space in Earl's Court's narrow streets, but timing played its part, as shortly after 5 p.m. one vehicle after another was pulling away from its metered space. Securing a spot just yards from the door of the Arawak High Commission, he fed the meter and then ran to the small flight of steps leading to the polished oak door.

As he entered the building, he heard the purr of a large vehicle and turning saw an aging black Bentley pull up at the kerb. He held the door open for the Caribbean man who now stepped through it to walk down to the car, and he knew from the clipped moustache, distinguished greying hair and well-tailored ensemble that this was H.E. Barclay Grant, the High Commissioner.

Drummond crossed the red carpet and told the middle-aged male receptionist that Lemay was expecting him. He was asked to take a seat and a few minutes later a very dark, attractive woman in her early thirties came to escort him to Lemay's office, where he was surprised to find Lal Sharma.

"Mr Sharma! This is an unexpected pleasure."

"Oh, good evening, Mr Drummond." Lal Sharma stood up, a tall, good-looking man with a spade-shaped beard; it was easy to see what Shirley saw in him.

"If I'd known you were coming this way, I could have given you a lift," said a mystified Drummond.

Lal Sharma grinned. "Quicker by public transport, Mr Drummond." He checked his watch. "I arrived fifteen minutes ago."

"Yes, quite possibly." Drummond frowned across at Lemay. "But I don't quite see…"

"Oh," declared Lemay, "Lal is a frequent visitor to the High Commission."

Drummond thought for a moment and then, none the wiser, shook his head. "I still don't…"

Lemay was enjoying this. "Tell him, Lal."

"I'm Arawakian, Mr Drummond," he said, resuming his seat.

It all came back to him: after the abolition of slavery, planters in the British Caribbean had imported Indian indentured labourers, thus explaining the presence of people like Cheddi Jagan in Guyana and V.S. Naipaul in Trinidad. And, it turned out, Lal Sharma in Arawak. Drummond instantly relaxed and broke into a self-deprecating smile. "What a fool I've been." He eased into the seat next to Mr Sharma. "Even so…"

"Lal has some distressing news, Roger. Your company's potential contract with Arawak may be in jeopardy." He pursed his lips and said again, "Tell him, Lal."

Rather like a doctor about to impart the bad news to a patient who believes himself to be in the best of health, Lal Sharma crossed his legs, folded his hands in his lap and moistened his lips.

"The company," he said, "is headed for financial difficulties. In the first place, sales of the new products have not been at all swift. Although the profit-margin is wider than usual, most of them remain in the warehouse. The German mark rose to new heights just as payment for the stethoscopes was due. Then the Benuegan government failed to renew its contract. The Libyans may well be willing to pick up where their clients had left off, but they are slow in doing so, with the result that M & T has expensive equipment in its warehouse with no prospect of moving it for some months. Finally, a large bill has been presented by the pharmaceutical institute that has just completed research on the new drug. You are presumably aware of much of this detail, Mr Drummond, but a forensic view of the books"—yes, he was just like a doctor!—" leads to the inescapable conclusion that we have insufficient cash to remain afloat. M & T has, for the first time in its history as far as I am aware, a cash-flow crisis."

Drummond felt as if he had been underwater, holding his breath for the time that Lal Sharma had been speaking. He now let it out somewhat noisily. Some of the responsibility for this parlous state of affairs, he knew, lay with him: the ideas for the stethoscopes and the new drug had, after all, been his. He looked across at Lemay seated behind his desk and wondered whether he realized that he shared in the guilt for urging him to undermine Uncle Joseph. He turned to Lal Sharma. "Is Mister Ronald aware of this situation?"

"No, but I have laid the facts before Mister Joseph. If he does not speak to Mister Ronald in the very near future, I shall have to do it."

Despite the seriousness of the situation, Lemay suddenly burst into laughter. "Mister Ronald! Mister Joseph! Is this really how you speak to each other at Merritt & Thwaite?"

Drummond and Sharma turned to each other and shrugged before directing their attention to Lemay, each giving him a shamefaced nod.

"But if, Mr Drummond..." Sharma attempted to continue.

"Roger! His name is Roger!"

"But if, as assistant exports manager, Roger, you feel that you should be the one..."

For Drummond, the pieces now fell into place: Sharma and Lemay had rehearsed this moment, with Lemay urging Sharma to make this suggestion as a further means of placing himself to succeed a discredited exports manager.

Although replying to Sharma, Drummond fixed his gaze on Lemay, letting him know that he was wise to his game. "Well, we'll make that decision if and when the time comes, Mr Sharma."

Lemay grinned across at Drummond and mimed the word "Lal."

Drummond ignored this. "You were saying, Garry, that the Arawak contract might now be in jeopardy."

Lemay shrugged. "Of course. If M & T goes under, there will obviously be no contract. If, on the other hand, it survives in straitened circumstances, the contract could well be on less friendly terms than we had hoped."

Drummond nodded grimly and turned to Sharma. "Is there a solution...Lal?"

"A loan—and soon."

"But sooner than that," said Lemay with a smile, "I suggest we relieve the tension by going for a drink. But first I must place some papers on the High Commissioner's desk that he needs to look at tomorrow morning. Give me a minute."

"Does Shirley know about this situation?" Drummond asked, simply making conversation, while Lemay was out of the room.

Lal Sharma nodded emphatically. "Oh yes, we tell each other everything."

Drummond was appalled. *"Everything?"*

Lal Sharma was puzzled for a moment but then broke into laughter. "Oh, you mean that thing at Christmas a few years ago! Yes, she told me about that." He smiled. "But don't worry. I've been in this country long enough to know that these things happen at Christmas parties. Besides, it was only kissing."

*

When the position could no longer be hidden from Ronald, Uncle Joseph walked into the old man's office like a man going to the gallows and emerged looking like a ghost, charged with raising a loan large enough to tide them over until the Libyan deal was concluded. Everywhere he went, however, he was confronted with impossibly high interest-rates. No one in the City, it seemed, was prepared to risk very much on a medium-sized company with little to offer in the way of potential other than contracts with unstable Third World governments.

In the middle of the crisis, Drummond received another call from Streeter.

"Hi, Roger!" he began breezily. *"Could you use a loan right now?"*

"Whatever for, Mr Streeter?" Drummond replied, unperturbed. He leaned back in his chair and smiled, prepared to enjoy the one occasion in his life when he would have a transnational on the hook.

"Whatever for!" Street echoed. *"I like that, Roger, very much. And the name's Phil. Come on, I know you're in trouble. If you don't raise some bread within a week, you'll have an appointment with the Official Receiver. So how about it?"*

"You tell me, Phil." Drummond replied coolly. "How about it?"

"Pardon me?" Street was taken aback by Drummond's swift change of tack.

"How about it? At what rate of interest? That seems a sensible place to start the discussion."

"How long for?" Streeter was all hard business now. He was like the man who has just clinched a date with the most

attractive and unapproachable woman in the office, unable to believe his good fortune but pressing on with the details of where and when to meet.

"Six months should be adequate, I would think. Give us enough time to sign a couple of sizeable contracts."

"Seventeen point five."

"That's a nice figure, but a little on the high side, Phil. Perhaps you'd better call me in a day of so."

"Come on, it's a lot better than you were offered in the City."

"But you're not the City, Phil, are you?"

"My point exactly. That's why it's so low, Roger."

"If your people want M & T, you'd better tell them it needs to be a lot lower."

"Or we could let you go under before we move in."

"But your people don't want to do that, Phil, do they? The last thing you want is to take over a company that has just gone under, thereby shaking the confidence of both suppliers and clients. You said it yourself, Phil: you want to present the image of the traditional, respectable, solid business run by men who learned their business ethics on the cricket pitches of this fair and green land. If we fail and you move in, you'll do so amid no little publicity, especially in some of our client countries, where the M & T name is the biggest in the field. Just think of it, Phil: M & T snapped up by the greedy imperialist transnational. I would have thought you would have wanted the transition to be rather more discreet than that."

"Okay." There was a short silence at Streeter's end. *"Fifteen."*

"Thirteen."

"Are you nuts? The minimum lending rate's twelve-and-a-half, for Chrissake!"

"And inflation is only 8.3 percent, so in real terms you'll pocket 4.7 percent. Divided by two, of course, as we're talking of only six months." Drummond paused and exhaled noisily through his nose. "Stop buggering about, Phil. Do you want M & T or not?"

"Are you serious about this? Is the old man really ready to let go of the reins?"

"I think I can engineer him into a situation where he won't have any choice."

"You're a sharp operator, Roger. I bet you didn't play much cricket, did you?"

"No, but that's not really the sort of person you want on your team, is it Phil? Apart from Ronald, as you said yourself, for a figurehead."

"Maybe not. Okay, I'll put your figure to my people."

"But we haven't discussed the amount—or is that not important to you?"

"I'm guessing half a million."

"A million."

"Dollars?"

"Sterling."

If, Drummond thought, Streeter had been Caribbean, he would have sucked his teeth; instead, he made a sound like air escaping from a punctured tyre.

"Which bank will you be using?"

"Philadelphia National."

"Alright. One more thing."

"Shoot."

"Were you serious when you said that we had about a week to go? Is that the feeling in the City?"

"Yeah—a week, ten days at most."

"I see. You'd better call me in five days, then."

"Are you crazy? A week may be the general feeling, but it could be a lot less. You need the money now, Roger."

"Five days, Phil. I know exactly what I'm doing. Trust me." He replaced the receiver.

Those five days were sufficient to allow Uncle Joseph to run through the remaining possibilities, none of which came to anything. At the end of the period, he seemed to have aged ten years. Although Drummond knew that he was more concerned with his pride than the good name of M & T, he felt some sympathy for him.

*

Ronald remained remarkably calm throughout the crisis. Drummond could only assume that he was taking it philosophically and with the dignity expected of one who had walked the corridors (or, rather, sailed the sea-lanes) of colonial power. It was a cardinal error to let the natives see that you were afraid, after all.

"Roger," he said, when he called him into the office, "you are aware that we are passing through a little crisis at the moment.

Joseph has just been to see me. He offered his resignation." He paused and regarded Drummond closely.

Although Drummond's heart missed a beat, he maintained an outward calm, apart from allowing one eyebrow to elevate in mild surprise. "I see, Mister Ronald…"

"But I did not accept it." He paused once more to gauge Drummond's reaction, but again was met with what appeared to be something bordering on indifference. "Instead, I told him to take a month's leave. I understand that he will be spending this in Kenya. As usual, I'd like you to take over his job until his return, Roger."

Ronald was certainly putting a brave face on things: in fact, he seemed to disbelieve the serious nature of the crisis.

Drummond nodded. "Of course, Mister Ronald."

Ronald smiled. "In due course, that arrangement may become permanent."

To demonstrate his modesty—which was, of course, entirely false—Drummond allowed a frown to crease his brow.

"Come now, we both know that Joseph is not quite up to life in the modern business community. You, on the other hand, appear to have a natural talent for it. If we can hang on until the Libyan money comes on-stream and the Arawak contract is signed, we'll pull out of the present difficulty. And I'm aware that you were responsible for that opportunity, Roger, although Joseph was quite happy to take all the credit."

Drummond shrugged. "Ohh…"

"Don't sell yourself short, Roger, just because Joseph is family. And from now on you can drop the 'Mister.'" He lay his head back and sniffed.

"Are you quite sure we're going to pull through, Mister Ronald?"

"Ronald. Positive." He looked Drummond in the eye. "Couldn't be more so. Do you have any thoughts on the matter, by the way? Any avenue we might investigate to secure a short-term loan?"

Drummond cleared his throat. "As a matter of fact, I do. I didn't mention it earlier because I was not sure how you would react."

"Go ahead, Roger. Let's hear it. I promise not to fire you for at least a week."

Drummond smiled uncomfortably. "There is a bank called Philadelphia National that will let us have the kind of money we require for six months at an annual rate of thirteen percent."

Ronald looked down at his hands, deep in thought. Then he chuckled and looked up, his clear blue eyes sparkling. "Americans? Dear me, and with poor Joseph not yet cold in his grave—not yet *in* his grave, in fact. But I would have thought that there must be a few strings attached for them to offer terms that are—comparatively, at least—so favourable." He folded his hands on his blotter and awaited Drummond's response.

"And that is why I've hesitated to raise the matter. You see, their parent company would rather like to buy us—you, that is—out."

Ronald leaned back in his chair, swinging sideways and stretching his legs. He reached for his gold paperknife and tapped it thoughtfully on his lips. "Yes, I thought there might be something like that involved. But why haven't they moved in for the kill already?"

"They want the world to see the traditional M & T flourishing and stable; and, besides, they don't want to enter the scene in a blaze of publicity."

"They want to preserve the character of the firm, d'you mean?"

"Very much so. They want their name kept in the background as far as that is possible. In fact, they'd like you to remain at the helm."

Ronald raised his eyebrows. "Interesting. Any chance of us accepting the loan on any other terms?"

"Only on the understanding that they will be allowed to buy you out sooner or later."

"How much later?"

"Just as soon as we've got over this rough patch and re-establish ourselves as an effective and reliable company—all of which could take place fairly swiftly, of course, once those contracts are signed and the money begins to flow again."

Ronald swung around to face Drummond, bringing his hand down onto the blotter in a decisive gesture. "Alright, but the terms are as follows: they advance the loan at twelve-and-a-half percent interest—but for a full year—and before the end of next year we'll sell them forty-nine percent of the company."

Thinking about it afterwards, Drummond thought his mouth may have fallen open at this point. "But how could I persuade them to agree to that?"

"Because, as they might phrase it themselves, they're not the only game in town."

"But Uncle Joseph and I have tried every possible City..."

"Oh, I know. That's the trouble with tradition, Roger: it stifles creativity." He winked at Drummond. "I had another chat with my MP friend a day or two ago. He is perfectly confident that, if the situation were explained to him, Col Qadhafi would sympathise with our plight and throw us a million quid at zero percent interest."

"Then why not approach him?"

Ronald laughed. "Well, you're obviously not inhibited by tradition, are you, Roger?" He fell silent, assuming a more serious mien. "I was tempted to do precisely that, my boy. Now, the choice before me is between letting almost half the company go to the Americans and placing it in a position of obligation to Col Qaddafi." He sighed. "No, Roger, put my terms to your contact and we'll see what comes of it."

Drummond got to his feet. "Very well, Ronald."

"Don't go just yet, Roger."

Drummond, pallid after Ronald's revelation, resumed his seat.

Ronald swung his chair sideways and stretched his legs, then picked up the gold paperknife from his blotter and began tapping his knuckles with it. "How long before we get a signature on that Arawak contract—any idea?"

"Well, as you know, they're recovering from the effects of the floods, but the bauxite revenue will soon be appearing on their balance sheet..."

"You're perfectly right, Roger: I *do* know that. I was rather hoping you'd be able to give me some inside information. I understand you're rather well-connected at the High Commission..." The blue eyes twinkled, the mouth smiled easily; for his age, Ronald was a handsome man.

Drummond told himself not to respond immediately, to slow down, take his time, and inspect the road ahead for booby-traps. He forced a grin. "All part of the job, Ronald. Of course, if you would like me to make enquiries before Uncle Joseph returns from annual leave..."

"I would, Roger, I would." He sighed and made eye-contact with Drummond. "In fact, I would like it even more if you could persuade them to open negotiations before Joseph returns from his hols—in which case you would be our representative." He grimaced. "He means well, but I hear on the grapevine that the Arawak people weren't best pleased with Joseph's patronising approach. You're the man for the job, Roger."

"Well, that's very gratifying, Mister Ronald, but presumably Uncle Joseph will be back in three weeks or so..."

"If you can start the negotiations before then, that will be the easy way of dealing with Joseph." He was now frowning down at his blotter, suddenly the hard employer. He looked up at Drummond and held his gaze. "If you can't, I'll have to deal with him the hard way."

At a loss, Drummond cleared his throat. "I see. Well, if that's all, Ronald…"

The tough face suddenly melted. "Not quite, Roger." He smiled. "How is Miss Evans doing?"

The afternoon was full of surprises. "Miss Evans? Actually, it…it's…"

"Yes, yes, I know it's Mrs Sharma now." He shrugged and tossed the paperknife back onto the blotter. "I just wondered whether you thought we should promote her." He twinkled a mischievous grin. "I know the two of you were pretty close a few years ago, and so I thought…"

In Drummond's mind, a hand descended onto a coffee table, silencing an alarm clock.

*

"Hils, I'll be late tonight. I have to go to the Arawak High Commission." Lemay had protested that he was snowed under with work and unable to get away.

"Not to worry, darling. In fact, I'll be out myself. Audrey called and asked me to go to a talk with her."

"Asked you to go for a walk with her?"

"No, darling, a *talk*. Will it be alright if you eat out, or do you want me to leave something?"

Preoccupied with the mission Ronald had assigned him, Drummond felt no urge to question Hilary's somewhat unusual evening excursion. Audrey was a neighbour, the wife of George Colson, a personnel manager whom Drummond had never really got to know. "No, that's fine. I'll eat somewhere in town."

He walked over to the window and groaned as he saw that the City streets were lashed with rain. It was 3.45, and it would take him forever to drive from the City to Earl's Court. The alternative—taking the Tube and then making the return journey later in order to collect the car and drive home to Acton—was, however, even less attractive. Besides, if he left immediately he would miss the worst of the traffic. Picking up his briefcase and grabbing his raincoat from the hat-stand, he made his way to the lift.

"Early day, Roger?" Ronald was adjusting his tie as he awaited the arrival of the lift.

Drummond laughed aloud as he was reminded of his late morning arrivals during his early weeks at the company, when he had often shared the lift with Uncle Joseph. "Far from it, Ronald. I'm off to see a man about a contract," he announced confidently.

The lift arrived and they stepped in.

"That's very...commendable, Roger," Ronald murmured with a smile but then, perhaps realising that his own early departure was unexplained, spent a moment inspecting the fingernails of his right hand. "I," he said finally, having cleared his throat, "have an evening engagement for which I must prepare."

Drummond, praying that Ronald would not use their few moments of privacy to once again allude to his adventure with Shirley Evans, was almost oblivious to the other man's discomfort.

His timing seemed fortunate, for he managed to slip through the City with minimum delay. Having traversed the Strand, he drove down Whitehall, across Parliament Square and into Millbank. From here, he would drive straight, turning right at Cheyne Walk before weaving his way to Earl's Court. Relaxed now, he had time to replay the events of the afternoon. Mister Ronald was turning into something of a mystery man, for even leaving aside his contact with Libya he must have several impeccable sources of information. How did the old man know that he was "well-connected" at the Arawak High Commission, and that the Arawakians had not appreciated Thornton's display of paternalism when he had visited their fair isle? Who could have been the source? Lemay? Of course: Lemay. Who else? It was at this point that he realised that Ronald had been uncomfortable in the lift, almost as if he had felt guilty at having been caught sneaking off early. But that was ridiculous, for Ronald was the guvnor and could come and go as he pleased—and, in fact, did so. His embarrassment, therefore, could only have been occasioned by the nature of his "evening engagement," which meant that it must be in some way connected with the matters they had discussed. If it concerned Arawak, this would mean that his source at the High Commission must be someone other than Lemay, for he was at this moment awaiting Drummond's arrival.

Did any of this matter? There was no particular reason why it should, but he had a feeling that it did. And how did the mention of Shirley Evans fit into all this? If Ronald thought so highly of her—and she *was* extremely good at her job—he surely would have promoted her long before now. No, Drummond suspected that the only reason her name had been mentioned this afternoon was to let him know that Ronald had witnessed them burrowing into each other's pants all those years ago. But why?

*

As previously, he was escorted to Lemay's office by Yvonne, Lemay's secretary.

"Okay, Yvonne, call it a day now. See you tomorrow." Lemay looked up as they entered his office and Drummond could see immediately that this Lemay was just a little more careworn than the one he'd last seen. While his desk was tidy, it probably held a great deal more paper than that of Barclay Grant. He waved Drummond into the chair opposite him and pushed his own back, expelling a mouthful of air as if he had been doing push-ups.

"The coffee-maker's half-full and it's still fairly fresh," said Yvonne from the door. "Please don't forget to switch it off before you leave."

Lemay gave her a mock salute, then smiled at Drummond. "Coffee?" He pushed himself from his chair and followed Yvonne into the outer office. Drummond heard him arguing with her, telling her to go home while he poured the coffee. "I hope," Lemay called as he filled the mugs, "you're the bearer of good news, because we surely could use some. Our credit-rating has been lowered, exports have declined, and Washington appears to be flying guns into the country, utilising the ganja trade."

"But the bauxite is being mined and things will soon start looking up," Drummond suggested hopefully.

Lemay re-entered the main office. "Hard to say how long that will last, though. If the bauxite mines had been well-established, I would think that the North American companies would now be slowing production as part of the destabilisation campaign." He placed a mug before Drummond and shrugged. "They can't really do that, though, as they've only just started production."

"Well, I *think* I bear good tidings." He took a sip from his mug and placed it down again. "The boss wants me to negotiate the contract with your people..."

"So you did it?" Lemay's mouth had dropped open.

"Nope, this comes from Ronald—don't ask me why. But he also wants to sideline Thornton with as little pain as possible, which means starting the negotiations within the next two weeks, before he returns from his Kenyan holiday."

"Shit. That's a tall order, Roger. And what do you mean 'starting' the negotiations? How hard will this be?"

"I want you to have the equipment at a knock-down price, Gary. That means you're going to have to beat us down. So do you have any mean negotiators in your health ministry?"

Lemay sat blinking at him while he digested Drummond's words and then began to smile, wagging a finger across the desk. "You bet we do! Do me a favor, Roger: amuse yourself in the outer office while I make a call home."

Drummond frowned and looked at his watch.

"It's mid-morning in Arawak, Roger."

*

"She'll be here next week," Lemay announced as he opened the door to the outer office and leaned on the doorpost.

"She?"

Lemay smiled. "Davinia Lee, our health minister. You're in for a rough time, Roger."

"No problem. That's exactly what's needed. But won't she feel slighted?"

"Slighted?"

Drummond spread his arms. "I'm a mere assistant exports manager, Garry."

"Ahh!" Lemay waved a dismissive hand. "Don't worry—I'll brief her on the situation. Besides, I assume that your MD will meet her for the actual signing."

"OK, as long as you're sure. By the way, I did some thinking while you were on the 'phone. Must be the adrenaline. We've overlooked a factor that could work in our favour."

"I'm all ears."

"You know what year this is?"

"1978."

Drummond sighed. "And what anniversary will be marked during the year?" He smacked the surface of Yvonne's desk with the flat of his fingers and smiled at Lemay. "The thirtieth anniversary of the formation of our National Health Service, Garry!"

"Yes," Lemay nodded, frowning as he sought to locate the significance of this event, "but how…"

"We have a Labour government, Garry. They will obviously want to make a big fuss of the thirtieth anniversary. They'll probably look upon it as restating their socialist credentials, despite—or maybe because of—the fact that Dennis Healey has handed responsibility for economic policy to the International Monetary Fund. Jim Callaghan could use some good press, so what better opportunity than this?"

"You mean..?"

"Exactly! On the thirtieth anniversary of the NHS, a Labour government makes a generous grant to assist a member of the Commonwealth in modernising its own health service."

Lemay was smiling now. "It sounds good, Roger. But won't this have to be agreed by your own health minister?"

"No, Gary. This will fall into the lap of the Minister for Overseas Development, who seems a decent sort."

"Yes, we're obviously familiar with her. But surely her ministry's budget will be already allocated this late in the day."

Drummond made a face. "Don't know. They must surely have a reserve for emergencies."

"What emergency?"

"We'll have to create one, Garry."

Lemay nodded. "I think I'd better call the Minister again."

*

Before driving home, Drummond took Lemay to Khan's in Westbourne Grove, just a mile or so from Lemay's flat. During the meal, the Arawakian began to have doubts regarding the possibility of a grant from the Ministry of Overseas Development. "Let's be realistic about this," he said, prodding his glasses with a forefinger. "How likely is it that the British government, which is fully supporting Washington in its attempt to destabilise our government, will put its hand in its pocket to help us out?"

"You may have a point there," Drummond conceded. "But the needs of your health service, and the plight of the Arawakian public, are going to be made very public." He broke off a piece of poppadom and brought it to his mouth, hesitating while he continued, "Whatever it's doing to support Washington, on the other hand, is behind the scenes, very secretive. In fact, it's possible that it will gladly come up with a few million just to indicate that its hands are clean." He shrugged and deposited the cracker in his mouth. "We'll see."

Lemay poured white wine for them both. "How are things with Hilary?"

"Bloody awful."

"Because you're working behind her uncle's back?"

"Oh, no—she let it be known quite some time ago that she doesn't give a damn about Uncle Joseph. In fact, she wants me to succeed at his expense." He looked at Lemay. "I hadn't realised how long it's been since we've had a chance to talk. Anyway, it was only this afternoon that Ronald sprang this latest departure on me."

"My, you're a fast worker, Roger."

"With Joseph due back in a few weeks, it's a case of having to be." He glanced around the restaurant to make sure they could not be overhead and then leaned forward. "There were a couple of other surprises in this afternoon's little tete a tete that I need to mention to you."

Lemay raised his eyebrows and, in Drummond's estimation, had no idea of what was to come.

"He knows that I am, as he put it, 'well-connected' at the High Commission, and he also knows that Joseph made a prat of himself in Arawak. Who at the High Commission knows that you and I are friends?"

Lemay smiled good-naturedly and shook his head. "Well, since you first visited us, all the people you've seen at the High Commission know about you, but before that...No, no one. They—the High Commissioner, for example—obviously knew that I had a contact in your company, but they didn't know who that was. Regarding Thornton's behaviour, that was known to practically everyone." He shook his head again. "But there is no reason why anyone would have spoken to your boss."

"Someone in the Arawak Support Group, maybe?"

"Oh, well...It's never possible to be absolutely confident about security in a broad solidarity organization, but I don't see what anyone would have to gain. And who would be in a position to know Ronald Mathews? But who did *you* tell, Roger?"

"That's just it, Garry: no one, apart from Hilary."

*

He drove to Acton by following the number 7 bus route on which, in another life, he had often worked as a conductor. Although the rain had stopped several hours ago, the glistening streets were almost empty and he made good time. As he arrived home at 11.15, the signs indicated that Hilary had returned and gone to bed. Having shed his raincoat, he made himself a cup of hot chocolate and sat over it in the kitchen, sketching out a negotiating plan for the following week but, finding that his brain had slowed, he soon tore the page from his pad, screwed it into a ball and walked across to the pedal-bin under the sink. As the lid lifted, he glimpsed a green A5 leaflet and bent down to gently ease it out, smiling as he saw that it was a Christian tract of some sort that urged the reader to avoid despair as "the LORD can give your life MEANING." This had obviously been pushed through the letterbox while Hilary had been out and she, upon her return, had placed it where it belonged. He returned it to its grave.

9

Later, Lemay would advise Drummond of the rapid pace of developments in Arawak following his last telephone conversation with Davinia Lee.

Within forty-eight hours, the *Arawak Chronicle* was on the warpath, running banner headlines about the parlous state of the health service in the small Caribbean country. Dengue, typhoid and tuberculosis stalked the country and yet where were the facilities to provide adequate care for all? In attacking the shortcomings of the self-proclaimed "socialist" government of Lester Robinson, the newspaper thought that it was serving the interests it had traditionally supported, i.e., those of the Arawak Democratic Party, the local elite, and foreign investors. However, although the idea had been put to Forbes Thomas, editor-in-chief and publisher, by a staunch and prominent ADP supporter, its origin could be traced (but of course never was) through a chain of intermediaries leading back to the office of health minister Davinia Lee. The campaign had an added attraction for the ADP and the owners of the few large local firms in that Davinia Lee was possibly the most left-wing member of the Cabinet.

However, her spirited rebuttal soon brought home to her detractors the fact that their campaign could inflict but limited damage on either her or the government. "It seems to have escaped the attention of our critics," she told a reporter from the country's only (and state-owned) television company, "that we have been in office for less than two years. If our health service has defects—and I would be the first to admit that it has, and that those defects are both numerous and major—our people know very well upon whom the blame should be laid. So when dem trow stone dem muss careful dem don't meck dem shiny glass house come crash down 'pon dem fat backside!" The press conference at which this warning was delivered dissolved into laughter at this point, and the anecdotal evidence indicated that the same effect was achieved with those who viewed television or listened to radio collectively, in downtown bars and outside tiny stores throughout the countryside.

Now the *Chronicle* was faced with a problem: how could it withdraw from the campaign it had started without appearing to be in full and undignified retreat from the wrath of Davinia Lee? Contact was made with her office, and it was explained that, while the newspaper's remarks about the current government's responsibility had perhaps been a little opportunistic, its main intention had been to focus public attention on this vital issue. This was not only in the public interest but was, surely, objectively supportive of Ms Lee's efforts as health minister.

"Are you saying," Ms Lee asked Forbes Thomas when she called him later that day, "that you wish to join with us in a crusade to modernise our health service?"

There was a brief silence at the other end of the line. But what could the man say? That he was now opposed to the idea? That he needed to take advice? "But," he said finally, "we have already started the crusade, Madam Minister."

"Will you join me in a press conference late this afternoon so that we can announce this new departure?"

"Of course, Madam Minister." Thomas did not sound particularly happy.

"Excellent. And would the ADP be prepared to join this crusade of ours—or perhaps I should say of yours?"

Now Thomas chortled. "How would I know, Minister?"

"The same way you always know, Mr Thomas."

"A little unfair, Minister. Well, we can ask—we are a newspaper, after all."

"And Mr Thomas?"

"Minister?"

"I'd take it as a personal favour if you could make sure that local stringer for the BBC is present. I understand his day job is with you."

"Gregory Beckford?"

"That's him. And one last thing, Mr Thomas."

"Minister."

"Hold the front page."

*

Given the size of the media in Arawak, press conferences were never huge, but this one was as packed as they got. Left or right, the media practitioners liked Davinia Lee because she always provided good entertainment value, but this time the word had gone around that something peculiar was about to unfold, and the atmosphere in the conference room of the Ministry of Health was electric with anticipation.

There could be no doubt that it was her show. At 5.30 she swept into the room, her slim body enclosed in a loose scarlet blouse and frock, and strode swiftly to the top table, which was festooned with microphones. Accompanying her was Forbes Thomas, a fifty-five-year-old, yellow-skinned man dressed in an incongruous three-piece suit. Struggling to keep pace with the woman who was twenty years his junior, he arrived at the table well behind her and nodded uncertainly to the *Chronicle*'s team before taking his seat.

She was a rich dark brown colour, and although, as indicated by her surname, her father had bequeathed her a certain proportion of Chinese blood, the only sign of this was in the eyes. Without waiting for an unnecessary introduction by the woman press officer who hovered at the edge of the table, she stood, both hands splayed on the table-top, and called the journalists to order. Then she straightened up and began. Immediately, a journalist at the back asked if a press release would be distributed. Throwing back her head, she sucked her teeth and gave the unfortunate man a mock scowl. "You want us fe write de dyamn story for you?" Then she smiled and said softly, "No, I'm sorry. No release yet. We just didn't have time, and we thought that this was something you needed to hear without delay." On the second "we," she turned to Thomas, including him in the decision, and he smiled in reluctant complicity.

She reminded them that at the press conference just a day before she had said that she acknowledged that the shortcomings of the health service were many, and she now listed them: the shortage of hospital beds, the insufficient number of hospitals or health centres in the countryside, the frequent shortages of drugs, the shortage of trained doctors, the absence of state-of-the-art equipment...On and on the litany went. And who should be held responsible for this lamentable state of affairs? The sense of anticipation reached breaking point, for now, surely, the tirade would commence. But Davinia Lee's voice was still not raised, and there was no anger in it. Just a day ago, she had pointed the finger at the ADP, but had she been fair to do so? Well, up to a point. It would be dishonest of her to claim that the ADP had made no improvements, just as it would be dishonest for the ADP to claim that those improvements had been sufficient. The ADP had been in office for ten years—hardly sufficient time to effect the complete transformation of a Third World health service. Prior to 1966, however, Arawak had been a British colony for three *hundred* years. Now her voice was raised, and she looked around the room as if wishing to ensure that all present had understood that last statement.

"Can we—any of us, whether we are ANP, ADP or no P— honestly say that the health service handed over to our country just twelve short years ago was adequate?" For a moment, she seemed to think that she was speaking at a public meeting or rally, although the more acute observers would have known that her statement was now being broadcast live over Arawak National Television in an extended news program. "After three hundred years in which our forefathers shed sweat and blood— some as slaves, others as indentured labourers—for the British, didn't our people deserve more than was handed over to them in 1966? And cannot we all—ANP, ADP or no P—put aside our differences and now speak to London with one voice, demanding that a start is made in redressing this injustice?" She sighed. "Let me return to that question later."

Lowering her voice, she simply told them what had happened over the past day or two. The *Chronicle* had run stories on the health service that she had interpreted as attacks on the government, so she had responded accordingly. But then, just this afternoon, she and Forbes Thomas had talked to each other over the telephone, and (here she began to depart from the truth a little) it had been a revelation for both of them. Forbes (this is what she called him now, although they had never been on first-name terms) had told her that his real purpose in all of this was to place the health service squarely in the public spotlight. If that was the case, she had wondered what they were arguing about.

"And so I asked myself why the government of the day and our country's only major newspaper—even if it usually supports the ADP—should not join forces to support and promote this very noble and patriotic cause." She glanced at Thomas. "And although I cannot speak for Forbes, I would like to think that the same thing occurred to him. Anyway, here we are, totally in agreement on this issue, prepared to work together." Suddenly she struck the table with her fist. "Not only is this a first in our country, but it shows what can be done if people forget party and class interest for a while and focus on the needs of our people." She turned again to Thomas. "Forbes Thomas, I salute your patriotism!"

A somewhat diffident Forbes Thomas got to his feet to claim that the *Chronicle* had always, regardless of the issue, had the best interests of the people at heart. However, its commitment to this particular cause should not be interpreted as blanket support for the government—and, indeed, if the *Chronicle* perceived that the government was faltering in its own commitment to improving the health service the newspaper would be the first to say so.

When the press officer called for questions, a radio journalist asked if the ADP had decided to join the health service crusade, whereupon a voice at the back, introducing itself as belonging to a deputy general secretary of that party, announced that the ADP had always supported the health service and would continue to do so, and if that meant singing from the same song-sheet as the government on this issue, so be it—although the tune would change at the first sign of government back-sliding.

A middle-aged woman from a monthly news-magazine now got to her feet, smiling broadly. "I'm sure," she said, "that our readers would like to know if the ruling party, which seems to have entered an alliance with the ADP and the *Chronicle*, really intends to continue with its relationship with the left-wing Workers' Party." Demurely, she resumed her seat, hands crossed on her lap, and waited to see how Davinia Lee would handle *that* one.

"You know, Miss Kempton, that really is a very interesting question, and I thank you for raising it." The health minister smiled indulgently in the direction of the journalist before proceeding in a reasonable tone, "We have seen this afternoon what can be achieved when people are guided by patriotism rather than privilege. The alliance we entered into two years ago with the Arawak Workers' Party was very similar. The AWP claims to be a patriotic party, and so far I have seen nothing to suggest that such a claim is dishonest. The alliance it proposed to us in 1976 was based on support for our policy of developing our own industrial base, which would surely be in the interest not only of the working people but of Arawakian businesspeople who want our country to have a degree of economic independence that it has never enjoyed before. Similarly, it supports our aim of modernising agriculture and developing a more independent foreign policy. At the same time, just like the ADP and the *Chronicle*, it has said that its support is conditional on the government pursuing each of these policies wholeheartedly, with no backsliding unless this is caused by factors outside our control.

"So you see, Miss Kempton, the only real difference between the Workers' Party and the ADP and the *Chronicle* is that the AWP has extended its patriotism to a range of policies rather than just one." She closed her eyes for a second. "Believe me, Miss Kempton, it is my dearest wish that other parties and interests in our country should also take a patriotic view of some of our other policies, because if they did so they would realise that they are worthy of support. In this regard, I am afraid that your own publication has not been particularly helpful. For example, regardless of any assistance we may receive from the international community, our health service is going to need money—*our* money. That money is less likely to be available if publications—with the occasional support of politicians—run scare stories aimed at dissuading investors from coming here and in general contributing to the atmosphere of destabilisation to the extent that our credit-rating is lowered, and we find it difficult to raise funds on the international market. I would be grateful, Miss Kempton, if you would pray for those misguided people in the hope that they will look at our country with new eyes and see the truth."

There was around the room a mixture of suppressed (for the sake of poor Miss Kempton) mirth and astonishment that Davinia Lee was able to be even more effective when she lowered her voice. Miss Kempton's figure was rigid, her stony smile a poor attempt to conceal the rage within her.

"Are you really suggesting," asked a man from the *Chronicle*, seeking to come to Miss Kempton's rescue, "that those who support the health-service campaign should also approve of your government's developing relationship with Cuba? Is that one of your patriotic policies?"

Frowning, the minister at first appeared to have difficulty understanding the question. "But isn't it obvious," she said after a moment's thought, "that the two are connected?"

Too late, fearing that, like Miss Kempton, he had laid his own trap, the man attempted an interjection. "And you indicated earlier, Minister, that Britain..."

Davinia Lee quieted him with a soft wave of the hand. "Yes, I'll come to Britain, but first let's talk about Cuba. I sometimes forget that many of our people—and not a few of our journalists—still look at Cuba through the eyes of Washington. Those who support the faltering first steps in our attempt to develop our country should understand that this is not so different from what Cuba has been attempting for almost twenty years. Now, why do I say that our policy on the health service is connected to our growing friendship with Cuba?" She paused, apparently wondering how far she should go, and then, pursing her lips and having made a decision, nodded. "You know, I was going to save this for a separate announcement, but it seems to me that this is the most appropriate occasion to tell you the assistance Cuba is preparing to extend to our health service."

As an expectant silence fell, she raised her head. "You remember the list of failings I told you about earlier? One of them was a shortage of doctors. One of the reasons for that shortage is that it costs so dyamn much to train as a doctor that only the sons and daughters of the affluent can aspire to it! And where do they train? Mostly in the USA. What do they do once they finish their training? Forty percent of them either stay in the USA and practice there, or go to Canada or Britain. Only the most committed return to practice here. The only way we can make sure we have the number of doctors our people need is to ensure that the children of the less affluent have access to training."

She looked around the room as if daring dissenters to raise their voices. She threw out her right arm in the general direction of Cuba. "Cuba... *Cuba*, ladies and gentlemen of the media, has agreed to train doctors from Arawak free of charge! There are conditions, of course: the students must come from deprived backgrounds, and once their training is completed they will be expected to return here to practice in deprived areas. You know what? If the Cubans had not stipulated those conditions, we would have suggested them ourselves! So, this is just one of the fruits of our friendship with Cuba." She looked at the *Chronicle* man. "That is how the two policies—on the health service and Cuba—are connected. And, yes, both policies are equally patriotic.

"Another item on my list was a shortage of drugs. Of course, there's not really a shortage of drugs, just a shortage of *affordable* drugs. The pharmaceutical industry is, as we know, dominated by the large American and European corporations. They will tell you about the astronomical cost of research and development—at best a partial truth. The larger truth is that those corporations are more interested in making profits than saving lives. Cuba, my friends...Cuba, struggling under a blockade of its economy, is developing its own pharmaceutical industry—to be more specific, generic drugs, which it will make available to us and other Third World countries at a fraction of the price charged for branded drugs. We won't get all the forms of medication that we need for the simple reason that our Cuban friends haven't developed them all yet, but those we do get will be of enormous assistance to us, both medically and financially. So yes, once again let me emphasise that our friendship with Cuba is a patriotic policy with benefits for the vast majority of our people."

Davinia Lee leaned towards Thomas, whispering, "Where's your man Beckford?"

Thomas nodded at a young man with a neat beard and woolen cap in the front row who had chosen this moment to reach up to the table and check that the tape in his cassette recorder had not reached the end of the spool. The Minister smiled at him, placed her hand over her microphone and murmured, "This is where I give you your British scoop, Mr Beckford, so make sure you have sufficient tape." Contriving to frown and smile at the same time, the BBC stringer nodded and resumed his seat.

"I said earlier," the minister continued into her mike, "that Britain had bequeathed us a health service that was itself in need of remedial treatment. Is it too late to demand that Britain remedy this?" She smiled and wagged a long finger from side to side. "Not. At. *All!*

"But before I discuss that, let's not forget that two years ago we did have a demonstration of British generosity—although not from its government—when we received a donation of medical equipment after the floods of '76. For that we must thank a company called Merritt & Thwaite. Since that time, I have ensured that our High Commission in London maintained contact with the company, because high on our list of priorities, once our economy has fully recovered from the floods and the bauxite revenue has begun to flow, will be health service modernisation—or as much of it as we can afford. In a few days' time, therefore, I will be flying to London to negotiate a package with Merritt & Thwaite." She held up a thick glossy document. "This is their catalogue. And Messrs. Merritt & Thwaite, as thankful as we are for your past generosity, allow me to say that if you think Arawak can afford those dyamn prices, you'd better listen to what Davinia Lee has to say!"

She dropped the catalogue on the table. "But that is only one of the reasons why I am going to London. The second is to have a little heart-to-heart with Sister Amanda Long. Who is she? Sister Amanda is the UK's Minister for Overseas Development. So am I going to London with the Third World begging bowl?" She threw back her head and laughed. "Naw sah! Sister Lee a go fe *demand* that Britain recognise it' responsibility. And this is just the right time for such a mission. Yuh know fe why?" A spirited thump on the table with her fist. "This year, the United Kingdom celebrates the thirtieth anniversary of its National Health Service! And what are we, after 300 years as a British possession, celebrating?"

Davinia Lee narrowed her eyes and smiled. "The answer to that question, ladies and gentlemen of the media, depends on the outcome of my trip to London, and I am both proud and hopeful that both Merritt & Thwaite and the Ministry of Overseas Development will know that I speak for the whole of Arawak, thanks to the patriotic support of the *Arawak Chronicle* and the Arawak Democratic Party!"

*

The *Arawak Chronicle* and the Arawak Democratic Party had for the time being no alternative but to admit, if only to themselves and each other, that they had been outmaneuvered by Davinia Lee. Thus, they played along, making tightlipped but supportive comments when it was unavoidable and sitting back to await the first opportunity to resume their partisan stances.

Following the dispatch from Gregory Beckford on the World Service, the BBC rang the M & T office seeking a quote. Ronald redirected the call to Drummond who, although taken aback by this dramatic development, spoke of the very warm relationship between M & T and Arawak, and said that he was looking forward to meeting the delegation in the next few days. He then called Lemay and told Ronald that he was going to the Arawak High Commission. Shortly afterward, Ronald took a call from Kenya, assuring Joseph Thornton (a keen World Service listener) that there was absolutely no need for him to cut short his holiday. The following day, both the BBC and ITN had television crews in Arawak, and British viewers were given brief glimpses of overcrowded wards and the long line of unfortunates snaking towards the casualty department of the Arawak General Hospital. The London broadsheets then began to pick up the story.

Upon his arrival in Earl's Court, Drummond was treated to Lemay's account of recent events in Arawak, supplemented by a recording of the Davinia Lee press conference which had arrived in the diplomatic bag.

"Well?" Lemay looked across his desk at Drummond, a broad smile on his face.

"Why?" Drummond looked ashen.

"Wasn't it you who said that we should create our own emergency? The stance of both M & T and the British government towards Arawak is now in the public gaze. If a little more pressure is required, all we have to do is turn the tap."

"But in one sense this is bad publicity for Arawak. How is this public airing of the deficiencies of the health service going affect tourist arrivals?"

Lemay, still smiling, shook his head. "This will all be forgotten in a few months' time. And in any case, while it's nice to have tourist receipts, at the end of the day tourism is not going to provide us with the solution to our problems—in addition to which, most of the high-end hotels and resorts in Arawak are owned by foreign corporations. If anything, this publicity will give those corporations an interest in seeing that healthcare in Arawak is improved." He paused, mouth half open, then a murmured "Wow, there's a thought." He reached across the desk for a notebook and scribbled a few words before grinning up at Drummond. "Memo to myself: 'Suggest Minister of Economic Development urges British hotel chains to pressure Amanda Long for grant.'"

"All forgotten in a few months' time?" Drummond echoed. "Does that include the bipartisan approach? Are you really willing to let go of that?"

For a moment, Lemay regarded Drummond silently, as if unable to believe his ears. Eventually, he drew down the corners of his mouth and swept off his glasses. "I'm sorry, Roger. I keep forgetting that you've had little political training." He sighed patiently. "We would be only too pleased if the bipartisan approach not only held but, as Davinia said, was extended to other policy-areas." He placed his elbows on the desk and leaned toward Drummond. "Do you really think that Forbes Thomas and the ADP leadership are comfortable with the position that Davinia has tricked them into? No, Roger, right now they will be working out how they can break out of it and resume the attack. And it's not just them, of course: they will be catching hell from Washington—and maybe London too—for allowing themselves to be trapped into supporting our health service drive."

"So what's the point, Gary?"

"The point, Roger, is that it buys us time. Time for you and Davinia to do your thing. Time for us to make *some* improvements, or at least get them agreed and financed. Soon enough, our opponents will revert to type. You think these people want to wait until 1980 to get us out of office? Not at all, man, not at all. And they will be playing for keeps, Roger."

10

At first, Drummond feared there might be disagreement over the venue for the negotiations, suspecting that Davinia Lee might take the view that as M & T was attempting to sell its product it should be prepared to travel to Earl's Court in order to do so. He therefore made it clear to Lemay that this would not be a problem. However, Lemay said that Ms Lee was perfectly relaxed on this point; her only concern was that the venue be within reasonable travelling distance of Westminster, as she would need to spend part of her time at the Ministry of Overseas Development. Then Drummond discovered a reason why the M & T offices should not be used: if the negotiations were protracted and overlapped Joseph Thornton's return, it would be difficult to exclude him. Earl's Court it was, then. The negotiations would commence on the Tuesday morning and proceed on the understanding that Ms Lee must be back in Arawak by Sunday.

Just as she had swept into the press conference a few days earlier, on Tuesday Davinia Lee entered the High Commission's small conference room like a whirlwind, followed by the grey eminence of Barclay Grant, the High Commissioner, and a male assistant clad in a black safari suit and carrying a bulging pigskin briefcase. Drummond, who had been sitting on one side of the modestly sized elliptical conference table with Shirley Sharma, nee Evans, his note-taker, slowly rose to his feet, unable to take his eyes from Arawak's health minister. Her wide smiling mouth unpainted, she wore a long, billowing sleeveless dress of emerald green and Drummond was instantly star-struck. Barclay Grant eased past her and extended a hand. "Good morning, Mr Drummond. May I introduce..."

"Davinia Lee," that lady interjected, thrusting her hand at Drummond as she gave him a dazzling smile.

He took her slim, cool hand. "Good morning, Ms Lee. It's a great pleasure to meet you. I'm Roger Drummond, M & T's assistant exports manager." Releasing her hand, he cleared his throat and stepped aside. "And this is Mrs Sharma, my assistant."

Davinia Lee nodded and smiled at Shirley. Instead of extending her hand, she waved it nonchalantly in the vague direction of the man in the safari suit. "George will be performing the same job for me," she said, making it clear that handshakes were not required and giving Drummond a small insight into the class distinctions that might exist even within an anti-imperialist government.

His Excellency the High Commissioner waved Ms Lee and George into seats on the opposite side of the table, pulling out the one at the head of the table for himself. Drummond watched as George emptied the contents of his briefcase onto the table, placing a few items (one of which, Drummond saw, was the M & T catalogue, probably the same copy Ms Lee had used so effectively as a prop at her press conference) in front of his employer and retaining the remainder at his side.

"Mr Lemay has told me so much about you, Mr Drummond," she remarked during these preparations.

"And being a public figure, Minister, you are no stranger to me," Drummond responded, careful to avoid giving the impression that Lemay had briefed him.

She appeared to consider this for a second; then she nodded with a tiny smile and turned to Grant. "And where *is* Mr Lemay this morning, Your Excellency?"

Grant peered over his glasses at her, the suggestion of a grin tugging at the corner of his mouth. "Other duties, Minister. He will join us shortly."

In a light-headed moment, Drummond found himself wondering whether these two ever dropped the formality and referred to each other as "Vinny" and "Barkers."

Barclay Grant now started to formally open the meeting, but hearing a sound behind him he halted, closed his eyes, and uttered a soft "Ah!" as he recalled the "other duties" upon which Lemay had been engaged. Lemay now entered, holding the door open for his secretary Yvonne as she brought in a tray laden with a pot of coffee, crockery, creamer and sugar. Yvonne poured and Lemay passed around the cups, saving the last for himself, which he carried to a chair next to the High Commissioner. Grant waited until everyone was creamed and sugared and then began again. We all recall the generous M & T donation...Mr Drummond deserves our gratitude...Needs of the Arawak health service still largely unfulfilled...Who else to turn to but M & T?...Straitened circumstances of Arawak a major factor...Nevertheless confident that negotiations will be conducted courteously and amicably...The ball appears to be in the Minister's court...

Drummond watched Ms Lee as Grant droned on. She scratched away on the A4-sized pad before her, a slight frown pinching her brow, but Drummond could hardly believe that she had left it this late to prepare her opening gambit. No, he thought, this is an act to lull me into thinking that she is ill-prepared. As Grant pronounced the word "courteously," she glanced at him sideways and raised her eyebrows, as if to say, "If you believe that, you'll believe anything," and when she then smiled across at Drummond the message was, "You won't know what hit you."

As Grant concluded, she let her pencil fall from her hand, leaned back in her chair and looked directly at Drummond, her face now expressionless. But Drummond, star-struck though he might be, appeared unmoved, paying her respectful if mildly amused attention. He was prepared. He had seen how she had behaved at the previous week's press conference and, expecting more of the same now, he had planned his strategy accordingly. As anxious as he was to assist Arawak in obtaining as much of its requirements at the lowest price possible for M & T, there could be no question of the company suffering a loss on the transaction.

And then it dawned on him that, far from attempting to intimidate him with this silent scrutiny, she was actually reading him, and by the time she opened her mouth to speak she would have joined together all the dots: he had said that she, being a public figure, was no stranger to him, meaning that he knew all about her outbursts of anger, was expecting to get the rough treatment this morning, and had prepared accordingly. He could see that she now knew all of that and was about to do something totally unexpected. Suddenly, Drummond looked and felt less assured.

Eventually, looking tearful, Davinia Lee waved a forearm in a gesture of inarticulate helplessness, placed her elbow on the table and clasped her forehead in her palm. She shook her head and then looked to Grant. "I'm sorry," she said. "I can't do this."

*

It was the only negotiations Drummond had attended where the first adjournment came before the haggling. He was now alone with Shirley Sharma.

"So, Shirley, any chance you can tell me what's happening here?"

She raised a dark eyebrow. "Isn't it obvious?" Shirley was remarkably calm.

"Not to me, no. Well, apart from the fact that she's just blown my negotiating strategy out of the water. I was prepared for the version of Davinia Lee I knew about, but she's presented me with one I know *nothing* about. If you have any insights, you'd better share them before she comes back." How, he thought, like a manager I sound.

"She knows you're attracted to her."

"Am I?"

"Of course you are."

He frowned at her for a moment and then sighed, as if deciding to humour her bizarre theory. "For the sake of argument only, how would my being attracted to her—not that I am, of course—be of assistance to her in this situation?"

It was Shirley's turn to sigh. "You can see she's stunningly beautiful. You know she's a strong character. The sudden collapse of that strength is intended to bring out the protective male in you. How can you play the hard-faced businessman when she's on the point of tears?"

"Oh, come on, that's so bloody corny it couldn't possibly work."

"But it has." She smiled. "Hasn't it?"

"Bollocks. Anyway, what do you know about Davinia Lee's strength of character? You hadn't heard of her until a day or so ago."

"Oh, I'm sorry, I thought I was married to an Arawakian."

Drummond felt himself reddening. "Oh shit, so you are. I'm such a prat."

There was something in her eyes. "Behave like that with Davinia," she said, "and you may get somewhere."

He pointed to the chair upon which he sat. "You fancy doing this job while I take the notes?"

He wondered why it had not occurred to him before: if Ronald knew that he was "well-connected" at the High Commission, and that Joseph had won few admirers in Arawak, surely Lal Sharma was his source. Or, given that they told each other everything, maybe even Shirley. Yes, and that would explain why Ronald was talking about promoting Shirley!

*

The brief interlude with Shirley had worked wonders, and suddenly he was at ease. Not for the first time, he reflected that their relaxed enjoyment of each other's company and their ability to swap banter had arisen from that feverish sexual encounter several years earlier and their unspoken agreement that no one else would ever know of it and that it would never—*need* never—be repeated. He sat perfectly calmly as the Arawakians filed back into the conference room, paying particular attention to Lemay in an attempt to divine whether he had been party to his minister's unorthodox negotiating ploy, but his friend's eyes were averted, his face a blank. Of course, thought Drummond, even if Lemay had previously known nothing of Davinia Lee's intentions, he would be privy to them now, for she must have explained her actions during the adjournment.

In reopening proceedings Grant, who appeared to be not at all flustered, simply cleared his throat, gave a tight smile and said softly, "Thank you for your patience, Mr Drummond. We will continue now." He nodded to Davinia Lee. "Minister."

The minister placed her hands, palms down, on the table before her, contemplated them a moment and then looked across at Drummond.

*

To the others, it must have seemed that Davinia Lee could do as she wished with Drummond.

He began by handing her a document of medium thickness containing lists of the items previously identified by her Health Ministry as being essential components of the package it wished to purchase. Each item was priced, and on the last page of the document there appeared a total for the whole package.

"As you will see, Minister," he began carefully, his voice low, "we have considered both your requirements and your available resources very carefully." He risked a tight grin. "If you care to compare these prices with those in our catalogue, it will be readily apparent that we have made significant discounts."

Davinia Lee spent a long two minutes leafing through the document, and what seemed like an even longer fifteen seconds riveting her gaze to the final page, before letting it drop to the table as a sigh escaped her. She looked across the table at Drummond, appearing to blink away tears, her mouth turned down in bitter disappointment. "You must..." she began, before covering her mouth with a slender hand and clearing her throat. "You are surely aware, Mr Drummond, that we could never afford these prices." She turned to an equally grim-faced Grant. "Maybe this was all a mistake, High Commissioner." She placed a hand on the arm of her chair, as if to rise.

"Minister." Drummond placed an outstretched hand, reaching out to her in a plea that she stay, palm-down on the table. A grin would be out of place now: he gave her a gentle smile. "Give me a chance to go through the figures again. Please. There may be some wiggle room." He turned to Grant. "It would be a great help if I could have the use of a telephone during a brief adjournment."

It was Lemay who rose and stepped to the side of the room, where a telephone sat on a small table. Somewhat demonstratively, he picked up the cord and, bending, plugged it into the socket. "All yours, Mr Drummond."

"Would twenty minutes be sufficient, Mr Drummond?" asked Grant.

"Thirty would be better, sir." Drummond glanced to Shirley Sharma, as if seeking confirmation. "Yes, thirty minutes, if we may."

Davinia Lee, who had been sitting with a hand covering her mouth, now gathered herself and stood. Before turning towards the door, she touched the tabletop with the tips of her fingers and gave Drummond a sad smile. "You will do your best, won't you, Mr Drummond?" Her eyes beseeched. "Please."

*

Thirty-three minutes later, Lemay rapped on the door of the boardroom and peered in, to see Drummond, his jacket draped over the back of his chair, pecking away at a calculator while Shirley Sharma scribbled furiously in her notebook.

"Need a bit longer, Roger?"

Drummond glanced at his watch, as if in disbelief at the swift passage of time. "Sorry, Garry. Another five?"

"Sure that's enough?"

"Positive. I'm just doing the final total."

Seven minutes later, Lemay re-entered the room, followed by the rest of the team. Drummond immediately stood and retrieved his jacket from the back of his chair, grinning sheepishly at Davinia Lee.

"Oh, please," she said, seemingly quite relaxed now. "It's a little warm in here, so feel free to leave off your jacket, Mr Drummond." She smiled. "In fact, I'm encouraged that you feel this is a job you need to roll up your sleeves for."

"Thank you, Minister, that's very kind. But all the same..." He went ahead and donned the jacket.

"Ah," she joked, "now I remember why I love coming to this country: that British modesty and sense of propriety."

For a moment, he appeared dazzled, hands folded in front of him while he sat contemplating this newly confident Davinia Lee. If he avoided appearing to be in a trance, this was possibly because Shirley kicked him under the table, leading him to clear his throat and pick up the sheet of paper in front of him.

"I hope you have a nice surprise for me, Mr Drummond," Davinia Lee purred.

It occurred immediately to Drummond that she could have said "for us" but had—apparently deliberately—chosen to say "for me." This, he suspected, should be filed under "Negotiating Tactics" rather than "Double Entendres."

"Well, Minister," he said, his tone apprehensive, "I hope so too." He passed a single sheet across the table. "You'll have to forgive my scrawl, but what I've done here, having made further reductions in a number of items—most of them, in fact—is to summarise the new total in each category of equipment, then provide the new overall total at the bottom of the page. I can give you the reductions per item if you wish, but you're probably more interested in the totals."

She took the page and ran her eye over it several times, her face impassive. Finally, she sighed and looked up at Drummond. No indication of real disappointment, no suggestion of tears, but no smile either. She sighed again. "Well, we're certainly moving in the right direction, Mr Drummond, but even so…" She shook her head, and her sad smile now was not in disappointment but in commiseration: poor Mr Drummond would have to try a little harder. "We not quite there yet, are we?"

It was Drummond's turn to appear distraught, dropping his eyes and slowly shaking his head. He ran a hand through his tightly curled hair and uttered a long, shuddering sigh before meeting her gaze once more. Where we are, his expression told her, is perilously close to a failed negotiation.

"There's only one area left for further movement, Minister," he told her in exasperation.

She raised her eyebrows and made an open-hands gesture, encouraging him to continue.

"And you may not like it. In fact, Merritt & Thwaite may not like it, either."

Davinia Lee transformed her raised eyebrows into a frown.

"I refer to the area of quality, Minister. Some of the items can be reduced in price if you're willing to consider cheaper models."

"Do you mean less safe, Mr Drummond?"

"No, not at all, Minister. If we sold you cheaper hospital beds, for example, they would be less comfortable, less attractive—perhaps even less hard-wearing."

She sighed in apparent relief. "We're a Third World country, Mr Drummond. For us, comfort and appearance come a long way after the ability to treat people at all. But less durable? Yes, that might concern us." She paused, chewing her lip pensively before making eye contact again. "Look, just tell me what kind of further reduction we might be able to achieve if—without impacting on either safety or durability—we went for lower quality on some items. Give me a ballpark figure."

Drummond sighed and glanced through his notes, flipping the pages. Finally, he shrugged and glanced up. "I'd need to go through the whole list item by item, but overall, given that not all items would be affected, the total might be reduced by a further five or six percent."

Safari Suit George, at the Minister's elbow, now made his first contribution to the meeting, taking Drummond's handwritten sheet, glancing at the figure at the foot of the page and murmuring, "That, Minister, would be, uh…"

"Yes, George," she snapped, "I went to school too." Then she slumped back in her seat and passed a hand over her eyes before looking across at Drummond. "Oh," she said softly, "then I'm sorry, Mr Drummond. I really thought…"

For several seconds Drummond was, in all but his eyes, which blinked nervously at a point in the middle of the table, a statue, arms akimbo, hands clasped before him, lips thoughtfully pursed. He was able to see, however, that the fingers of Grant's right hand, which rested on the table, were gently lifted and he sensed that the High Commissioner, perhaps feeling that he should break the tension, was about to speak.

Drummond lifted his head sharply and directed his gaze to Grant, forestalling his intervention. "With your consent, High Commissioner, I'd like to propose something entirely unconventional."

In the few moments before Grant was able to reply, Drummond surveyed the faces on the other side of the table: there was an amused twinkle in Grant's eye, while those of Davinia Lee were narrowed in calculation as she coolly surveyed this strange Englishman; Safari Suit George appeared confused; of the four, it was probably Lemay, who was looking straight at Drummond with a tiny smile which may have betokened admiration as much as amusement, who approached an understanding of what was happening.

Grant cleared his throat. "Well, Mr Drummond," he chuckled, "you have my consent to make the proposal, but whether that will extend to us accepting it will rather depend on precisely what you put forward."

"Of course, sir." Drummond sat straight in his chair and continued without pause. "I would like to suggest that the Minister and I continue to discuss this matter alone. No notes. Off the record." At his side, he sensed a tightening of Shirley Sharma's muscles, as if she were repressing a gasp.

He smiled at Davinia Lee. "I realise, naturally, that this would require the agreement of Ms Lee."

That lady was now smiling—presumably at his impertinence. Only Lemay had not changed his expression. Grant appeared to be in a quandary. "Well, look, Mr Drummond, if there is the possibility of further progress, we can surely…"

"High Commissioner," Drummond broke in, "I have absolutely no wish to mislead you: there is no possibility of Merritt & Thwaite agreeing to a further reduction in the price I have quoted, subject to some movement—five or six percent, as I've said—in the area of quality."

"But then what," asked Davinia Lee, "would we have to talk about, Mr Drummond?"

"I'd like to explain to you—and you alone—*why* it's not possible for me to agree a further reduction." He hoped he was coming across as earnest, honest and committed.

"But if this involves some commercial secrets or…sensitivity," said a very proper Barclay Grant, "it would surely be a mistake for you to…"

"Let's do it, High Commissioner" said Davinia Lee. She glanced across at Drummond, a reassuring smile on her lips. "As Mr Drummond has said, this will be off the record, and if there is indeed any commercial sensitivity involved it seems that he feels that he can trust me. If it were otherwise, he surely would not have suggested the discussion."

*

As Davinia Lee sat calmly, her hands folded on the table, her smile had a neutral quality about it. "So, Mr Drummond…"

Now, for the first time, Drummond—eyes lowered, thinking furiously—was nervous, although he reasoned that it would do his case no harm if he allowed her to see this. He raised his eyes and sighed.

"Minister…"

"Davinia."

Oh shit. He swallowed. "How much has Garry Lemay told you about me…Davinia?"

"Well, Mr Drummond…"

"Roger."

She laughed; he chuckled. They were both at ease now.

"He's told me that you are a good friend to Arawak, Roger, that you were the moving force behind the donation of equipment after the hurricane…"

He nodded. "Good. Because I want you to know that I intend to go on being a friend to Arawak."

"But what would prevent you?"

"I meant being a friend in my current employment." He uttered a sigh of exasperation and threw out a hand in the direction of the sheet containing his calculations. "Look, it must be obvious to you that I'm not a businessman. You've twisted me around your little finger this morning." He wagged a finger at her. "There was I, expecting to be confronted with a firebrand, and you present me with this vulnerable woman."

She grinned. "It's somewhat tiring, being a firebrand all the time, Roger."

"But that's alright. To be honest, I've never *wanted* to be a businessman. It was only when I began to take an interest in some of the countries that Merritt & Thwaite deal with that I decided to stay with the company."

Davinia Lee was drawing circles on the table with her index finger. "But I still don't understand, Roger."

He leaned forward in his chair, elbows on the table, and locked onto her gaze. "I really have gone as far as I can with these prices, Davinia. Any further and I would be out of a job, or perhaps demoted, and therefore unable to help Arawak in the future."

"Ah," she said, leaning back her head and thoughtfully stroking her long neck with a finger, "I see." She smiled warmly across the table. "But why did the others have to leave before you could tell me this?"

"Because the others, with the exception of Garry, would not have understood. I watched the recording of your press conference last week and was impressed by the level of your understanding, and the depth of your feeling." He struck his chest with an open palm. "Well, although in radically different circumstances, I have some of that feeling too, and I just want you to know that I'm not some sharp businessman trying to get the best deal possible for my company. I'm on your side, Davinia."

She was as softly feminine as she had been all morning, cocking her head to one side and smiling across at him with what looked like genuine affection. "What a sweet man you are, Roger."

He decided to make a joke of it, clearing his throat as he collected his papers together and replying gruffly, "I may not be a hard businessman, but I'm not sure how I feel about being described as sweet." He shrugged his shoulders and returned her smile. "I'm just sorry we were unable to come to an agreement."

"Oh, but we have, Roger."

He dropped his papers onto the table. "Excuse me?"

"Now that you've convinced me that there is no more, ah...wiggle room...Hah!" She dissolved into laughter and brought a hand to her mouth. "Oh, Roger, when you used that phrase I could hardly keep a straight face. Wiggle room!"

As she threw her head back and laughed unrestrainedly, Drummond was visited by a tremor of concern. "Davinia, please." He nodded at the door. "What will they think if they hear you?"

"Oh, they'll probably think that I'm enjoying myself." She wiped an eye with the back of her hand, looked across at him and shook her head. "I'll say it again: what a sweet man."

"But you were saying, Davinia..."

"Ah yes. I'm now convinced that you can go no further, so we'll just accept your last proposal."

*

"I hope that wasn't too trying for you," Lemay said as he shook Drummond's hand at the street door.

"Not at all; I rather enjoyed it."

"So did the Minister."

"Oh, I'm sure. She's quite an actress."

"You're not so bad yourself, Roger." He leaned close and lowered his voice. "I especially liked your request for the telephone. I assumed you would be calling your boss during the adjournment to clear your next offer."

Drummond glanced over Lemay's shoulder. Shirley waited patiently on the pavement. "That was the idea, yes."

Lemay wagged a playful finger. "Strange then, that our switchboard tells me that there was no call made from the boardroom."

Drummond took it in his stride. "That's right. I decided it wasn't really necessary."

Lemay looked into his eyes for two seconds and then smiled. "Oh, okay. Well, I'll let you know how tomorrow afternoon's meeting goes."

*

"Would I be correct in assuming," said Shirley Sharma as Drummond drove them away from Earl's Court through the light lunchtime traffic, "that he was asking you why, having asked for a telephone, you didn't use it?"

"You would, Shirley."

"And why didn't you?"

"Because," he replied as, just before the lights changed, he turned right into High Street Kensington, "it was all an act. But you knew that."

"To be honest, I wasn't sure."

"Mm. So I was that good."

She chuckled. "On a more serious note, are you sure that Mister Ronald will be okay with the price you agreed?"

He overtook a number 28 bus as it entered the bus lane. "Mister Ronald," he said with a disrespectful sneer, "will be bloody ecstatic." He flashed his eyes at her, noting her puzzled frown. "You see, Shirley, by adopting the negotiating tactic you suggested—and I must thank you for that—I was able to get Ms Lee to agree to a sum somewhat in excess of that which, yesterday afternoon, Ronald and I agreed should be our bottom line."

"Oh bugger."

"Yes, I know what you must be thinking: English businessman tricks poor Third World island nation out of thousands of pounds. And, of course, you're right—or you would be if that was all there was to it. But that was not my intention. I wanted to let her have the goods at the cheapest possible price, but the more I thought about her helpless-little-girl act, the more pissed off I became. So I put on an act of my own."

"So you got the better of her."

"Not really: if she's successful at the Ministry of Overseas Development tomorrow, the UK government will end up bearing the cost."

Shirley Sharma clapped her hands and laughed, delighted by this twist.

11

When he arrived back in his office at 2.30, he was told that a Mr Streeter had left a message that he return his call as soon as possible.

"Streeter."

"Good afternoon, Phil."

"Roger! Where the hell have you been?"

"I *beg* your pardon?"

An exasperated sigh. *"Sorry. I've been trying to get you forever, Roger. Frankly, I thought the boot would have been on the other foot."*

"Not sure I'm with you, Phil."

Another sigh. *"It's your company that's desperate for a loan, Roger. I thought you'd want to know how my people reacted to your proposed terms."*

"Oh, I see. Well, yes, I'd be interested to hear their reaction. To be honest, however, we're not nearly as desperate as when we last spoke. The Arawak contract is as good as signed—that's where the hell I've been this morning, Phil—and I think Ronald may have another source of funds."

"You don't say." Streeter was, it seemed, not at all perturbed.

"That seems to be the case, yes."

"Do you want to hear my news or not?"

"Oh, go ahead, Phil. I'm all ears."

"My people found your terms absolutely outrageous, Roger." A pause for dramatic effect. *"Nevertheless, they're willing to agree."*

"Oh, that's wonderful, Phil. I must let Ronald know right away."

"Their agreement, however, is subject to two conditions."

"Ah, here we go. Let me guess: they want fifty-one rather than forty-nine percent of M & T."

"Bullseye!" Streeter seemed amused. *"But that's the easy one, Roger. Any idea what the second condition might be?"*

"Not a clue, Phil."

Brief though the pause was, Drummond later realized that Streeter had used it to banish all traces of levity from his voice, replacing it with cold steel. *"Make sure that your company stays well away from Libyan money. Do I make myself clear?"*

*

"Ah, good afternoon, Roger!" Ronald looked up from his desk, smiling in expectation of good news. "How did it go this morning?"

"It went very well, Ronald, very well. We're almost there."

"Oh, excellent!" He paused, a frown creasing his brow. "But you look less than overjoyed, Roger. Is there a problem?"

"I have just spoken to my contact with International Enterprises, Ronald," came the tentative reply.

"Oh, I see." One raised eyebrow. "Bad news?"

"That will be for you to say. The loan from Philadelphia National is available, but subject to conditions."

"I assume they want fifty-one percent; that was to be expected. Anything else?"

Roger laughed. "Yes, I guessed that first one myself. In addition, however, the company must have nothing to do with Libyan money."

"How the blazes did they know…? You didn't…?"

Drummond shook his head vigorously. "No, of course not."

"A friend at the High Commission, maybe?"

"No one, Ronald."

"Not even Hilary?"

Drummond was somewhat surprised that Ronald would refer to his wife, whom he had only met once, by her forename. "Especially not Hilary."

It was Ronald's turn to look surprised. "Why *especially* not Hilary?"

"Her outlook on international affairs is somewhat…conventional."

Ronald nodded. "Ah, I see." He inclined his head to one side, eyes slightly narrowed. "But you trust her in…other matters?"

Failing to see the relevance of this area of enquiry, Drummond hesitated.

"I'm sorry, Roger. That's none of my business. I had no right to ask."

"No, that's alright." His silence now was thoughtful. "Funnily enough, I've never given much consideration to the question myself. So yes, I suppose I trust her." He grimaced. "Or, as she might see it, take her for granted."

Ronald grinned and spread his hands. "Alright, let's leave that." He sighed. "I suppose your man…"

"Streeter."

"Your man Streeter will be expecting a response."

"He will indeed, Ronald."

Ronald inserted a knuckle into his mouth, biting. "Well, tell him we'll accept—minus his second condition. If he presses you on it, you can tell him that in this country we don't appreciate foreigners telling us how to conduct our business."

"And I could also tell him that whether or not we need to borrow from Libya is to an extent dependent upon the successful outcome of our negotiation of the Arawak contract."

A nod. "You could." A quiver of concern. "But that's not in doubt, is it?"

"Not at all. As I said earlier, we're almost there."

This assertion would, however, turn out to have been a trifle optimistic.

*

Late the following afternoon, he received a call from Lemay, asking that he come to the High Commission to hear the bad news.

"They turned you down?"

"They did, Roger."

"Any explanation?"

"Better come and hear it from the horse's mouth."

Drummond stepped into Ronald's office. Ronald appeared to be preparing for another early departure, slipping documents into his briefcase.

"There's a hitch in the Arawak business, Ronald."

Ronald's face dropped. "Oh?"

Drummond sighed. "Yes. It turns out that the Arawak government was relying on a grant from the UK government in order to purchase the equipment. The Minister for Overseas Development has just turned them down."

Ronald grimaced. "Well, that's a bugger!" A pause, during which the cloud seemed to lift from his brow. "Still, I expect the Arawakians will now go back into campaign mode, won't they?"

That had not—yet—occurred to Drummond. "Well, yes, I suppose they might."

"They certainly created enough fuss a week ago."

"You're right, Ronald. So it may be that all is not yet lost..."

Ronald gave him a tight grin. "I would hardly think so, Roger." He snapped his fingers as a thought came to him. "Have you spoken to that American fellow yet?"

"Streeter? Not yet, no."

"Good! You can now tell him that we'll definitely need the Libyan money now, so there can be no question of us accepting his second condition." Seeing a frown beginning to form on Drummond's brow, he winked. "Trust me."

"And the fifty-one percent?"

"No, tell him they can have fifty, price to be negotiated once we've weathered this storm."

Drummond nodded and got to his feet.

"Oh, and Roger?"

At the door, Drummond turned. "Ronald?"

"Get on to Streeter right away, while the Arawak thing is hot news."

*

"Good afternoon, Phil."

"Hi, Roger. What can you tell me?"

"The Ministry of Overseas Development has just turned down Arawak's request for a grant for its health service. This puts our Arawak contract in jeopardy, and so we will certainly need the cash that Libya is offering."

Streeter seemed to take it in his stride. "Any more glad tidings, Roger, or is that it for today?"

"Couple of things, Phil. First of all, we can't let you have fifty-one percent of M & T; fifty-fifty is as far as we're prepared to go."

"And the price?"

"That will have to be negotiated once we've overcome these current difficulties."

"I see." Streeter fell silent for a while, and Drummond wondered whether he had replaced the receiver. But then Streeter uttered a long sigh. "What would you say, Roger, if I told you to go to hell?"

"Oh, I'd probably say that we'd have to struggle along on what the Libyans might be able to spare us."

When Streeter failed to reply, Drummond assumed that he was no longer taking it in his stride.

"Anything else, Roger?" Streeter said finally, somewhat testily. "You said there were a couple of things."

"Yes, Phil," said Drummond, speaking evenly, as if totally unaware of the tension on the line, "the final thing is that if the Arawak contract falls through, we would struggle to find the thirteen percent you're asking for the loan."

"But thirteen was the figure you suggested!"

"True, but that was before this Arawak problem." Drummond was now speaking without authority, but what could go wrong?

"I'll have to get back to you," Streeter snarled.

*

"Hello, Hils. I have to go to the High Commission, so no dinner for me. I'll eat out."

"Oh, that's alright, Roger. In fact, I was just about to call you, as I'm going out myself."

"Okay, I'll see you later."

Having replaced the receiver, Drummond spent a few moments frowning down at the instrument. Then he shrugged and got to his feet, patting his jacket pockets for his car keys.

12

As Drummond pulled out onto the street, he glanced in his rear-view mirror and saw Ronald reversing his black Mercedes from his parking bay. Although the rush-hour approached, the weather was fine, and he made good time. Passing the House of Commons, he caught sight of a group of vaguely familiar figures, although he was driving down Millbank by the time their identity came to him: trade union activists with whom he had had a fleeting acquaintance when, in another life, he had worked on the buses; they had probably been at a meeting at Transport House in Smith Square and were now making their way to Westminster station. A sudden flash of nostalgia took him by surprise, and he found himself wondering if, had he been strong enough to resist Hilary's ambitious plans for his future, he might have been happier if he had stayed on the buses, perhaps graduating to driver, possibly even becoming active in the union. That, of course, would have meant no house and a cheaper car, but so what! He would have survived. More importantly, maybe, surely Hilary would not have stood for it. Ha! Again: so what! He laughed aloud at this reckless thought. Worth thinking about? He shrugged his eyebrows and spent a few moments reflecting on the possibilities.

Arriving in Earl's Court, he easily spotted a parking space and walked back to the High Commission, where he found Lemay, Davinia Lee and Barclay Grant seated in the small boardroom. He helped himself to a chair and looked around at the other three, raising his shoulders in enquiry.

"I smell a rat," said Davinia Lee. She wore an emerald trouser suit which set off her brown skin. She did not seem to be particularly upset.

"To tell you the truth, Mr Drummond," rumbled Barclay Grant, "I think we all smelled that rat."

"As expected," explained Lemay, "Mrs Long told us that the budget for her ministry had been set some time ago and that it would be quite impossible to make a grant to Arawak at such short notice." He sighed. "But she looked very uncomfortable as she trotted this out, Roger; I would go even further, in fact, and say that she looked as if she didn't believe what she was saying."

"And that," said Barclay Grant, "was the rat we all smelled."

Davinia Lee frowned. "You know, Barkers,"—a movement in the corner of her eye attracted her attention and she glanced at Drummond, to see him hastily bringing up a hand to conceal his grin—"on second thoughts I'm not sure I entirely go along with that. Oh yes, there was certainly a rat. But Sister Amanda's discomfort was just the tail of that rat. We all thought—didn't we?—that pressure had been brought to bear on her by either Callaghan, the Prime Minister, or Foreign Secretary David Owen, to deny this request for a grant..."

"But surely that stands to reason, Minister," said Lemay. "And Callaghan and Owen would, in turn, have been pressured by Washington."

Davinia Lee waved a dismissive hand. "That would hardly have been necessary, surely. Even so, it's entirely possible that Sister Amanda was under instruction from Callaghan, Owen or both." She paused. "But I suspect that the real rat was that civil servant who sat alongside her. Did you notice how she was constantly turning to him."

"Tall, slim, one of those middle-aged white guys who always look younger than their age. Grey hair, neatly cut. Speaks with a bit of a lisp; probably one of those public schoolboys that Westminster is reputedly full of." Lemay was addressing Drummond, as if he might recognise the man from this description.

Drummond shrugged. How would he know?

"Yes, you may very well be right, Minister." Barclay Grant turned back to Drummond. "We were in his company for a few minutes before Mrs Long arrived." He snorted. "His idea of small talk was a little surprising."

Recalling that brief discussion, Davinia Lee laughed. "You can say that again!" She turned to Drummond. "You wouldn't believe it, Roger"—she gave no indication of noticing the briefest exchange of glances between Lemay and Barkers at this use of Drummond's forename—"but he expressed the view that Arawak would find it much easier to navigate international waters if our socialism were of the British variety.

"And how did you respond to that, Minister?"

She hesitated, and seemed to be about to tell him to call her Davinia before thinking better of it. "I told him I was Health Minister and that responsibility for the economy lay in other hands, but that if he was suggesting that Arawak should duplicate Britain's National Health Service he would meet no argument from me."

They all laughed. "And did that shut him up?" asked Drummond.

"Oh, you should have seen his face!" said Lemay. "What a picture!"

"What I found surprising," said Barclay Grant in almost a whisper, as if fearing that what he was about to say might be considered undiplomatic, "was that here was a person with, one gathered, considerable power and influence, and yet he appeared to be—how can I say?—not particularly *bright*."

"I think the same might be said," responded Drummond, "of a great many members of the British ruling class." He looked across at Davinia Lee. "But what will happen now, Minister? Will you be returning to Arawak immediately?"

She laughed. "Roger, I recall you saying that you were familiar with Davinia Lee! Do you think we've just been sitting here waiting for you since we returned from the Ministry? No, Roger, a news release has been produced and sent to all the media that picked up on the original story last week…"

"Along with the left-wing press and the London-based Caribbean newspapers," supplemented Lemay. "I've also spoken to the Arawak Support Group, and tomorrow afternoon they—along with others, hopefully—will be demonstrating outside the Ministry of Overseas Development: a further follow-up story for the media."

There was a knock on the door, followed by the appearance of Yvonne, Lemay's secretary.

"Excuse me, Minister. The BBC just called to say that they're on the way. There are also a few print journalists outside."

Davinia Lee snapped her fingers and got to her feet. "Just in time for the evening news! I'd better get out there, gentlemen."

"No, Minister," intervened Barclay Grant, "it would surely be more appropriate if you and I met the journalists here, during which Mr Drummond and Mr Lemay can retire to Mr Lemay's office."

Davinia Lee nodded. "Good point, Barkers. It would in any case be a mistake for Roger to be spotted by the media: that would create the impression that it's his company which is lobbying for government money. And Roger? Stay until I'm finished and I'll buy you dinner."

"I couldn't possibly accept that, Minister," Drummond replied. "Dinner's on me."

*

"She's right about the media spotting me," Drummond remarked once they were seated in Lemay's office, "but I have to say I would have liked to watch her deal with the media, particularly if she's going to perform as she did at the news conference in Arawak last week."

Lemay laughed. "Yes, me too."

"Well look, Garry, you don't have to stay with me if you want to..."

Lemay waved a hand. "It's alright, Roger."

Drummond sighed. "Garry, I'm wondering why you asked me along here this afternoon. I could make no meaningful contribution to the discussion, and..."

"It was the Minister's suggestion that you attend, Roger." Lemay grinned. "I think she likes you."

*

When Drummond extended the dinner invitation to Lemay, Davinia Lee could barely conceal her relief when he demurred, saying that he would visit Alex Preston, who lived a few doors away from him, and check on the arrangements for the Arawak Support Group's demonstration the following day.

Drummond suggested they go to Khan's and so drove through the early evening traffic towards Notting Hill Gate.

"Tell me something, Roger," said Davinia Lee as they drove up Kensington Church Street.

"Anything, Minister."

"Davinia," she said, patting his arm. "Why were you grinning when I told the High Commissioner that I didn't quite agree with him about that rat we all smelled?"

"Because, Davinia, you called him Barkers, and I had wondered whether you called each other Barkers and Vinny when you were alone."

"How delightful! Well, you were only half right, because he would never call me Vinny—or even Davinia, come to that."

"Whyever not?"

"Fear, Roger. I seem to have that effect on some people."

Drummond laughed.

She sighed. "That has its advantages, but it also limits the number of close relationships I have."

His heart skipped a beat. Should he say this? "I'm not afraid of you, Davinia."

She smiled. "I know. That's one of the things I like about you."

At the lights at Notting Hill Gate, he turned right into Pembridge Road.

"Won't your wife be expecting you home for dinner, Roger?" asked Davinia Lee.

"No, she's out tonight."

"Anything exciting?" When she saw him frown, he placed her hand on his arm. "Oh, I'm sorry. That's none of my business."

He smiled to reassure her. "No, that's alright, Davinia. To tell you the truth, I have no idea what she's doing. That's why I frowned."

"Oh," she said. "I see."

A few moments later, she pointed to a turning on the left. "I'm staying in a flat down there, by the way. The High Commission keeps it for visiting members of the government."

Drummond filed away that information and changed the subject. "I should warn you, Davinia, that we may have trouble getting a table at Kahn's. It only opened last year and it's very popular; there's often a queue."

"Well, we'll see. It's midweek and so maybe it won't be a problem."

Westbourne Grove was fairly busy, judging from the numbers on the pavements, but Drummond found a parking space some fifty yards from the restaurant. He alighted, but by the time he reached the passenger door Davinia Lee had already let herself out. She grinned and took his arm. Arm in arm, then, they walked eastwards in the balmy, early spring evening, looking like lovers or a married couple and attracting attention, she in her emerald-green trouser suit and he in his light grey, single-breasted suit.

"What do you feel when you see people looking at us?" asked Davinia Lee.

He looked at her and smiled. "I feel like a very lucky man," he said. "But what do you suppose they're thinking?"

"They're thinking that we're an attractive couple."

"Now *there's* a thought."

As Khan's was on the other side of the road, they walked until they stood opposite the restaurant, peering across in an attempt to see if there were tables available; there was no queue.

Suddenly, Davinia Lee stiffened.

"What's wrong, Davinia?"

"You see the man, slim with short grey hair, at the table in the middle of the restaurant? That's the rat."

"Oh, Christ!" He turned, guiding Davinia Lee away. "Let's go back to the car, Davinia."

"Why? Do you know him?"

"No, but I know the man sitting with him."

13

Davinia Lee leaned over him and gently stroked his head.

"You're going grey at the temples, Roger."

He opened his eyes and was confronted by her small brown breasts. "Mm, I know. I have a stressful life."

"Are you feeling stressed now?"

He smiled. "Not at all."

"So what *are* you feeling?"

"Hopefully, the same as you're feeling."

"That's possible." She sighed. "You know this is crazy, don't you?"

He raised his head and kissed a nipple. "Yes, but I don't care."

She brought her face to his and kissed him on the lips. "Me neither. For now."

*

Leaving Westbourne Grove, Drummond had driven back to Notting Hill Gate, where they dined at the Chinese restaurant near the Underground station.

"Aren't you afraid of being recognised, Davinia?"

She shook her head dismissively, holding her chopsticks in mid-air. "Roger, I'm the Health Minister of a small Caribbean nation. Who's going to recognise me?"

"Caribbean people?"

She looked around the almost empty restaurant. "You see any here?"

"Well, you've been getting a lot of publicity lately and…"

"A few minutes—if that—on a news broadcast here and there. Believe me, Roger, it takes a great deal of exposure before public recognition becomes a problem."

"Where did you learn to use chopsticks?"

She frowned at him. "Are you indulging in all this small talk in order to avoid telling me about the man in Khan's?"

"Yes."

"Well, I've seen through it, so tell me about him."

"His name—or so he says—is Streeter, Phil Streeter. He's American, and claims to represent a company called International Enterprises, which is interested in taking over Merritt & Thwaite. They've also offered us a loan to help us over the rough patch we're currently going through."

"So what would be his connection with a British civil servant?"

Drummond grimaced. "I now suspect that your rat can only be described as a civil servant in the broadest definition of that term, Davinia."

She paused reflectively. "I see. And what would have been the purpose of their meeting this evening?"

"I think you'll discover that tomorrow."

"Will I? How?"

"Unless I'm completely wrong, you'll get a call from Amanda Long saying that there's been an awful misunderstanding and that your request for a grant has been approved."

She laid down her chopsticks and looked up at him. "Well, that would be good news—wouldn't it? Who do we have to thank for that?"

He grinned. "Well, me—in part at least."

"Why?" Her frown almost became a smile. "What did you do, Roger?"

He reached across and patted her hand. "Let's see if I'm right first, Davinia." He cleared his throat. "Now, your use of chopsticks..."

Davinia Lee laughed. "Alright, I think I understand." She held up her chopsticks. "These? Have you forgotten my surname, Roger?"

*

"Well, Davinia," he breathed as he drew up outside the High Commission's flat, "it's been a pleasure, and hopefully one we can repeat before you return to Arawak."

She turned to him, her face trying not to betray disappointment. "You won't come in?"

"You haven't asked me."

Her smile was one of relief. "Would you like to come in, Roger?"

"I would like that very much, Davinia."

The flat was neat, although not luxuriously furnished, but it had not been dusted recently.

She waved in the direction of the sofa. "Can I get you a drink, Roger?"

"Do you know what I would really like, Davinia?"

She came close to him, lifting her face in invitation. "I can probably guess."

He kissed her soft lips, drawing her to him, feeling her body warm against him. "Actually, you probably can't guess," he said softly as their lips parted. "I'd like to watch *News at Ten*, Davinia." Seeing her eyebrows rise in something like outrage, he added, "For your interview."

Her outrage was replaced by laughter. "Ah, of course." She glanced at her watch. "Five minutes to go. And it won't be the lead item, so you can at least give me another of those nice kisses."

His lips touched hers for just a moment before he drew away. "ITN did turn up, did they?"

"Oh, yes. A bit late, but they were there."

That one kiss led to others, and before long the jacket of Davinia Lee's trouser suit lay on the floor and Drummond was unfastening her bra. Suddenly, she held up a restraining palm and dashed across the room to switch on the television and ensure that it was tuned to Channel 3. Then she was back in his arms, looking up at him as if to say, "Alright, please continue," and he was struck with the thought that, for all her beauty, Davinia Lee might not be as practiced in this activity as might be expected; it apparently had not occurred to her that she could take the lead. He swung her onto the sofa and, falling to his knees, buried his face in her small, firm breasts.

"*Meanwhile,*" said Sandy Gall, "*the government appears to have found itself in trouble with one of the smallest members of the Commonwealth.*"

They now sat side by side, elbows on knees, as Sandy read further into the piece. They must, thought Drummond, look quite ridiculous, Davinia Lee half-naked and he still in his suit. As she had made no move to undress him, he now stood and began to strip off while watching the news-piece unfold.

"As viewers may recall, last week the small Caribbean island of Arawak demanded that Britain take action to modernize the island's badly under-equipped health service. Now, just days later, Health Secretary Davinia Lee is in London to pursue that demand at the Ministry of Overseas Development. At a meeting this afternoon, however, Minister Amanda Long ruled this out for the foreseeable future. ITN spoke to Ms Lee at the Arawak High Commission."

And there was Davinia Lee, lips pursed and eyes blazing, as she replied to a question from the ITN reporter.

"Our health system is in a parlous state because that was how Britain left it when it departed from Arawak in 1966. In this year—the thirtieth anniversary of Britain's own National Health Service—it is surely appropriate that Britain should begin to make amends for its crimes and oversights of the past. What crimes? Why, slavery, of course! Britain's industrialization in the 19th century was made possible by the capital accumulation generated by the slave trade and the sugar industry, and so in a very real sense Britain is indebted to Arawak and the other Caribbean nations.

"Today, Mrs Long has said No. Well, make no mistake, Mrs Long, Arawak is not prepared to take that for an answer, and we—along with, I might say, the many Britons who support our cause—will continue to campaign on this issue until we have justice."

Back to Sandy Gall in the studio. *"We obviously haven't heard the last of this particular story, and ITN will advise you of further developments as they occur. Meanwhile, in other news..."*

"Was that...? Why, Roger, you've..."

"Yes, I have." He had disrobed, a process of which Davinia Lee had been quite oblivious, and now stood there in his underpants. "What were you about to ask, Davinia?"

She covered her face with her hands for a moment, and when she removed them it was clear that she had been embarrassed. "I was going to ask," she said, "if my performance was okay."

He fell to his knees and kissed her lightly, taking her face between his hands. "Of course it was, Davinia. It was more than that: it was superb." He regarded her closely, smiling gently, and could see that she was genuinely pleased by this verdict, which could only mean, in turn, that she had not been at all confident.

"Of course," she said, "if you're right about this Streeter fellow, it will have been all for nothing."

"But, my darling..." What was he saying? Somehow, the use of this word, hitherto so middle-class and false-sounding, felt so right when applied to Davinia Lee. "But, my darling, no one will ever know about Streeter's role." His hands, already cupping her face, exerted a gentle, reassuring pressure. "The victory will be all yours."

She beamed, positively beamed. "Oh, Roger, Roger, Roger." She threw her arms around him, whispering, "Take me into the bedroom, please Roger. Now."

*

She was so nervous and reticent that he found himself taking every initiative—except kissing, and he assumed that this was because kissing, which could be done without undressing, was something with which she was more comfortable. It seemed that striking fear into those who might otherwise have become intimate with her had, as she had said, exacted a toll. He made love with her slowly, gently, protectively.

"Am I really your darling?" she whispered after the first time.

"Oh, I certainly hope so, Davinia. Will you be my darling?"

Her voice was still a whisper. "Yes, I would like that."

"I'm sure, though, that many men must have called you their darling."

She regarded him silently for a while, and then: "Not so many, my sweet."

My sweet!

"But how can that possibly be?"

"As I told you: fear."

He smiled and kissed her on the mouth.

"But we must be careful, Roger."

"Yes, I understand that, sweetheart. If your political opponents could see us now, for example, they would probably say that you had seduced me in order to influence our negotiations."

She laughed. "They would have a hard time arguing that, Roger, as the negotiations were completed yesterday."

"Ah. Well, I was going to tell you about that, my darling. Strictly speaking, they're not completed."

She stiffened. "You surely don't intend to demand a higher price in view of the grant from the UK government—if it materializes."

He smiled. "Quite the contrary, Davinia. When we finished yesterday, I still had a little wiggle room..."

She giggled. "Wiggle room again!" Suddenly, she frowned. "Then why didn't you use it?"

"To be honest, Davinia, you had irritated me with your little-girl-lost act..."

"That, Mr Drummond, was not entirely an act."

He nodded. "Yes, Ms Lee, I can see that."

"So what are you proposing, my sweet?"

"A further reduction of three percent. I'll have Mrs Sharma make the necessary amendments to the notes, if you'll ask your man to do the same."

"And now?"

"And now, my darling, I think maybe I had better make tracks."

She frowned playfully at him. "You *think maybe*. That doesn't sound very decisive, my sweet. I was hoping, as I still have a little wiggle room..."

*

It was 1.30 by the time he reached Acton. The house was in darkness, the curtains closed, and so he assumed that Hilary was in bed. Once inside, he gently eased the door closed behind him, removed his shoes and padded silently upstairs. Finding the bedroom empty, he dropped his shoes on the floor and made his way back downstairs, thinking that he might have a cup of hot chocolate to ease him into sleep mode.

Luckily, he heard the car draw up before he had entered the kitchen or switched on a single light. Drawing the front-room curtain aside just an inch, he saw Hilary stepping out of an expensive vehicle. A black Mercedes. He dashed back upstairs, hurriedly tore off his clothes and was in bed, apparently asleep, by the time Hilary crept into the bedroom.

14

As he drove into town in the morning, Drummond found that the knowledge that his employer was probably having an affair with his wife made little impact on him. She had still been asleep when he had prepared to leave the house without bothering to make himself breakfast, and he had chosen not to awaken her. Now, he listened intently to the *Today* programme on Radio 4 but there was nothing on Arawak. It was too early: it would almost certainly be mid-morning before the Ministry made a decision and close on midday before that decision was made public.

When he arrived at the office, he found that the parking bay reserved for Ronald was still empty. Well, the old boy had presumably had a hard night. Feeling his stomach growl as he pocketed his keys, Drummond decided, for the first time in years, to visit the sandwich bar around the corner.

"Good morning, Luigi."

"Good morning, sir." The proprietor, a thickset Italian with a harelip, at first frowned and then smiled as recognition dawned. "Gordon Bennett! Been a while since you was 'ere, innit?"

"A few years," Drummond replied with a grin. "Didn't have time for breakfast this morning."

Luigi closed his eyes in concentration, holding up a forefinger to forestall Drummond's order. "Don't tell me...Bacon sarny and a cappuccino."

Drummond laughed. "Why not, Luigi? For old time's sake."

He took a table close to the counter. As most regular customers were by now in their offices, the café was almost empty. A bus crew now entered, hurrying to the counter.

"Two coffees, please, Luigi," ordered the driver, a tall good-looking man in his early thirties. "Better make 'em a bit milky coz we're out in seven minutes."

"Okay, mate, take a seat and I'll bring 'em to you."

As the crew took the table next to Drummond's, he noticed that the driver was wearing a red TGWU badge on his lapel.

"Didn't see you at the branch meeting last night, Ted." said the driver.

The conductor, a tubby middle-aged man who parted his hair in the middle, grimaced. "Nah, I'm past it, Geoff. Don't suppose I missed anything, did I?"

The driver seemed genuinely amused. "You 'aven't 'eard, 'ave you?"

Interested now, the conductor leaned forward. "Go on."

"Jimmy Watts reported back on the wage negotiations. You won't believe this, but they've agreed to"—he stabbed the table with a forefinger—"London Weighting,"—second stab—"unsocial hours payments"—stab number three—"and an 'efty increase in the basic rate."

Drummond, halfway through his bacon sandwich, couldn't help himself. "Bloody hell!"

The driver, perhaps suspecting that Drummond might be an irate rate-payer, frowned across at him.

"Sorry, mate," Drummond apologized, "but I couldn't help overhearing. I was on the buses myself for a while at Middle Row."

The driver instantly relaxed. "Ahh, I see. We're out of Bow."

Luigi brought the crew their coffees and placed them on the table.

"We've changed our minds," quipped the conductor. "Got any champagne, Luigi?"

*

It was just before eleven when he received a telephone call from Davinia Lee.

"First things first, Roger: I'd like to thank you for a wonderful evening."

"The pleasure was all mine, Davinia."

"Not quite all yours, Roger."

"I know: I keep on having flashbacks."

She was silent for a moment and then, almost guiltily, she admitted, *"Yes, me too."*

"Will I see you again before you return to Arawak?"

"Yes, you will. But I'll come to that. It turns out you were right, Roger. Sister Amanda just called: terrible mistake; accounting problem; HM Government delighted to make this grant to one of the most loyal members of the Commonwealth."

Drummond laughed. "Wonderful!"

"Isn't it? She also suggested that we have a celebratory dinner. I told her that I could not afford to be seen in a swanky West End restaurant, so I nominated a Caribbean restaurant in Shepherd's Bush."

"Goodness! How did she take that?"

"Not a problem. She is Labour, after all. I also suggested that our supplier should be represented by the man who did all the work and its MD. She agreed to that too. So that will be you and your boss Gerald…"

"Ronald."

"Ronald. And your wives."

Every silver lining, thought Drummond, has a cloud. "Our wives?"

"Yes, darling. For obvious reasons in your case—obvious to the two of us, that is."

She called me darling! "But Ronald is a widower."

"Oh, well, tell him he can bring a…partner."

"And when will this be, Davinia?"

"Tomorrow evening. Short notice, I know, but it can't be helped. Your wife won't have another appointment, will she?"

Drummond smiled grimly. "Highly unlikely, Davinia."

*

As he entered Ronald's office, his secretary was just placing the day's correspondence in his in-tray. It hardly seemed enough for a day's work.

"Ah, Roger! What news from the front?"

"You've obviously not been following the news, Ronald."

Ronald waved his gold paperknife at the younger man. "Now that is not strictly true, Roger. I caught the interview with the Arawak health minister over breakfast—replayed from last night, I gather." He winked. "Pretty lady, that, wouldn't you say?"

"She is rather attractive, yes."

"At that point, however, Mrs Amanda Long—Mandy to her friends—had turned down the request for a grant." He raised an eyebrow. "Any recent developments there, Roger?"

"Why don't we stop playing around, Ronald?"

"Playing around, Roger?"

"You had a pretty good idea that Amanda Long's decision was going to be reversed, didn't you?"

Ronald sat bolt upright. "Reversed? Has it been, Roger?"

Drummond maintained his laconic delivery. "If you tune into *The World at One*, Ronald, I think you'll find that it has been."

Ronald brought his palms together. "Why, that's wonderful!" He then controlled his excitement, speaking in a lowered voice as he regarded Drummond through narrowed eyes. "Now, what makes you think that I knew this would happen?"

"Because you had worked out that Mr Streeter was not exactly what he claimed to be. I told him that, with the Arawak contract lost, there was no way we could avoid accepting the Libyan money, and he then had a word with someone claiming to be a British civil servant, presumably telling him that Washington would simply find it unacceptable for a British company to be using Libyan money."

"How do you know this, Roger?" Ronald looked amused.

"Pure luck: I saw them together in a restaurant last night."

"So you know this civil servant?"

"No, but Davinia Lee does; he was in the meeting at the Ministry of Overseas Development yesterday afternoon."

"So you think he's MI6?"

"Not necessarily, but he probably reports to them."

"And you worked out that your Mr Streeter must be CIA."

"Yes, but you were there ahead of me, weren't you, Ronald?"

Smiling now, Ronald held up his hands. "Guilty, Roger." He chuckled affably. "It was the name of his company that first set me thinking. *International Enterprises?* It has CIA written all over it. That's the sort of name they give to what I believe are called their 'proprietary companies.' You know the sort of thing: Air America, the Pacific Corporation, the Western Enterprises Company, and so on."

Drummond found himself wondering what such a well-informed, intelligent man could possibly see in a woman like Hilary. He smiled. "And was there really any Libyan money?"

"Oh, they've helped out in Benue and they'll certainly be taking a generous supply of our vaccine and placing an order for hospital equipment. But an interest-free loan to Merritt & Thwaite?" He grinned and shook his head. "Not a single dinar, Roger."

"So will you be taking Streeter's loan?"

Ronald played with his paperknife meditatively, describing circles, ellipses and treble clefs on his blotter. "It's now possible that we can scrape by without it, Roger. But see to what extent they're willing to lower the interest-rate."

Drummond frowned, unable to see how this could work. "But their condition is that they buy half of the company, Ronald. You've offered a 50-50 arrangement."

A grin from Ronald. "Yes, I have, haven't I?"

"Do you think they seriously want to buy it?"

"Oh, I think so, yes. You can see how it would be of use to them: dealing with the health services of several Third World countries, exerting influence in those areas where they feel it's most needed..."

"But any loan will be tied to the eventual sale."

Ronald sighed a little impatiently. "But it cannot be tied to the *terms* of the sale, Roger. We've said, after all, that no part of the company will be relinquished until the company is returned to good health—when, in other words, it will fetch a hefty price."

"But surely CIA proprietaries have deep pockets."

Ronald tossed the paperknife onto his blotter and chuckled. "Well, if we end up taking a loan from them, I'll probably allow Joseph to talk me out of the sale."

Drummond was momentarily stunned. "Uncle Joseph is coming back?"

Ronald shrugged. "Why not? The Arawak deal is done and dusted and so Joseph is not in a position to do any damage..." He glanced at his watch. "Nearly time for *The World at One*, Roger."

"Yes, but it will hardly be the lead story. There's one further thing to tell you, Ronald: Mrs Long is hosting a celebratory dinner tomorrow evening, and you and I are invited—along with our partners."

"Oh, that sounds nice. Where are we eating? Savoy Grill?"

Drummond faltered. "Er, no. Ms Lee has said that she cannot afford to be seen eating in anywhere too up-market, so Mrs Long has agreed that they will dine at a Caribbean restaurant in Shepherd's Bush."

Ronald took it rather well. "Ah. I see." He grinned. "It will, I suppose, be an experience."

Drummond studied Ronald closely. "And you will be coming with a partner?"

"Oh, yes." He smiled at Drummond. "No problem there, Roger."

15

It was one of those places where customers usually turn a blind eye to the very basic décor and furnishing knowing that, by reputation, the food will be out of the ordinary. In this case the proprietors had quite deliberately placed a minimalist stamp on the restaurant to create the illusion among less knowledgeable customers that this was how a Caribbean restaurant was *supposed* to look. This evening, of course, as members of the British and Arawakian governments and the Arawakian High Commissioner were to be among the guests, some of the minimalism had been forsaken. The oilcloth coverings of the tables, placed next to each other with six seats on each side, were now hidden beneath gleaming white tablecloths; the electric lighting had been dimmed and was supplemented by Tilley lamps, placed on vacant surfaces about the room, to convey the impression of a humble Caribbean abode predating the arrival of electricity. Four statuesque waitresses, wearing long black skirts, white blouses and colourful madras headwraps, greeted the guests upon arrival and ushered them to a separate drinks table. Scratchy reggae music issued discreetly from small speakers placed on the walls.

Drummond found himself beaming. Oh, he was going to enjoy this! He guided Hilary to the drinks table, where a fifth waitress dispensed soft drinks, golden Appleton Estate rum and Red Stripe beer, and around which the guests stood chatting, drinking and, some of them, smoking. Drummond gave a grin to those he knew and to Mrs Long whom he did not; the one exception was Davinia Lee, stunning in a long, off-the-shoulder black dress and headwrap, who received a warm smile. Just then he felt the pressure of Hilary's fingers on his forearm, drawing him aside.

"Darling," she whispered to him, "do we really have to stay? I have a feeling that this is going to be just *dreadful*."

His mouth tightened. "Yes, we *do* have to stay. Anyway, how can you say that when we've only just arrived."

"It just gives the impression of being so...*tacky*."

"Hilary."

She looked up at him.

"Bollocks."

Her mouth dropped open, as if he'd slapped her. It would, however, be swiftly closed by his next remark.

"Oh, look, there's Ronald and his partner over there. Let's go and say hello."

"Ah, Mrs Drummond!" exclaimed Ronald as they approached. "How very nice to see you again. Come and meet my niece, Audrey."

Ronald's niece was in her twenties, slim and flat-chested with a wan face and lifeless dark hair. Hilary took her narrow hand in hers and smiled at the young woman with what appeared to be—unaccountably to Drummond—familiarity. She then regarded Ronald with something like relief and, offering him her hand, breathed, "Yes, so nice to see you again, Ronald."

Alright, alright, thought Drummond, don't overdo the act. Feeling someone touch his elbow, he turned to see that Lemay was offering him a bottle of beer.

"See if Red Stripe agrees with you, Roger. Jamaican, as is the rum."

"Shouldn't we be using glasses?"

Lemay gave his head a curt shake. "This is how it's done in the Caribbean—and increasingly here." He tipped the bottle to his lips and took a swallow.

Drummond followed his example, nodding appreciatively as he withdrew the bottle. "Yes, nice. But listen, you haven't met my boss, have you?"

He turned and introduced Lemay to Ronald and his niece. Lemay and Hilary, who had met occasionally over the years, exchanged cursory nods.

"A pleasure to make your acquaintance, Mr Lemay," boomed Ronald. "As I understand it, the contract we have just agreed owes much to your friendship with Mr Drummond."

Yes, no doubt about it: one or both of the Sharmas had kept Ronald well-informed, thought Drummond. And there, across the room, having just arrived, were Lal and Shirley!

Discerning Drummond's interest in these recent arrivals, Ronald gave him a mischievous grin. "Yes, I gave Mandy a call and wangled invitations for Mr and Mrs Sharma. He is from Arawak, after all."

"Mandy?" inquired Lemay.

Ronald chuckled. "Mrs Long. Amanda. Mandy for short—although of course I don't call her that to her face."

"I wasn't aware that you knew her," remarked a surprised Drummond.

"Oh, I don't really *know* her," he replied, swilling his rum around his glass. He glanced briefly at Drummond, adding mysteriously, "We have a...mutual acquaintance."

Drummond silently speculated whether this would be the MP with Arab connections.

Ronald drained his glass and looked across at Lemay. "This Appleton Estate really is excellent stuff!" he pronounced. "Whenever we docked in Kingston, I would send my steward ashore to have a case sent on board in bond." He lifted his glass. "Time for a refill, I think."

"Did you ever risk the overproof white rum?"

"Only once." Ronald grimaced and then, turning to his niece as she took his glass: "Oh, thank you, dear."

"If you will excuse us, Ronald," said Drummond, "Mr Lemay and I have one or two things to discuss."

"Of course, dear boy. I'm sure your charming wife will keep me entertained."

"Yes, I'm sure she will." He manufactured a grin for Hilary. "Won't you, darling?"

As they walked away, Lemay frowned. "What do we have to discuss, Roger?"

"Absolutely nothing, Garry. I just wanted to get away from them."

Lemay shrugged. "Okaaay. By the way, did you spot the arrival of the party-pooper?"

"I came in with her, Garry."

Lemay laughed aloud and playfully slapped Drummond's arm. "Oh, come on, now; it's surely not that bad."

"I can assure you, Garry, that it's worse. But who did you have in mind?"

Lemay shrugged his eyebrows at a spot across the room. "You remember the civil servant our Minister called the rat? There he is, large as life. Don't make it obvious that you're studying him."

Yes, that could well be the man he had fleetingly glimpsed as he sat next to Streeter in Khan's the other night. Dressed in a well-tailored light-grey suit, his slender form was next to Amanda Long, counting off something on the fingers of his left hand. Drummond wondered whether he was enumerating the things he expected her to do or say, and it was with some amusement that he saw the Minister turn and seemingly snarl at him: there were, apparently, limits to what even a member of a Labour government could be instructed to do. Apparently exasperated, the man tightened his lips and drifted away.

"I do believe," said Drummond, "that she's told him to piss off."

"Good for her," said Lemay. "Although he's certainly not leaving the restaurant. In fact, he's heading towards your boss."

"Well, he won't get any joy there."

"Anyway, Roger, I'm glad we have this opportunity for a chat, because there *is* something I have to tell you."

"It may have to wait, Garry, because I see we're being approached by the representatives of two governments."

This was true, as Davinia Lee had linked arms with Amanda Long and was now leading her in their direction.

"Sister Amanda," Davinia Lee announced upon arrival, smiling broadly, "you've already met Mr Lemay from our High Commission, and it is my very great pleasure to introduce you to Mr Roger Drummond of Merritt & Thwaite, the company which is supplying us with the medical equipment we so desperately need. It was Mr Drummond who negotiated the contract with me." She grinned mischievously at Drummond. "And, oh, what a hard bargain he drives!"

"But I thought, Sister Davinia," said Mrs Long with a smile, using a form of address she would not normally employ, "that the company made substantial discounts."

Davinia Lee held up a finger. "Indeed it did, Sister Amanda—but only because I drive a harder bargain than Mr Drummond!"

Each member of the group contributed to a gale of good-natured laughter during which Mrs Long, a tall, handsome woman approaching fifty, soberly attired in a grey knee-length dress, looked anxiously over at the small group around Ronald.

"You must allow me to introduce you to our managing director, Minister," said Drummond, having noted the direction of her gaze.

"Surely that should be *Ministers*, Mr Drummond," remarked Davinia Lee mischievously. "You seem to have overlooked the fact that I have yet to meet your Mr Donald."

Drummond leaned forward, comically mouthing, "Ronald."

"Ah, of course: *Ronald*."

"But you're quite right: you've not met him, and I apologise for the oversight."

"Shall we, then?" Davinia Lee turned towards Ronald's group.

"If you don't mind," interjected Mrs Long, "I'd rather wait until he's finished his conversation with my…"

"Minder?" The word was out before Drummond could stop it.

Lemay and Davinia Lee, possibly fearing that some form of protocol had been breached, immediately dropped their eyes, but Mrs Long merely gazed at Drummond in amusement, weighing him up. Having apparently decided that he was to be trusted, she gave him a slight nod, murmuring, "Yes, my minder. I'm afraid that Mr Hesketh-Brown and I rarely see eye to eye."

"By the look of it, he's also having that problem with my MD," observed Drummond.

The grey man had been with Ronald for several minutes and now, having spoken his piece, was receiving what appeared to be a spirited response.

"Are you two men going to carry those beer-bottles around all evening?" asked Davinia Lee.

Drummond lifted his empty bottle. "In fact, I thought I would have another while we wait for Ronald to dispense with Mr..." He turned to Mrs Long for assistance.

"Hesketh-Brown."

"Can I get you anything ladies?"

"A rum and coke would be lovely," replied a grateful Mrs Long. "Easy on the coke."

"And a 7-Up for me," said Davinia Lee.

Lemay handed Drummond his empty bottle. "Same again for me, Roger."

As Drummond returned from his errand, two beers and a 7-Up (with straw inserted) in one hand and a rum and coke in the other, the song coming over the speakers was a reggae version of "Red Red Wine," to which Mrs Long was swaying in time. Once Drummond handed her the glass, however, she gave it serious attention, taking a large swallow and then, eyes closed, uttering, "My goodness, I was ready for that!"

Looking around the room, Drummond saw many brown faces and several happy people. A pall of blue smoke hung over the drinks table, soon to be dispersed when two of the waitresses plugged in powerful fans; from the kitchen came the odour of spicy food. Drummond took a swig of his beer and thought that he could get to like a place like this. He saw that Mrs Long was not the only one swaying to the music; even Ronald's knees were moving as he pretended to listen to Hesketh-Brown. Hilary, on the other hand, appeared glum and motionless, clutching her second or third rum and frowning as she attempted to decide whether she agreed with Ronald or Hesketh-Brown.

"Ladies," said Drummond, having realised that he had an appetite, "I think we should complete the introductions before they start serving the food."

"Good thinking," said Davinia Lee, sweeping the room with her gaze. "We'd better find Barkers, in that case."

"Barkers?" inquired Mrs Long with a frown as Davinia Lee swept across the room.

"Mr Barclay Grant, the High Commissioner, ma'am," Drummond explained with a grin.

"Ma'am? I'm not royalty, Mr Drummond." She held up her empty glass and cast a longing eye at the drinks table.

With a subtle bow, Drummond reached for her glass. "Allow me, ma'am."

As he walked to the drinks table, he heard a shriek of laughter behind him and wondered whether Hesketh-Brown's only instruction to Mrs Long might have been that she should not get pissed.

They gathered around Ronald (almost as if he were the most important person in the room), and the introductions were made.

"A great pleasure to meet you, Mr Mathews," intoned Barclay Grant, "although you may rest assured that your company has been very ably represented by Mr Drummond."

"Oh," Ronald replied, although with an eye to Davinia Lee, "he's very good at what he does. Did you find that, Ms Lee?"

Davinia Lee accorded Drummond the briefest of glances before directing her smile at Ronald. "As the High Commissioner said, Mr Mathews, your company was very ably represented."

"I do hope, Mr Mathews," said Mrs Long, lowering her voice, "that you did not find Mr Hesketh-Brown too bothersome."

Ronald sniffed and glanced at his empty glass before handing it to his niece, who scampered across to the drinks table. First things first. "Bothersome?" he repeated. "*Bothersome?*" He turned down his mouth at the corners and shook his head. "No, dear lady, he was not bothersome; he was damned impertinent!" He looked across the room to where Hesketh-Brown had retreated. "Know what he said to me?" Ronald had had a few. "Said he hoped that I had taken the decision to *eschew* funds from a certain Middle Eastern country. *Eschew!* What sort of person introduces a word such as *eschew* into normal conversation? *Eschew*, indeed! Bloody Eton bum-boy, if you ask me. Anyway, I told him to bugger off." He raised an eyebrow in Mrs Long's direction. "I hope that does not meet with your disapproval, dear lady."

Instead of replying directly, Mrs Long grinned and raised her glass. "Your health, Mr Mathews."

Having made a brief sobriety estimate and thinking ahead, Davinia Lee asked her hostess, "Will you be saying a few words after dinner, Sister Amanda?"

"Oh, yes, I think I must, don't you? I mean, after the...But yes, I shall make a brief speech."

"Very well, and I will respond if you are comfortable with that. But I think that you might also say a few words, Mr Mathews."

"Glad to, madam." He chuckled. "I'll dream up something while I listen to you two. And please call me Ronald."

The restaurant's proprietor, a tall black man with a short, greying beard, emerged from the kitchen area and, hands clasped before him, announced that dinner was about to be served. The waitresses now led the guests to their seats, which were indicated by cards bearing their names. Drummond found himself placed next to Davinia Lee; to her right sat Lemay and the Sharmas. They faced, on the table opposite, Barclay Grant, Mrs Long, Ronald and Hilary, and, at the very end, Audrey and Hesketh-Brown. There was a spare place next to the Sharmas, and Davinia Lee explained that this was intended for the official photographer that Mrs Long had arranged. That gentleman now arrived and, having placed his camera equipment on a spare table just inside the door, waved across the room to his employer; Mrs Long scowled at her watch and waved a finger at him.

"Who is responsible for the seating arrangements?" murmured Drummond, inclining his head to Davinia Lee.

She smiled. "Who do you think? Do you approve?"

"It's inspired, absolutely inspired," he chuckled.

"Because we're sitting together?"

"Well, yes, but I also had in mind Hesketh-Brown, perched on the end of the table with only Ronald's niece to talk to."

"Yes, I thought I'd place him where he would be unable to do any damage."

Drummond grinned. "I'm wondering whether he'll suffer any damage at the hands of Audrey." Noting her puzzled expression, he explained: "She has a somewhat manic look about her; I think she might be religious."

Their conversation was interrupted by the arrival of the first course: Arawak chicken soup.

"Mm, this is nice and spicy. Talking of which, what do you make of Ronald?"

She giggled at the allusion. "A saucy old devil. He gave the impression that he knew about us. But that's surely not possible." She regarded him from the corner of her eye. "Is it?"

"No." He flinched. "On second thoughts, yes."

The appalled look which now appeared on Davinia Lee's face pierced him with deep disappointment.

"I suspect that either Lal or Shirley Sharma has now and again passed Ronald information concerning my connections with the High Commission."

"But surely they can't know about us!" She was leaning forward over her soup dish, her voice an urgent whisper.

"No, but during the adjournment the other day Shirley remarked that I was obviously attracted to you."

Another pause while one of the waitresses filled their wine glasses.

Davinia Lee's soft expression now went a considerable way to assuage his disappointment. "Oh, well...No harm done, I suppose," she murmured.

"Davinia, is this the last time I'll see you before you fly home?"

She nodded. "Yes, I'm afraid so, Roger."

"God, that's awful!"

"Yes, it is, but what can we do?"

The soup dishes were cleared away, followed by the arrival of the main course. Drummond was having the curried goat, rice and peas, while Davinia Lee had opted for Arawak oxtail.

"Oh, this is so delicious!" commented Drummond as he sampled the goat. "First, I'm tasting tender goat and then, like a delayed reaction, the curry flavour bursts on my tongue. So subtle, it's a miracle."

Pleased, Davinia Lee smiled. "That's how it should be, Roger."

Drummond leaned back in his chair and drew the attention of Lemay. "Garry, why didn't you tell me about this place before?"

Lemay grinned and shrugged. "The occasion didn't arise. Besides..."—he cupped his right hand to hide his mouth—"it's not cheap."

Drummond nodded at Davinia Lee's plate. "What are those balls, Davinia?"

"Fried dumplings. We call them johnny cakes. Would you like to try one? Here, take one."

Drummond speared a dumpling with his fork and transferred it to his plate. "Ohhh, yes: crispy on the outside, but so light and fluffy on the inside! Davinia, I honestly can't recall when I had a meal as tasty as this. I'm really enjoying myself."

She looked across to the table opposite. "You're not the only one by the look of it."

In a literal sense, this was true. Barclay Grant wore an appreciative grin as he savoured his curried chicken, while Mrs Long, accustomed by the job she did to the cuisine of equatorial nations, alternated a mouthful of goat with a swig of wine; occasionally, words were exchanged between the two, and from the snatches Drummond was able to catch they seemed confined to the repast they were both so obviously enjoying. Given his naval background, Ronald was also no stranger to Caribbean fare, and he too, like Mrs Long, was taking an appreciative bite followed, after chewing, by a swallow of wine. Greatly amused, Drummond saw that their actions were often not only synchronised but in time with the reggae instrumental which drifted softly from the speakers. Chuh-cha-chung, chuh-cha-*chung*—sip! Chuh-cha-chung, chuh-cha-*chung*—bite! Chuh-cha-chung, chuh-cha-chung, chuh-cha-*chung*—chew! Chuh-cha-chung, chuh-cha-*chung*—sip!

But Davinia Lee had not said that *everybody* was enjoying themselves. Hilary, having presumably chosen jerk chicken as the safest option, seemed to be taking two sips of wine for every small mouthful she rather hesitantly lifted on her fork, and maybe just as well, for the wine had lightened her sullen demeanour. If Audrey was eating little, this was not through any dislike of the food but because she was more intent upon convincing Hesketh-Brown to come to Jesus (the sibilance of her saviour's name had travelled quite audibly across to Drummond's ear on several occasions). And if Hesketh-Brown appeared to concentrate upon the food before him, this was due less to a voracious appetite than to his vain attempt to ignore his dinner-partner's insistent evangelization.

Drummond inclined his head to Davinia Lee, murmuring, "Seems I was right about Audrey."

"Yes," Davinia Lee chuckled. "Did you notice a little while ago, that when he looked across at the photographer and rolled his eyes, she thought that she was getting through to him and that he was casting his gaze to heaven?"

"It seems rather strange that she should pick on Hesketh-Brown who, I imagine, would be a hard nut to crack. I would have thought that Hilary would be the better bet."

After dessert (a choice of rum cake, mango cheesecake and several coconut-based sweets), rum and mixers were placed on the tables and the men were offered Jamaican cigars. Hesketh-Brown took this opportunity to escape from Audrey to have a brief exchange with the photographer, who crossed to the table where he had placed his equipment and began pointing his light meter at the table where Mrs Long sat. This was Hesketh-Brown's next destination, where he placed a small card before Mrs Long before retreating out of range. Mrs Long glanced at the card before turning it face-down and placing her empty wine glass upon it. Audrey, with the departure of Hesketh-Brown, now devoted her attention to Hilary, who had engaged her in discussion. To Drummond's dismay, his wife appeared to be quizzing the evangelist about her success, or lack of it, in bringing Hesketh-Brown to the Lord. Drummond now recalled the brilliantly-coloured A5 leaflet he had found, following one of Hilary's evenings out, in their kitchen. That evening, he remembered, she had told him that she was going to a talk with

Audrey: she had not lied, but it was now apparent that she had been with Audrey Mathews rather than Audrey Colson.

Having allowed a decent interval for after-dinner discussion, Barclay Grant rose to his feet and tapped on his glass with a spoon. He thanked the UK government for its hospitality and the proprietor and staff of the restaurant for providing such a memorable meal, and then called upon Mrs Amanda Long to say a few words.

Mrs Long had, of course, endured a stressful week and it had stamped her features. As she flicked aside a stray lock of greying hair from her forehead, the shadows beneath her eyes were all-too apparent although, being quite drunk, she was still able to project an impression of strength and resolve.

"Your Excellency Barclay Grant, Minister Davinia Lee, Mr Ronald Mathews and dear friends," she began, "I shall be brief." She took a deep breath, and when she spoke again her voice filled the room, drawing staff from the kitchen. "It was—on my part, anyway—with the deepest sense of pleasure and gratification that, on behalf of the UK Government, I was able to make this grant to the people of Arawak, enabling them to re-equip their health service. When Health Minister Davinia Lee—Sister Davinia, as I have come to call her, and she calls me Sister Amanda..."

"I call her Mandy." Even at the best of times, Ronald was incapable of a *sotto voce* delivery, and this, after his considerable intake of alcohol, came out as, rather than a whisper in Hilary's ear, a bark that was clearly audible about the room, causing a ripple of amused laughter from everyone except Hilary and Hesketh-Brown.

"When Sister Davinia," resumed Mrs Long, "launched her campaign recently, I saw immediately that Britain must make a generous contribution. More than that, I agreed with the reasons Sister Davinia used to explain *why* that contribution must be made. The condition in which my country left Arawak's health service when independence came in 1966 was nothing less than shameful. And I am of the view, ladies and gentlemen, that that word *independence* should have real substance. It is not for the United Kingdom—or, indeed, any other foreign power—to attempt to dictate the means by which Arawak chooses to develop its economy and lift its people out of poverty,"

Hesketh-Brown was now very agitated, waving in a vain attempt to attract his minister's attention. The photographer, a not particularly neat man in his thirties with a tangle of unkempt hair on top of his head (Drummond suspected he might freelance for one of the marginal members of the left-wing press), was now in action, his flash exploding in rapid fire; he probably regretted, in view of the nature of Mrs Long's comments, that he had no audio.

"Even more shameful, of course," said Mrs Long, "is that in more remote history the relationship between our two countries was characterised by slavery. And that is something for which this modest grant does not come near to compensating."

That got her a round of applause.

"At first, though, it looked as if the grant to Arawak would not be made." Mrs Long looked rather pointedly in the direction of Hesketh-Brown. "I don't think it would be helpful to go into the reasons for that initial...misunderstanding. I take the view, however, that when we consider extending the hand of friendship to another people, particularly in such a vital area as healthcare, the ideological orientation of that people, or its leaders, should play no part in our decision."

Hesketh-Brown was on the verge of explosion.

"Poor Mrs Long," Drummond whispered to Davinia Lee, "obviously doesn't know why that decision was reversed." Seeing Davinia frown, he realized that he had still not given her a full explanation. He sighed. "If I ever get the chance, I'll fill you in on the details."

"Why not now, Roger?"

"It wouldn't be appropriate."

"When *would* it be appropriate?"

"When we're alone together."

She smiled and shrugged her eyebrows. "Well, we'll see."

Mrs Long lifted her glass, brimming with rum. "In conclusion, let us drink to peace and friendship between our two peoples!"

"Peace and friendship!" echoed all, with the exception of Hesketh-Brown, with raised glasses.

"That has a bit of a Soviet ring to it," murmured Drummond.

Mrs Long sat down rather too abruptly, splashing her hand with the remaining rum in her glass.

Without waiting for Barclay Grant's introduction, Davinia Lee now rose to her feet.

"I would like, ladies and gentlemen," she began, "on behalf of the people of Arawak, to thank Sister Amanda for the generous grant that her government has made and, on behalf of those present this evening, to express our appreciation for this celebratory meal. I must also express my admiration for her warm and courageous words of solidarity to our struggling nation." She blinked as the photographer depressed his flash button.

"You can be assured, Sister Amanda, that the medical equipment purchased with your grant will receive a heartfelt welcome when it arrives in our capital, Arawak City, before being delivered to hospitals not only in the capital but also in the countryside. We are all aware, I think, that although it was I who negotiated the contract for this equipment with Mr Roger Drummond, who sits on my left, much credit must go to the High Commission, where Mr Drummond has been no stranger, and in particular to Mr Garrison Lemay, with whom he has a longstanding friendship." She placed a hand on shoulder of Lemay, seated to her right. "It is, therefore, with great pleasure that I can announce that the High Commissioner has decided that Mr Lemay should accompany the equipment on its voyage to Arawak, and that I have agreed that, following its arrival, he should monitor its distribution."

Warm applause greeted this announcement. As Davinia Lee resumed her seat, Drummond leaned forward and said to Lemay, "So that was your news?" Lemay, a broad smile on his face, nodded.

"Any more surprises up your sleeve, Davinia?" Drummond asked.

She presented her slender bare arm. "No sleeve, Roger."

Barclay Grant, beaten to the punch by Davinia Lee on the last occasion, rose swiftly to his feet.

"Ladies and gentlemen," he intoned in his deep baritone, "the company which has provided the medical equipment to Arawak has long been our good friend. Some years ago, in the wake of the terrible floods which caused such damage to our little country, Merritt & Thwaite donated—completely free of charge!—a considerable supply of medical hardware. The company has been in existence for over a century, would you believe, and I now ask you to give a warm welcome to its managing director, Mr Ronald Mathews!"

"I call him Ronnie!" called Mrs Long with a shriek of laughter before the applause greeting Ronald could drown her out.

Hesketh-Brown had his head in his hands.

Drunk though he was, Ronald had listened intently to the previous two speeches, occasionally jotting a note on a paper napkin, which he now held before him as he rose to his feet.

"Your Excellency," he began, with a nod to Barclay Grant, "I thank you for that warm introduction." He looked around the two tables. "Many of you, of course, had never set eyes upon me before this evening. I therefore hope that you have not been misled by anything Mr Grant has said into thinking that I have been at the helm of Merritt & Thwaite for the whole of the one hundred and twenty-odd years of its existence."

They laughed. They liked him. Drummond considered the handsome face, wreathed in smiles, and realised that Ronald was an adept public speaker, probably having gained proficiency by addressing the ship's company; and there, too, he may have been bolstered by rum.

"I listened to Mrs Long and Miss Lee with a great deal of interest and found that I agreed with much that they had to say. Independence should have *substance*, said Mrs Long. Of course it should! For something like the last decade, we have been witnessing something called *détente*—the relaxation of tensions between the Soviet bloc and the West. I like to think that this has come about because certain people have begun to accept that the world has changed, and that if we are to survive we must all learn to live together." He shrugged, a wry grin on his face as he glanced in the direction of Hesketh-Brown. "I could be wrong about this, of course." A pause for laughter. "But this period surely brings great opportunities: the chance of small nations like Arawak to diversify their foreign relations, seeking out those relationships which will most assist them in their struggle to develop." He picked up his glass. "My first toast, then: To *détente*; long may it continue!"

"To *détente*!" came the echo.

"Now, I am of the view," continued Ronald, his voice rich and gravelly, "that just as this period brings opportunities for needy nations, it also brings possibilities for companies like my own. Traditionally, as you may or may not know, Merritt & Thwaite has concentrated on trade with the Commonwealth countries. Should we not take this opportunity to branch out, spread our wings a little wider?" He rapped the table with his knuckles. "Yes, I say! In this connection, I am *delighted* to report, we have just concluded a contract with Libya." He grinned across the table to Drummond. "Yes, Mr Drummond, the deal is done!"

The first thought that came to Drummond was whether, rather than taking enforced annual leave in Kenya, Uncle Joseph had been, for at least part of the time, in Tripoli. This was followed by a golden oldie: what can this clued-up, clever man possibly see in Hilary?

"Now, I have been told—and quite recently, at that—that my company should eschew Libyan money. *Eschew!*" His gaze roved over the other celebrants as he played with the word, a wide grin for *es* followed by an exaggerated pout for *chew*. "Now there's a word for you! But if there's anything I *eschew*"—his eyes were now on Hesketh-Brown—"it's unsolicited advice from grey men with political agendas!" He smiled. "And so I also agree with Mrs Long when she says that when extending the hand of friendship—or, in my case, of trade—our decisions should not be guided by the ideology of the people concerned."

Some of the applause greeting this was a little reticent, although that from Mrs Long was enthusiastic.

"Finally, allow me to say a final word about Mr Drummond. In the absence of Joseph Thornton, our exports manager, Roger has performed tirelessly, and I will therefore ask him to continue to represent our company with regard to the Arawak contract. It is surely appropriate that, when our medical equipment leaves Tilbury in a fortnight's time, he should join Mr Lemay on the voyage which will take it to Arawak, where I am confident, madam,"—a roguish grin to Davinia Lee—"that you will ensure he is given the warmest of welcomes."

Drummond was momentarily stunned. The applause which greeted Ronald's last remarks was, he realized, directed in part to him, congratulating him on his good fortune. It was hard to see how Hilary was taking it: the alcohol she had consumed gave her the appearance of an Alzheimer's sufferer as she glanced from Ronald to Drummond, as if not entirely sure what was happening. He dared not look at Davinia Lee, who had turned to beam at him.

PART TWO

16

The alarm bells rang and men hurried to the lifeboat stations. Lifeboat drill came twice a week as something to be endured, and so the men hurried not out of any manufactured sense of danger or urgency but in order to get it over with. The paler their skins, the redder their eyes: some of them spent their afternoons sleeping in their cabins while others decorated the crew deck with their brown bodies, indulging in that peculiar act of vanity they called, in their merchant navy slang, "bronzying." The brown ones appeared alert, their orange lifebelts secured about their necks, walking smartly to their stations, while the white ones shuffled sleepily, pulled from their bunks by the bells, the strings of their lifebelts trailing untidily behind them. It was 1615 hours and many of them wore their cook's trousers and whites, ready to turn to in the galley and prepare dinner once this tiresome ordeal was over.

As Tilbury lay eight days behind them, this was the third time the sixty passengers had been treated to the ritual, and so they paid it no attention. Most of them, having run through the permutations of new friendships and conversations, were thoroughly bored and disappointed with each other and so spent their afternoons in their cabins, like the white-faced seamen.

At the after end of the ship, Drummond turned his back on the rest of the *TSS Burgos*, its passengers, its crew and its ritualistic boat drill, and looked out to sea. He liked the sea, its moods and its movements. While they were still in the North Atlantic, he had often come up on deck when all the others were safely below, to feel the deck plunge and roll beneath his feet and allowing the sharp spray to collect on his face. He had felt exhilarated and alive. The further the ship ploughed into southern waters, the more Drummond sensed that the words "New World" had not been ill-chosen. It *felt* different, new. The old world contained all the despair, and if he had felt its dead air beneath his nostrils on this ship it could only be because the people had brought it with them. The old world, *his* old world, was empty of purpose and meaning. What had he back there? The job at Merritt & Thwaite, and Hilary. Now that the Arawak contract had been signed, he doubted whether the job would hold much interest for him. And Hilary? Ha!

The sea had changed again. This morning there had been flying fish sparkling silver against the blue, and islands of sargassum lying like dead things brought to the surface by some underwater explosion; but now it was a choppy emerald green as cloud formations, more gorgeous and inventive than those smoky grey things that were pushed across English skies, gathered above and on the horizon, and a light, tepid rain began to fall. Drummond closed his eyes and lifted his face, almost in a gesture of acceptance. The rain touched his forehead and cheeks, his bare shoulders, collected on the hair at the back of his head and rushed refreshingly down his neck and back. When he opened his eyes, he saw the captain looking down at him from the deck above, the brows beneath the peaked cap tugged together in incomprehension and just a suggestion of disapproval. Involuntarily, two fingers of Drummond's right hand shot out. He controlled himself in time, though, keeping the hand at his side. All the same, he suspected that the captain had seen the half-completed gesture, so he smiled mockingly and brought the two fingers to his forehead. "Carry on!" he called out, and then walked below to his cabin, leaving the captain's mouth to open and close impotently.

*

He sat at his table in the dining saloon, waiting for Lemay to appear, and ran his eye over the rest of the passengers. Once more wouldn't hurt; he might even find something overlooked on previous inspections. But there was nothing.

Ellen Listor appeared interesting if a little intimidating, but she had teamed up with the boorish Brian Garner, a man who claimed to be a company lawyer but who sounded like a used-car salesman: anyone who saw anything in him couldn't be all that interesting. Then there was the slender Jean Parris, a woman in her late thirties who appeared to have that peculiar strength derived from an acceptance of loneliness. The rest, couples and family groups, ranged from an estate agent from Barnes with a wide commercial smile to a minister in some obscure Caribbean revivalist sect who was travelling home from a prolonged sojourn in the immigrant areas of London and the Midlands. The estate agent (Barnes & Barnes of Barnes) seemed to have sold the idea of marriage to his wife in much the same way that he might have unloaded a house to a gullible client, for she had the disappointed look of someone who had woken up to discover that her roof leaked and her walls were subsiding. The Reverend Mr Bassfield Thomas of the Wrath of God Holy Gospel Mission was taken to delivering sermons to anyone mistaken enough to speak to him first; after the first few days, no one was. He was travelling with four females aged between twenty and thirty-five who sat with him now, clothed as they always were in their very proper long black dresses. Say what you will, however, it had to be admitted that the Bassfield Thomas group *was* interesting.

These were the two extremes, to be avoided at all costs, but the rest were merely gradations of these two primary colours. Of the officers, only a junior officer called Berry, a round-faced man still in his late twenties, evoked a spark of sympathy in Drummond; this was probably because he had overheard two other officers discussing Berry, running him down for drinking in the crew quarters. As punishment for this transgression, the captain moved him around the dining saloon from night to night, if possible from boor to boor. Tonight, he sat with Ellen Listor and Garner. Drummond noticed that three seats at this table usually occupied by the Pattersons (who spent their days, and presumably their nights, with their heads bent together over a Scrabble board) and their daughter Xanthe (who had been born with yellow hair), were vacant.

The stewards, each of whom wore a badge bearing his forename, were a strange lot. George was a horse-faced, white-haired man who looked to be well beyond normal retirement age and made his way from the galley to the dining saloon and back again taking very small steps, acting deferentially towards his passengers but never encouraging familiarity. During the early part of the voyage when the *Burgos*, a mere 8,000 tons, had been tossed about like a matchstick by the North Atlantic, Drummond had been one of the few passengers who, suffering no seasickness, had managed to stumble to the dining saloon, and he had fully expected George to have a bad time of it; but the only difference in the old man's performance was that, in anticipation of a roll, he would pause, tray expertly balanced on one hand, and patiently wait until the movement was completed. When, at breakfast one morning, a passenger remarked, "Damn rough today, George!" the old man glanced over his shoulder, as if seeking the nearest porthole, and replied, with not the flicker of a smile, "Yes, a bit choppy this morning, sir." Drummond wondered how many times over the years George had made this rejoinder.

Young Jimmy, short and sharp-featured, was anything but deferential to his "bloods" and at the end of a service their tablecloths often bore stains caused by spilled soup and other inefficiently served liquids. One evening, as Jimmy took a breather between courses, standing at the rear of the saloon with a tall Irish colleague with a ginger moustache, Drummond overheard him explain this indifference to the concept of customer care. "I miss the Oriental Line," he hissed. "At least on that line you knew there was a prospect of getting a decent dropsy from the bloods at the end of a cruise. No chance of that with these tight bastards. Just ask yourself: what kind of person takes a cruise on a banana boat?" Jimmy's time with the Oriental Line had been lucrative in at least one other way, for on another occasion Drummond overheard him tell the same Irish steward that, during a Mediterranean cruise season, he would purchase an accordion in Italy on the first trip and, docking in Southampton, pay the customs duty on it before scarpering ashore to sell it. On each subsequent visit to Italy, he would purchase another accordion and, upon arrival in Southampton, present the customs officer with the customs receipt for the one he had purchased on the first trip, thereby evading duty and greatly increasing his profit-margin.

Nicholas, although only a little above medium height, gave the impression of being taller by the erect manner in which he held himself. Drummond was reminded of a character in a Raymond Chandler story—or was it a novel? —in which Philip Marlow describes an evidently gay young man as moving like a dancer, with no movement above the waist. Nicholas's blondness was almost Teutonic, his even features cold and cruel, and he treated his passengers with a disdain which the middle-aged women among them tended to overlook.

And there was Cecil, the head waiter, slender and tanned with chiseled features, his dark hair swept back over his head, paying obsequious attention to the women passengers, showing two rows of even white teeth as he smiled down at them.

Drummond wished Lemay would hurry up and get there. He hated having to sit alone, looking at everyone looking at him. Miss Parris looked directly at him, and a smile panicked its way onto her face. He returned her smile and looked away.

Finally, Lemay arrived, flustered and apologetic.

"You look worried, Garry. What's wrong?"

Lemay's eyes scanned the saloon before focusing on Drummond. "Every day, Captain Ferris receives a summary of UK and international news by telex." He frowned gravely. "The news from London is that Mrs Long has been replaced as Minister of Overseas Development."

Drummond grimaced. "I daresay Hesketh-Brown had something to do with that." He made a gesture with his right hand, indicating that there might be two sides to this story. "Even so, some of the remarks she made at the dinner she held for us, and her general behaviour, couldn't have gone down well with her masters."

"Probably not, Roger. And, as the government grant is, so to speak, in the bank, her sacking can't do us any harm."

Drummond lowered his voice. "So it must be something else that's causing you concern."

Lemay took another glance about the saloon and leaned forward. "The latest from Arawak is that there have been a number of what they're calling 'armed incidents' in the capital."

"What kind of incidents? Robberies? Terrorist attacks?"

"As you may have heard, a few months ago, our Defence Force apprehended a light aircraft which was found to be carrying a shipment of small arms. That aircraft, it turned out, had been making the trip every few weeks, bringing in arms and loading up with ganja for the return trip to Florida."

"A CIA operation?"

Lemay nodded. "The arms were probably coming in preparation for a major destabilization effort, so, yes, the CIA was almost certainly involved."

"And the arms were going to the Arawak Democratic Party?"

"Not necessarily. While certain key people in the ADP were probably aware of the shipments, there would have been no need for the involvement of the wider party at this stage." He grinned sourly. "In a poor country like ours, it only takes a few dollars to enlist the services of men—lumpen men—as gunmen, with, perhaps, professional criminals being paid to store the guns."

"You haven't answered my question, Garry: what kind of incidents?"

"The office of the Arawak Workers' Party was sprayed with gunfire..."

"It might just be an anti-communist thing, then."

"And there was an attack on the life of a left-wing Assembly member and another on Jules Robbins—he's the Home Affairs minister, also on the left."

Drummond, his mind on Davinia Lee, drew a hand through his hair. "Shit! But why now?"

"My own theory—and that's all it is, until I have more information—is that their original strategy was long-term: to create such misery and terror over the next couple of years that a large portion of the electorate would vote against Robinson at the next election just to have the violence stopped. That's how the CIA works. Now, however, it's my guess that some of the locals have finally accepted that their supply of arms has dried up, so they've decided to use what they have, maybe as a prelude to some kind of coup attempt."

"How likely is that to succeed?"

"At the moment, not very, but situations like this can change very swiftly."

"But why would they choose to start something like this at the moment, when the Robinson government's popularity-rating is bound to bounce up when it takes delivery of our medical equipment?"

"Good question, Roger." He shrugged. "At first glance, it makes no sense, but we'll have to wait and see what the opposition has to say about it."

"Excuse me, Mr. Lemay, Mr. Drummond..."

Unnoticed, Ellen Listor had approached their table, her soft, tanned throat thrusting out of her unbuttoned shirt, hands jammed into the back pockets of her tight jeans.

"The Pattersons are all down with sunburn tonight, and so Mr Garner and I were wondering if you would like to join us." She turned on an air-hostess smile. "You won't turn us down, will you?"

They did not turn her down. They would have liked to, but there was no way to do it without appearing rude. As they made their way to where Garner was sitting with Berry, Drummond noted with some alarm that Ellen was making a detour to rope Miss Parris into the party.

"Well," said Garner as they were all seated. Drummond guessed that Ellen had press-ganged Garner into this arrangement as well. "Well, Ellen...that is, we...were wondering if we could all go ashore together in Port of Spain tomorrow. That is, if you've not made arrangements already..." He was the kind of man who exuded good health and heartiness, forcing those about him into the fervent hope that some incurable disease would silence him forever. But tonight his freckled face was unsure of itself, as he had been maneuvered by a sharper intelligence and a stronger will into doing things he would rather not.

"Oh, if we'd known sooner…" Lemay responded with a swiftness which both surprised and pleased Drummond. "You see, I've already arranged to take Roger on a tour of the trouble-spots during the 1970 rebellion." He cleared his throat and joggled his glasses on his nose. "Some of them are still quite dangerous places to walk, you understand." Whenever Roger had delivered a verdict on a fellow passenger, Lemay had always laughed with genuine amusement, gracefully stopping short of actually agreeing with his assessment; it was now clear, at least as far as Brian Garner was concerned, that his agreement was total.

Pleasure flushed Garner's face. "What a pity. Not to worry, though."

"But I think it's a marvelous idea!" said Jean Parris, clapping her hands together in delight. "The three of us could still go ashore together, couldn't we?"

Ellen, who had received the news that Lemay and Drummond were unavailable rather badly, bounced back. "Yes, of course we could! Brian would love that, wouldn't you Brian?"

Garner's face was painful to watch.

"And perhaps you could join us, Mr Berry."

"I'll be on duty, I'm afraid," said Berry with his northern twang.

17

The new world!

Drummond leapt from his bunk and stepped quickly to the porthole. It was 6 a.m. A block of foliage was floating past and at first he thought this must be Trinidad itself, but then came a stretch of sea, followed by another block of greenery. The ship was edging through the small islets which lay off Trinidad. How very green they were! He had never seen such a green. A new green, the green of the New World! He showered quickly and pulled on his white jeans and a short-sleeved shirt, pausing only to arrange his hair before the mirror. The face which stared back at him was tanned and healthy, the eyes glowing with a spark that in recent years had been absent.

Up on deck, the beauty of the morning overwhelmed him. Again, he gazed upon the small islands, each completely covered with a thatch of green, glowing in the pristine morning light. The ship was moving slowly now, barely disturbing the perfectly flat surface of the sea. The air, already warmed by the young sun, was pure balm, and Drummond wanted to gulp it in and rejoice in it. Then, sadly, he realised that he would never in his life know this moment again. The sun would rise in the sky, growing older and more oppressive, the clear light would thicken and become hazy; these islands would be left behind and he would never see them again.

Further aft, Jean Parris was standing with Berry, the junior officer, she tall and a little angular in a bright print frock, he short and stocky in his tropical whites. They turned and smiled silently as Drummond approached, perhaps reluctant to shatter the tranquility with human speech.

Berry's hands rested on the rail, the thick black hair that covered his wrists standing out against the white of his shirt as he toyed surreptitiously with an unlighted cigarette. As the last of the green islets drew level and began to slide past, he uttered a deep sigh and placed the cigarette in his mouth. Drummond now realised that another reason he liked Berry was because he was not, and did not affect to be, as blasé as his colleagues. The other officers and crew members liked to convey the impression that they had seen everything worth mentioning, that these things—the outstanding examples of the world's beauty and ugliness—were only worth mentioning if you had *not* seen them, that, in reality, they were disappointing.

Jean Parris had not seen everything. She stood, her hands gripping the rail as if its metallic hardness might reassure her that this was all real, an expression of total enchantment on her face. Below, the aged engines pounded at slow speed with a steady thump-thump-thump, the sound travelling to the islets and coming back as an echo. Jean Parris cupped a hand to her ear and, directing it at the passing island, said, "Are those drums I hear?"

Berry tried to keep a straight face, failed, spluttered, and lost his cigarette over the side.

*

Lemay was still worried.

He appeared at breakfast, a copy of the *Express* folded under his arm, his mouth working agitatedly. He had obviously rushed ashore as soon as they had tied up, for Drummond had waited in the foyer, by the purser's office, for the newspapers to come aboard, but by breakfast they had still not arrived.

"Something wrong?"

"The situation at home doesn't look so good, at least according to this morning's *Express*. Protest demonstrations against the shortages yesterday."

"Spontaneous, or organised?"

"Good question. As the demonstrations took place in three separate places on the same day, I would say organised. They were fairly modest in size, but this is just the start."

"And who is doing the organising?"

"The ADP, of course. Hand in hand with the traders who are creating the artificial shortages in the first place."

"By hoarding?"

"Correct."

Drummond's eyes narrowed in concern. "Do you think there's any danger that Captain Ferris might bypass Arawak?"

Lemay grinned. "Hardly. There's our medical equipment to be offloaded and, of course, he needs to return home with a cargo of bananas. What he may do is give AC a miss and unload our stuff on the north coast."

"So the unrest is confined to AC?"

"At the moment, yes."

"And what about his bananas?"

"There are a couple of banana ports up there, so he wouldn't be leaving Arawak with an empty hold."

As Jimmy served them breakfast, Drummond described how his first glimpse of the New World had affected him. Lemay smiled at his words in a way that suggested that he was taking them as a personal compliment. Then the smile dimmed.

"Yes, there is a great deal which is beautiful in our part of the world," he said wistfully. He sighed. "There is also plenty that is ugly. The same as a lot of places in the world, I suppose. The beautiful and the ugly can exist together, side by side, for years, during which neither threatens the existence of the other. But there comes a time, there *always* comes a time, when one must perish if the other is to survive."

"But how could the beauty of what I saw this morning ever be destroyed?"

"In any number of ways. The islands you saw—were they a little bigger—could become dotted with holiday apartments. The sea could become polluted with oil and plastic waste. Any number of ways, Roger. More fundamentally, those who *perceive* that beauty could be, if not destroyed, at least changed. If some of the people can be chained to machines and the rest forced into hunger and crime, the beauty you talk about, natural beauty, will certainly cease to exist—*for them*—but beauty will also cease to exist *in the people themselves.* You worked in a factory once, right? How many of the men or women you worked alongside had any appreciation of beauty? Any beauty. It had been forced out of them. Art? Literature? Music? Natural beauty? I'm willing to bet they had no *time* for all that, that they thought it was not their *concern.*"

*

Lemay had told him that Trinidad was, because of its oil, the richest island in the English-speaking Caribbean, and yet how poor it was! What a reservoir of ugliness existed beneath the green hills! What was happening to beauty in Trinidad? And if Trinidad was the richest island, what would things be like in Arawak and Jamaica?

They rode into Port of Spain in a battered American car that alternated between bursts of speed and spells of low-gear work whenever a pothole was approached. The aging Detroit ambassador took them past ramshackle wooden houses on which the paint had long ago peeled and blistered, where women sat on verandas with folded arms. Beneath the oppressive sun, the colours were garish and painful to the eye. Children, some well-dressed, some half in rags, others wholly in rags, waved and shouted excitedly as they rode past. Drummond smiled sadly. Did they know what awaited them, these children? No, because if they had known their bright faces would not have been so quick to smile. They were too young; they did not yet look at the adults about them and think: one day I shall be like that.

The adults themselves were struggling. Amazingly, hope had not yet completely vanished. The ragged shirts which rubbed shoulders with the smart business suits were, it seemed to Drummond, by no means tokens of despair. He watched a man slowly pedaling an old bicycle on the other side of the street. Carefully, the man lifted his hat in mock salute to a white-shirted man who stood with his arms folded, maintaining a proprietary stance outside a bar and boarding house. Before replacing his hat, the cyclist leaned clear of his machine and spat adroitly onto the street. Then he replaced his hat and, back straight, pedaled slowly onward. The gesture seemed to sum up most of the people on the street. Anyone who cared enough to spit with such style and finely-honed contempt had not yet surrendered to despair. Hopes may have been betrayed, but all hope had not been consumed. If these descendants of African slaves and Indian indentured labourers—"coolies"—were the kind to give up hope, they would have done so long ago. And yet how was it generated, this hope that never died? From the defiance which had been revealed in the cyclist's gesture, a stubborn refusal to lay down and die? Yes, but that, presumably, had its roots in the collective sense of defiance born of slave rebellions.

As he and Lemay left the taxi, the first person Drummond saw was an Indian woman, begging on the sidewalk. He hoped that she would prove to be the exception to the rule, but her eyes were dead and flat, lifeless. It was no wonder, as the spark of hope could not possibly have lived in that fleshless shell of a body. He pushed a note into her hand and quickened his pace to join Lemay, who had walked ahead.

"Now you see the ugliness, eh?" Lemay said, pushing his hands into his trouser pockets and keeping his eyes to the front.

*

He could take no more of it. After they had walked only a short way, Drummond asked Lemay if they might step into a bar, out of the heat, away from the suffering. But there was more than just suffering: the way some of the people, especially the young men, looked at him. What was it exactly? As if he was...an enemy? Yes, an enemy, because he was white and presumably English.

The unfairness of this almost made him angry. After all, he was highly sympathetic to the suffering he had seen. He could do nothing about it, and it wasn't his fault, it had not been caused by anything he had done, but the looks he received appeared to accuse him of exactly this.

The bar had a frontier air to it, like so many bars throughout the Caribbean. Men came here to get drunk, swear and spit and obtain some relief from the rigours of life outside. The colours stood out against the grayish-brown woodwork: a red shirt here, a pair of blue overalls there; ice-cubes dancing in a glass of golden-brown rum, jiggling and clinking deliciously against the side of the glass; faces from almost black to almost white; blue tobacco smoke; a smiling, full set of white teeth here, a decimated collection of tobacco-stained stumps there.

If Drummond had—or thought he had—encountered enmity of the street, he was presented here with its opposite, for as he entered the bar an old man drew his thin, poorly-clothed body erect with the cry: "Teeenn-*shun!* Hofficer approachin'!" Good-natured, easy laughter filled the bar. Perhaps he had imagined the hostility out on the street. Race apart, there seemed to be little difference between the men here and those he would have found in the pub opposite the factory in Acton. They were working men, the same as...Yes, here lay the explanation: the young men who had glared at him outside had probably been unemployed and bitter.

Lemay listened to Drummond's observations and smiled. "Yes and no, Roger. First, you attribute far too much anti-colonial consciousness to the average Caribbean male. Only a few of those guys on the street would have a deep enough understanding of the colonial relationship to be angry about it. And most of them don't have a deep-rooted hatred of whites. True, Trinidad did have the Black Power thing some years ago, but those young guys you refer to would have been children then. So, you're probably right when you guess that some would be unemployed. But there's another possibility: they may have mistaken you for a seaman—passengers, even of the *Burgos*, would be rarely seen in this part of town—and assumed that you were out whoring. Some of them may have been church-goers." He shrugged and chuckled with genuine amusement. "The scene is not as politicised as you imagine."

The bar occupied the whole of the ground floor, although it was cut in two by a wall running down the middle into which a series of arches had been hewn. A counter ran almost the whole length of this, the front half, while a hatchway served the other half. Round metal tables and uncomfortable folding chairs were placed about the floor. Next to the dividing wall, a short flight of steps ran up to a door through which couples would sometimes pass, to return in thirty minutes or so.

Lemay ordered rum and cola for them, and they sat at one of the tables. He removed his glasses and polished them with his handkerchief. He looked up and smiled kindly. "I'm sorry it's upset you, Roger...but what did you expect?"

Drummond drew a hand through his hair and snorted in exasperation. "Oh, I don't know. I honestly don't know, Garry. Look, it's not the poverty so much, it's the..."

"Ugliness?" A mischievous smile played on Lemay's lips.

"Yes, seriously, that *is* it: the ugliness. Things don't *have* to be like this, and if that's true it means that they *are* like this because someone or something makes them so. The ugliness lies in the cause, whatever it is, and needs to be rooted out."

"So let's drink to that." He raised his glass.

Drummond took a sip, followed by a good swallow. "This is good stuff, Garry. I could get used to this."

Lemay ignored this, lacing his fingers together and holding them up. "Remember what I said about beauty and ugliness?"

"Yes, of course I remember. I also remember what you said about beauty having been forced out of people in England. That's very true. You know what it feels like when someone says something that you've only felt, that you have never been able to put into words?"

Lemay drew the glass back from his lips and smiled, nodding.

"That's exactly how I felt this morning when you made that remark." Drummond grinned. "It seems to be a talent you have: at that meeting of the Arawak Support Group two years ago, your analysis of the situation had the same effect."

Above the hubbub of the drinking men, a scream came from upstairs. No one paid any attention to it. Then the scream turned into a laugh.

Drummond gulped down the remainder of his drink, realising that he wanted to unlock his tongue. He drew a wad of red Trinidadian currency from his back pocket. "Could we get a bottle here?"

Lemay seemed about to object and then reconsider. He readjusted his glasses on his nose and laughed. "Yes, we could do that," he said pleasantly. "But put that money away before you lose it."

They bought a bottle of Old Oak and two cans of cola, topped up their glasses and drank. The bar seemed more real to Drummond now. He looked at one old man, broad-shouldered with leathery brown skin, a battered trilby jammed onto his grey head. He watched this man as he argued a point with a friend, noting the strong yellow teeth and the work-hardened hands, all of which were brought into play to deliver the argument, and he thought: yes, there is humanity. In a strange way, he felt himself expanding in all directions, reaching out for everyone in this bar and drawing them closer to him. He drank again and placed his glass on the table, turning it thoughtfully between thumb and forefinger.

"How are things between you and Hilary?" asked Lemay.

Drummond's eyebrows shot up. "Whoah! Didn't see that one coming, Garry. We've been together for over a week and you leave it till now to ask me that!"

Lemay grinned. "The first few days were hardly conducive to that kind of intimate conversation, what with both of us being thrown about by the North Atlantic." A thoughtful pause. "Besides, just now you appear to be...taking stock."

Drummond sighed. "Yes, I suppose that's what I'm doing." He took a drink, smacking his lips as he set the glass down. "You know what I did in that factory I worked in? I turned out tiny electrical components for a long-term government contract. Nobody—certainly nobody on the shop floor—knew what purpose those things served, whether they were used to save life or destroy it. After a while, I stopped caring. All I knew was that, as the factory never operated at less than full capacity, and as the cars in the directors' car park were never more than two years old, it must be a fairly profitable activity. Three years of soul-destroying emptiness, stagnation. Then they closed the factory, making us all redundant."

"But I thought you said it was profitable."

"Oh, it was: they just moved production up north, where wages were lower. Mind you, I got my own back."

"You did?"

"Mm. The day before I left, I let all the tyres down in the directors' car park."

Lemay laughed into his drink, spilling it onto his lap. Then his face softened with the kind of sympathy Drummond did not welcome.

"Yes, I know, I know. I didn't really get my own back, did I? You don't have to look at me like that, Garry. Three years of spiritual and intellectual stagnation and the most creative response I could dream up was to let a lot of tyres down. Rather proves the point, doesn't it? They didn't even know that it was me who did it. Pathetic. Impotent."

"Then, I think I remember you telling me, you went on the buses. What was that like?"

Drummond nodded, a small smile of reminiscence on his face. "Surprisingly okay. Yes, I liked it. I attended meetings of the union branch, but I didn't get involved in union work. I sometimes think that was a mistake."

"In what way, Roger?"

"I think that if I'd become involved I would have had a reason to resist Hilary when she was persuading me to try something else—something, as she said, 'with a future.'"

"Aaahh, now we get to Hilary...So she introduced you to Joseph Thornton and..."

"And I went along with her suggestion that I work for Merritt & Thwaite."

Lemay looked mystified. "But that's been okay, hasn't it?"

"Not totally, Garry. At first, I couldn't take the place seriously, with its olde worlde ways, and with Ronald and Joseph seeming to believe that they were doing Commonwealth countries a favour just by being in business. But then I became interested in the countries we traded with, broadened my reading and then, of course, made contact with you at the Arawak Support Group. From that point on, I took a much greater interest in what I was doing for a living." He uttered a long sigh. "But I don't see how that can last. With the Arawak contract done, dusted and—almost—delivered, what will I be going back to at M & T?"

Lemay scratched his beard. "I thought that you were going to step into Joseph Thornton's shoes."

"So did I, but that won't happen now. But even if it did, what would I end up doing? I'd just be a younger version of Joseph, selling stuff to countries which desperately need it but, for the most part, can't really afford it. And fending off the Yanks, of course."

"Where do the Americans come into the picture?"

"We'll need another drink for this part of the story, Garry." He leaned forward, poured more Old Oak into their two glasses and added cola.

Lemay held up a hand and waved to the bartender. "Can we get some ice over here?"

The bartender sent across a boy, not be much older than eleven or twelve, who placed a blue plastic dish on the table. Lemay dug into his trouser pocket and gave him a few coins, then dropped a large ice cube into each of their glasses. He looked at Drummond and smiled. "We're all set."

Over the next few minutes, Drummond related the Libyan saga and the role of Streeter.

"So Davinia saw this CIA guy sitting with Hesketh-Brown?" asked Lemay when the tale was concluded.

"She did, although at the time she didn't know that's what he was."

"And so she doesn't know why Mrs Long reversed her decision on the grant?"

"I've yet to give her a full explanation, although I've told her in outline. I don't suppose Mrs Long knows why she was told to do a U-turn, either. I told Davinia that I would explain it to her at an appropriate time; I couldn't very well go into it at the dinner."

"No, I suppose not. You think Thornton was in Libya for the past few weeks?"

Drummond nodded. "That's the only conclusion I can draw. This, after all, was a man who was supposed to have been forced to take annual leave due to his mismanagement, and yet here he is, back in London in his old job."

"And that means that you've been..."

"Yes, fooled! Not just by Ronald but by Joseph as well!"

Lemay shrugged. "But what was the point of it all?"

"I can only assume that the point of fooling me was so that I, in turn, would fool Streeter." He grunted. "I suppose I've been *used* rather than fooled, but I have to say that it doesn't feel any better for that."

"But don't you think that, in sending you to Arawak, Ronald is in a way compensating you?"

"I might have thought that at one time, Garry, but I'm now cynical enough to suspect that he's sent me to Arawak to get me out of the way."

"While he does what?"

Drummond threw up his arms. "I don't know, Garry. How *could* I know? My mind would have to be as devious as his to work that out."

Lemay frowned. "You know, you surprise me, Roger, because I thought you had a bit of admiration for Ronald Mathews."

"Well, I do: the figure he cuts; the progressive things he was saying at the dinner...But I certainly don't admire his deviousness and the way he's used me!"

Lemay chuckled.

"What's tickling you, Garry?"

"I just find it surprising that these earth-shattering revelations have come out of a discussion which I began by asking how things were between you and Hilary."

Drummond laughed. "Yes, you're right." He leaned back in his chair and lifted his gaze to the corrugated-zinc ceiling. "Well, in a sense, I *have* been talking about Hilary, because none of this would be happening if I were not with her."

"Every cloud, then..."

Lemay could have meant any number of things by this remark, but Drummond suspected he had Davinia Lee in mind and therefore let it pass without comment.

"You know, I thought Hilary was having an affair with Ronald..."

"With *Ronald?*"

"That's not as far-fetched as it sounds. He's a good-looking man for his age, and he's worth a few bob."

"But you were mistaken?"

Drummond nodded. "I think so." He lifted his glass, gave Lemay a glance and drank. "I don't know whether you noticed at the dinner how Hilary was behaving with Ronald's niece, Audrey. At one stage, I was wondering why Audrey was spending so much time on Hesketh-Brown, when Hilary would have been the easier target. Then, when Hesketh-Brown escaped, it was obvious, from the way Hilary was talking to Audrey, and the questions she was asking, that she was already in the bag."

Lemay threw back his head and laughed. "Are you sure about this?"

"Pretty much. It all adds up. Some time ago, after Hilary had been out for the evening, I came home and found a religious leaflet in the kitchen. I thought it had come through the letterbox that morning, so I threw it away. More recently, Hilary was dropped off home in the early hours by Ronald's Mercedes. I pretended to be asleep and didn't ask her about it. Now, it seems pretty obvious that although it might have been Ronald's car, it was driven by Audrey."

Lemay gazed down into his drink, then lifted his eyes to regard Drummond from beneath a furrowed brow. "And now you have a thing with Davinia Lee?"

Drummond was surprised that he was able to greet this question so calmly. "Do I? To be honest, I'm not sure." He grinned wryly. "Anyway, you're not supposed to know about it."

"All I would say, Roger," said Lemay sympathetically, "is that you should be careful. For your own sake." He made a gesture with his left hand. "Davinia Lee may be more complicated than she appears."

Drummond nodded. "Yes, I think you may be right."

Lemay's nod indicated that this part of the discussion was concluded. "So what are your plans now?"

"I don't know. You see, what you said this morning was absolutely correct: beauty has been forced out of many English people. They're selfish, narrow and empty. It's as if there's nothing behind their eyes. But in the factory where I worked there were a number of West Indians—Jamaicans mostly, but a couple from Arawak—and they seemed different somehow. There was something about them which shone, there was something alive in them. Even those people we've just seen have more going on inside of them than many English people do. Do you see what I mean?" He snorted.

Lemay leaned forward, speaking softly now, eager to convey his earnestness. "Yes, I know what you mean, of course I do. But don't be too hard on your own people, because it's not entirely their own fault. At the same time, don't make the mistake of romanticising *my* people."

"Not entirely their own fault? How do you mean?"

Seeing that Drummond was calm, Lemay also relaxed, leaning back in his chair. "I tell you, the study of history is a wonderful thing"—a laugh broke from his throat—"and maybe it's just as well that you're sharing a drink with someone who's studied it. Seriously now, I'm saying it's a wonderful thing because it enables you to trace, over the centuries, the formation of national characteristics. Now let's take this vibrancy you notice in Caribbean people. How do we explain that? Do we say that the spark of life exists in these people because they're black—which is how some racist black politicians explain it? No, of course not. It exists as a result of historical conditioning and, naturally, it is not confined to either the Caribbean or to black people."

"But it *is* lacking in the English."

"*Some* of the English. And even in those it may not be the case all the time." He held up his hands. "Okay, we'll come to that. But what do you think it is that gives other peoples—*some* other peoples—this particular characteristic? Why do they seem more 'alive,' what is this something that, to use your word, 'shines' in them?" Lemay was the lecturer, Drummond the student.

"The word you used this morning seemed to fit the bill: beauty."

A somewhat dubious Lemay almost shrugged. "Okay, but let's say this beauty is that which reflects the good in humanity, which works *for* the good of humanity. But it is not always possible—or easy, we'll say—for people to keep this alive in themselves. It becomes particularly difficult when they find themselves divorced from the strivings of their fellows. Do you follow?"

"Yes!" Drummond's mind was working hard. "I think I can see now why the quality we're discussing exists in the Caribbean—

because the people have more often found themselves united, striving first for freedom…"

"That's right, first for freedom from slavery, then against colonialism and now… Both the level of the struggle and the degree of unity have been uneven, but nevertheless it's true to say that the more advanced members of our different communities in the Caribbean have been united against a common enemy and that this unity has filtered through the societies. I think that goes a long way towards explaining the phenomenon."

"And its absence in Britain?"

Lemay raised his eyebrows. "Surely that's obvious. The people there have only been united to any degree for very short periods—during the Second World War, for example. Certainly, if you go back far enough, perhaps to the Chartists, you'll find a considerable movement against the existing order, but the whole process was really interrupted—at least diluted—by the advent of what I would call the imperialist age. In fact, it's here that both explanations converge. Britain was exploiting the Caribbean and the rest of its substantial empire, and the peoples of those colonies were coming together at various levels to resist; while in Britain, the unity of the people was broken to a considerable extent by the ability of its rulers, with all this colonial wealth at its disposal, to sweep a few crumbs from the table. The people of Britain—and this isn't a judgment, merely a statement of cold historical fact—have been corrupted, Roger. There lies the answer to your question."

18

Most of the passengers had drifted back to the ship for dinner, perhaps not trusting the cuisine in this strange, poverty-stricken place (the richest island in the English-speaking Caribbean!). This could not be said of the Reverend Bassfield Thomas, of course, and yet his entourage was assembled at their customary table, the ladies in their long black dresses, hands folded in their laps, eyes modestly downturned as they awaited the arrival of the leader of their congregation. Drummond suspected that the Reverend was too mean to eat ashore, that he insisted on receiving all he had paid for.

"I have been robbed!"

There was a clatter as items of cutlery were dropped onto plates at the wrathful sound of the Reverend Bassfield Thomas's voice. Heads turned in the direction of the door, from where Thomas's large blacked-suited body moved purposefully towards the captain's table. His brows were locked in an unquenchable fury, his jaw set in a determination to secure, if not retribution, at least recompense. Both captain and purser, having overcome their initial surprise, began to move in an attempt to stop him short, but the towering figure, quivering with anger, cast its shadow over the table before Captain Ferris had the opportunity to do more than stand up and push back his chair.

"Mr. Thomas..." Concern for the reputation of the company and his own, already fading, hopes of promotion gave his face a mobility it had never had before. The left corner of his mouth gave birth to a tic, while his right eye showed a sudden tendency to close in a slow wink.

"I have been robbed!" the Reverend Bassfield Thomas repeated, as if there were some chance that he had not been heard the first time. "During the afternoon, while I was ashore talking to colleagues in Port of Spain, my cabin was burgled and my money stolen. I demand justice, Captain Ferris..."

Ferris's mouth worked but no sound emerged. The purser, Ferguson by name, stepped in. "Perhaps we had better go to my office and discuss this matter, Reverend Thomas."

"Why? So that your precious passengers won't know just how lacking this ship is in security measures? I demand to know what you intend to do. Why is it that a man can't go about God's work without having his cabin burgled and his money—his church's money!—stolen? Answer me!"

"Why didn't you place your money in my safe, Reverend Thomas? It would have been quite secure there. Now, let's go to my office and we'll see exactly what happened and what can be done."

"I want this whole ship searched until the money is found, Captain Ferris! You hear me? Why don't you speak, man?"

Ferris eventually gained control of both his features and his voice. He cleared his throat. "Just how much money have you lost, Mr Thomas?"

Thomas opened his mouth to reply and stopped. He looked from Ferris to the purser, licking his lips thoughtfully. "Maybe it would be better if we went to your office, Purser," he said.

Drummond and Lemay watched as the group exited from the saloon.

"Bassfield Thomas is an interesting figure," mused Lemay. He lifted his eyes to Drummond's. "He's spent some time behind bars, you know."

"Really? Some financial scandal?"

"Not at all." Lemay chuckled. "Oh, there were always allegations of that sort of thing, but his supporters would never accept that the money they gave him was misused. No, they're very loyal, and look upon Bassie Thomas as a kind of hero. He did his time before independence."

"For what?"

"Sedition. He was a fierce anti-colonialist. And," he added, giving Drummond a wink, "he may have his uses in the current situation."

"In what way?"

"Maybe you'll see for yourself before too long."

19

"I've been bloody well robbed!"

At breakfast, four hours before the *Burgos* put into Arawak City harbour, knives and forks once again clattered onto plates and heads were turned towards the door of the dining saloon where the wrathful roar of the Reverend Bassfield Thomas was being emulated by Brian Garner, but all he could manage was impotent anger. Red-faced, he strode to the captain's table, his arms waving aimlessly, frustratedly, as if seeking something to snatch and smash. Ellen Listor, already seated, brought her hands up to her open mouth. The Reverend Bassfield Thomas smiled, booming to his entourage: "It is some consolation, children, to learn that this thief is interested in the property of mere mortals and not merely that of the Almighty." The four ladies smiled and bowed their heads.

"I've been bloody robbed, Ferris! Someone entered my cabin during the night and took all my valuables."

"While you were in the cabin, Mr Garner?" Captain Ferris faced this problem unafraid. Unlike the huge Mr. Thomas, Garner was totally unable to inspire fear and awe; as for promotion... well, Captain Ferris's prospects had not been particularly rosy in any case. He seemed to have decided that if he was going down, he would do so with a smile on his face. "You mean to tell me that while you were asleep someone was able to enter your cabin and steal your valuables without waking you?"

"Well, no." Garner flushed, realising that he had made a mistake by blustering into the saloon in this way. He leaned close to the captain and lowered his voice. "No. I, er, was not in my cabin last night."

"You weren't in your cabin, Mr Garner? You surely didn't spend the night on deck?" Ferris's voice was still loud enough for most of the passengers to hear.

"You see," intoned the Reverend Bassfield Thomas, "the sins of the flesh must be paid for, my children." The four ladies nodded solemnly, the ghost of a smile touching their lips.

"Shut up, you!" Garner barked over his shoulder. He turned back to Ferris. "Now, I want to know what you're going to do about this. Everything is gone—money, traveler's cheques, my camera..."

"And your dignity, Mr Garner. Now be quiet and we'll go along to the purser's office and make a list of the items missing. We'll radio ahead and alert the police in Arawak City so that they can be ready to come aboard and conduct a search. Frankly, though, I wouldn't put much hope in ever seeing your valuables again. The police in Port of Spain turned the ship inside out in the attempt to recover Mr Thomas's...er, belongings, but all to no avail."

Ferris stood up to lead Garner to the purser's office. Garner turned and saw that the whole saloon was looking at him. He reddened. He could not leave like this, having made a fool of himself, so he stabbed a trembling finger at each table. "One of you has done this to me. One of you is responsible, and if I find out who it is there'll be a murder aboard."

The captain took his elbow and pushed him in the direction of the door. As they passed the table of the Reverend Bassfield Thomas, Garner tripped and sprawled onto the deck. Thomas bent down, ostensibly to help him, and whispered, "The next time you tell me to shut up, I'll cut your ears off, you little creep." He straightened up, winking at the lady opposite him. She withdrew her foot beneath the folds of her black skirt, clasped her hands in front of her and winked back.

*

Captain Ferris had told Lemay that although he had considered bypassing AC he had, after consultation with company headquarters, decided against this; the unrest appeared to be moderate and directed at members or supporters of the government, and so he had merely advised his passengers to take great care when venturing ashore and to avoid certain areas.

Arawak City shimmered in the noonday sun. The city was bigger than Drummond had expected. Having originally sprung up around the harbour, one of the largest in the Caribbean, it now stretched for several miles on either side of what were known locally as the "old docks" (a new terminal, for which the *Burgos* was destined, had recently been built on the western outskirts of the city). The middle-class suburbs reached inland, the northernmost of these having invaded the foothills of the mountains whose blue mass dominated the backdrop. Even from where he stood on deck, Drummond could see that it was a city of contrasts. Tall, white multi-storied buildings bearing the names of well-known banks stood out against more modest structures of wood and dull brick. The pilot came aboard and guided the ship past the hideous oil storage depot and into the new terminal.

The police were waiting for them on the dock, a surly collection of men with striped shirts and hats whose visors almost completely concealed their eyes. An officer with a swagger-stick paced up and down while they waited for the *Burgos* to tie up and the gangway to be lowered. Dockers with tattered khaki shirts huddled at the stern end, now and again casting distrustful glances towards the policemen.

Lemay was standing with Drummond on the forward deck. Both were in their going-ashore clothes, Lemay in a tan safari suit and Drummond in white slacks and a checked short-sleeved shirt.

"Do you think, Garry, we need go to our cabins and wait for the search party?"

"I don't think so, Roger. As soon as the gangway is down, we'll go and have a word with the officer."

"How will you persuade him to let us disembark?"

Lemay grinned. "I'll simply ask him if he's prepared to incur the wrath of Davinia Lee *and* the Prime Minister."

"They're coming to meet us?"

"Yes, and no: Davinia Lee may be coming to meet you, but she and the Prime Minister—along with us—will also be conducting a bit of a ceremony in front of the offloaded cargo for the sake of the media."

A sceptical Drummond peered onto the quayside. "No sign of media, Garry. Maybe they're running on Arawak time."

Lemay bit his lip. "Maybe, but this *is* a little worrying." He brightened, though, when he turned to gaze further down the dock. "Ah! Here come the trucks! They'll be transporting the equipment to a warehouse by the General Hospital."

"But still no media. Or government bigwigs."

Lemay frowned in disapproval. "Alright, alright." He sighed. "Let's see if we can find out what's happening."

*

"Mr Lemay?" inquired the officer with the swagger-stick. He removed an envelope from his side pocket and offered it up. "Chief Inspector Crawford, sir, with a message from the Minister of Health."

They were standing outside the purser's office, just a few feet from the gangway. Lemay took the envelope and, standing back against the bulkhead to allow the search party to pass, ripped it open. Expressionless, he swiftly scanned the letter before passing it to Drummond.

> Dear Mr Lemay,
>
> As you may be aware, the security situation in Arawak City has deteriorated over the past few days, and it has therefore been decided to postpone the media event.
>
> Please tell Mr Drummond to leave his luggage aboard the ship and arrange to sail with it tomorrow, remaining as a passenger until Port Santiago, where it is possible that our media event will be held in a few days' time.
>
> Chief Inspector Crawford, the bearer of this letter, will now convey you and Mr Drummond to me; I will explain the situation which necessitates these precautions.
>
> Sincerely yours,
>
> Davinia Lee,
> Minister of Health.

"So you are to take us to Ms Lee, Chief Inspector?" asked Lemay as he took back the letter from Drummond.

Crawford, a tall, light-skinned man in his early forties, nodded. "Indeed, sir. But first I have business aboard this ship."

"You're not going to supervise the search, are you?" asked Lemay, half in jest. "That's surely not a job for a man of your rank."

"You are quite correct, sir," chuckled the Chief Inspector. "No, I'll just make sure my men know how they're expected to behave. Can't have them upsetting the tourists, can we?"

"As we're both packed, I assume that your men will not be searching our cabins, Chief Inspector," said Drummond. "Where would you like us to wait for you?"

"It's entirely up to you, sir." He grinned. "But as you'll be staying aboard until Port Santiago, you might use the time to *un*pack."

"Yes, very droll, Chief Inspector."

"Hadn't we better oversee the unloading of our cargo?" suggested Lemay.

Drummond nodded. "Yes, of course. But first I must see Mr Ferguson to arrange my passage to Port Santiago."

The business with the purser was soon concluded, the latter agreeing to advise the company to bill Merritt & Thwaite for the extra meals and mileage. As Drummond was about to leave the purser's office, there were sounds of a scuffle outside, and the door burst open to reveal the somewhat disheveled figure of the steward Jimmy in the grip of a police constable on one side and a sergeant on the other.

"Mr Hicks!" exclaimed the purser, his mouth dropping open. "Surely you're not the thief!"

"No, Boss, of course I'm not, but someone has fingered me."

The purser turned to the senior man with narrowed eyes. "Sergeant?"

"We have information that this man has a record of dishonesty, Purser, having defrauded your Customs people in the matter of accordions!"

*

When Drummond and Lemay had witnessed the boxed medical equipment lifted from the hold by a crane and then transferred to flatbed trucks by forklifts, Drummond went back on board to exchange half of his travelers' cheques for red Arawakian currency.

"Not thinking of buying a house here, are you, Mr Drummond?" quipped the purser.

"Ha ha." And why not? In truth, he didn't know why, other than an uneasy feeling that it might be needed, he was withdrawing so much money.

"This'll make a bit of a bulge in your pockets, Mr Drummond," said the purser with a frown. "I should put it in a bag, if you have one."

"Yes, I'll get it from my cabin. What happened about little Jimmy?"

"Little Jimmy's cabin was searched," replied the purser with a sigh, "and was found to be clean as a whistle. Seems another crew-member—somebody with a grudge, I suppose—told the police about his accordion trick. What he did, you see..."

Although he had overheard the story from the horse's mouth, Drummond let the purser repeat it, not wishing to cause trouble for the Irish steward.

Mr Ferguson purser chuckled. "Clever little trick that."

"Was Jimmy hurt?"

"Oh, they roughed him up a bit, but nothing too serious. Poor little bugger was crying, though."

"Can nothing be done about that?"

The purser looked Drummond in the eye and shrugged. "What can we do? I got their inspector to give the two men a bollocking, but that's about it. I suppose I could write a letter of complaint, but I can't see that doing much good."

*

Once Lemay's luggage had been loaded in the boot of the police car, Crawford, who sat in front with the driver, leaned over and passed a blanket to Drummond, who sat, a black shoulder bag on his knees, in the back with Lemay.

"Put this over your head, Mr Drummond, until we're well clear of the docks."

"Whatever for?"

"Because we don't want you to be identified. Ms Lee, I am sure, will explain this to you."

"Ah," said Lemay as they approached the dock gates, "I can see part of the reason. There's a crowd of media people at the gates, being kept out by the police."

Drummond heard the click-whirr of cameras as they passed through the gates.

The driver turned right and accelerated.

"Are they likely to follow us?" asked Lemay.

"No, my men will hold them there for a good fifteen minutes. You can take that off now, Mr Drummond."

Across the street, Drummond saw a huddle of shanties with corrugated zinc roofs. Children, the boys in ragged shorts, the girls in equally ragged frocks, stood looking across at the docks, perhaps imagining the places the *Burgos* had visited.

They were on a dual carriageway now. On one side of the road stood the oil storage depot, grey and depressing, while on the other green land, uncultivated, swept up to meet the blue of the mountains in the distance. Every now and again the driver would drop down to second gear to maneuver around the potholes which studded the road.

"Well, this is AC," Lemay announced as they entered the outskirts of the city.

They passed the old docks. It was surrounded by bars, most of them dingy affairs of wood and stone. Here and there a prostitute sat outside alone, there being little business in mid-afternoon. They entered Jetty Street, which ran right along the waterfront, and at first the buildings were not much smarter; but gradually, as they moved east, the shiny concrete and glass bank buildings began to appear. The people moved slowly, looking about them as if expecting something to happen. Some of the men had transistor radios jammed to their ears and Drummond asked Lemay if the situation were so tense that people were waiting minute by minute for news.

"No," he replied wryly. "There's a test match in Barbados at the moment."

Some of the buildings and all the lampposts were festooned with posters and stickers advertising meetings and calling for various forms of action:

FIGHT IMPERIALISM—DEFEND THE ROBINSON
GOVERNMENT—ARAWAK WORKERS' PARTY MEETING
SUNDAY NIGHT

ROBINSON MASH UP THE COUNTRY—RALLY AGAINST PRICE
RISES WEDNESDAY—ARAWAK DEMOCRATIC PARTY

COMMUNISM IS THE DEVIL'S WORK—BILLY JOE HARRISON
CONCERT AND RALLY, 22 JUNE

The car took a left turn and they entered one of the main shopping streets. A few windows, broken in the recent demonstrations, were boarded up.

"My god." It was Lemay. He sounded both saddened at this evidence of the last few days' events and a little daunted by the thought of the tasks ahead.

Drummond's thoughts turned to Davinia Lee, with whom he would be reunited in a matter of minutes. Was she in danger? Would she want to renew their relationship? Did she retain any of the affection she had displayed during their hours together in the Notting Hill Gate flat? How would she behave with Lemay present? He cast back his mind to that evening, but this time there were no flashbacks.

Lemay was looking with some concern as the landmarks as they flashed by. "We're not going to the Ministry of Health, Chief Inspector?"

Crawford shook his head. "Too obvious, Mr Lemay. We'd be besieged by the media if we went there."

They drove to the northern suburbs of AC, leaving behind both poverty and brash commercialism and entering an area of exclusive sub-divisions concealed behind dense green hedges and protected by checkpoints manned by private security guards. They entered one of these and drove past two-story houses and bungalows, each worth a lifetime's wages for a worker in this small country, until at the end of a cul-de-sac they saw the large bungalow, set in an expanse of green lawn, guarded by two members of the Arawak Defence Force.

Chief Inspector Crawford led the way to the front door, nodding to the ADF men before ringing the bell. The door was opened by a neat woman in her mid-thirties—it was not clear whether she was maid or secretary—who led them into a comfortably furnished living room. She gestured to a sofa and turned to Lemay. "Please take a seat, Mr Lemay. Ms Lee wishes to speak with Mr Drummond for a few moments."

She then led Drummond into a small library, and there stood Davinia Lee, beautiful in a red trouser suit. It was apparent from her slightly confused expression that she had no idea how she should behave and Drummond therefore knew that he must act. Hearing the door close behind him, he strode to her and threw his arms about her, planting his lips on hers before she could protest. He drew her closer, feeling her small breasts against his chest before releasing her lips to plant kisses all over her face, murmuring, "Davinia, Davinia, Davinia," letting her know that this was not mere desire but devotion.

Eventually, she shook her head. "You mustn't. Roger, you mustn't."

"But you know you want to."

"Yes, but you mustn't. *We* mustn't." She placed her palms on his chest and eased him away. "We need to talk, Roger."

"You can say that again."

"Roger, be *serious! Please!*"

Seeing that she was indeed in earnest, he sobered and, removing his shoulder bag, allowed her to lead him to a small table where they sat opposite each other. She pushed a copy of that day's *Arawak Chronicle* across the table and tapped the front page. "You'd better read that."

MED FIRM LINKED TO LIBYA

UK GRANT "TAINTED," SAYS ADP

The Arawak Democratic Party has charged that Merritt & Thwaite, the British company supplying medical equipment to this country, has links to Libya, the Middle Eastern state widely suspected of sponsoring international terrorism.

Speaking to the media yesterday, ADP leader Maynard Lewis announced that his party had been advised by "unimpeachable sources" that Merritt & Thwaite had not only contracted to supply medical equipment to the rogue state but had recently been attempting to negotiate a loan from that same country.

"Our party," said Mr Lewis, "was only too willing to join Health Minister Davinia Lee in her crusade for the modernisation of our health service, and we fully approved her intention of seeking a grant from the government of the United Kingdom for this purpose. Unfortunately, that grant has turned out to be tainted.

"Why do we say that? We make this claim because it is an irrefutable fact that Ms Lee's negotiations with Merritt & Thwaite *preceded* the UK government's final decision to accede to her request—or *demand* as she so characteristically termed it—for the modernisation grant. Thus, it was *known* that these funds would go to a company with links to Libya, a country which has displayed implacable hostility to Israel, with which our country has the warmest relations, and the United States, which provides much of our foreign investment.

"This was certainly known to Ms Lee. I have no idea whether it was known to the UK government, but it may be significant that Mrs Amanda Long, who as Minister for Overseas Development acceded to Ms Lee's request for a grant, has in recent days been replaced. Perhaps our own Prime Minister would like to consider following a similar course of action."

The medical equipment provided by Merritt & Thwaite is due to arrive in Arawak City today aboard the TSS *Burgos*. Also aboard will be that company's representative, Mr Roger Drummond, who is expected to participate in a hand-over ceremony with Ms Lee.

"I am sure," says Mr Lewis, "that the people of Arawak will give Mr Drummond the welcome he so
richly deserves, leaving him in no doubt that they heartily disapprove of a company which, for
commercial gain, climbs into bed with an enemy of freedom and democracy like Libya."

Having read the story, Drummond allowed the newspaper to fall back onto the table. "I see," he said calmly. "Well, Lemay did wonder what the opposition would have to say about our mission." He looked up at her and shrugged. "Now we know."

"And now you see," said Davinia Lee firmly, "why there can be nothing between us. Whenever we meet in public—and that will probably be just once, at the hand-over ceremony—there must not be even the merest hint that our relationship is anything but professional."

He regarded her in silence for a few moments. Her eyes, he noted, avoided him, darting from the newspaper which lay between them to the spot above his head where the ceiling fan turned. He suspected that, should Lemay ask him again if he had a "thing" with Davinia Lee, he would have no alternative but to reply in the negative. But what a waste! Look how she sits there, angry and yet vulnerable, her insecurity masked by a display of pique, and I know that if I were able just to touch her lovely face she would crumble, be mine again. Will I be able to get through the weeks and months to come without really knowing whether she intended this break to be final? Should I seek confirmation? Yes, let's risk it.

"And when we're not in public?"

Now she looked him in the eye, her mouth resolving itself into a thin, determined line as she slapped the table with her palm. "The *only* time we will meet is in public! Do I make myself clear?"

"Davinia, don't you think you might be over-reacting somewhat?" This was said almost as a sigh, sadly.

This caused a further eruption. "Apparently, I am *not* making myself clear! Consider my situation: yesterday, I was on the brink of a political triumph; I, Davinia Lee, had launched a campaign to modernise our health service by forcing the UK, albeit in a small way, to make reparations for its previous sins; to prosecute this campaign, I had ventured into the lion's den—London; when our demand was at first rebuffed, it was I who stood before the British media and shamed the UK government into reversing that decision; today was to have been the crowning moment as the medical equipment arrived on our shores. Had it all gone to plan, the whole population would have been singing my praises now!

"But what is the reality?" She slapped the newspaper which still lay before her. "This! The equipment Davinia Lee has secured is 'tainted.' She has been treating with a company that deals with Libya! She is such a pariah that the leader of the opposition is practically calling for her to be dismissed!"

"But you knew that Ronald was dealing with Libya. You didn't seem to be upset when he announced it at the dinner!"

Almost rising from her seat, both palms pressed to the table, this was not the woman Drummond had been with in London but a different being entirely, her face distorted, made ugly with rage. And she responded without thinking. "Because it was not then a threat to my career!"

Ah. It was out. He regarded her coolly, recognising now what previously he had failed to see: personal ambition. He held her in his gaze, knowing that she realised that in speaking so unguardedly she had diminished herself in his eyes, watching her almost writhe in embarrassment. Time to take her down a further peg.

"But we both know, Ms Lee, that it was not you who forced the UK government to reverse its original decision regarding the grant." He could barely resist a grin as, immediately giving him her full attention, her eyes flashed at him. "You remember when we saw Hesketh-Brown sitting in the Indian restaurant? The man with him was a CIA officer called Phil Streeter. Earlier that day, I had told Streeter that, with the Arawak contract lost, Merritt & Thwaite would have no alternative but to pursue the Libyan loan that he, Streeter, had been so keen on dissuading us from taking. When I saw them together, it seemed obvious that Streeter was telling Hesketh-Brown that a U-turn would be in order." He grinned, albeit a little bitterly. "But there was never going to be a Libyan loan. Streeter purported to represent a company called International Enterprises, which had first expressed an interest in acquiring Merritt & Thwaite and then, when we seemed to have hit a rough financial patch, offered a loan. Ronald worked out that this was a CIA proprietary company, and so concocted the fiction of a Libyan loan in order to force Streeter to moderate his terms." He chuckled. "Ronald's a clever chap."

Davinia Lee was becalmed, no wind in her sails. "And so..." she faltered. "And so he will take a loan from this CIA company? Or even let them buy the company?"

Drummond shrugged. "Who knows? I'm not as privy to Ronald's thinking as I once thought." It occurred to him that, either way, Davinia Lee was in a difficult position: at the moment, the right could attack her over "Libyan money," whereas if Streeter's case prospered the left would be up in arms over the CIA connection. Unless, of course, she turned the tables on the ADP.

"It seems to me, Minister," he commented, tapping the newspaper with his forefinger, "that this attack can be countered fairly easily."

"Oh, Mr Drummond?" replied a dubious Davinia Lee, although no doubt gratefully maintaining the formal note he had introduced. "And how do you suggest I do that?"

He spread his hands. "You surely need to ask who Mr Lewis's 'unimpeachable sources' are. Surely Mr Streeter, or his employers, can be fingered on that account. Indeed, who else could it be?" He sighed. "So, while the ADP complains of a Libyan connection—of which, of course, you were entirely ignorant until our contract had been signed and sealed, that party had received its information from a foreign intelligence agency." He cocked an eyebrow. "Isn't the CIA seeking to meddle in the internal affairs of Arawak?"

Seemingly recovered from her spell of doubt and depression, Davinia Lee brought her palms together. "Of course!" She closed her eyes for a moment and, when she reopened them, for a moment looked directly at Drummond, giving him a slight nod. "Thank you, Mr Drummond." She checked her watch. "I have called a news conference for five o'clock, and so I think we had better ask Mr Lemay to join us now."

"Before you do so," Drummond replied, "can I ask why, when we drove past the press at the dock gates, I was asked to hide under a blanket?"

She almost gasped, bringing a hand to her mouth; obviously, something had slipped her mind. "Of course." She pushed the *Chronicle* back towards him. "You surely read the last paragraph of this story, Mr Drummond. The ADP has made you a target, and so the last thing any of us want is to have your photograph splashed across tomorrow's front page." She got up and walked to a small bureau situated between two bookcases.

Drummond let this information sink in. A target? Strangely, the prospect did not make him particularly nervous.

"Whenever you're ashore, try not to look like a businessman," she said as she stepped to his side. "Those clothes you're wearing are just about right. But you should also take this for your own protection." She leaned forward and placed an automatic pistol on the table in front of him. "It's a Browning .22. Ten shots in the magazine." She picked it up and demonstrated the safety mechanism before handing it to him. "Here, put it in your bag. And don't tell anyone where you got it."

He did as she instructed, placing the bag before him on the table. She remained standing beside him and, looking up at her, he felt the urge to touch her, but she sensed this and turned away, walking to the door to ask Lemay to join them.

*

"Have you had a chance to read the lead story in today's *Chronicle*, Mr Lemay?" asked Davinia Lee.

Lemay nodded. "Yes, Minister, your secretary provided me with a copy."

"What do you think?"

Lemay grimaced. "Sadly predictable, I'm afraid, Minister. In fact, a few days ago, when Mr Drummond asked me what these gun attacks could accomplish when you were about to deliver the government a sizeable victory, it occurred to me that the opposition might spring something to diminish that victory."

"And do you think we were justified in calling off the hand-over ceremony today?"

"Under the circumstances, yes," Lemay replied after a moment's thought. "Might I ask what the arrangements will be for Port Santiago, Minister? The equipment, after all, is now warehoused at the General Hospital."

"The equipment destined for the Port Santiago hospital and the other medical centres will be transported overland, timed to arrive in Port Santiago just before the *Burgos* docks. Mr Drummond will come ashore, where he will be joined by me, the Prime Minister, yourself, Mr Lemay, and the British High Commissioner. The formal hand-over ceremony will then take place on the dock—witnessed, of course, by the media. Following the ceremony, you and Mr Drummond will, if the security situation permits, then oversee the distribution of the equipment to the hospitals and medical centres, starting in Port Santiago itself."

"And if the security situation does not permit, Minister?" asked Drummond.

"Then, Mr Drummond, I regret to say that you will need to reboard the *Burgos* and stay aboard until she reaches England."

"Or," interjected Drummond, "I could simply fly back, as was the original intention."

"You could," Davinia Lee nodded solemnly. Then she brightened, giving them both a dazzling smile. "But I hope that this Libyan nonsense will have been defused by then, gentlemen, in which case you will be able to complete your mission as originally planned."

"Might I ask how, Minister...? Lemay began.

She reprised her smile. "I have a news conference at five, Mr Lemay."

"Ah, I see. In that case, Minister, might I ask what arrangements have been made for my accommodation?"

"All taken care of! We've booked you into The Crown."

"As a matter of interest, Minister," asked Drummond, his brow furrowed in thought, "do you recall which hotel our Mr Thornton stayed at when he was here?"

"Yes, I believe he also was at The Crown."

"In which case, I think it would be advisable to make other arrangements for Mr Lemay. You see, according to Mr Streeter, the hotel at which Mr Mathews stayed is owned by International Enterprises."

"The CIA proprietary company?"

"The very same."

"Oh, listen," said a thoroughly perplexed Lemay, "I can stay at my brother's house, so that's no problem."

Davinia Lee fell silent, stroking her chin. "I wonder," she speculated eventually, "if your Mr Streeter is here..."

"Well, if he's following up the case..."

"And if so, where he might be staying."

Drummond shrugged. "The Crown, I would have thought."

"Exactly." She grinned and lifted a forefinger. "Let's try something." She walked to the door and called for her secretary. "Lydia, can you get me the number of The Crown?"

Davinia Lee stood in the corner of the room at a small table upon which sat a white telephone. When her secretary entered the library and handed her a slip of paper, she dialed.

"Hello. Yes, good afternoon. Put me through to Mr Streeter's room please." A pause of some seconds, and then: "Oh, he's not in his room? No, that's quite alright, I'll try again later."

20

Lemay persuaded Crawford to drive them to his brother's house, back towards the city centre. Crawford was not happy about leaving them both there, but Lemay assured him that he would ensure that Drummond got safely back aboard the *Burgos* in time for dinner.

"And now," said Lemay, having greeted his sister-in-law, his brother being at work, "I suggest we find a bar that serves food."

"And that has a television."

"A television?"

"You wouldn't want to miss the minister's news conference, would you?"

They walked onto the street and began to look for a taxi.

"Maybe we should have asked Mr Crawford to wait for us," suggested Drummond.

Lemay laughed. "No, I don't think it would be a good idea for us to be seen getting out of a police vehicle in the area I'm taking you to."

Passing through the parts more susceptible to fly-posting, Drummond's attention was drawn to the posters advertising the forthcoming concert by Billy Joe Harrison.

As they paused in traffic, Drummond gestured through the window with his chin. "Who is this guy?"

"Billy Joe Harrison?"

"Who else?"

"All I know is what I read in the *Weekly Arawak Chronicle* in London. Seems he's a Christian rock singer. American, of course."

Drummond was incredulous. "A Christian *rock* singer?"

"It's a newish genre," explained an amused Lemay. After a thoughtful pause: "You know, after liberation theology arose in the left wing of the Catholic Church, the countries of Latin America—Cuba excepted, of course—found themselves suddenly inundated by evangelical Protestant sects putting out a right-wing message. Most of them imported from the USA. Well, I suppose Billy Joe Harrison has been sent to do a similar job here."

"But does liberation theology have much of a following here?"

Lemay grinned. "No, but we have a government with liberation politics."

"Ah, of course. Won't he have a hard time putting his message across?"

"In AC he would, yes. But this concert you see advertised is in the countryside, so I imagine his thinking—or that of his promoters—is that the audience there will be a little more backward."

"And will it be?"

"Possibly," Lemay acknowledged. "It will depend on how much work the AWP and the ANP have done in that area."

*

Lemay told the taxi driver to drop them off on West Princes Street, the last east-west major thoroughfare before the harbour. It was clear that AC had not been planned in any real sense of the word. True, the streets were all set neatly at right angles to one another, rather like those of New York, but poverty and riches were thrown together quite haphazardly. The main streets had nothing of interest which could not be found in England— AC even had a Woolworth's and several Kentucky Fried Chicken outlets. The streets—or "lanes" as the smaller side-roads were called—which lay behind the main shopping streets contained the poor, their children and their dogs, and it was down one of these that Lemay led Drummond, presumably to reduce the risk of a sighting by journalists or other interested parties. Crouching in the shadow of the big bank buildings, ramshackle rooming houses and even, here and there, shacks built on stilts, provided shelter for the those employed in the lower-paid occupations and the unemployed—along with petty criminals and prostitutes. The sight of a white man was a rarity in the lanes and so he was watched with some curiosity. The only hostility he sensed was from the older women, who suspected with some disapproval that he was a seaman on the lookout for girls (although the presence of Lemay should have ruled out this possibility), and from some of the younger men and youths, those with Rasta-coloured tams perched atop their plaited locks, who thought the colour of his skin probably put him on the side of the exploiters. But most seemed to think him a curious irrelevance, looking up from their chores, blinking and then dismissing what they saw with a shrug of the shoulders.

"What made you choose this area, Garry?" Drummond tried, with a fair degree of success, to keep any note of concern from his voice.

Lemay chuckled and gave him a glance. "A number of reasons. First, it's just a short taxi ride from the *Burgos*. It's rough, as you can see, but it's pretty safe. This is Lester Robinson's constituency, so most of the locals are on our side. And rather than take you to some tourist spot, I thought that you'd like to take a look at the real AC. Did I get that right?"

Drummond returned his glance and nodded. "You did, Garry."

Towards the harbour, Lemay halted outside a bar.

The Antonio was fronted by a small flight of steps, at the top of which sat three young women, fanning themselves and swapping stories. Inside, a jukebox blared. Taking a breath, Drummond followed Lemay up the concrete steps, meeting the girls' expectant looks with a smile and a quiet "Excuse me" as he stepped around them. At the bead curtain which hung across the doorway, he turned for a moment and looked back into the street. It was like a dream, the sun beating down on this crumbling lane where people called to each other in a dialect he could barely understand, children shrieking as, barefoot, they pursued each other among the debris and, somewhere further down towards the harbor, metal rang upon metal in a car repair shop. The girls stopped talking and looked after him. The jukebox began to play an old Aretha Franklin record. Suddenly, there was nothing strange in the scene at all: they were all just people, the same as people anywhere. The only strange thing about it was that he should be here. He turned and brushed aside the bead curtain. Behind him, the girls resumed their conversation.

The bar was empty apart from a group of youths playing dominoes in the back room, slapping the pieces down vigorously and noisily onto the metal table-top. At the sight of Lemay, the barmaid—or maybe she was the owner—brought her palms together.

"Lord God! Garrison Lemay! Wh'appen to you all these years, m'dear?" In her mid-thirties, she was a large woman with a pleasant face and a gap between her front teeth.

"Just come from London, Lurleen." He turned to Drummond. "The Antonio was one of my haunts during my younger years."

He jerked a thumb over his shoulder. "We passed the place where I was born just up the lane."

Lurleen gestured towards his safari suit. "And *look* at you! You is politician now?"

"No, no," Lemay laughed, "just a small diplomat. But listen, Lurleen, mi have two very important question fe you: do you still serve that chicken in orange sauce; and is your tv in working order?"

She slapped the bar. "Two yesses! But first you want a beer, right? You fren too? Okay, first round on de house."

He and Lemay began by drinking Red Stripe but soon went onto rum and cola. After a while, Drummond began to feel mellow. He sat on his barstool, feeling the sweat trickle down his sides and listening to the cool, pleasant sound of the ice-cubes as they clinked against the side of his glass. The jukebox alternated reggae and soul. A wave of well-being began to spread through his body.

Drummond cast his eye about the bar. On the wall behind him, someone—no Michelangelo—had painted a pink woman with huge breasts and a lopsided grin. On the wall behind the bar, by the side of the small television set, were portraits of Kwame Nkrumah, Martin Luther King and John F. Kennedy. Try as he might, he could not see what they had in common.

"Would you mind if I asked you a personal question, Roger?"

"Go ahead, Garry."

"Actually, I'll be repeating something I've asked you before."

"Oh, *that* question." He grinned and lifted his glass. "The answer is no."

Lemay laughed. "You don't seem to be particularly upset about it."

"I probably will be, later." He shrugged. "Possibly tonight, as I lay in my bunk, thinking of what I'll be missing for the rest of my life."

"Perhaps she'll be thinking the same thing."

"Ha! Not a chance, Garry. She'll be thinking of her"—he held his glass before him and realised that he was becoming a little tipsy—"*career!*"

"Ah. Well, I did..."

"Yes, you did, Garry, you did."

When the food arrived, Lemay declined Lurleen's offer of a table, telling her that they would eat at the bar.

"So why yuh aks bout mi television, Garrison Lemay?" she enquired as she handed them their cutlery.

"At five o'clock, Lurleen, your Health Minister will be holding a news conference."

"Dat Chinee gal?" Lurleen snapped her fingers. "Bway, she hot, eh? Me like de weh she give dem ADPs some *hard* licks!"

Lemay gave her a smile. "In that case, Lurleen, I don't think you'll be disappointed at five o'clock."

"But they won't show her news conference live, will they, Garry?" asked Drummond. "Surely they'll just show the highlights in the early-evening news."

"We only have one TV channel here," explained Lemay, delaying his first bite of the chicken, "and it's government-owned. If the station is told to show it live, that's what they'll do."

Lurleen nodded at Drummond's wrist. "What time yuh have dere, sah?"

"Five to four. But please don't call me sir, Lurleen."

"Oh, pardon me," said Lemay. "Lurleen, this is my friend from London, Tom Lomax."

The gold bangles on Lurleen's wrist jangled as she extended her hand to Drummond.

As Lurleen turned and made her way to the other end of the bar, Drummond frowned at Lemay, mouthing "Tom Lomax?"

Lemay gave him a wink, whispering, "Don't forget you're a target."

When they had finished their meal, the three girls came in from their spot on the top step and persuaded Drummond to buy them drinks. Being suffused with a feeling of wellbeing, he did not need much persuasion. Having bought the round, he sat back and studied his three new companions. The boldest of them, Monica, was tall and slim with long, violently red fingernails. She put on airs when she spoke to Drummond, locating the aitches in all the wrong places. The second, Mavis, was a stocky girl who at one time had been cut about the face with a broken bottle. However, she looked the type who might just as well deal out that kind of treatment to anyone who crossed her, and Drummond averted his gaze whenever she looked at him, afraid that a glance from him might be misinterpreted as interest and his subsequent refusal as bordering on treachery.

Tina was different. She was the youngest of the three, barely twenty, Drummond estimated, and as yet the kind of life she must be leading had not soured her as it had the other two. Yes, she had the most attractive face and body, but there was something else, too: the light in her eyes was not yet deadened by hopelessness. This may have meant that she was still naïve and too inexperienced to know that any hopes she might have would go unfulfilled, but it was an attractive characteristic just the same. As Drummond sipped his way into another rum and Coke, he found himself more and more looking across at her, his eyes sweeping her body from the firm breasts which thrust forward beneath her white T-shirt to her smooth, brown, unmarked face. Before long, Monica and Mavis saw they were being left out in the cold and moved to a table, Monica giving Tina a look quite openly charged with envy and malice. "Don't think you're always going to be young," the look said. "You'll be like us one day."

Drummond encouraged Tina to talk about herself, of her childhood in the countryside, of how she had been forced to come to the city in search of work two years ago, of the life she had led since. The pathos of her tale combined with the rum to produce a wave of sympathy. Looking at her finely-formed features as she turned to smile at him, he could not stop himself from leaning across to kiss her. At that moment, he loved her. He loved her youth, her beauty, her poverty, her still-alive spirit. He also loved this bar, the lane outside and the people in it. He wished all his dead-alive former workmates in England could be here so that they could love all these things too—except Tina, of course. He wanted to love her on his own.

Lemay brought him back to earth. Although he had been chatting with Lurleen, one ear had obviously been cocked to catch the activity of the couple next to him. Now came the sound of Lemay's teeth being sucked in consternation. He spoke to Drummond, but his words, uttered in a gruff, authoritarian tone inflected with dialect, were obviously intended for Tina. "Cho, man, wha' yah a-deal wid? When dis news conference finish, wi gahn, yunnerstan?"

As five o'clock approached, people began to drift into the bar—workers who lived locally and who had the smell of honest toil about them. Most of the men slapped a few cents onto the bar and received a small glass of potent white rum. Some of them drank it neat, tossing it back and grimacing, while others mixed it with water and drank slowly. Each was silent until he had put a drink between him and work, and then he would turn to the others and enter into conversation. Gradually, almost visibly, the tension slipped from their bodies and they began to smile and laugh. Maybe it was the alcohol, but Drummond felt comfortable, at home. Almost free. He recalled the hope he had expressed to Hilary all those years ago—"To dance beneath the diamond sky, with one hand waving free"—and realised that this was the closest he had ever come to experiencing that feeling. The prospect of a return to Merritt & Thwaite—and Hilary—suddenly filled him with something like dread. Surely, he belonged here, or somewhere like it, surrounded by workers and friends. Did he have friends in London? Really only Lemay.

One of the men slapped a one-dollar note on the bar. "Lurleen, gimme change fe de jukebox nuh!"

Lurleen held up a restraining palm. "Leff it till five-thirty or so, m'dear." Her hand turned in the direction of Lemay and Drummond. "These two genklemen want fe watch a TV ting at five." She laughed—a throaty thing. "Me too, m'dear!"

The man, in his forties and wearing a short-sleeved grey work-shirt, looked interested. "What dem a-show, Lurleen?"

"Health Minister gwine speak to de nation!"

The man turned to Drummond and placed a hand on his shoulder. "So you want fe see our sweet Davinia?"

Drummond found himself at a loss to know how to reply. Leaving aside his relationship with Davinia Lee, how was an Englishman expected to respond to such a question put by a rough, middle-aged Caribbean worker? "Oh, ra*ther!*" Or "Yes, *I'll* say!" He chuckled inwardly but thought that, pleasant though this was, maybe it was not home.

Lemay came to his rescue, leaning forward and telling the man, "Im wan fe listen, not look."

When Lurleen switched on the television, it slowly flickered into life until there appeared the black-and-white image of a young woman presenter, who announced that the station's normal schedule was being interrupted to allow the broadcasting of a news conference by Ms Davinia Lee, Minister of Health.

Lurleen slapped the bar. "Alright, ladies and genklemen, mek we all keep duhn de nize so we can hear what de sister haffe seh!"

Amazingly, she was instantly obeyed, and all heads turned towards the television. The two youths who had been playing dominoes in the back room sauntered into the bar and found chairs.

Davinia Lee stood behind a small table and tapped the microphone with a slender forefinger. With a face like thunder, she then gazed into the single television camera.

"Bway, she look fierce!" commented one of the workers.

"A smaddy gwine get some licks!" responded another.

"*Shhhhhh!*" hissed Lurleen.

*

"*My fellow citizens,*" the Health Minister began, "*today should be a day for celebration. As you know, last month I returned from London, having secured a grant from the UK government for the partial modernisation of our health service. I also negotiated with Merritt & Thwaite, the company that would provide the equipment necessary for the modernisation. Today, that equipment has arrived in Arawak City.*
"*But we are not celebrating, are we? Why?*"
She held up a copy of that day's *Arawak Chronicle*.
"*We are not celebrating because this newspaper, which just weeks ago effected to join me in a campaign to put our health service in order, has chosen to use its front page to run a story based on the lies and distortions of the Arawak Democratic Party.*"
"What mi a-tell you!" came a remark from behind Drummond. "Yes, Davinia! Lash dem, lash dem!"
"*They say that the equipment that arrived today to serve our sick is 'tainted.' Tainted! Why? Because, so they say, Merritt & Thwaite, the company providing this equipment, was recently seeking a loan from Libya, a country which, according to ADP leader Maynard Lewis, promotes terrorism and is an enemy of the United States. Mr Lewis claims that this information has been received from an 'unimpeachable source.'* She nodded at the camera, chuckling ironically. '*Unimpeachable? Unimpeachable? In a minute, I'll tell you who that source was, and let you, my fellow citizens, decide if such a person is unimpeachable.*"

She stood before the camera, fists on hips, presenting to the nation the fighting Davinia Lee, scourge of the wealthy and powerful. She must know, thought Drummond, that all over the country people with access to a television set or radio would be cheering her, urging her on. Certainly, that was the case in the Antonio Bar. He stole a glance at Tina, and could see that she understood little.

'*Before I talk about the facts—or lack of them—in Mr Lewis's statement, I think we should ask ourselves what he is saying about this medical equipment. Is he saying that it should be rejected, so that our sick should continue to be treated with the shabby, obsolete equipment we have in our hospitals? Is he, to score a cheap political point, prepared to see that happen?"*

She lowered her voice, narrowing her eyes.

"Or is Mr Lewis simply intent upon bringing shame to Davinia Lee and the government of Lester Robinson? Didn't he hint that Mr Robinson should dismiss the tainted Davinia Lee? Do you think that, if the Prime Minister took his advice, Mr Lewis and his so-called Arawak Democratic Party would rest there?"

She waved a fist and once more raised her voice.

"No! They would not rest there, my fellow citizens! Their aim is to drive this government from office. They want to see this government gone—this, the only *government since so-called independence to seriously attempt to raise up the poor and give our nation* real *independence!—so that they and their supporters, the hoarders and the price-gougers, can crawl back into Government House and the Assembly and take away all the gains the working people and the poor have won! But I know that you will not allow that to happen!"*

She had the support of the Antonio Bar. Fists were raised along with voices, slogans shouted and support affirmed.

"Now, my fellow citizens, let's examine that statement of Mr Lewis to see if we can find a shred of truth in it. Did I know of any Libyan connection while I negotiated with Merritt & Thwaite to get the best possible deal for Arawak?" She shrugged. *"How could I have known? Mr Ronald Mathews, the managing director of Merritt & Thwaite, only announced that his company had secured a contract with Libya—which I assume is similar to the one it signed with Arawak—after our negotiations were concluded! He made this announcement at a celebratory dinner hosted by the then Minister of Overseas Development.*

"Mr Lewis does not leave it there, of course. He warns us that Libya has promoted terrorism." She threw back her head. *"Well, first of all, the contract I signed was with Merritt & Thwaite, not with Libya. But Mr Lewis, surely, is hardly qualified to take the moral high ground when it comes to terrorism! Who placed guns in the hands of those who attacked the offices of the Arawak Workers' Party, and attempted to gun down Jules Robbins, our Minister of Home Affairs, and our Assemblyman? Curb the terrorists in your own party, Mr Lewis, before you begin to lecture others on terrorism!"*

Davinia Lee picked up the newspaper and pointed to the front-page splash.

"And what does Mr Lewis mean when he is quoted in this story as saying that Mr Roger Drummond, the Merritt & Thwaite

representative who has accompanied the company's medical equipment to these shores, should be given 'the warm reception he deserves,' leaving him in no doubt about what the people of Arawak think of a company with links to Libya? What is this but an invitation to attack Mr Drummond?" She narrowed her eyes and pointed a finger at the camera. *"Maynard Lewis, let me give you fair warning: if Mr Drummond suffers any harm while he is in Arawak, the police will be coming for you!"*

Drummond's heart was skipping. Lemay looked at him out of the corner of his eye, murmuring, "You sure you don't have a thing?" Drummond did not reply. Did she still care for him? Probably not.

Once more, Davinia Lee allowed the newspaper to drop to the table.

"But wait! Mr Lewis also says that Merritt & Thwaite had recently attempted to negotiate a loan from Libya. That is untrue. How do I know this? I know it because I have my own unimpeachable source. Unlike the source of Mr Lewis, mine really is unimpeachable.

"Mr Lewis's source, on the other hand, is not only impeachable but...tainted, shall we say. Who is he? My fellow citizens, he is a man called Philip Streeter. Mr Streeter claims to represent a company—really a conglomerate—called International Enterprises. This conglomerate was established by the Central Intelligence Agency of the USA. In recent decades, the CIA has established a number of such companies, which are known as CIA proprieties. Mr Streeter is, therefore, a CIA officer." She grinned. *"As I said earlier, Mr Lewis's source is very impeachable.*

"But why should this CIA officer tell Mr Lewis that Merritt & Thwaite had been attempting to secure a Libyan loan if this was not true? To be fair to Mr Streeter, it must be said that he did not know that this was untrue. As I understand it, Mr Streeter's initial task was, by liaising with his British intelligence contacts, to dissuade the British government from agreeing to the grant which I travelled to London to secure. Our government is rather too pro-people for Washington's liking, and so it will do anything to lower the public's support for us. Davinia Lee gets on her soapbox and announces that she will go to London to demand money for the modernization of our health service; she arrives in London and is turned down; she therefore returns empty-handed, a failure. Would this have increased our popularity? Of course not. Quite possibly, I would have been out of a job. And the UK government did, at first, refuse my demands.

"So what happened to change the mind of the UK government?

"Mr Streeter had been in contact with Merritt & Thwaite for some time and had initially proposed that the company should be sold to International Enterprises. Had that happened, of course, Merritt & Thwaite would have become another CIA proprietary company, and you can imagine what kind of mischief it would have been used for in developing countries like our own. Anyway, once the UK government had turned down our request, Merritt & Thwaite told Mr Streeter that in these circumstances it had no alternative that to avail itself of an interest-free loan from Libya." She grinned. "Mr Streeter swallowed this."

Davinia Lee held up her hands in mock horror.

"Ahh, Libya! Anything but that! And so Mr Streeter conferred with his British contact and had the decision of the government reversed.

"And then, seeking to make the best of a bad thing, Mr Streeter came to Arawak and whispered in the ear of Maynard Lewis. The grant had been made, the medical equipment would arrive, but it must now be portrayed as a thing hardly worth having, tainted by the Libyan connection.

"So, in conclusion, Mr Lewis's source is the CIA—one of the most impeachable sources imaginable. Anyone who doubts that merely has to read the book which Philip Agee, a former CIA official himself, published a few years ago. This organization has sought to meddle in the affairs of Arawak, and still seeks to do so. Otherwise, why would Mr Streeter remain in Arawak?"

Hitherto, directing her remarks into the sole television camera, Davinia Lee had addressed herself to the people of Arawak, so anyone who did not know that this event was described as a news conference would be unaware that she was surrounded by journalists, whom she now addressed directly for the first time.

"Yes, ladies and gentlemen of the media, this CIA officer is in the country at this very moment. If you doubt my version of events, I suggest you go to interview him at his hotel. He's staying at The Crown—which, surprise, surprise, also happens to be a CIA proprietary company, part of the International Enterprises empire. And maybe you will give him the kind of warm reception that will leave him in no doubt regarding what the people of Arawak feel about foreign intelligence officers who dare to meddle in their affairs!

"Thank you for your attention."

*

Lemay and Drummond exchanged glances, that of Lemay displaying rather more concern than Drummond's.

Drummond: "Wow!"

Lemay: "Jesus!"

"Why the worried look, Garry?"

"Do you think it will be only journalists that will make their way to The Crown?"

Two or three men in the bar now proved Lemay's point, loudly stating their intention to descend on the hotel and "give dis Yankee some licks" and/or to "mash up de place."

"No, no, breddas," Lemay urged. "Wait, wait, wait. What yuh tink appen if yuh a-do dat? Dis time tomorrow yuh see President Carter on dat screen,"—he threw out an arm behind him—"sayin im send marines to Arawak fe protect US lives an property. No, no, breddas, leave dis to de govament!"

"An who you is?" demanded a thin, disheveled man with a patchy beard,

Lurleen slapped the bar. "Yuh don't knaw Garrison Lemay what was born in dis lane?" she asked in a tone of disbelieving astonishment. "De first college bway from duhntuhn AC?"

Several of the men now wrinkled their brows in recollection and recognition.

"Ahhh, you is de pickney of Mama Louise?"

"Laahhd God, is mi classmate Garry!"

"An im not speaky-spokey like dem udda college bway-dem!"

Noting the turning of the tide, Drummond now sought to consolidate the peace. "Lurleen, a drink for everyone—on me!"

"You is a Yankee-man?" This from the man who, in another life, had wished to play the jukebox.

Drummond laughed. "You hear Sister Davinia mention Roger Drummond, the man who brought the medical equipment to Arawak? You're looking at him!"

Lemay was at first dismayed by this indiscretion but then, seeing the press of bodies around Drummond, his hand pumped, his shoulder slapped, he shrugged. He looked at Lurleen, who grinned and shook a finger at him, murmuring, "Is a lie yuh tell me."

The man with the patchy beard was still sceptical, asking Lemay with a frown "Yuh wuk fe govament?"

"Kind of. At the High Commission in London."

"How yuh gwine mek sure dis Yankee gone?"

Lemay turned to Lurleen. "Yuh have telephone?"

Lurleen reached down and placed a large black telephone on the bar.

"But it's locked, Lurleen."

She held up a finger as a request for patience and pulled on the gold chain around her neck, dragging up a key from her cleavage. "Last year," she explained as she unlocked the instrument, "de bill dem send mi come to some fantastic money, so mi aks dem what de rass dem a-play. Dem mek mi know mi mek call to Miami, call to New York an even call to Canada, to rass! Den mi tink of all mi friend-dem mi let use de dyamn ting..." She pushed the telephone towards him and asked, in mock seriousness, "Is local call yuh mek?" They both laughed.

Lemay had been giving the next step some thought. Who to call? Davinia Lee would presumably, be uncontactable, on her way home. Should he call Government House and ask to speak to the Prime Minister. He would probably get through, but how then to tell Lester Robinson his business? When they had parted that afternoon, Davinia Lee had given him her business card, writing her home number of the back, a transaction that Drummond had pretended not to notice. He turned to Drummond now.

"Roger, can you recall the name of the Minister's secretary?"

Drummond thought for just a moment. "Lydia."

Lemay took the card from the breast pocket of his safari suit and dialed the handwritten number on the reverse side.

"Good evening. Is that Lydia? Lydia, this is Lemay. As the Minister is probably not home yet, I wonder if you could get a message to her. It's very urgent. As you probably saw in the Minister's broadcast, she suggested that journalists besiege Streeter, the CIA man, at The Crown. Fair enough, but the danger is that the more demonstrative of the government's supporters will also choose to visit him, leading to the possibility of a major international incident. However, this can be immediately defused if the Prime Minister would..."

"Garry, Garry!" Drummond was directing his attention to the television screen, where the image of Lester Robinson had just appeared.

"Lydia, the Prime Minister is on television now, and so this call is probably superfluous. But if the Minister wishes to contact me, I can be found at this number." He read off the number on Lurleen's telephone and replaced the receiver.

Lester Robinson, light-skinned with wavy grey hair, faced the camera with an air of solemnity.

"My fellow Arawakians, a little while ago Ms Davinia Lee, our Minister of Health, made a broadcast in which she revealed that an officer of the USA's Central Intelligence Agency has been willfully and maliciously meddling in the affairs of our country—to the extent, indeed, that he had passed false information to the opposition Arawak Democratic Party with the intention that this be used against your government.

"I have just put down the telephone after speaking to Mr Herman Cassidy, the US Ambassador. I told Mr Cassidy that such activity, and those who undertake it, are wholly unacceptable to the people of Arawak and that Mr Streeter—the CIA officer in question—should be withdrawn from these shores without delay. Mr Cassidy, while declining to confirm that Mr Streeter is employed by his country's Central Intelligence Agency, has agreed that it would be in the best interests of the relationship between our two countries if Mr Streeter were to depart—which he will do by 3 pm tomorrow.

"Our Health Minister also revealed that The Crown, the hotel at which Mr Streeter is staying, is, through a company called International Enterprises, effectively owned by the CIA. When I put this to Mr Cassidy, he was unable to confirm whether this was indeed the case. In the days to come, therefore, my government will investigate this matter, having particular regard to international law.

"My good friend and colleague Ms Lee concluded her broadcast by suggesting that members of the media might wish to interview Mr Streeter at The Crown. Now this is a perfectly innocuous suggestion—although, admittedly, Mr Streeter might not think so. However, it strikes me, and Ms Lee, that it might be misinterpreted by patriotic Arawakians to mean that they should also visit The Crown in order to demonstrate their disapproval of Mr Streeter's activities. This, I must stress, is not my wish, nor was it Ms Lee's. The government has dealt with this situation swiftly and effectively and so, fellow Arawakians, I urge you to stay at home and stay peaceful.

"Thank you and good night."

The audience in the Antonio Bar applauded their Prime Minister, some displaying clenched fists. The man who had doubted the government's intention to act extended his hand to Lemay.

Lemay turned to grin at Drummond. "That was timely, Roger,"

"It was, Garry. What did you make of the fact that he referred to Davinia Lee as his 'good friend and colleague?' Was there anything between the lines there?"

"I think he was telling her—and the country—that, although he might be pissed at her, she's not in trouble."

There came a ringing on the other side of the bar. Lurleen hauled out the telephone and hurriedly unlocked it. Having greeted the caller, she passed the receiver to Lemay.

"Hello?"

"Good evening, Mr Lemay. My secretary tells me that you called."

"Ah, yes, Minister, but Mr Robinson's broadcast has really dealt with..."

"The Prime Minister has been on the air?"

"Just a few minutes ago."

"About the Streeter affair?"

"Yes, he said the US Ambassador has agreed to get him out of the country..."

"Yes, I knew he was going to request that. Anything else?"

"He said that, as the matter had been dealt with, people should stay at home and not go to demonstrate at The Crown..."

"Did he say anything about me?"

Lemay smiled and glanced at Drummond. "He referred to you as his good friend and colleague."

There was a brief silence at the other end of the line and then a relieved *"I see."*

"I'm still a little concerned, though, because he didn't say anything about sending security to The Crown."

"Do you think we should be shooting at our own supporters if they're misguided enough to turn up?"

"No, Minister, but it's not beyond the ADP to send a bunch of roughnecks there in an attempt to create the international incident the Prime Minister wants to avoid. In fact, Streeter may be advising them to do just that as we speak."

"Make no mistake, Mr Lemay: I also want to avoid an international incident. But you're right. I'll speak to the Prime Minister. But where are you, Mr Lemay? It's awfully noisy there."

Lemay winced. "I'm surrounded by your admirers, Minister. At a bar in downtown AC."

A silence, then: *"A bar, Mr Lemay? Is Mr Drummond back on board his ship?"*

"No, Minister, he's with me."

"Tell me, Mr Lemay, are there...prostitutes there?"

Lemay rolled his eyes. "Well, it is a..."

"*Bar in downtown AC.*" With this, Davinia Lee answered her own question.

"But Mr Drummond is perfectly well-behaved, Minister." Change the subject, Garry!

"Well, apart from the fact that he disclosed his identity. I think he was inspired by your broadcast, Minister."

"*He did WHAT?*"

"Yes, Minister, at first, I was as appalled as you obviously are. But really, there's no harm done. In fact, he's being treated as a hero. And, of course, there are no cameras here." He paused. "Minister, it does occur to me that as the Libyan thing seems to have been well and truly disposed of, largely thanks to your broadcast, it might surely be possible to return to the original plan regarding the handover ceremony and the distribution of the equipment, rather than delaying it until the *Burgos* reaches Port Santiago."

"*Oh, that's what you think, is it, Mr Lemay? Well let me tell you that the security situation is by no means clear as yet. That being the case, you will escort Mr Drummond back to the* Burgos *immediately. Do you hear me loud and clear, Mr Lemay? Immediately!*"

"As you wish, Minister. Would you like to speak to Mr Drummond?"

There came the sound of Davinia Lee replacing her receiver with some force.

"Marching orders?" enquired a somewhat amused Drummond.

Lemay nodded. "Marching orders."

As, following a round of genuinely fond farewells, the pair left the Antonio Bar, the jukebox resumed activity with Jimmy Cliff's rendering of "Wild World."

"Appropriate," commented Lemay.

Drummond, who remembered the words from the Cat Stevens original, nodded sadly. "In more ways than one, Garry."

21

Things had not stood still during Drummond's absence. There had been what Ellen Listor referred to, when she later related the news to Drummond, as "certain developments."

The Reverend Mr Bassfield Thomas had been prevented from landing. The police sergeant who led the search of his cabin had entered the force in Thomas's parish and had, in fact, had a hand in arresting him some fifteen years earlier, and their unexpected reunion now was an occasion for rejoicing on one side and contemptuous ejaculation on the other.

"Bassie Thomas!" The sergeant's eyes lit up as do the eyes of many policemen when they are unexpectedly presented with an harassabble, if not arrestable, member of the public. They may not find the stolen valuables, but at least the day would not have been spent in vain.

"Kiss mi neck, Norris! What devil's work yuh a-do on dis ship? And don't call me Bassie."

The sergeant smiled and folded his arms across his broad chest. "*Me* doin devil's work, Bassie? *Me?*" He smiled with the air of a man who suddenly had all the time in the world. "Come now, tell Mr Norris where you hide de white people' ting-dem. You know this almost de lass cabin mi search? De *lass* dyamn cabin, Bassie." He shook his head at his own foolishness. "All me had fe do was look down de passenger list and see your name and me coulda save miself a whole heapa trouble."

Thomas drew himself up to his full height, waxing indignant. His bloodshot eyes widened with anger and his right hand, reaching forward to grasp the policeman by the collar, was checked just in time and became a gesture of accusation, one finger wagging in Norris's face like the tail of an angry dog. "You know me fe tief, Norris? You know me fe tief?"

"Do I know you fe tief? What you been doin in Henglan, den— eh? Yuh get poor God-fearin people fe part wid dem money after yuh a-tell dem a few lie? Yuh don't call dat tief, eh? Eh?"

"Listen me nuh, you rass..." If the wrath of God was anything like the wrath of the Reverend Mr Bassfield Thomas, it was truly terrible, for Thomas was now like a volcano on the point of eruption, his cheeks quivering and his hands forming into fists which desperately wanted to rain retribution onto the head of the policeman.

"Yessir, Bassie, say the word nuh. Me see de dog-collar mean juss as much to you as it did in de old days." He smiled his sweetest smile at the preacher and, turning his head, barked over his shoulder: "Okay, search the cabin!"

Two constables entered the cabin, glancing at Thomas with a respect inculcated in school. In return, they received a glare in which respect was entirely wanting.

"Yuh search my cabin, Norris? Yuh search my cabin when I myself have been robbed?"

Norris's eyes narrowed. "*You* been robbed, Bassie?"

"Yes, dyamn it, while the ship was in Trinidad, just like that white fool Garner. We teck a trip ashore an when we come back de money gone." He turned to the constables. "Yuh handle mi ting-dem wid care, yunnerstan? An yuh mek sure them put back where dem belong."

The sergeant was stroking his chin thoughtfully. "An who is dis 'we' yuh a-talk bout?"

Thomas opened his mouth to reply and then groaned as he realised what he would have to submit to now.

"Yuh have travellin companion, Bassie?" Norris pursued in a caricature of sweet reasonableness.

"I am travellin wid some sisters of the Wrath of God Holy Gospel Mission," he intoned, with just a whiff of the martyr's air about him, knowing that he was about to be bated.

"Oh *really*. Wrath of God Mission. Sisters." He tapped one of the constables on the shoulder. "Yuh fine anyting bway?"

The constable checked himself as he began to react to the touch on his shoulder. "No, Inspector, not a ting."

"Now tell me, Bassie, where might dese...ah, *sisters* be found?"

Thomas appeared to be doing breathing exercises, his huge chest expanding and contracting rhythmically, air noisily entering and leaving his nostrils. "Nex two cabin—sixteen, seventeen," he volunteered in a rush, between gasps.

Norris jerked his thumb at the door. "Fetch dem come," he ordered the constable he had previously tapped on the shoulder.

The four women, black from head to toe, duly presented themselves for inspection. Coolly holding their heads aloft, they regarded Norris with little short of disdain.

Norris inspected each in turn, his eyes travelling over every inch of their figures in such a way that it would be obvious to them all that he was attempting to gauge what lay beneath their formless black dresses. Reaching the end of the line, he chuckled, scratching his chin in admiration.

"Well, Bassie, me haffe confess yuh have taste. *Mm!*" Grinning lasciviously, he turned to Thomas and lowered his voice, although anyone within ten yards would have been able to hear him perfectly well. "Tell me, Bassie, which one yuh sleep wid? Dis one?" He went systematically down the line. "Dis one? Ah, dis nice lickle one, I bet! Or dis one? She have plenty bubby unner dis black ting by de look of her. Or maybe dem teck it in turns, eh Bassie?"

He had, of course, gone too far. They all knew it, even the constables, whose faces looked as if they were watching someone inflate a balloon which was about to burst. The only one who didn't know it was Norris himself, as he was so used to having his victims completely at his mercy that he had forgotten there was any other kind. It was all over in a second. Thomas kicked him hard in the shins, put a hand to each of his epaulettes and thrust his bull-like head into the other man's face. The two women standing behind Norris obligingly moved away as he fell back against the open door and slid slowly to the deck, blood trickling from his brow, making a detour around his moustache, down onto his striped shirt.

"An don't call me Bassie, mi tell you!" Thomas spat at the prone figure.

"Oh God, Missah Norris," bleated one of the constables. "Lord God, why yuh vex de man so?"

*

Ellen Listor, of course, knew of this incident in only the broadest outline, as did everyone on the ship. With regard to the sequel, however, she could claim eye-witness status.

At the time, she had been standing in the queue of perspiring passengers—when in port, the air-conditioning became extremely temperamental—at the purser's office waiting to change some money. The purser himself had been called below to some commotion and so the notes were being laboriously counted and doled out by the chief steward, a man of limited mathematical prowess. Brian Garner, despite Ellen's efforts to persuade him to lie down and cool off in his cabin (he was by now proving to be, among other things, an embarrassment), was at her side, pouring his outrage and seething, impotent anger into her finely moulded ear.

"Oh, if only I could lay my hands on whoever is responsible, Ellen." He waved those very hands, red instruments of strangulation in search of a victim, before Ellen's face. She closed her eyes, tilted her head the other way and pressed his hands down with one of her own. "Yes, Brian, I know you're upset, but you really must try to get a hold of yourself." She was acutely aware that his oafish threats were drawing looks of "Oh, why doesn't he shut up?" from others in the queue. In rebuke, she turned and looked straight at him in the schoolmistressy way which some middle-class English women can affect. "*Please!*"

At that moment, she caught sight of Drummond at the head of the queue. Oh God, don't say he's going ashore straight away!

"Oh, why doesn't this queue *move!*" she muttered urgently almost to herself, like a shopper at the supermarket checkout visualising her bus pulling away from the stop. She groaned inwardly as Drummond made for the gangway, where he was joined by Lemay.

Garner had noticed the direction of her gaze and one more ingredient was added to the already explosive mixture churning within him: jealousy. "I see you've got your eyes on Drummond."

"Don't be ridiculous! Frankly, Brian, I want to be on my own this afternoon, so I'd appreciate it if you'd just leave me alone. Go to your cabin as I suggested. Can't you see that you're simply causing..." She drew a tissue from her handbag and twisted it nervously in her fingers, hoping that tears would get rid of him.

He changed now, fluttering about her in a conciliatory manner, anxious to stem the tide of tears. knowing only too well that when the woman with you started crying, you lost the sympathy of all around you. "Come, now, Ellen love...Causing what?" He put an arm around her shoulders. "What am I causing, pet?"

She shrugged off his arm. "Embarrassment. Can't you see that you're upsetting me? You've been upsetting me since that scene at breakfast. Oh, God, I hope I never live through anything as embarrassing as that again!"

He was about to plead extenuating circumstances when the commotion came up the companionway ahead of them and made for the pursuer's office. The purser himself led the way, followed by Sergeant Norris, partly recovered but still bloodstained and leaning on the arm of a constable. Next came the Reverend Mr Bassfield Thomas flanked by two constables who made a poor pretence of holding him (violence in a righteous cause seemed to have increased his size by half again). The four sisters of the Wrath of God Holy Gospel Mission drew up the rear, surrounded by the remaining constables.

It took five seconds for Garner to work it out: Thomas was held by two officers and was therefore vulnerable to a lightning attack; by the time he had landed a few blows, the officers would drag him to safety or, failing that, they would pile on top of Thomas to prevent him from committing a further crime. His manhood would be confirmed to both himself and to Ellen, and he would escape without a scratch.

"They've caught the thief! What have you done with my money, you cheap crook? Aaaaarrrgh!"

This "Aaaaarrrgh" was emitted as Garner launched himself at the Reverend Mr Bassfield Thomas, who at that moment was on the point of entering the purser's office. He raised his eyebrows in mild surprise and distaste, having other things on his mind at that moment, and let Garner come. One of the sisters—the same one who had tripped him in the dining-saloon—once again placed a foot in his path. He tripped and, it was later established, broke his jaw.

Confusion reigned for some minutes while the ship's doctor was called and Thomas and his followers were shepherded into the purser's office. The queue, once Garner's prone and moaning body had been shifted alongside a bulkhead, now formed itself into a semicircle about the office, the noses at the front all but pressing against the window. The chief steward was sent to disperse them. Ellen Listor, however, as it was assumed that she wished to remain with her fallen lover, was allowed to remain.

So she heard it all. First, Sergeant Norris telephoned ashore and requested that an immigration official come aboard immediately.

"Why Immigration?" the purser was heard to enquire.

"Because this man is an undesirable alien," came the reply.

The captain arrived at this point, touching his cap to Ellen as he strode into the office, stopping in his tracks to glance down at Garner and mutter "Good Lord" before moving on.

"Spot of trouble, sir. Police officer assaulted by Mr Thomas, I'm afraid."

"Good Lord. Which one? Oh, I see. Quite."

"Sergeant Norris, Captain Ferris. Sergeant Norris has sent for Immigration, Captain. Claims Mr Thomas is an undesirable alien, even though his passport is Arawakian."

"Good Lord. That right, Sergeant? Man an alien in his own country?"

"Undesirable, anyway, Captain."

The Immigration official, a man called Davis, so light-skinned he could have been white, arrived shortly from his office on the dock. He walked over to where Ellen stood beside Garner. "This him? Well, we don't take dead ones, that's for sure, ma'am. Heh heh."

In the ensuing discussion, it became apparent that both captain and purser did not look forward to having a man as violent as the Reverend Mr Bassfield Thomas with them on their return voyage. The ship's doctor arrived at Ellen's side and knelt, opening his bag. As his fingers prodded and probed, he murmured his suspicions. Concentrating on what was happening in the purser's office, Ellen Listor replied distractedly.

"In the current political situation, I think we can say that we're fully justified in denying this man permission to land," the Immigration official was saying. You say he was previously jailed for sedition, Sergeant?"

"Correct," Norris replied, "and possession of unlicensed firearms. He was preparing to launch some kind of uprising." Then, turning to Ferris, "Believe me, Captain, I would love to get him ashore after what he has done to me." He laughed wheezily. "But maybe this is a greater punishment for him, anyway. He obviously came back with some scheme up his sleeve, and by keeping him out we'll be frustrating his plans. Besides, separating him from his sisters here isn't going to make him very happy. They can land, Mr Davis?"

"Oh, they can land," replied the Immigration official.

"Good Lord. Well, if that's the way you people feel about it, I suppose we've no option but to keep him with us."

"Tell me, Doctor," Ellen asked, "I would have no difficulty in changing my travelers' cheques ashore, would I?"

The doctor shook his head without looking up. "No trouble at all. Plenty of banks on the main drag."

She began to walk to the gangway.

"But Miss Listor...I thought you were with Mr Garner. Poor sod's got a busted jaw."

Ellen Listor looked over her shoulder and smiled sweetly. "No, Doctor, I'm not with Mr Garner."

*

Drummond skipped dinner that evening.

Instead, he lay on his bunk and thought. At first, he thought of Tina. She was, wasn't she, sweet? If, that is, a prostitute could be described as sweet. Very soon, his mind turned to Davinia Lee. Did she still care for him? He recalled the way she had pointedly ignored him as she had handed Lemay her card. And then, when Lemay had asked if she wished to speak to him, she had slammed down the phone. These had not been positive signs. But she had—hadn't she?—asked Lemay if there were prostitutes in the Antonio Bar, following which she had insisted that he be escorted back to the *Burgos* without delay. These, surely were hopeful signs. And that kiss and embrace when he had first arrived at her home that afternoon! She had, until she collected herself, responded as warmly and passionately as she had in London. And, yes, here was a flashback! Maybe all was not lost.

22

With Lemay departed, Drummond ate breakfast alone the next morning. Looking across the dining saloon, he was surprised to see the Reverend Bassfield Thomas, also alone. Catching his eye, the clergyman raised a finger in greeting, which he reciprocated.

"I didn't expect to see you here this morning, sir," remarked Jimmy as he placed grapefruit and coffee in front of him.

"Bit of a complication, Jimmy."

The steward grinned. "Yeah, I was watching the news in a bar last night and I got the drift of what had happened."

"While we're on the subject of surprises, Jimmy, I didn't expect to see Mr Thomas this morning."

Jimmy grinned. "Yeah, bit of a kerfuffle yesterday afternoon. I don't really understand it, but they're not allowing him ashore."

"And what about your own kerfuffle, Jimmy?"

"I've been thinking about that." He held up a finger. "Listen, let me see to my other bloods first and, if you like, we'll have a bit of a chat about that when I bring your fry-up. The usual, sir?"

Drummond nodded. "Yes, the usual. And let's have that chat, by all means."

"As you heard me say to the pursuer," Jimmy murmured as he took his time placing Drummond's fried breakfast on the table, "somebody put the finger on me. The question is: who?"

"How many people did you tell about the accordions?"

"On this ship, only one, and he's a friend, so he's in the clear."

"That would be Liam, the Irish bloke."

Jimmy brought his small body erect. "How did you…?"

"I overheard you telling him."

"Oh, Jesus. D'you think anyone else…?"

Drummond shook his head. "No, I was the only one close enough to hear. So who do you suspect?"

"Well, I've been asking myself if there's any crew member on this ship that also did those Mediterranean cruises with me."

"Fresh pot of tea for Table 6, Jimmy." This was Cecil, the head waiter.

"At once, Cecil. And how about you, sir? More coffee?"

Drummond deliberately dawdled over his breakfast until Jimmy returned with a frankly unwanted fresh pot of coffee.

"And there's only one," the steward announced in a low voice as, minutes later, he picked up the empty coffee-pot and laid down the new one. "Nicholas."

"*Really!* Shouldn't you be telling this to the purser, Jimmy?"

"What? That he'd sailed with me before and knew about the accordions and so he'd probably fingered me?"

"But you must suspect that he's the thief."

"Of course, but his cabin's been searched twice and nothing was found."

"Look out, Jimmy." Cecil was walking in their direction.

"To be continued, sir," said Jimmy as he scooped up Drummond's plate and cutlery.

*

The *Burgos* would not sail until the afternoon and Drummond found himself at a loose end. He was tempted to go ashore, but to where? The Antonio Bar, the only place with which he was familiar? He wandered up on deck and gazed over the rail at the activity below, most of which took place around a much larger vessel belonging to a Scandinavian line, berthed ahead of the *Burgos*. A crane hoisted cargo from the hold as forklifts stood ready for duty. Gaily dressed passengers streamed down the gangway, off to experience an exotic Caribbean city. Now and again a taxi would pull up to the *Burgos* to be quickly surrounded by porters as passengers for the ship's homeward journey would step out.

"Ah, there you are!"

Drummond turned to see Ellen Listor, in a pretty print frock, twirling a parasol as she advanced towards him.

"Good morning, Ms Listor. I didn't see you at breakfast."

"Please, it's Ellen." She grinned and patted her stomach. "Trying to control the pounds. I was hoping to go ashore with you yesterday, but you shot off with Mr Lemay before I could change my travelers' cheques."

"Oh, maybe I should have told you that I had business ashore."

"Of course: to do with your medical equipment, I suppose. Well, thanks to you," she added with a pretence of anger, "I was forced to spend the evening fighting off men smoking evil-smelling cigars at that big hotel in town—The Crown, is it? I was back on board by—*imagine!*—ten-thirty, and treated myself to an early night."

"Oh, I beat you to it: I was back long before that and went straight to bed. Any excitement at The Crown?"

"Oh, they had live music—you know, a reggae band, as you might expect, but nothing to write home about."

He chuckled. "No, I meant, you know, a disturbance."

"Yes, at one point the reception was swarming with journalists, but the person they wanted to see wasn't available; eventually, the staff persuaded them to leave."

"And that was it?"

"Oh, a little later a bunch of rough-looking characters turned up outside, shouting things I was unable to understand, but by that time there were police and soldiers on the forecourt, so they were dispersed."

Drummond kicked himself for not having picked up a copy of that day's *Chronicle* from the table outside the purser's office where, when the *Burgos* was in port, the shoreside newspapers were usually to be found.

"Well, you certainly lead an exciting life, Ellen. And where was Mr Garner during all this?"

She frowned. "Brian? In the General Hospital, of course."

"I beg your pardon?"

"Oh, you haven't heard, have you?"

There followed the story of the Reverend Mr Bassfield Thomas and the ill-fated charge of the light brigade—light in the head, she said gleefully—in the person of Brian Garner. Drummond wondered why, apart from mention of a "kerfuffle," Jimmy had told him none of this; but there had, of course, been other things on Jimmy's mind this morning.

"How long will he be in hospital?"

"I haven't the slightest idea. According to the pursuer, if he's well enough they'll transport him to Port Santiago so that he can rejoin the ship there, but that's a bit doubtful, unless it's a very minor fracture. So the purser says, anyway."

"You haven't been to see him?"

She seemed surprised by this suggestion. "It's not as if he's my husband or my brother, Roger!"

"Oh, my apologies; I thought you two were…"

She removed her eyes from his and glanced over the rail, the fingers of her free hand fluttering dismissively. "It was nothing more than a brief shipboard flirtation, Roger. Luckily, he revealed his true colours before it was too late."

Without being really interested, Drummond found this amusing. "His true colours?"

"Well, for example, that scene at breakfast yesterday! It was *awful*! I've never been so em*barr*assed!"

But, Drummond thought, Garner had spent the night prior to the accident in her cabin, so what did she mean by "too late?" Too late for what? Now, the man not only had a fractured jaw but was penniless, so it was easy to see how he might have lost much of his attraction for her. There was, he could plainly see, rather too much of Hilary about Ellen Listor for his liking.

"Anyway." Her sigh was accompanied by another fluttering of the fingers. "I've put it all behind me now." As she looked up at Drummond now, there was about her expression something which could only be described as flirtatious. "Shall we go ashore, Roger?"

"I'm afraid," Drummond was able to say with relief, "that, like Mr Thomas, I am confined to the ship, at least while we're in AC."

She blinked. "I'm not sure I understand, Roger."

"I take it, then, that you didn't see yesterday's edition of the *Arawak Chronicle*."

"Do you know," she responded irrelevantly and with a distinct note of distaste, "I would sometimes see the weekly edition in my newsagent's in London. I often wondered what I would find if I bought a copy, but I failed to see how it would interest me."

Then why, Drummond asked himself, would she have come on a cruise to Arawak? Briefly, he explained his situation.

"Oh, my goodness, Roger. How awful for you. Aren't you rather scared?"

There was, he detected, beneath this show of concern, genuine disappointment that they would not be going ashore together. "No reason to be scared, Ellen. I'm safe enough here."

"Well," she persisted, "maybe we can go ashore in the next port, if there's time."

"Oh, there'll be plenty of time. John Crow Bay is the banana port. But whether it will be worth going ashore is another question."

*

Ellen Listor had planned to move across to Drummond's table now that she was relieved of Garner and LeMay had disembarked, but as they entered the saloon at lunchtime the Reverend Mr. Bassfield Thomas attracted them with a wave.

"Ah, good people, I insist that you keep a wronged old man company over lunch," he boomed.

Two people found this inconvenient. Cecil, the head waiter, now had two empty tables, something he usually tried to avoid. Moreover, Drummond had previously been served by Jimmy, while the table occupied by Ellen Listor and Brian Garner had been waited on by Nicholas, and the elderly George had served the Reverend Mr Bassfield Thomas and his four ladies. Now he had to rearrange things so that duties were equitably distributed. He hovered around the Thomas table, biting his lip and furrowing his brow, briefly considering raising an objection to this unilateral action by the bloods; but then, reasoning that things would sort themselves out with the arrival of the new passengers, his expression relaxed and he drifted away.

Jimmy's concern was less easily assuaged. He had stationed himself at Drummond's former table, as, keen to resume his revelations about the recent spate of robberies, he awaited his arrival. When that arrival coincided with that of Ellen Listor, his face dropped; as both were invited to join the Reverend Mr Bassfield Thomas, his mouth fell open. As Drummond walked past, he gave Jimmy a "What can I do?" shrug, which Jimmy acknowledged with a nod.

"Mr Drummond, isn't it? And Miss Listor?"

"Mrs I'm divorced."

The Reverend Mr Bassfield Thomas smiled and bowed his head in acknowledgement of his error.

"You don't disapprove?" Ellen asked teasingly.

"My dear, I am on earth to do God's work, and at the moment God has more important plans for me than probing into people's private lives. The way people live their lives can be changed by inner, spiritual conversion, but the answer, my master tells me, lies in the temporal sphere. Our task at the moment is to provide the conditions in which the spirit may flourish." He chuckled throatily. "Unfortunately, this seems to conflict with the aims of the people's temporal masters. Never mind." He made a brushing motion with his hand. "They shall be swept away."

Ellen was leaning forward, chin cupped in her palm, as if enthralled. "Are you really what they say you are?"

He lifted a spoonful of soup to his mouth. "All depends which 'they' you mean, my dear. One 'they' say that I'm a charlatan out to take people's money for myself. They're wrong, a bunch of liars whose aim is to fool the people as to my true mission. The other 'they' say that I'm a violent revolutionary out to stir up the people to revolt against their betters." His eyes twinkled merrily. "They come closer to the truth."

"I don't think you believe in God at all," Ellen accused with enough good humour to make the charge acceptable even if it turned out to be incorrect. She was the attractive younger woman teasing the irascible older man.

"In a way, you're right," he admitted cheerfully. "I don't believe in the god they push down poor people's throats"—he waved his spoon in the direction of dry land—"any more that I believe that it's the God-given lot of these people to be poor while others are rich. What I do believe in is God's Will. Now, there's always a struggle between the different interpretations of God's Will. That's been the case ever since men felt the need to believe in a god. The side with all the money and land tend to see God's Will as keeping things as they are, and the people with nothing—or at least their more perceptive representatives—take the view that God's Will is to overturn a few tables and even things up. I take the latter view."

"What will you do back in England? Drummond asked. He had been drawn to Thomas's table against his will, but there was clearly more to the man than he had first thought.

"England!" Thomas repeated scornfully, pausing to make sure that he could not be overheard. "What makes you think I'm going back to England? You think I'm going to let them bar me from entering my own country?"

Drummond and Ellen exchanged glances. "So, your followers are making a legal challenge to the Immigration people?" Ellen ventured cautiously.

"No time for that. No, my young friends," he confided in a whisper, "I shall be off this ship tonight. And by tomorrow I will have embarked upon my mission of seeing that His will be done."

Drummond cleared his throat and moved his chair closer to the table, now completely under the man's spell. "But I don't understand why you're telling us this. What's to prevent us going to the captain?"

"Well, I'm perfectly sure that you won't be the one to do that, young man. Your spirit and that of Captain Ferris were simply not meant for union, from what I've seen. Also, I had a word with your friend Lemay before he disembarked." His heavy mouth broke into a grin. "Oh yes, we are acquainted, Mr Lemay and I. We sometimes disapprove of each other's methods, but we have a large amount of common ground. Anyway, he seems to think that your heart is in the right place."

"But that still doesn't explain why you're telling us this," Ellen broke in impatiently.

"I am telling you, my dear child, simply because I want to ensure that when I leave this ship, I leave behind two honest, perhaps even sympathetic, witnesses. You've seen yourselves how casually people tend to ascribe unscrupulous motives to me. Well, they are not above crediting me with acts in which I had no hand in committing, either: my deeds tonight will, I am sure, be exaggerated and embroidered until they are no longer congruent with that rather flexible notion that men call truth. I want you to watch everything which I and my followers do and then if anyone later decides to offer a more colourful version, either to the press or to the authorities, you will be there to set the record straight."

23

At five o'clock that same afternoon, John Crow Bay appeared on the horizon as a ribbon of deep green. As they pulled in closer the ribbon was broken into individual palms and breadfruit trees, the trunks of which were not brown, as Drummond and his classmates had painted them in junior school but a whitish, luminous green. Soon Berry was able to point out the narrow dusty road which followed the shoreline around the bay, the shed where the bananas were stacked prior to loading, the wooden, barrack-like building where the loaders took their meal-breaks and, up on the green hillside, the wooden shacks where the loaders lived. Dotted along the road were three other buildings: bars. As the *Burgos* tied up there was not a sound to be heard ashore. They seemed to have entered an entirely magical realm of peace and tranquility.

"Oh, isn't it all you've ever dreamed of?" Ellen declared ecstatically, hugging herself with pleasure at the mere sight of it.

"Yes, I suppose it is," Drummond said more thoughtfully. "But it can only be a dream, can't it? For us, I mean."

"Shut up, you miserable bugger. Will you take me ashore tonight?"

"Where will we go, for heaven's sake?"

"We usually go to the bars," Berry admitted.

I bet they're nothing like the cocktail lounge at The Crown, Drummond thought. He smiled. "Ok, fine. We'll go ashore tonight."

*

After dinner, the three of them, joined by the Reverend Mr Bassfield Thomas, stood on deck and watched the loading of the bananas, which had begun immediately after the *Burgos* had tied up. It was Captain Ferris's plan to load up and get around to the north coast as swiftly as possible as Port Santiago and the surrounding settlements, being the centre of the island's tourist industry, were considerably richer and the political climate was consequently less tense.

On the jetty, women and youths ran from the banana shed to the ship's loading bay with 28-pound boxes of bananas balanced expertly on their heads. Each time they delivered up a box a bell rang, and Drummond saw that they were given a token of some kind. The women amazed him, with their straight backs and proud carriage. Once in a while, the loaders would knock aside a tourist who, stepping from the gangway of the ship, stumbled into their paths; or a scuffle would break out as a queue-jumper was cursed and pulled back.

"My, wherever do they get the energy?" marveled Ellen.

The Reverend Mr Bassfield Thomas smiled sadly. "You hear that bell?" he asked. "That is the tally-bell, my young friend. Each time someone brings up a box, the bell rings and they are given a tally which they cash in at the end of the job. The few cents they receive for each box means that to earn enough to feed themselves and their children they must load as many boxes as possible. But there are only so many boxes on the one hand and so many loaders on the other. If one person loads more, another will load less. That's why you see fights breaking out from time to time. The tally bell-bell does the same job as the whip back in slavery days. From the point of view of the employer, I suppose the bell is preferable to the whip, as the whip made them rebel against the slave-master, while the bell simply makes them fight among themselves." He paused. "Oh, their anger when they rise will be terrible to see!"

At this last, he had raised his face to the night sky and his fist rose and fell. It was clear to both Drummond and Ellen that he would be most disappointed if the people's anger turned out to be anything less than terrible. He quickly collected himself and pointed to the shed, still full of boxes stamped with the name of the shipping company, which had until recent years owned banana groves on the island. An American giant had moved in and now the shipping company was merely its British subsidiary.

"You see those boxes? And you see the lorries coming down the road with yet more boxes? Thousands of them. Well, these people will not stop until they are all loaded. Don't count on sleeping tonight, because that bell will be ringing well into tomorrow. And the people will still be running."

"Why doesn't the company install a conveyor-belt?" Ellen asked.

The temptation to marvel at her naiveté was resisted. "Oh, they did, several years ago." For what followed, Thomas coated his words with a heavy layer of sarcasm, speaking as if he were in the pulpit on a Sunday morning. "Oh, truly they did. These kindly gentlemen had, perhaps, been told of how hard these poor people worked and so had, possibly, wept with pity in their boardroom in the United States of America and, perhaps, had run anxious fingers over their wise grey heads as they thought of ways and means of lightening the load, to devise some means whereby not so many of these poor, hardworking people would have to exhaust themselves by running all through the day and into the long hot night. The wages bill would then have been even lower but, surely, these kindly and wise gentlemen had not been thinking of that but of the welfare of the workers who live in that cluster of wooden houses up there on the hill.

"There would be no alternative work for those displaced by the conveyor-belt, and work was scarce anyway, as only two ships a week at most put into John Crow Bay, but the wise and kindly gentlemen could not have foreseen this because they were, after all, thousands of miles away in their boardroom in America. The workers were wise and understood all this. Yes, they knew that the men in the boardroom were trying to help them and could not have been expected to know about things like unemployment and hunger. So they made sure that their own feelings on the matter would not be misunderstood. They tipped the conveyor-belt into the sea and continued to load by hand."

He turned to Ellen and Drummond. "So you see, my young friends, the conveyor-belts must wait until a few tables have been overturned."

"But those tables are protected by police and soldiers," Drummond objected, nodding to the foot of the gangway, where three policemen stood, arms folded across their chests as they watched the loaders, whom they clearly saw as a lower caste, with ill-concealed disdain.

"Oh, them. They're supposed to prevent me from going ashore, you realise. Fearsome-looking bunch, aren't they? The sort who beat you senseless in the cells. That's when the odds are in their favour, of course. Reverse the odds and you'll see some very frightened policemen, as human as you or I. Have you ever seen a frightened policeman? Watch."

What the Reverend Mr Bassfield Thomas did next filled Drummond with horror. He took a pace forward, gripped the rail with his huge hands and summoned at the top of his voice: "Brethren! Brethren, stop your labours and listen to me." He paused while the loaders gradually slowed to a halt and looked up at him.

"My God, it's Bassfield Thomas!" cried one woman, dropping her load on the jetty. "Wh'appen, preacher, yuh come back to lead us from de land of de Pharaohs? But what a lang time since we see you!"

Slowly, boxes were lowered to the ground and the loaders gathered around the woman who had recognised him first, looking up at him, a sea of expectant, black, sweat-bathed faces. "Yes, Reverend, give us de word! Give us de word like you used to afore dem lock you aweh!" shouted one man in a ragged straw hat.

Thomas glanced over his shoulder. "I didn't tell you, did I?" he whispered. "This is my home parish."

"Yes, brethren," he continued to his assembled flock, "I have returned to give you the word. They locked up my body, but my spirit remained free! And you, brethren, your bodies are free, but your spirits are in chains. Together we will carry out God's Will and the spirit shall be free."

"Lead us from de land of de Pharaohs!" implored the first woman.

"No, sister," he boomed back, "I will not lead you from the land of the Pharaohs because we are not *in* the land of the Pharaohs. What we must do is cast out the Pharaohs from *our* land. The Pharaohs come from the United States, from Canada, from England, from Germany, to rob and plunder our land, bending your backs beneath the weight of the riches they steal from us. We must drive them out!"

A chorus of agreement came from below, filling the hot, black night. When they fell silent once more, Drummond noticed for the first time just how hot and still it was. He saw that Thomas's face was bathed in sweat, shiny-black and powerful. The policemen, although not yet afraid, were becoming increasingly nervous and concerned, fingering their holsters.

"But Lester Robinson, your Prime Minister, has been trying to do exactly that, even though his heart has at times failed him."

A confused murmur passed among the crowd. "Yes," someone said, "Robinson not a bad man at all."

"Den why we so hungry?" another demanded.

"His heart sometimes fails him," Thomas elaborated, "because the people have failed him. They have failed to push him into more courageous, more resolute action against the Pharaohs. How is he to know what is God's Will if the people do not show him? God's Will resides in the people, my brethren, in the people!"

He captured the enthusiasm of the loaders once more, and a volley of exclamatory cries shot through the night. "Yes!" "We is God's Will!" "We want the Pharaohs out!"

"But because he has been unsure of which way to go, the Pharaohs have been able to force Lester Robinson into doing things which have hurt you. And you, in turn, have begun to turn aside from him, allowing his opponents to stir you into disaffection, urging you to violence against the government. But who are these opponents? Who are these men who call upon you to throw out Robinson? Are they men like you, working people and small farmers, people who work with their hands? No, they are the big men, the money-grubbers who have become rich by clinging to the coattails of the Pharaohs. It was they who invited the Pharaohs into our country after Independence in the hope that they could get rich by accepting a few crumbs from the Pharaohs' table. Now they say they want no more of this government, even though they, like the government, want to get rid of the Pharaohs. But there the likeness ends, brethren. The government—or so it claims—wants the Pharaohs out so the people can claim their inheritance, their birthright. But the rich men want them out because they now feel that they themselves are big enough and strong enough to take over from them. They do not want to give the country back to the people who have created all its wealth. No, they want it for themselves!"

*

Jean Parris was convinced that Nicholas, the gay steward, was the burglar. She lay now, alone in her cabin, and, as that rather frightening man, the Reverend Mr Bassfield Thomas, apparently conducted some form of service up on deck, ran over the evidence, circumstantial though it was.

When Brian Garner, whom she thought a terrible show-off, much too full of himself, had burst into the dining-saloon during breakfast and created his scene, she had smiled to herself. She was not one to laugh at other people's misfortunes, but she permitted herself the one small luxury of a smirk on this occasion because she was *glad* he was upset. The fact that he was upset because he had lost all his money and many of his valuables was unfortunate and, perhaps, to be regretted: it was his *being* upset that pleased her. The gods had revealed themselves to be not always on the side of those with the beautiful bodies and the silver tongues. This, in her experience, was rare, for ever since she had been called Lean Jean by her workmates at the first job she went to after school, she had been convinced that the world's favours were reserved for the Brian Garners and the Ellen Listors, rather than for people like herself.

No matter how desperately she wanted a man to love and understand her, she was certainly not going to throw herself in *his* direction. And she could have, oh yes, she could have. One day, as he had passed her as she made her way to her cabin, he had, even though he was seeing that divorced woman at the time, patted her bottom and made some perfectly crude remark—so crude that she had forced herself to forget it.

Oh, there was no mistaking what he was about! Mind you, she—the Listor woman—wasn't much better: no sooner had Brian Garner landed himself in the Arawak City hospital than she had turned her attention to Roger Drummond. Yes, she seen them talking together on deck this morning. Then at lunch there they were together, bold as brass, at the Reverend Mr Bassfield Thomas's table. Roger *was* a disappointment to her, she didn't mind admitting.

Her second reaction was one of shocked realisation, for she suddenly found a picture in her mind which she had played no part in summoning up. She saw Brian Garner and the Listor woman sitting together in the bar, he pecking at her neck and murmuring in her ear, while Nicholas, whose duties on a small vessel like this included clearing up in the bar as it was about to close, hovered nearby with the obvious intention of eavesdropping. This was succeeded by a second, equally damning picture: this one had the Reverend Mr Bassficld Thomas about to go ashore with his ladies in Port of Spain while Nicholas, who wasn't even their steward, wished them a pleasant evening and enquired whether they would be needing anything on their return. "No, not this evening, young man," Thomas had replied. "We shall be back quite late."

So Nicholas had known when Brian Garner would be sleeping in the Listor woman's cabin and he had known in Port of Spain that the coast would be clear as regards Mr Thomas for several hours. Nicholas was obviously the burglar.

But who could she tell? She had no proof, and a lifetime spent in the shade had made her wary of advancing into the light of public scrutiny. On previous occasions she had always made sure of her facts before making a move, for while her plain features caused the world to treat her with indifference, she knew only too well that people like herself drew scorn and ridicule once they advanced an incorrect opinion or made an ill-judged decision. The Garners and the Listors could get away with it, but what little self- confidence she possessed would have evaporated in the face of such a defeat. This being the case, she could not very well go to the captain or the purser. Another point worthy of consideration was that, should her accusation fail to be proven, she would have to endure Nicholas's resentment for the remainder of the voyage. Oh, that was unthinkable. She would die of embarrassment.

Berry, the nice little junior officer, was a possibility, but he was the one person on board who treated her as a human being and it was for this reason, paradoxically, that she did not go to him. She feared that if she revealed her suspicions to him and was eventually proven wrong, his friendship would be lost, especially if he got into trouble over it. Captain Ferris did not appear to think very highly of Berry, after all, and would probably seize any opportunity to discipline him.

Now, however, an opportunity had come her way, for she had spotted Nicholas stalking his new victim: Roger Drummond. At dinner, as old George served them in his slow but sure way, it was Nicholas who stood at the station behind Mr Thomas's table, polishing cutlery with his napkin while he eavesdropped. There was, after all, a way out: she could relate her fears to Roger Drummond, and with a little planning on his part Nicholas might be caught red-handed. (To arrive at this decision, she had to overcome the initial temptation to let Nicholas go ahead, as this would have been Roger's punishment for taking up with that silly woman, but he was such an inoffensive man compared to Garner that she resisted the temptation.)

The Listor woman, however, allowed her no opportunity. She stuck by his side right until the moment, at ten o'clock, when they stepped ashore together. Jean Parris, who was continuing her ruminations on deck, watched them go, pushing between the loaders, who seemed to have stopped work to listen to the Reverend Mr Bassfield Thomas's impromptu sermon, and made their way onto the dirt road. Damn, damn, damn!

"Cheer up, Jean lass," a voice beside her said.

"Oh, Mr Berry! You shouldn't come up behind a person like that."

"There's lots of things I shouldn't do," he confided, winking in his comic way, "but that doesn't stop me from doin' 'em." He laughed, an open, curiously honest sound.

She blushed. "Where do people go in this place?" she asked, anxious to demonstrate her ability to at least carry on a normal conversation with a man without sinking into a quicksand of embarrassment. "I've been watching them for some minutes now, walking up that road. Mostly members of the crew, I think, although Mr Drummond and that ...and Mrs Listor have just gone ashore."

"There's only three places to go in this place, love: the first bar, the second bar or the third bar...Why, would you like to go?"

Jean was not at all sure whether she actually wanted to go ashore, but if Berry was inviting her such an evening might accomplish two things: she could consolidate her friendship with him and may have an opportunity to warn Roger about Nicholas. But she was not at all sure that Berry *was* inviting her. She would have hated to force him into making the invitation by saying that, yes, she *would* like to go. So she stalled. "Do you often go ashore here, Mr Berry?"

He made a pretence of shame. "Er ...Yes, I 'ave been once or twice. Just to keep an eye on the lads, you understand. But it's not a place for a nice girl like you."

"Some of us 'nice girls' are nice through choice, others because the rest of the world decides to make us that way, Mr Berry." Goodness, what *was* she saying! She did not know what had come over her to make such a bold statement.

"In that case, Jean, let's bloody well go! And for God's sake call me Norman, will you?"

"Okay Norman, let's bloody well go!"

24

"Are you carrying your worldly goods in that?" Ellen Lister asked, nodding in the direction of his black shoulder bag as they descended the gangway.

"Pretty much," Drummond acknowledged.

"Wouldn't it be better to leave it on board?"

He laughed. "It can't have escaped your attention, Ellen, that there have been a couple of robberies aboard our ship."

"Oh, of course." For some reason, this confirmation that Drummond was carrying at least a good proportion of his immediately accessible wealth seemed to lower her spirits.

The Reverend Mr Bassfield Thomas was still holding forth from the deck and Drummond and Ellen Listor therefore had to squeeze their way through his congregation, Drummond noting the grimace of distaste that his companion was unable to disguise as she encountered the odours generated by several hours of exertion. Drummond gave the policemen an appreciative nod as, when it was almost too late to be of assistance, they cleared a way for them. Their vehicle, a dusty Land Rover, sat at the side of the road just beyond the dock gate.

They made slow progress along the dirt road. Within minutes, Drummond had stumbled into the undergrowth on the right-hand side, falling amid curses and oaths only slightly tempered by Ellen Listor's presence. They had not realised that the road was totally unlit, making it impossible to see more than a foot or two ahead. To their left, fireflies whirled, ghostlike and silent. The silence, however, did not extend to the rest of their surroundings, for darkness had awakened a host of insects and other forms of nocturnal life—crickets, croaker lizards and frogs. The racket these sent up somehow made the darkness more frightening, giving the imagination something to work on. The road itself was far from even, for it had rained a few days previously, after which the sun had hardened the ruts left by the trucks laden with sugar for the ship which had then been in John Crow Bay, forming treacherous ravines. It was this latter feature of the terrain that had caused Drummond to plunge into the undergrowth.

Ellen seemed to be having little difficulty, however. She had removed her shoes and placed them in her shoulder-bag and after Drummond's fall it was she who led the way. She appeared totally unafraid of the darkness or what it might conceal, and this increased Drummond's anger at his own clumsiness, causing him to mutter darkly to himself. She laughed lightly and, using a hand placed on his neck to guide her in the darkness, drew close and kissed him on the cheek. He caught the warm, damp smell of her beneath her evaporating perfume. He told himself that he did not want this.

They rounded a bend and there, in an island of yellow light, was the first bar. A languid Chinaman in a floppy hat, apparently the proprietor, sat outside smoking, while inside two seamen sat at the bar, served by the Chinaman's wizened wife. As they passed, the Chinaman lifted his hat and spat neatly into the dust.

"Good evening," said Ellen, automatically taking his gesture to be one of greeting.

To Drummond's dismay, Ellen decided that she did not want to stop at this particular watering hole as it was far too quiet. The two seamen turned and followed them with their eyes. One of them lifted his glass, as if toasting their courage in coming ashore in John Crow Bay. The other said something and they both laughed. The Chinaman's wife dropped her eyes and hid her mouth with her hand. With some reluctance on Drummond's part, they prepared to grope their way to the next bar. As they were about to enter the darkness once more, however, they heard a cry behind them, and turning they saw Jean Parris and Berry coming up the road behind them.

They now made better progress, for Berry knew the lay of the land and was an expert guide. He explained that it was important to keep the whirling fireflies well to your left, as they marked the mangrove swamp. And if you lost your sense of direction, all you had to do was stand still and wait, until the sound of a jukebox pointed the direction of the next bar. He insisted that this theory be tested, so they all came to a halt and waited, holding hands slippery with sweat. Sure enough, scratchy reggae rhythms soon began to waft down the road, giving them an audial landmark.

The second bar was filled to overflowing with seamen and, curiously, girls. Seeing that some of the latter wore high heels and makeup, Drummond knew instantly what they were. He and Berry exchanged glances.

"Wherever do these women come from?" Jean Parris enquired. "They don't look like loaders at all."

"They're..." Berry began.

"Prostitutes," supplied Ellen.

"From AC," Berry continued. "They follow the ship around the coast—to John Crow Bay, at least; they only go as far as the north coast if they've got a special boyfriend. The north coast has its own...girls."

"Dear me," said Jean Parris.

The third bar, a crude wooden structure with a lean-to tacked onto the side, was almost empty. Three very young seamen sat in a small bar-room at the side of the building, nursing their beers and slapping at mosquitoes. They looked up as the four newcomers entered the lean-to, and Drummond suspected that their look of relief meant that they were fearful that the girls were coming this way and that they would be forced to behave like hard, whoring seamen.

The lean-to contained three long wooden tables and matching benches. At the far end of one of these three locals sat moodily over their white rums, raising their eyebrows and chuckling derisively at the new arrivals. Whenever one of the young seamen got up to feed change into the jukebox, the locals would call out the numbers to be punched, smug in their superior taste and knowledge.

"Do you think those... girls...will be coming to this bar, Mis...I mean Norman?" Jean Parris asked. Her first flush of boldness seemed to have passed.

"Oh, almost certainly, Jean," Berry replied matter-of-factly. "I did tell you that this place wasn't..."

"Oh, don't be silly, Norman," she said, recovering her confidence. "They don't bother me. In fact, I find it all rather fascinating. What makes them do it, do you think?"

"You saw the women loading the ship? Well, they work three days a week at most and some weeks, when there's no ship to load, not at all. Their husbands, if they have husbands, are no better off. They may have a little bit of land on which they can grow some food, but it's never enough. Their daughters face the choice of following in their footsteps or going to AC. If they go to AC, they'll probably end up like these girls. But at least they'll eat meat regularly and have clothes on their backs. What would we do in their situation? I know what I'd do."

"Well, thank goodness we don't have such problems in England," she said, side-stepping his question.

"We have them, alright, Jean. It's just a matter of degree, just a matter of degree." As he spoke, his words seemed to issue from a sense of personal shame, almost self-disgust, and Drummond realised that coming to sea might well have been an escape for Berry. He thought, for the first time in hours, of Tina, and anger boiled within him. In his mind he became an avenging knight, cutting down injustice with his terrible sword. And yet what, in reality, could he do about such injustice? The anger quickly drained, to be replaced by a sense of his own uselessness. He was unable to see where he fitted in to all this.

In time, the seamen and the prostitutes drifted up to the third bar. The seamen were almost all drunk and Berry explained that this was merely the continuation of a binge commenced in AC. Drummond watched as beauty and ugliness locked in conflict. The men pawed at the girls, barked demands at them, snarled curses, mouthed obscenities. The lean-to was filled with their noise and a blue fog of cigarette smoke. One of the young seamen in the side room struggled manfully to overcome his embarrassment and sense of inexperience as a girl draped her arms around his neck and whispered in his ear. His companions laughed guardedly, relieved that she had chosen him and yet anxious in case she should transfer her attention to one of them. Eventually, half-unwilling but, by the rules of behaviour laid down by tradition for hard, whoring seamen, unable to back down in front of his shipmates, he allowed himself to be led, white-faced and swallowing hard, to a room at the back.

And yet Drummond wondered if this *was* a clear-cut fight between beauty and ugliness, with the former represented by the girls and the latter by the men. Surely this very battle was being waged *within* both participating sides. It was merely the fact that ugliness had won in the seamen and beauty appeared to reside in the girls because they were the oppressed. But in fact, ugliness was present within them also, carrying on its insidious, corrupting work, present within them as a result of their poverty-stricken lives and now fighting for possession of their souls. This must be true, for look how they submitted to the indignities at the hands of the seamen with never a word of protest. And that girl over there, wearing high heels and such a heavy coating of makeup (makeup obviously intended for white women) that she looked like a ghost. Who could say that ugliness and evil did not hold her in their grip?

If the battle was being waged within the men, though, where was that spark of goodness? Drummond could see it nowhere. A man in his late fifties, insisting on paying for the next round, swayed uncertainly as he got to his feet, one hand jammed into his pocket as he groped for his money. He lost his balance and sat down, his head falling forward onto the table where it struck and shattered a glass. The golden rum mixed with red as it formed a pool and began to drip off the edge of the table. His friends laughed. At the opposite end of the same table, two men were engaged in a tug-of-war over a girl. One finally gained control and pulled the girl to him, seating her at his side. Unwilling to accept defeat, the other lunged at the back of the girl's dress, ripping it to the waist. The victor stood up and flicked out with the back of his hand, knocking his rival onto the seat of his pants. He sat there, a look of confusion on his face as he fingered the trickle of blood coming from his nose. Everyone thought this extremely funny and he too, seeing no other way out, sought the approval of his peers by laughing also.

"By Christ, I'd like to shoot the lot of them!" Drummond muttered almost unconsciously. They represented all that was bad in the British working class, all that had driven him to despair at that factory in Acton. Before he spoke, he had been fantasising, wishing that an armed band of the Reverend Mr Bassfield Thomas's supporters would descend the hill. He wondered how bravely these seamen would act with a couple of submachine guns pointed at them. Oh, if only it would happen!

"You shouldn't be too hard on them, Roger," Berry said. He had been watching Drummond and knew exactly what had been going through his mind because the same thoughts, almost the same fantasy, had plagued him on his first few trips. "It's not all their fault, you know. They're at sea, most of them, because they're running away from failure, from shitty jobs, broken marriages and lousy housing. They act this way because they've been shat upon all their lives and..."

"And so they think they're evening things up by shitting on people who've had it even worse than them!" Drummond cut in angrily.

"I'm not saying I approve of their behavior," Berry continued patiently. "I disapprove just as much as you do. What I *am* saying is that their behaviour is understandable. They're taking it out on people even more unfortunate than themselves because they've got no sense of direction, they don't know how to put things right back home. In fact, I'd be surprised if many of them know why they *do* behave in this way, that things *are* wrong back home."

"So how are they to be given a sense of direction?"

"How the bloody hell should I know?" Berry had lost his temper at last. "If I knew that, I daresay I wouldn't be wasting my time at sea."

And I, thought Drummond, wouldn't be throwing away my life in the service of Merritt & Thwaite. Now *there* was a thought! Hang onto that one Roger, so you don't lose it in drunkenness.

Berry stood up. "I'm going outside for a bit of fresh air."

Drummond went with him.

"Actually," said Berry, "I came out for a piss." He unzipped his trousers and a few seconds later sent an arc of urine into the foliage. Having restored his equipment to its home, he took out a cigarette and lighted it.

Drummond was about to resume his discussion with Berry when, from behind him, came a voice.

"Good evening, Mr Drummond." And then, when Berry was the first to turn, a nodded "Mr Berry."

Jimmy stood there, not totally drunk, holding a Red Stripe bottle by the neck. Drummond had not noticed him in the press of men inside.

"Can I have a word, Mr Drummond?"

"No problem, Jimmy."

A mystified Berry studied the reddened tip of his cigarette for a moment, then looked up at Drummond. "I'll see you back inside, Roger."

Jimmy took a sip of beer and then let out a sigh as he gazed out at the blackened bay, beyond the mangrove. "I've been doin' a lot of thinking, Mr Drummond."

Drummond nodded. "Obviously."

"Yeah, about those Med cruises." He looked Drummond in the eye. "On one of 'em, you know, we had a few burglaries, just like we've had on this one."

"So now you're sure that Nicholas is your man, right?"

"Oh, yeah, but there's more to it than that."

Just then, there came the sound of the grinding of gears as a banana truck made its way around the nearest bend, bound for the dock. As it drew into view, Drummond saw that, precariously seated atop the boxes of bananas, were six people: two youngish males and four females, each in a long black dress.

Drummond knew what was about to happen.

25

As Liam described it later to Jimmy, four women (who looked oddly familiar) and a small group of young men had joined the crowd late and were now forcing their way to the front. The Reverend Mr Bassfield Thomas, having, with considerable effort, obviously prolonged his address until the overdue arrival of this group, now seemed to sigh in relief as he delivered his peroration.

"Brethren, our local Pharaohs care nothing for the Will of God or for the well-being of the people. If they should succeed in their scheme, it will not be long before the people realise that they have been cheated. But that does not worry them, for they will be relying on policemen and soldiers to keep you at bay." He threw down a finger in the direction of the policemen. "There are the palace guards of our local Pharaohs, the men who will shoot the people down should they be so bold as to demand their birthright!"

The policemen all turned to their accuser, just as Thomas had intended they should. The two women who had pushed to the front of the crowd lifted their dresses and each took out a pistol, which they pointed at the policemen's heads. The youths moved in quickly and disarmed the constables who, just as Thomas had predicted, were now showing signs of humanity.

"Yes, brethren, they told me that I would not be allowed to land in Arawak, this beautiful land of my birth, but they forgot that a man who is carrying out God's Will has friends everywhere."

Prodding the policemen ahead of them, the young men stepped up the gangway and joined the leader of their church. Thomas took one of the pistols confiscated from the constables, whom he ordered bound and gagged. When this was done, he turned to the deck above, where Captain Ferris and the purser, Mr Ferguson, had been standing throughout.

"Captain," he called up, "I would be obliged if either you or the purser would meet me at the office right away. There is a little business we must settle before I take my leave of you."

Ferris, caught between horror at what was happening on his ship and relief that Thomas appeared intent on leaving, ordered the purser down to his office.

By the time Thomas and his group reached the office, Ferguson was already behind the window, attempting to appear as relaxed as normal, to act as if Thomas were merely a passenger like any other, about to disembark.

"You will recall, Purser," said Thomas, "that the amount stolen from my cabin was the equivalent of twenty-five thousand American dollars."

"That is correct, Mr Thomas."

"It is my belief that this money is still on board this ship. A reasonable supposition, wouldn't you agree?"

"Yes, I think that's quite reasonable. If the person who burgled your cabin was the same person who burgled Mr Garner's, we know at least that he or she did not get off at Port of Spain."

"Right. Now, I care little how you go about finding my money, you understand. That, quite frankly, is your problem. What I would like you to do now is to count me out twenty-five thousand American dollars—or their equivalent—from your safe. When you find the original sum stolen from me, you may keep it. This is fair, is it not?"

The purser's mouth had fallen open. "But Mr Thomas, we don't *have* that much in American currency."

Thomas leveled his pistol at him. "Please pay attention, Purser. Twenty-five thousand American dollars *or their equivalent*. Any convertible currency with do. I want no more, but no less, than what was taken from me."

"But that will take *all* of our currency, Mr. Thomas," the purser began to protest.

"Again, that is *your* problem, Purser. You might tighten up the security in your passenger accommodation so that this sort of thing does not happen again. Besides, you can contact your home office and have a sum of your choosing wired to any bank in Port Santiago. Now start counting, please."

The purser did as he was bidden. From this point, the whole operation took some fifteen minutes as, under pressure, the purser's mathematics turned out to be not much more advanced than the chief steward's. By the time he had finished, the counter was dotted with neat piles of sterling, US dollars, Trinidad dollars, Arawak dollars and Bermudan pounds. But the Reverend Mr Bassfield Thomas was not quite finished.

"Now make out a receipt in my name, with a carbon copy, for the amounts you have before you. You keep the carbon, as proof that I have only taken what was due to me."

An unloaded banana lorry was commandeered for his escape. As he stepped onto the running board, he turned one last time to the loaders. "Steel yourselves for the struggle ahead, brethren!" he cried. "Pharaoh is arming himself against you." Outside the dock gate, he hopped from the running board and shot out all four tyres, and the spare, of the police vehicle. Then he was gone, the lorry bouncing up the dirt road. In the silence that descended, the sound of the engine ricocheted across the bay for the next five minutes, the sound rising and falling as the driver changed gears on the bends.

*

The last piece of information imparted by Jimmy was, thought Drummond, devastating, and he fell into a thoughtful silence as he pondered how he might use this intelligence.

"Okay, Jimmy," he said eventually, "I need you to confirm the dates of that cruise. Can you do that?"

Jimmy nodded. "It'll be stamped in my discharge book. But that's in the purser's office. They stamp the book at the end of a trip before they return it to you."

"Can you make some excuse to get a glimpse of it? Then let me know?"

Jimmy was not exactly enthusiastic. "I suppose so."

"And I need to know Nicholas's surname."

"Listoff."

"What?"

"Listoff." He shrugged. "His family came from somewhere in Eastern Europe."

"Ah, I see."

"You're not gonna involve me, are you, Mr Drummond?"

"I'll try not to, Jimmy."

"So what are you gonna do?"

"You'll see. At least, I hope you will."

Drummond went back inside to rejoin Berry and the two women, while Jimmy returned to his raucous friends.

*

Seeing that they were in danger of losing the two men to a bout of drunken philosophising, Ellen suggested that they dance. The four of them moved to the space in the centre of the lean-to and began to move their limbs, many of the seamen quietening now that they noticed Berry for the first time. The girls giggled and whispered among themselves as they watched Jean Parris move awkwardly to the unfamiliar music. The owner of the bar, an old man with a creased, leathery face, shouted above the music: "Yuh see mi get fine ladies an genklemen ina mi place! Soon mi ave no use fe whore an sailor-man!"

Midnight came and went and Jean Parris had still had no opportunity to warn Drummond about Nicholas. Perhaps she might have a chance on the walk back to the ship, she thought, although no one showed any sign of leaving just yet. The lean-to was packed tighter than ever, making it impossible to dance, so the four sat, drinking and talking and trying to pay no attention to the uncivilised behaviour about them. The girl who had taken the young seaman into the back room had, Drummond noticed, since been back for one of his friends, and was now entertaining the third.

It was at this point that they heard, from the direction of the dock, a few seconds apart, *pop! pop! pop! pop!* And then, almost as an afterthought, a fifth *pop!*

Drummond and Berry exchanged glances.

"Do you know what that sounded like?" asked Berry.

Drummond nodded. "I do."

"Do you think it was?"

"I'd put money on it."

"Maybe I'd better get back."

"There's probably no need for that, Norman." He looked around the lean-to. "No one else seems to have noticed it."

Minutes later, there was the sound of a truck approaching from the dock. Strangely, it stopped outside the bar, and there came two shots.

A mass exodus took place at once, the girls shrieking like sinners being thrust down into hell, the men cursing to give themselves courage. The drunken man who had cut his face on the glass was lifted by the armpits and dragged out into the road. The young seaman in the rear room with the girl staggered into the lean-to, his mouth open wide with fright, his trousers held up with one hand. As he attempted to run into the road, his hand lost its grip, his trousers slipped and he was brought down face-first. He rolled over, pulled his trousers up and buckled the belt, then crawled out into the road on his hands and knees, whimpering pathetically.

Berry had ordered his three companions to lie flat under the table. Jean Parris found herself next to Drummond. She pushed herself close to him and leaned towards his ear.

"Roger, I know this is hardly the time or place, but..."

"Now look, Jean, I..." he began, more terrified by her hungry look than by the danger of bullets.

"*Listen*, will you! I've been trying to tell you all evening and haven't had the chance. I think Nicholas is the burglar and that you're next on his list, so *please* keep an eye on him. And please don't tell anyone what I've told you. I should hate to be wrong."

"Alright, Jean, thank you very much. I must admit, however, that that doesn't rate very highly on my list of priorities at the moment.

Silence had now returned to the lean-to. From somewhere inside, the owner could be heard whispering self-pityingly, "Dem want fe drive all mi customer-dem away. What de rass dem a-play at?"

"Anyone still there?" a voice from outside shouted.

Recognising the voice, Drummond sighed with relief. "Yes, Mr Thomas, I'm here with Mrs Listor, Miss Parris and Mr Berry."

"Are there any fornicators left in there?"

"No, they've all gone."

"Good. We just wanted to frighten them, Mr Drummond."

"You frightened us, too."

"Sorry about that, Mr Drummond, but if innocent people don't want to get caught up in the manifestation of God's Will, their best plan is to be somewhere other than the place that manifestation is going to be...manifested."

"In future, perhaps you'd be good enough to tell us where that is likely to be."

"Wherever evil is found in abundance, my young friend."

"But I thought you said," objected Ellen, "that God's Will had more important things to worry about than butting into people's private lives."

"That is true, good lady, but prostitution is a sign and a consequence of the Pharaohs' rule. And besides, it's about time somebody told those seamen that the British Empire is no more."

"Fair dues, Reverend," Berry commented, "fair dues."

"Ah, is that young Berry?"

"It is, Reverend."

"Mr Berry, I saw the light of righteousness in your eyes more than once. The fact that your own Pharaoh disapproves of you is an additional point in your favour. Go in peace now. All of you, go in peace."

As the truck moved off, the Reverend Mr Bassfield Thomas fired once more into the air.

"There was no mention of this in the brochure," said Jean Parris, and Berry could see that, after a few drinks, she might be fun.

*

On the walk back to the dock (which seemed to be accomplished in far less time than their original stumbling trek), they saw that the customers that had evacuated the third bar had simply made their way to the second to resume their carousing. Drummond fully expected Berry to issue a mild warning, reminding the men that they would be expected back at work in a few hours, but he remained silent.

Outside the first bar, they stepped off the dirt road to allow the passage of a banana truck commandeered by the three policemen who had been stationed to prevent the landing of the Reverend Mr Bassfield Thomas. The truck paused at their side, one of the policemen on the back leaning over to ask if they had caught sight of the fugitives. It was Berry who waved his arm several times at the dirt road, indicating that they were long gone.

Outside the dock gate, they came across the police Land Rover, each of its wheels resting in a puddle of rubber, explaining the first shots they had heard. Glancing up, Drummond saw the notice which, walking out of the gate earlier, they had failed to observe.

PROPERTY OF THE UNIVERSAL BANANA COMPANY

OF THE UNITED STATES OF AMERICA

STRICTLY NO TRESPASSERS!

The loaders were back at work, and the tally-bell was ringing.

26

Like a veil, night was peeled away from the island of Arawak and the dense heat seemed to lift. Beneath the blue porcelain sky, the tall, giraffe-like breadfruit trees around John Crow Bay bowed their heads as if weary from the ordeal of night. Had it not been for the loaders thumping along the wooden jetty with their bare feet and the ringing of the bell, the bay would have lain as green and silent as only an island, cut off from the rest of noisy humanity by miles of sparkling sea, can be silent. Drummond, who had a headache this morning, wished that such was the case, and he knew that he would not be able to tolerate the thumping feet and tinkling bell for very long.

He had left his cabin to come up on deck to greet the day. Below him, on the after deck, one of the ship's two bakers strolled out into the fresh air after two hours' work and lighted a cigarette. He removed his apron, shook the flour from it and then leaned against the rail, appearing to marvel at the beauty which lay before him. Drummond had seen him ashore the previous night, carousing with his shipmates, and yet it he was able to appreciate this scene there was, Drummond thought, hope for him yet.

He was sure that Jimmy and Jean Parris were right, and that Nicholas was the burglar. In the early hours, as they had come back on board, Nicholas had been hanging around, obviously waiting to see if Drummond would be spending the night in Ellen's cabin. When Ellen had suggested this, Drummond had demurred, claiming fatigue, but hoping that she would understand that he was simply not interested.

Nicholas was in evidence again this morning, floating about the station behind their table with that studied grace, a superior smirk twisting his lips. Drummond and Ellen Listor sat at the table that had once been the Reverend Mr Bassfield Thomas's, to which today Norman Berry had also been assigned by the captain. And now Jean Parris arrived, her hand fluttering nervously about her hair. "Good morning, everybody. I'm awfully late, aren't I? It must have been all the excitement last night. I was really out like a light." She sat down opposite Berry, her eyes meeting his as she unfolded her napkin. "Good morning, Norman," she breathed almost inaudibly, crimson touching her cheeks.

Drummond effected not to notice this, directing his attention about the dining saloon, where the occupants of each table seemed to be engrossed in excited chatter concerning the events of the previous night.

"You're looking a bit rough this morning, Roger," Berry murmured.

Drummond grunted. "Feel it, too."

"How bad?"

"Not so bad, Norman. I'll be okay after breakfast. How do I look?"

"Eyes a bit puffy."

Cecil glided by, frowning as he saw that Jean Parris had relocated without his permission. George shuffled up to the table and laid down a basket of breakfast rolls and was dismayed to discover that, due to the arrival of Jean Parris, he was one short. He looked across at Cecil with raised eyebrows, as if to suggest that this surely could not be allowed but, when Cecil merely shrugged, he turned and began to shuffle back towards the galley to collect one more roll. Realising, however, that this would not be making the best use of his time, he stepped back to the table and asked for their orders.

"Oh, golly!" Ellen cried as Jean was ordering. "I still have to post that letter to my parents! There isn't a post office here, is there? But if there is, I can't say I look forward to going ashore after last night."

"Oh, I'll take it ashore for you, Ellen," volunteered Drummond. "I'm quite used to the sound of gunfire now. Is there a post office up the road, Norman?"

Berry nodded. "Sort of. The mail's picked up from the second bar."

Jean Parris paused halfway through her order, her eyes seeking Drummond's as she moved her head from side to side, indicating that it would be a mistake for him to leave his cabin unguarded.

"But don't be daft, Roger," Berry insisted. "I'll be glad to take it ashore."

Jean Parris sagged in relief and continued her order.

To her horror and disbelief, however, Drummond would not be dissuaded. "No, really, there's no danger now. I'd really like to take it. Besides, I want to pick up a bottle of that rum we were drinking last night. I'll nip ashore at about ten. Be gone for half an hour, forty-five minutes, I suppose. Do you have the letter with you, Ellen?"

"As a matter of fact, Roger, I do." She reached down for the bag at her side and took out an envelope, which she passed to Drummond.

Drummond glanced at the Earl's Court address and lifted his own bag, unfastening the clips and dropping the envelope inside. "Do your parents live with you, Ellen?"

"Since my divorce, yes." She cleared her throat. "Still carrying your worldly goods around with you, I see."

"Can't be too careful," he grinned.

Understanding, Jean Parris relaxed. Nicholas, pretending to concentrate on the folding of his napkin, seemed less pleased.

"Oh, if you've got any valuables in that bag, you should really leave them in the purser's office," suggested Berry.

"And how secure was that last night?" Drummond came back, causing Berry to blush.

*

Drummond took his time over breakfast, patiently awaiting the departure of his fellow diners. Jean Parris and Berry were the first to leave, and Drummond suspected that they would be whispering endearments until parted by Berry's necessity to return to duty. "I think I'll have another coffee," he announced. He didn't suggest that Ellen Listor have one for fear that she would agree.

"But that will be your third, Roger."

"So it will. Need to keep awake after last night."

She dropped her napkin on the table and rose. "Well, I've no need to keep awake and so I think I'll lie down for a while."

Drummond asked George for another coffee and then watched him make his slow way to the galley, noting that Jimmy, who had kept his eye on the table throughout breakfast, now followed him.

Minutes later, placing the coffee before him, George laid a slip of paper alongside it, murmuring, "From Jimmy, sir."

Drummond unfolded the paper, noted the details of a summer cruise on the Orient Line in June 1977, and placed it in his shirt pocket. He tipped a generous amount of milk into his coffee cup and hurriedly drank it. Next stop, the purser's office.

"Good morning, Mr Drummond!" Ferguson greeted him at the window. "Fully recovered from last night?" There was no telling whether he was referring to the excitement of the revolutionary clergyman's escape or the drinks Drummond may have consumed ashore.

"On the way to recovery, Purser!" Drummond replied. He leaned closer to the window, lowering his voice. "I wonder, Purser, whether I might have a quiet word with you. In your office. There's a rather delicate matter I need to discuss."

Given the apparent respectability of the person making this request, the purser unlocked and unbolted his door and swung it open, ushering Drummond inside.

"How may I be of help, Mr Drummond?"

"Could you tell me, Mr Ferguson, whether it's possible to contact Scotland Yard from the ship?"

*

He felt Nicholas's eyes on him as he walked down the gangway. Stepping deftly through the loaders, he turned to smile back at Jean Parris, who stood at the rail, and sure enough, just a few paces behind her stood Nicholas. He continued to the edge of the compound, marked by the sign which had so angered him.

In the building where the loaders took their meal-breaks, which was really no more than a roof supported by poles, a handful of women and youths were taking a late breakfast, mopping the juice left by their fried bananas with chunks of unwholesome-looking bread. They watched him with eyes shining with defiance this morning, as if he were the Pharaoh they were to rise against. They looked at him the way those youths in Trinidad had looked at him, except the latter had not had their strength. Thomas had stirred them, that much was plain. And yet he did not feel wronged as he had done in Port of Spain, for since then he seemed to have broadened his understanding to the extent that he was able to shrug off their hostility with the thought that Bassfield Thomas, were he here, would have explained to them that Drummond too had his Pharaohs to contend with.

He entered a realm of silence which was invaded only by the sound of the high palm fronds as they were stirred into sibilant susurrus by a gentle breeze. The sun, climbing to the centre of the blue dome above, beat down relentlessly, and he could feel his shoulders burning through his shirt. Breakfast had not been as restorative as he had hoped, and he wished he had brought a hat with him.

Reaching the second bar which, at this time of day, was entirely deserted, he unclipped the flap of his shoulder-bag and threw it back. At the bottom of the bag, next to Ellen Listor's letter, nestled the pistol which Davinia Lee had given him, a sight he found strangely reassuring. He drew the letter from the bag and handed it to the proprietor.

"How much?"

The proprietor, a tall man in his forties, light-skinned and losing his hair, glanced at the address. "Air mail?" He might have been a sub-postmaster in London, administering the mail as a sideline in his newsagent's shop.

"Yes, air mail."

"Fifty cents."

The transaction completed, the sub-postmaster looked at Drummond and smiled. "Hair of the dog?"

Drummond grimaced. "Is it that obvious?"

The man grinned and nodded.

"Is your Red Stripe cold?"

"The coldest in John Crow Bay."

Drummond sighed. "Then let me have the coldest you can find."

He took his beer outside and, sitting at a small table under the awning, drank it slowly, relishing the sensation as the cold beverage hit his throat. He had never been a strict believer in the "hair of the dog" theory, possibly because he had never really been a hard drinker, and he was pleasantly surprised when his headache seemed to lift.

Apart from the occasional clink of bottles as the proprietor restocked the shelf and refrigerator that last night's activities had diminished, all was silent. Then from his right came a sound, faint at first, that ricocheted along the narrow dirt road, gradually filling the silence, until around the nearest bend came a car, ploughing through the dust like a ship through a rolling sea. It was a US, left-hand-drive model, and as it passed the bar the driver, headed for the port, threw him a glance. Next thing he knew, the car had braked to a halt just past the bar and there came the sound of reverse gear being engaged. Drummond unclipped the flap of his shoulder-bag and made sure that the pistol was in a position where he could swiftly retrieve it if the situation seemed to demand such a precaution. The car stopped and the driver stepped out.

"Bit early for that, Roger."

Lemay!

Drummond stood up and greeted his friend as if they had not seen each other for months.

"Join me?" he asked, jerking a thumb in the direction of his almost-empty Red Stripe bottle.

Lemay nodded with a degree of enthusiasm. "With pleasure." He grinned. "Hot work driving from AC."

The sub-postmaster brought two beers, nodding respectfully to Lemay as he set them on the table.

"You're a sight for sore eyes, Garry! What brings you here?"

Lemay pulled the bottle from his mouth, smacking his lips in appreciation. "I bring tidings from our health minister, Roger."

Drummond leaned forward in anticipation. "Oh?"

Lemay laughed. "Nothing of a personal nature, unfortunately. The feeling is that, as the level of risk seems to have reduced, Plan A should be reinstated."

"So my presence is required back in AC?"

"Correct."

"Why didn't you just send a telegram to the ship?"

"And how would you have traveled to AC?"

Drummond snorted, pointing the neck of his bottle at Lemay. "Good point, Garry."

"We should make a move soon and get back to AC while it's still light."

"So the level of risk has only been reduced during daylight hours?"

"It's *always* risky travelling on country roads at night, Roger."

"Doesn't worry me, Garry" I'm a veteran. Did you hear about that little bit of excitement with the Reverend Mr Bassfield Thomas last night?"

Lemay chuckled. "Yes, I've been listening to the news on the car radio. Did you witness it?"

"Some of it. I was in the bar up the road, and he stopped to wish me a fond farewell before taking off in his commandeered banana truck, discharging his firearm in the air."

Lemay shook his head in amusement. "Bassie, Bassie, Bassie."

"By the way, Garry, I need to be in Port Santiago when the ship arrives."

Lemay thought for a moment, then nodded. "Should be possible. But why—we're flying home, aren't we?"

"We are, but there's a situation on board. I'll explain as we drive to the port."

27

Understandably, the purser was surprised to learn that Drummond was returning to AC.

"But we've booked you to Port Santiago, Mr Drummond."

Drummond shrugged. "I'm sure your company can work it out with my employers, Purser."

"Ah, Mr Lemay!" cried the purser, having recognised Drummond's companion. "Thought for a moment you were rejoining us, sir."

"Unfortunately not, Purser. Mr Drummond and I have business back in AC."

"And what about the matter you discussed with me a little while ago, Mr Drummond?"

"No worries, Purser: I intend to meet you again in Port Santiago in a few days' time, to resolve any difficulties that might arise with the local constabulary."

A furrow of concern appeared on the purser's brow. "The local constabulary, Mr Drummond?"

"Well, it's hardly likely that Scotland Yard will be sending out their own team," he explained with a grin. "Far more likely that they'll ask the locals to act on their behalf."

"Ah, I see." His eyes turned in the direction of Lemay. "And does Mr Lemay...?"

"I've explained the situation to Mr Lemay, Purser, and given him the job of making sure that I arrive in Port Santiago in time for your arrival."

"Would you like me to have a steward give you a hand with your luggage, Mr Drummond?"

"That would be most kind of you, Purser. We are, in fact, in a bit of a hurry."

After his luggage was stowed in the boot of Lemay's car and he and Lemay were about to descend the gangway, Drummond was spotted by Jean Parris.

"You're surely not leaving us, Roger!"

"I must, I'm afraid, Jean. Duty calls."

"But what about...?"

"All taken care of, Jean."

Open-mouthed, Jean Parris was thoroughly confused. "What shall I tell Ellen?"

"Nothing, Jean."

*

Lemay's car—government issue, of course, so, with the aircon not working, they drove with the windows wound down—careered around bends and hurtled over hump-backed bridges, its horn blaring as it struck fear into infrequent pedestrians, birdlife and, on one occasion, a mongoose streaking across the road ahead.

As the vehicle cut its way inland, they passed an ugly cement works and Drummond asked Lemay whether it was foreign-owned or Arawakian. From the expression on Lemay's face, Drummond would have thought that the cement works had once been his personal property, taken from him the way a finance company repossesses the car or the furniture when the payments are not made. "Foreign," he replied sullenly.

Drummond wondered whether the Reverend Mr Bassfield Thomas might think this sense of ownership misguided, that it made little difference whether the cement works were owned by foreign or local Pharaohs.

The breeze flowed around them, tempering the effect of the sun. The mountains stood in the background, blue and immovable, while greenery of all descriptions flashed past them. Lemay noticed that Drummond was drinking it all in and nodded sagely. "Nice, eh?" he said, although what he meant was, Drummond suspected: "You see, this Arawak of mine can be beautiful if only people would give it a chance."

The view produced in Drummond a charge of elation, a great sense of freedom. He was no longer tied to the ship by a ticket which said "Destination: Tilbury." He was, for a while anyway, free! He recalled Kristofferson's words: "Freedom's just another word for nothing left to lose." In the villages they passed through, people moved slowly and smiled quickly. When the car came too close to a pedestrian, the arm which was waved and the names which were called seemed to carry no anger or malice. Now and then a truck would go by in the opposite direction, carrying cane-cutters to the canefield, men in tattered shirts and trousers tucked into gum-boots, their hard hands gripping machetes. Drummond wondered if they, as they sped to work aback their lorries, felt the same sense of freedom as he. He suspected not. Invisible chains bound them to these trucks as they carried them to canefields owned, as likely as not, by a group of faceless men thousands of miles away, the Pharaohs of his own country.

Soon, they were passing mile upon mile of banana groves. A large painted sign, the paint scorched and peeling under the sun, depicted two hands of bananas, one yellow and healthy, the other bruised and mottled. Each was accompanied by a prosaic sign. *They Pay a Lot for This in England* and *But Nothing for This.*

Lemay paused at a crossroads before turning left towards AC. Some thirty yards on, a little elderly woman in a straw hat bedecked with flowers waited patiently for a bus, several bags of produce at her feet. Lemay brought the car to a halt and leaned across Drummond.

"Whe' yuh a-go, Mammy?"

"Is AC mi a-go," she replied, "fe Wednesday market." Today was Tuesday.

"Jump in, Mammy."

The woman smiled toothlessly, gesturing to the bags at her feet.

"Plenty room," said Lemay. "Roger?"

Drummond sprang out of the car, opened the rear door and placed each of the bags on the seat, leaving room for at least one little old lady.

Miss Spriggly, as she introduced herself, told Lemay that she was 62 years old and had seven children.

"An' you still a Miss?"

A throaty chuckle issued from Miss Spriggly. "Yuh know de weh it go, chile."

Lemay nodded silently.

They passed a neat little house, set back from the road, with a car outside and goats in a paddock. "All yuh need fe live in Arawak," mused Miss Spriggly. "House, cyar, animal-dem fe live off." She frowned and sighed, seeming to wonder why, if these demands were so modest, they had never been fulfilled for her and so many others.

*

A few miles outside the city limits, the police had stopped a bus. As their car approached, a constable stepped out into the road and waved them in behind the bus.

Lemay looked over his shoulder. "You stay here, Mammy. Roger, you come with me."

They stepped out of the car and walked slowly and calmly to the side of the green bus, where the passengers were lined up, two deep. Drummond noticed that several of the windows were either cracked or missing. Somewhere in the back of the bus, a chicken squawked. An officer with a swagger-stick was walking down the line, paying close attention to each of the passengers. Catching sight of Drummond, he smiled and approached him.

"Good afternoon, sir. American?" The teeth flashed in a sycophantic smile.

"English."

"Ah! Was in England during the war, you know. RAF." He spoke in a gross caricature of the clipped tones he must have heard his wartime officers use. "Fine country, England, fine country. Can't say she's done us a favour by abandoning us, though. Life was so much simpler before this blasted independence lark: if things got out of hand, you declared a state of emergency; if the commies stirred things up, you interned them. You a businessman, sir?"

"Sort of, yes." Drummond was peering over the officer's shoulder, mystified by the activity of a constable who walked swiftly down the road, picking up various items as he went. "Whatever is that chap...?"

The officer followed Drummond's gaze and burst into laughter. "He is collecting the ganja, sir." He waved a hand. "Unless I'm mistaken, when the driver spotted our road-block he would have announced this to his passengers. The criminals amongst them would have immediately taken whatever illicit items they were carrying from their bags and thrown them out of a window." He shrugged. "Happens every time. We can't prove who was carrying what, of course, but at least we will have confiscated their ganja."

The constable who had been collecting the packets now ran up and dumped them at the officer's feet.

"Right, what do we have here?" The officer poked among the parcels with his stick, then gouged a hole in one. "Ganja." He looked up at the constable. "That all?"

"Yes, sir, juss a lickle ganja. No weapons."

Drummond assumed from this that they were looking for followers of the Reverend Mr Bassfield Thomas.

"Well, tell these dung-spreaders to get their belongings down from the bus. Then we'll search everything." He returned his attention to Drummond. "Where are you coming from, sir?"

"John Crow Bay."

That caused his eyebrows to jump. "John Crow Bay! Were you there during the excitement last night?"

Drummond smiled. "I was, yes. No one hurt, though."

The officer paused for a moment. "Yes, that was the work of the man who calls himself the Reverend Mr Bassfield Thomas. He's a scoundrel, but really only peripheral to the state of affairs in which we presently find ourselves. I shouldn't worry too much about him if I were you. He will be brought to justice; you have my word on that. Now, if you'll excuse me."

Having brought down their bags, the passengers stood on the shady side of the bus, the men with their hands in their pockets, the women with their arms folded over their breasts. Resentment and fear rose almost tangibly from them, like a fine mist.

"You!" the officer shouted at the crowd, waving his stick. "Get away from that bus and form up over there." He indicated a spot where there was no shade. The sun continued to beat down unmercifully, although lifting his eyes to the west, Drummond could see that a bank of dark clouds, slipping down from the mountains, was forming over the city.

The officer stalked over to where the passengers stood, sagging in the heat, and began to work his way down the line, prodding with his stick, barking interrogatively and occasionally dealing out a slap. The constables followed him, ordering each person to tip their belongings into the road and then replace them in the cases and boxes, one item at a time.

"You!" The swagger-stick waved menacingly before the face of a male passenger in his late twenties. "I know your face. What's your name?"

"Gardner," came the sulky reply. "Erle Stanley Gardner."

"I've heard that name before, too. You ever been arrested?"

"Plenty time."

"On what charge?"

"You muss have charge now?" The large brown eyes, entirely passive, did not move from the officer.

The swagger-stick came down onto the man's shoulder. He winced but did not move. All heads were turned to him in silent admiration at his courage and wonder at his foolishness.

"Mi ask yuh what charge!" the officer repeated, reverting to patois, the sinews in his neck standing out as he felt his ability to inspire fear blunted by the man's calm insolence.

"If you have mi on record, all you haffe do is look it up. Right now, mi is a innocent man going about him business an' you break the law by assaultin' me." He turned his head to the rest of the people. "Yuh see how dem treat people like you an' me? An' then see how dem treat dis yah backra man, skinning dem teeth at him like im better than we. Lick up an' spit down!"

The stick came down onto the side of the man's head and he fell in a heap. On the officer's orders, two constables lifted him and began to drag him to a police van parked on the opposite side of the road.

"No, no, no. Inspector." Lemay, hitherto silent, had stepped forward. "This man has committed no crime. Release him."

The officer lifted his chin, eyes wide as he turned to regard this interfering member of the public. "And who, may I ask, are you?"

Lemay took his wallet from his back pocket, retrieved an ID and handed it to the policeman. "I'm currently working with Health Minister Davinia Lee, and Mr Drummond"—a nod in Roger's direction—"represents the company which has provided new equipment for our health service. As this has been in the news in recent days, you must be aware of it."

It was a chastened officer who now regarded Lemay. "I see."

"And tell me, Inspector, does Chief Inspector Crawford approve of your methods?"

Instead of answering the question, the officer gestured to Lemay's car. "On your way, Mr Lemay."

Lemay shook his head. "No, Inspector, I think we will stay here until you have completed your business with the passengers of this bus."

The officer gave that a moment's thought and then turned his attention to his constables. "Yuh finish? Yuh fine anyting? Okay, back to the city!"

Drummond and Lemay watched as the police party crossed the road, boarded their vehicle, and drove off. As the van disappeared from view, the passengers besieged Lemay, thanking him for his intervention. Drummond found the man whom the officer had assaulted and raised an eyebrow.

"Erle Stanley Gardner?"

The man laughed.

"I wonder how the old lady is taking this," said Drummond as they waited for the bus to resume its journey, waving to the passengers.

When they returned to the car, they found the back seat empty.

"Well," chuckled Lemay, "we know now what was in those bags, beneath the mangoes and breadfruit."

Drummond nodded. "Just as well they didn't search me, Garry."

"Why? You have ganja?"

Drummond opened his bag and showed him the pistol.
"Where the hell did you get that, Roger?"
"Can't say."
"Ah, Davinia." He grinned. "Maybe she still likes you after all."

*

As they entered the suburbs of AC and the houses grew closer together, the influence of kung-fu movies became evident as children on every sidewalk attempted to administer kicks to each other. Rubbish and rubble began to pile up at the roadside and there was no more of that good-natured name-calling and profane arm-swinging they had seen in the countryside, but hard stares and quietly desperate people.

28

By late afternoon, AC sweltered beneath a dense carpet of cloud that trapped the heat, packing it to the earth. Their car nosed its way forward and suffering AC passed by: broken-down bars, small stores where goods were sold in the smallest possible quantities, betting shops and cinemas all needing a coat of paint. At the corner of most lanes, small groups of men stood discussing their problems and swinging their forearms in time to the nearest jukebox. A bus driver, spotting a friend across the street, brought his vehicle to a halt and entered into a conversation, oblivious to the noisy protests of traffic building up behind him.

Below them, most of AC lay exhausted, bubbling lazily with people going home from work, green buses ferrying them here and there, diesel and petrol fumes throwing a thin blue veil over the city. The discipline of the streets, so strict in their lay-out, seemed to be at variance with their poverty. They formed, these streets, a well-trained but poor army that marched, struggled, up from the waterfront. Here and there the glistening white column of a bank pointed to the fact that this army had an officer-corps of foreign mercenaries, but mostly it was made up of poor privates and lance-corporals. Glancing northwards, Drummond saw the middle-class homes of City Heights, the white houses reddened by the dying sun. Each house was some considerable distance from its neighbour, each a little plot of privilege on the hillside.

As Drummond and Lemay drove, they came across a large, quite professionally painted slogan, its two-feet-high lettering occupying a whole wall: PUBLIC EXECUTION FOR ALL GUNMEN, it read, a reference to the political gang warfare that had occupied the headlines during the last election.

They passed the old Government House that resembled nothing more than a large detached house in a small garden. The new legislature stood on a street corner, as might a bank, and it closely resembled just such a building, with its clean stone walls and glass doors. A policeman with hands on hips, one hand resting just above his pistol, stood by his patrol car like a black Rod Steiger.

"Where are we going, Garry?" Drummond enquired. "The Minister's house?"

"Not this time, Roger. She's waiting for us at her office." He glanced at his watch. "We're running a little late."

"No time for a drink, then?"

"Nope." He glanced at Drummond and grinned. "You seem to have developed a taste for Red Stripe, Roger."

"What I've developed is a huge thirst. It's so damned hot, man!"

"Well, I'm sure the Minister will be able to offer you something."

The Ministry of Health building, like the service it administered, had, in contrast to the legislature, seen better days, its stone surfaces weathered and its exterior wooden doors and window frames faded. As they arrived, most of the staff appeared to be knocking off for the day, leaving the building in ones and twos. The man on the main door had obviously become familiar with Lemay over the past couple of days, for he nodded in greeting and immediately led the way up three flights of stairs to the office of the Minister.

Davinia Lee occupied an office of generous size. She sat at her desk, running her eye over a single sheet of paper.

"Mr Lemay and Mr Drummond, Minister." The two dusty travelers were ushered in.

She looked up from her desk, swiftly removing a pair of unostentatious spectacles and smiling with what appeared to be genuine pleasure as she stood and walked around the desk. She wore a simple floral-patterned dress, indicating that she had spent the day in the office, having had no engagements.

"Mr Lemay!" she exclaimed. She checked her watch. "Hardly late at all."

Seeing that she was not at all serious, Lemay grinned. "We were delayed by a police roadblock, Minister."

"And Mr Drummond! How nice to see you again."

Her smile had a warmth which told Drummond that the pressure of previous days had lifted from her shoulders. This was the Davinia Lee he had known in London.

"The pleasure is mutual, Minister," he murmured.

She regarded him for a moment before uttering a sibilant "Yes." She blinked. "Well, come and sit down and tell me all about your adventures."

They sat opposite her at the desk as Drummond related the Bassie Thomas incident and Lemay, complaining bitterly of the action of the inspector, told her of the police roadblock.

"That officer," she said when they had done, "sounds like a certain Inspector Pearson." She grimaced. "Not what you would call a reliable element, and he certainly does not support our government."

"Nearing retirement, surely?" said Lemay suggestively.

Davinia Lee smiled at him and nodded. "Yes, I'll see if anything can be done to expedite that." She turned to Drummond. "As for the Reverend Mr Bassfield Thomas, I can only apologise, Mr Drummond. I hope you weren't unduly alarmed."

"Not at all, Minister. In fact, I think he looked upon me as a friend." He noted a slight clenching of her eyebrows as he employed the formal form of address and knew that, had it not been for Lemay's presence, she would have wished him to call her Davinia.

"Oh," she said thoughtfully, inclining her head, "that's interesting."

"Might I ask, Minister, what arrangements are in place for tomorrow?" asked Lemay, returning the discussion to business.

Davinia Lee tightened her lips. "Right!" She picked up the paper she had been studying before their arrival. "At eight-thirty tomorrow morning, we will have the postponed handover ceremony at the General Hospital. Apart from the three of us, that will be attended by the Prime Minister, the British High Commissioner and someone representing the British Ministry of Overseas Development…"

"Really?" interjected Drummond. "Do we know who that might be?"

She shook her head. "We do not, Rog—I mean, Mr Drummond. Any ideas?"

He grinned at her slip. "Not a clue...Minister."

She barely suppressed a grin of her own, while Lemay maintained an uncomfortable silence.

"Tomorrow afternoon, we'll visit Palmerston in the interior, and the following day we'll be in Port Santiago on the north coast. The day after that, you're both booked to return to London, via Miami, from Port Santiago airport."

"That's a tight schedule, Minister," remarked Lemay.

"Well, we lost a couple of days, so we've had to compress the schedule."

"You used the word 'we' several times, Minister." Drummond cocked his head to one side and narrowed his eyes. "Does that mean you're coming with us?"

"That's right. After the handover ceremony, it will be the three of us, a driver, and the police escort. And, of course, the trucks carrying the equipment." Avoiding Drummond's gaze, she turned to Lemay. "Talking of which, Mr Lemay, "will the car you drove today survive the trip?"

It was Drummond who replied. "The aircon does not work, Minister."

"Oh, well, if you find that too uncomfortable, Mr Drummond..." It was difficult to know whether the sarcasm was intended.

"I was thinking more of your comfort, Minister."

"Oh, I see." What a sweet smile! "Thank you, Mr Drummond. We'll have to take my official car, then. Tell me, Mr Lemay, are you still staying with your brother? I'm rather concerned about what we do with Mr Drummond tonight."

"Oh, my brother's house is very small, Minister..."

"Oh dear." She chewed her lip. "We can't very well have him stay at that CIA hotel, can we?" She snapped her fingers. "Look, Mr Drummond, I have a spare room—two, in fact—which you're welcome to occupy tonight. That way, Mr Lemay, we can pick you up at 8 o'clock tomorrow and make our way to the General Hospital together. Is that acceptable to you both?"

*

"Would you mind eating at a restaurant this evening, Roger?" asked Davinia Lee after Lemay had left the office. "I owe you a meal, after all."

Her use of his forename caused Drummond's heart to lift. "That would be nice, Davinia, but I need to shower and change."

She smiled. "Oh, of course. No aircon, so you drove with the windows down."

He nodded. "We did."

She bit her bottom lip. "The problem is, it's my staff's night off." After a moment's thought, she shrugged. "Oh, well, you can clean up at home, then we'll go out."

When Davinia Lee had mentioned her official car, Drummond had imagined something rather more luxurious than the Morris Marina into which the driver loaded his suitcase. It started first time, though.

The drive to the gated community in which she lived took less than ten minutes. The Arawak Defence Force sentinel at her front door had apparently been withdrawn. After the driver had brought Drummond's suitcase into the house, she said she would call him if he was needed later, failing which he should present himself at 7.45 sharp the next morning.

She showed Drummond to one of the spare rooms and then, once he had dropped his suitcase on the floor, led him to the large and gleaming bathroom. He was sitting on the side of his bed when she came back with towels and a bathrobe. He stood up when she entered the room. Ever since they had arrived at the house, his whole body had been tingling, alive to her proximity, wanting to touch her, hold her. As she handed him the bundle, he bent to kiss her, but she smiled and gently pushed the towels into his chest, easing him away, and miming, "Shower."

Fresh from his shower and wrapped in his bathrobe, he went in search of her and found her in the kitchen, bent before the refrigerator as she examined its contents. Hearing his quiet step behind her, she turned and addressed him as if sex were the furthest thing from her mind, but he knew that this was the lack of self-confidence he had observed in London.

"We have some cold chicken, Roger, and so I was wondering..." she began, looking up at him.

He eased her away from the refrigerator, closing its door and wrapping his arms around her as he planted his mouth on hers, which opened instantly. That kiss seemed to last forever, and when it was over she pressed herself to him, gasping rapidly "Yes, Roger, yes! This is what I want. This is what I always want from you, even when I act like a bitch. The last time you were here, I behaved so badly, so selfishly. Can you ever forgive me?"

He leaned back and looked down at her. When she turned her head, avoiding his gaze, he placed a gentle hand of her face, easing it around so that she looked him in the eyes. "Can I ever forgive you?" He watched as she returned his smile. "What does it look like, Davinia?"

29

The following morning, Drummond, Lemay and Davinia Lee stood at the entrance to the General Hospital. In order to discourage questions before the handover ceremony began, they carefully avoided the glances of the assembled media representatives, who had been herded into a cordoned-off area several yards away. They were soon joined by the hospital's senior administrator, a tall brown man who, having greeted them, cast his careworn eyes at the grey sky and remarked that, with luck, the rain would hold off.

Drummond's attention was drawn to a long line of patients who, at the far end of the building to their left, queued to consult a doctor. He turned to the senior administrator.

"Dr Ransome, would you mind if I..." He gestured in the direction of the queue.

The administrator frowned in confusion. "You wish to interview them, Mr Drummond?"

"No, no, Doctor. I just want to see the length of the line and what lies at the end of it."

A shrug. "Feel free, Mr Drummond, feel free." He glanced at his watch. "Unfortunately, I am unable to accompany you, as the Prime Minister will be arriving at any minute."

Davinia Lee sucked her teeth and threw Dr Ransome a look. "Come, with me, Mr Drummond."

"Would he really have been in trouble if he wasn't there to greet Lester Robinson?" Drummond asked as they walked towards the queuing patients.

Another suck of the teeth. "Of course not! He's just an old worrier."

As they proceeded past the line, Drummond could see that it extended deep into the hospital. Many of the patients were elderly, with symptoms not apparent to the naked eye, while several of the younger ones wore bandages; and, of course, there were babes in arms. All were quite visibly poor. Davinia Lee was, inevitably, recognised, and Drummond was impressed both by the warmth with which she was greeted and by the naturalness of her response. She was, Drummond could see, genuinely popular, and that her popularity was explained not just by her policies but by her demeanor.

"How long have these people been waiting?" Drummond asked.

"Some—those near the head of the line—since daybreak. Those further back will be here until at least mid-afternoon. The equipment you're handing over today will unfortunately not assist with this, Roger. We need more doctors, and that's where the Cubans will help us."

As they continued on their way, Drummond noticed that a confusion of wires and cables protruded from the ceiling; a lift was posted with an "Out of Order" sign.

Drummond had been expecting to find, at the head of the line, a reception area with a number of nurses dealing with three or four patients at a time, ascertaining their symptoms and assigning them to the appropriate department. Instead, there was a single doctor, a short, middle-aged white woman who, despite the size of her workload, appeared unflustered and calm.

"Dr Lane, allow me to introduce Mr Drummond, the representative of Merritt & Thwaite," said Davinia Lee. To Drummond, she remarked, "Dr Lane is now a citizen of Arawak. She decided to stay with us after Independence and, as you can see, she is making a huge contribution to our health service."

"You obviously have a busy day, Doctor," Drummond said as he took the woman's small hand, "and so we won't interrupt your work."

She smiled up at him. "This and every other day, Mr Drummond, but that's what I'm here for." She nodded. "Thank you for the contribution your company has made; we're all very grateful."

As he and Davinia Lee retraced their steps, Drummond felt the pangs of guilt. What right had he to accept the gratitude of that little woman? What was his contribution, or that of Merritt & Thwaite, compared to her own?

"I wonder if the Prime Minister has arrived yet," he pondered as they made their way back to the entrance.

"No, he's not here yet," responded Davinia Lee.

"How do you know?"

"We would have heard the people cheering."

Lester Robinson had, indeed, not arrived, although the British High Commissioner had—along with an unwelcome guest.

Once Davinia Lee had introduced Sir George Porter to her team, he coughed and, almost in embarrassment, indicated his companion. "And this is Mr Hesketh-Brown of the Ministry of Overseas Development."

The only person who shook his hand was Dr Ransome. There was an awkward silence while the other three merely glanced at Hesketh-Brown and looked away. It was Drummond who finally spoke.

"Isn't this somewhat irregular, Sir George?"

"Not sure I'm with you, Mr Drummond."

"Well, surely Her Majesty's Government is represented by the High Commissioner…"

"Ah, got you now." He wagged a finger. "Yes, you're quite right, of course, but in this case the Foreign Office was quite keen that Mr Hesketh-Brown should be present."

"Mm. I wonder why."

Sir George, who appeared to be perfectly comfortable with this questioning of Hesketh-Brown's qualifications, nevertheless shrugged. "Not for me to say, old chap."

"Should I ask him?"

Sir George checked a grin. "That would be quite improper, Mr Drummond." He swallowed. "Not that I can stop you, of course."

"Well, Mr Hesketh-Brown, how about it?"

Throughout this, the grey man had been standing expressionless, but now the left corner of his mouth lifted in a sneer as he turned to confront Drummond. "I will not be provoked by you, Mithter Drummond."

It was with something of a jolt that Drummond realised that this was the first exchange he had had with Hesketh-Brown; the lisp took him by surprise.

"Are you perhaps standing in for your friend Mr Streeter, now that he's been declared persona non grata?"

"I know no one called Thtreeter," replied the grey man calmly.

"But you shared a meal with him in Westbourne Grove a few weeks ago, Mr Hesketh-Brown." Drummond smiled in encouragement. "Surely you remember Phil Streeter: the CIA man who told you to make sure the British government's rejection of the grant to Arawak was reversed." He inclined his head to one side. "Ring a bell now?"

Sir George Porter had been enjoying Hesketh-Brown's discomfort, but now he stiffened. "I sincerely hope, Mr Hesketh-Brown," he uttered through tightened lips, "that there is no truth in this."

Hesketh-Brown opened his mouth, about to reply, but was interrupted by a loud cheer from the line of waiting patients: the Prime Minister was arriving.

Lester Robinson, tall and slender, light-skinned with wavy grey hair, stepped from his official car (superior to that assigned to Davinia Lee, although by no means ostentatious) and waited while a fellow passenger exited from the opposite door and walked around the vehicle to join him. This latter, much darker than the Prime Minister, and dressed like him in a light-coloured safari suit, smiled across at the media representatives as they walked towards the small party gathered at the entrance of the hospital, a gesture that marked him as a guest rather than a member of the Robinson administration.

As protocol dictated, Robinson first greeted Sir George Porter before giving a nod and a smile to Davinia Lee and Dr Ransome and turning his attention to Drummond and Lemay, greeting them warmly and thanking them for their efforts on behalf of his small island nation. He then frowned at Sir George and flicked his eyes in the direction of the grey man standing behind the High Commissioner's shoulder.

"Ah, yes, Prime Minister, this is Mr Hesketh-Brown, representing our Ministry of Overseas Development."

"Oh, really!" There was more than a trace of irony in Lester Robinson's smile. "Ms Lee has told me so much about you, Mr Hesketh-Brown."

Hesketh-Brown, visibly overawed by the charisma of the man whose hand he was shaking, found himself unable to speak.

"Sir George, I am sure," continued Robinson with a smile, "is familiar with my guest, as is Ms Lee, and so, gentlemen"—a smile to Drummond, Lemay and Dr Ransome—"it is with great pleasure that I introduce you to"—a hand on the shoulder of the dark man with whom he had arrived—"Señor Fernando Policarpio Perez, the Cuban Ambassador." He turned now to Sir George Porter. "You will be aware that the Cuban government has agreed to train doctors for us. As the schedule for that programme has now been finalised, Ms Lee and I thought it appropriate that Sr Perez should join us this morning, I trust that you find this acceptable, Sir George."

"Of course, Prime Minister, of course." What else could he say? Watching closely, Drummond saw that Hesketh-Brown, as he began to show signs of discontent, received a subtle elbow in the ribs from Sir George.

Lester Robinson looked to his left and right before turning to Dr Ransome. "Shouldn't some of the equipment be on display for the cameras, Doctor?"

"What we thought, Prime Minister," intervened Davinia Lee, "was that after the speeches we would lead the cameras around the corner so that they could catch the equipment emerging from the warehouse. The equipment for the General Hospital is the furthest in, so that the loads for Palmerston and Port Santiago can be moved out ready for the road."

Lester Robinson nodded sharply. "Very well." He sighed. "We'd better make a start, then."

With everyone's attention elsewhere, Drummond edged closer to Hesketh-Brown.

"There's potential embarrassment for you in this situation, Mr Hesketh-Brown," he murmured.

"Whatever do you mean?"

"I'm thinking of what the British newspapers will make of this. Can't you just see the front page of the *Daily Mail*? They'll almost certainly pick up pictures from one of the agencies, so there you are, standing next to Señor Perez, under the headline: CALLAGHAN'S MAN CELEBRATES LABOUR GIVEAWAY WITH COMMUNIST ENVOY."

"Nonthenth! For one thing, I'm not Callaghan'th man, but a career thivil thervant!"

"Oh, we both know what you are, Mr Hesketh-Brown, but it would be a mistake to expect that the more sensationalist members of the British press will strive for accuracy when, with a general election due within the next year, there's a chance to throw mud at a Labour government."

Drummond left Hesketh-Brown pouting at the ground and walked back to join Davinia Lee. "Do you think he'll try to cause trouble?" he asked her.

"Oh, I don't think so. Look!"

She lifted her chin in the direction of Lester Robinson, who was listening intently as Sir George Porter appeared to be explaining, somewhat apologetically, something about the grey man at his side. Robinson shrugged and gestured in the direction of the hospital entrance, seeming to say that if Hesketh-Brown was feeling unwell, he could not be in a more convenient place. Hesketh-Brown attempted a grin, shook his head and, having offered his hand to the Prime Minister, turned and walked towards the High Commission's vehicle, which Sir George has presumably made available to him. Lester Robinson looked at Drummond and gave him a subtle nod, indicating that he had overheard at least some of his exchange with the grey man.

*

"Have you enjoyed your first visit to our little country, Mr Drummond?"

To his very great surprise and pleasure, Drummond found himself at Government House with Lemay and Davinia Lee, sitting around a table with Lester Robinson. The speeches and the photo-ops at the hospital had gone smoothly enough; the only concern had been whether the local press representatives would behave themselves, but even they had seemed tame. When the *Chronicle* man had remarked that the training of doctors in Cuba might ruffle feathers in Washington, Lester Robinson had thrown a question back at him: "Is the *Chronicle* suggesting that the mighty USA would seek to deny tiny Arawak the number of medical personnel it needs?" He smiled. "I am sure, however, that your newspaper would never think of telling its readers that this generous gesture by the government of Cuba should be rejected." After that, all had been plain sailing. At the end of the proceedings, as the British High Commissioner drifted away, Robinson had looked at his watch and suggested elevenses. "A trifle early, I know, but I would like a chat. I think you'll still have ample time to get to Palmerston and complete your day's business. I'll drop Señor Perez at his embassy and see you back at Government House."

"It has been fascinating, Prime Minister," Drummond replied now.

"Oh, I'm sure! But have you *enjoyed* it?" The look Robinson gave Drummond was penetrating but friendly, giving the impression that he genuinely sought an honest reply.

Drummond had little idea where this was leading but nevertheless smiled and nodded, saying in all sincerity, "Yes, it has been very enjoyable. I've seen another way of life and have met another kind of people." He spread his hands. "I like it here, Prime Minister."

Lester Robinson took a sip of his coffee. "Mm, so glad to hear it, Roger." He flicked a glance at Davinia Lee, grinning mischievously. "Davinia tells me that Garry even found time to introduce you to life in downtown AC."

So this was where it was leading! "Yes, he did. And do you know, Prime Minister, after a while I felt completely at home in that bar."

Davinia Lee and Lemay tittered nervously, while Lester Robinson gazed rather wistfully at Drummond. "Do you know, Roger," he said slowly, "one of my great regrets is that my position prevents me from going to such places, from just sitting with ordinary people with a beer in front of me, listening to the jukebox and feeling good about it."

"I think I can understand that, Prime Minister. But surely there must have been a time before you were elected to high office..."

"Not really, Roger," Robinson laughed. "No, not really. You see, I come from what is known as one of Arawak's"—two fingers of each hand to indicate quotation marks— "'leading families.' Such places have always been off-limits to me—except, of course, when I'm campaigning."

"When there's neither bar, beer, nor jukebox," Drummond supplied.

Robinson threw back his head in laughter. "Exactly!"

Lemay and Davinia Lee remained silent, not quite sure how to take this discussion forward. It was becoming apparent to Drummond that when the Prime Minister had said that he would like a chat, he'd had in mind a chat with him.

Robinson took a biscuit from the plate before him and dipped it in his coffee before inserting it in his mouth. "Excuse me," he said with an upward glace. "Been a habit since childhood."

"That leaves the rest of us free to follow suit," said Drummond, holding up a biscuit before dunking it in his coffee.

"Yes," chuckled Robinson, "feel free. No need to stand on ceremony with me." Suddenly he became more serious, bringing the fingers of his right hand down onto the table. "That's *another* thing! When people come here, they always assume that they must stand on *ceremony*. I almost never—*almost never*—get the opportunity to behave naturally." He frowned, calling to mind something he had been told. "Is it true, Mr Drummond, that you started off as a factory worker?"

"That's perfectly true, Prime Minister."

"And what was that like?" Again, he really wanted to know.

Drummond grimaced. "It was perfectly mindless, and I stayed there far too long."

Robinson looked disappointed. "But then you worked for London Transport?"

"Yes, but first I treated myself to several weeks of leisure."

"Oh. You went abroad?"

Drummond smiled. "No, I stayed in London, but I did a lot of reading."

"Ahhh." As if this explained something.

"And then, after I was married, I went on the buses."

"And how was that, Roger?" He clearly expected something now.

A thoughtful pause from Drummond, then: "In fact, it was perfectly pleasant. I travelled all over London, got to meet large numbers of the public, and because of the shift system I sometimes had a lot of time to myself, so I could continue my reading. My workmates were a mixed bunch, but on the whole I got on well with them..."

"Were you active in the union?"

"I attended meetings, but it didn't really go beyond that." He drew his lips together. "I sometimes wish I had been more active. If I had been, my life might have taken a different turn."

"Oh, yes, certainly. You know, Roger, before I entered politics, I led one of our trade union federations."

"I wasn't aware of that, Prime Minister."

Although he had offered this piece of information, Robinson had obviously no intention of discussing it further. No, he was more interested in Drummond's past than his own. He narrowed his eyes. "So how did you make the transition to Merritt & Thwaite?"

A sigh escaped Drummond's lips. "It was my wife's suggestion; her uncle was—and still is—the exports manager."

Robinson's eyebrows shot up. "Joseph Thornton? The man who came here with the gift of equipment a while back? He's your wife's uncle?"

Drummond gave him a rueful smile. "Yes, I'm afraid so."

Robinson laughed and inclined his head, regarding Drummond sympathetically. "Any regrets?"

"About the job?"

Robinson laughed again. "Yes, let's restrict ourselves to the job; the other matter is none of my business."

"Well," Drummond sighed, "I obviously don't regret what little assistance I've been able to give to Arawak, and from time to time there have been other aspects of the job which I've found to be interesting and even rewarding, but…At the end of the day, the job is about making money for the owners of Merritt & Thwaite, and so, yes, there have been times—and still are—when I wish I was doing something else."

"Mm, yes," Robinson murmured, nodding almost somnolently. "You and I have a certain amount in common, Roger." Then he seemed to come alive. "You know, I often wish that I could just work away at an ordinary but useful job, alongside ordinary people, earning enough to keep my family alive. A bit like you on the buses, I suppose, Roger. The job not too taxing, leaving me enough time to deepen my understanding of the world. Maybe become involved in the union at ground level, making a difference there. As you probably know, Engels once said something about freedom being the recognition of necessity…"

"You read Engels, Prime Minister?"

"Not recently, Roger," he said with a grin. "That, anyway, is how I would look upon such a life, telling myself that circumstances and the prevailing social order had placed me there, and that the only way to make such a life meaningful would be to throw myself into it, while at the same time working to bring about a better social order. Wouldn't you say that would be a kind of half-freedom?"

Drummond once more recalled the discussion he had had, years ago, with Hilary about that Bob Dylan song. "Yes," he said now, "I would agree with that, Prime Minister."

Finally, Lemay spoke: "But surely, Prime Minister, what Engels said about freedom being the recognition of necessity surely applies to all of us, regardless of our station."

Robinson waved a finger at him. "Oh, you're a sharp one, Garry Lemay. Yes, it applies to all of us. But when I recognise my necessity, it means accepting that for the foreseeable future I will be surrounded by people who insist on standing on ceremony and prevented from leading a more natural life." He smiled ruefully. "I may have to recognise it, but I don't have to like it!"

He brought both palms down onto the table. "But enough of this! I've really enjoyed our chat, Roger, but I'm delaying you and your colleagues from completing the important work you have before you, so I must say goodbye and bon voyage!"

*

"Well," remarked Drummond as he walked with Lemay and Davinia Lee towards the Morris Marina, "I've certainly learned something about Lester Robinson today!"

"And so," said Davinia Lee, "have we."

30

As they set off, the rain that had been threatening all morning finally came down, sweeping through the streets of AC and sending people scattering for shelter. They had despatched the three trucks carrying the medical equipment ahead of them before joining Lester Robinson at Government House, telling the drivers that they would catch up with the convoy by early afternoon; that now began to look doubtful as the wiper on the driver's side struggled to clear the windscreen. The police vehicle leading the way, mystified by the Marina's poor progress, first slowed, and then halted. The Marina's driver gently pulled alongside the police Land Rover and asked Lemay, who occupied the passenger seat next to him, to wind down his window.

"Defective wiper!"

The driver of the Land Rover wound down his window. "What yuh seh?"

"Defective wiper. Mi cyan't hardly see!"

The inspector seated next to the police driver rolled his eyes. "Okay. Follow us." He gave the driver instructions, pointing to the road ahead, and the Land Rover moved off slowly; five minutes later, it led the Marina onto a covered forecourt under a Shell sign; to judge from the vehicles parked inside, the building adjacent to the cashier's office appeared to be a workshop.

A constable alighted from the rear seat of the Land Rover and, obviously under instruction from the inspector, bent over the bonnet of the Marina to examine the wiper. After a few seconds, he raised his eyes to the windscreen and shook his head before walking back to the Land Rover from where, once the man had made his brief report, came the raised voice of the inspector. The constable walked to the edge of the covered area, then sped through the rain to the cashier's office. A minute later, he was dodging the rain again, on his way to the workshop. When he re-emerged, he was accompanied by a tall, middle-aged man in blue overalls who, upon reaching the Marina, wiped his hands one last time on the rag he carried before stowing it in his pocket and bending to the wiper. After the briefest of inspections, he turned and, without a word, walked back to the workshop.

"I feel reassured," said Drummond as he watched the mechanic walk away.

"And why is that, Roger?" asked a bemused Lemay.

"Because there is a man who knows what he's doing."

Then the man was back, stripped the wrapping from a new wiper arm and blade and letting it fall to the forecourt. The defective unit was removed and likewise discarded, following which the man, who was very black, set about installing the replacement. His job done, he straightened up, stretched his back, and nodded to the driver. "Try it nuh," he said, making the injunction, with a rising intonation on the final word, sound like a question. The driver switched on the engine and smiled as the wiper blade described a perfect arc back and forth.

By now, the inspector had disembarked and was walking back to the Marina. He frowned down at the driver. "Yuh tink yuh fit to drive a govament minister?" He raised a meaty finger. "Next time, you check your vehicle afore yuh start out on a journey. Yunnerstan?"

"Yuh hear what the man a-tell yuh, Wilkins?" asked Davinia Lee with barely repressed anger.

"Yes, ma'am."

"Alright, now get this vehicle back on the road..." the inspector began. "Oh, wait!" He inclined his head and, smiling sarcastically, purred, "Yuh have full tank?"

The driver nodded dejectedly. "Yes, Boss."

"Ok, hit the road!"

"Wait!" This came from Davinia Lee. "The mechanic must be paid!"

The mechanic, having heard that there was a government minister in the car, was leaning to the driver's window, peering into the back seat. Recognising Davinia Lee, he broke into a broad smile. "Oh, it's you, Miss Lee! No need for payment, ma'am. It's on the house."

"Of course you must be paid! Yuh have money, Wilkins?"

"No, ma'am."

Drummond wound down his window and handed out a few notes. "Will this cover it?"

The mechanic took the notes, counted them and handed two back. "Thank you, sir."

"Oh, no, thank *you*," said Davinia Lee. "You were perfectly wonderful." She leaned across Drummond. "Let me shake your hand, Mr…"

"Biggs, Errol Biggs, ma'am." He looked at his hand. "But…"

"Oh, don't be silly! Give it here." She took his huge hand with her right, clapping her left on top of the handshake. "Thank you again, Mr Biggs. May your business prosper!"

"Is this your constituency, Minister?" Drummond asked as they drove away, following the police Land Rover.

"As a matter of fact," she replied, "no."

"Twice in one day," said Drummond, turning to give her a smile.

"What?"

"Reassurance."

*

Soon they were leaving the outskirts of AC and driving north into country parts. The rain ceased as suddenly as it had started, causing the driver to suck his teeth and mutter "Would you believe it!" Drummond and Davinia Lee shared the rear seat, with her overnight bag between them. Also between them was their memory of the previous night spent together: Drummond was having flashbacks and he suspected that she was also, as from time to time her gaze would slide in his direction. After thirty minutes, Lemay, seated next to the driver, started to nod off, and Drummond lifted his hand across the bag and touched the arm of Davinia Lee. She smiled, murmuring softly, "Why don't you move this bag and shift over?" He lifted the bag and placed it at his right side, next to the door, and moved closer to her. Checking the rear-view mirror, he noted that the driver was able to see him but not Davinia Lee. She clasped his hand and placed it in her lap.

"How long to Palmerston, do you think?"

She checked her watch. "It's 12.30 now. We should be there by around 3.30. We have to drive over the shoulder of the mountain; it will be quite slow going there, steep and twisty."

Soon they were passing through an area of dense woodland where the tall trees, their broad green leaves still dripping from the recent rain, allowed little sunlight to penetrate, and Drummond imagined that 150 years ago this forest might have echoed with the terrible crack of muskets as red-coated British soldiers put down Arawak's largest slave rising. He thought it likely that the soldiers would, when no rebels were in sight, have whistled to keep up their spirits as they trudged through the semi-darkness.

Davinia Lee's head fell against his shoulder, and she began to breathe deeply and evenly. Drummond tried to avoid sleep himself, as he did not want to miss any part of this journey; but, as the forest continued monotonously on each side of the road, before long he too fell into a doze.

He came awake as the Marina engaged a lower gear to climb a steep incline. Davinia Lee opened her eyes and, realizing that her head was on Drummond's shoulder, shook herself and straightened up.

"Oh, my! Pardon me, Mr Drummond."

"No problem, Ms Lee."

She leaned forward and peered through the windscreen. "Ah, we're going over the shoulder now."

"Trying to, anyway."

She slapped his knee. "Behave yourself, Mr Drummond."

As they rounded a bend, not quite sharp enough to be described as hairpin, the police Land Rover was visible on the long straight stretch ahead of them.

"They seem to be slowing down. Do you think they're in trouble, Garry?"

"I doubt it, Roger." Lemay had been awake for some time and had, turning his head, been amused to see Drummond and Davinia Lee, head-to-head and hand in hand, dozing on the back seat. "They're probably holding back to make sure that we manage to get over the mountain."

"Ah, I see. God knows how the trucks are coping with this gradient."

That became clear after they cleared the next bend: ahead of the Land Rover were the three trucks, inching up the gradient at a crawl, black diesel fumes belching from their exhausts.

"This looks as if it might take a while," Drummond commented.

"Don't worry," replied Davinia Lee. "It will be all downhill in a while."

When they crested the shoulder around thirty minutes later, Drummond released a long breath, almost as if he had been climbing the gradient under his own steam. Vegetation up here was sparse, the trees having been completely removed or bent double by the hurricanes of generations past.

"Stop here for a moment, driver," instructed Davinia Lee.

She alighted and led Drummond and Lemay to the narrow verge at the edge of the road. "There," she said, with a sweep of her right arm. "As we're here, we might as well, see the sights."

And what sights! Maybe three miles from the foot of the mountain lay what could only be the town of Palmerston, little more than an expanded village really, with arteries issuing to the south (the road they by which they would soon enter the town) the east and the west and (the road they would take tomorrow morning) the north.

"You can see the hospital from here," said Davinia Lee, pointing to one of the largest buildings in the town; even so, it was small as hospitals went.

"And where do the roads lead to the east and west?" ask Drummond.

"To the farms and plantations," she replied. "Sugar, bananas, a little tobacco."

"Surely they don't ship those crops over the mountain," said Drummond thoughtlessly.

Davinia Lee was almost severe with him. "Of course not! They're shipped out of Port Santiago—which, if you look carefully, you can just see on the horizon."

Yes, there it was, barely visible in the far distance, beneath a slight pall of urban pollution, a lone ship anchored at its dockside.

"That's surely not the *Burgos*, is it?" This from a somewhat alarmed Lemay.

Drummond shook his head. "Can't be: the purser told me they're due in tomorrow."

And there, just south-east of the city, was the airport from which Drummond and Lemay would be flying to Miami in two days' time. Saddened by the thought, Drummond turned to Davinia Lee and wondered if she could read his mind. Her expression told him that she could; she grinned bravely.

Drummond switched his attention to Palmerston. "I wonder where we'll be staying tonight," he speculated.

"A mere guest house, I'm afraid," said Davinia Lee, "but I'm sure it will be perfectly comfortable." She consulted her wristwatch. "We should be going now."

"There's one thing," Lemay said as they walked back to the car, "that I meant to ask the Prime Minister, but it completely slipped my mind."

"Oh?" said Davinia Lee, pausing as if considering that this might lead to a discussion not fit for the ears of the driver.

"Yes, I wanted to know how Bassie Thomas could be denied entry to the country of which he's a citizen."

Davinia Lee laughed. "Oh, I raised that with him. Someone at Immigration made a huge mistake. We all know that Mr Thomas was in favour of insurrection back in the colonial period, but some fool in Immigration seemed to think that he would be preaching revolution against the present government."

"So he's not wanted at the moment."

"Well, yes and no. He did, after all, taken a large amount of money from the Burgos..."

"No more than had been stolen from him on board that ship," Drummond interjected.

"True, but his cohort did disarm the police at the dock and confiscate their weapons."

"Although no one was harmed."

"Also true." She clenched her brow. "Look, if it can be confirmed that Mr Thomas lost that money on the *Burgos*—and even better, if it can be located and the thief identified—his problems will be largely over."

"There may be news on that front tomorrow, when the *Burgos* docks in Port Santiago," said Drummond.

Davinia Lee whirled on him. "What do you know about this, Roger?"

He grinned. "Ask me this time tomorrow."

She sighed. "Well, if he can just report to the government—and I *do* mean the government, not the local police station—I get the impression that he won't have too much to worry about. Of course, we don't know where he is..."

"That may change in the near future," said Lemay mysteriously.

*

It was true, as Davinia Lee had predicted, that it was all downhill now, but, as the trucks had to negotiate the gradient with caution, the speed of the convoy was not greatly increased. But eventually they were down, and the Land Rover now overtook the trucks to lead them triumphantly into the town of Palmerston.

"Has any thought been given to changing the name of this town?" Drummond asked as they entered.

"Yes, but we can never agree on what the replacement should be," replied Davinia Lee.

"You know Palmerston was sympathetic to the Confederacy during the American Civil War?"

"Oh, I thought he opposed slavery."

"He did, but he thought it might be a good thing if the United States was dissolved."

"He wasn't all bad, then," chuckled Lemay.

"Jesus Christ!" Drummond's attention had been drawn to something on the roadside.

"What is it, Roger?" asked Lemay.

"The place is full of posters advertising that Billy Joe Harrison concert!"

"Well so it is," mused Lemay, gazing through his window. "But I told you his concert was going to be out in the sticks, didn't I?"

"What's the date today, Garry?"

"June 22. Why?"

"It's tonight! The concert is tonight!"

"Why are you so excited, Roger?" enquired Davinia Lee innocently. "Are you a fan of this singer?"

Lemay found this uproariously funny.

"A fan? Of course I'm not a fan! This Harrison character is a religious nut. He'll work the crowd into some kind of anti-communist hysteria, and who knows what will happen then! And this at a time, Davinia"—a glance at the driver's image in the rear-view mirror—"at a time, Minister, when you are in town. Can't you see you're in danger?"

"Oh, the minister will have plenty of protection, Roger, so don't you worry," said Lemay soothingly.

Davinia Lee smiled and patted Drummond's hand. "You see?" She leaned forward to peer through the windscreen. "Now, driver, follow the trucks around the square and you'll see the hospital over to your right."

The town square was fairly sizeable—capable, Drummond estimated, of holding a couple of thousand people. Some fifty or sixty were there already and, taking the arrival of the convoy from AC as a signal, others were drifting in from the surrounding streets. Billy Joe Harrison's roadies were already on the job, placing a generator van close to the concrete podium at the far end of the square.

The upper floors of most of the buildings about the square were, Drummond noted, wooden and, thus, easily combustible should an anti-communist mob be let loose on them. He called to mind the anti-communist outrages in certain parts of Portugal after the 1974 revolution, and the destruction of neighborhoods during racist pogroms in the USA earlier in the century. He realised that he was being silly, however: the people who would later crowd into this square either lived in Palmerston or in nearby villages; why would they destroy their own property? He relaxed.

They joined the trucks, which had parked by the side of the hospital. And that hospital was, indeed, small, a single-storied structure which, like most of the buildings in the town, had concrete lower walls and a wooden superstructure from which the paint had peeled.

"I don't suppose we'll be delivering much of the equipment here," remarked Drummond as they walked from the car to the hospital entrance, where a small group of grinning dignitaries awaited them.

"More than you might imagine," replied Davinia Lee. "We also have to leave supplies for the clinics out in the countryside, on the eastern and western sides of the island. They'll use their own transport to collect their allocations in the next day or two." She turned to Lemay. "Are the allocations clearly marked, Mr Lemay?"

"So they assured me at the warehouse, ma'am."

At the entrance, they were greeted by the hospital administrator, a large woman in early middle age, a short, thin man in a shirtjac who turned out to be the town's mayor, and two senior doctors. A microphone stand unobtrusively occupied a corner just outside the glass doors.

"Ah, Sister Bradley!" Davinia Lee advanced on the hospital administrator, taking both of her hands in hers. "It's so good to see you again!"

"Oh, Minister! I've dreamed of this day! You don't need me to tell you that!" Dr Bradley, positively beaming, was quite beautiful when she smiled. "New equipment at last!"

Davinia Lee leaned closer and lowered her voice. "How many porter yuh have on duty, Sister? You cyan spare dem to help the men unload your truck?"

"Already taken care of, Minister." How those eyes sparkled! Dr Bradley really was a happy woman.

"And you, sir, must be Mr Wilfred Elkins, the mayor of this fine lickle town!"

"I have that honour, ma'am," said the little man with considerable enthusiasm, "and on behalf of Palmerston I bid you a very warm welcome!"

The introductions completed, Davinia Lee turned her attention to the street. The four-man police contingent had now stationed itself, evenly spaced, three or four yards from the hospital entrance, hands clasped behind their backs as they regarded the two or three hundred people who had drifted over from the square to hear the message from their Minister of Health. Not surprisingly, there were no journalists present.

After a white-clad hospital orderly had positioned the microphone stand, Mr Elkins stepped forward to give the welcoming speech, but found it necessary to call the orderly back into service as the microphone was positioned too high. Witnessing this, some in the crowd tittered affectionately, Mr Elkin's height being much remarked-upon in Palmerston. But this little mayor of the fine little town proved to have a surprisingly powerful voice, and he quickly claimed the attention of his audience. Given the warmth of his address, Drummond assumed that Mr Elkins was a member of the ruling party; and if, he thought, the people of Palmerston had elected an Arawak National Party member as their mayor, it was hardly likely that they would be easily persuaded by the message that Billy Joe Harrison would be bringing them later. More reassurance.

"You're next, Roger," said Davinia Lee as Mr Elkins invited his audience to celebrate the great honour bestowed upon their town, "so why don't you let me have that bag."

Drummond took the strap from his neck and handed the shoulder bag to Davinia Lee.

"My goodness, it's heavy! What have you got in here, Roger?"

For reply, Drummond simply looked into her eyes and grinned, an eyebrow raised.

Her mouth fell open. "Oh, my god! I'd forgotten all about that!"

With Mr Elkins acting as compere, Drummond and Lemay delivered their brief speeches, much the same as the ones they had recited in AC that morning. Then it was the turn of Davinia Lee.

"Fellow citizens! Bredren and sistren!"

This alone got her applause and cheers: here was a government minister who could not only speak the language but was not ashamed to do so. For the most part, her speech followed the same lines as her remarks to the media that morning: she was thankful for the fact that Britain had finally agreed to make partial reparations for its neglectful colonial stewardship, grateful for the efforts of Roger Drummond to assist a small country he had never visited until now, and she acknowledged the hard work of Garrison Lemay at the London High Commission.

"But we must do more to help ourselves! What is the meaning of this so-called independence we achieved in 1966 if we're always beholden to others? We, the people of Arawak, must develop we own economy! That's the only way we can be truly independent. And to do that we haffe *act* independently, working to serve the interests of the people of Arawak instead of the interests of other countries like America and the foreign companies that suck the wealth out of our little island!

"And you know what? I'm so *glad* to have this opportunity to speak to the people of Palmerston, because at the last election you showed that you understand this. Here, in the country parts, so often ignored by politicians in AC, looked down upon because they say you're backward and behind the times, you showed them that when it comes to knowing what this country needs you're way ahead of them, voting for a government—and, I must say—a local administration! —that will fight tooth and nail to bring about that real independence.

"Stand proud, people of Palmerston, and be ready to defend your gains!"

As the crowd erupted in applause, Lemay stepped forward and spoke urgently to Davinia Lee. When she nodded her approval, he took the microphone.

"One last message, people of Palmerston! What your health minister said about your understanding is right! But you go a few mile down the Manchester road to the east or the Plymouth road to the west, and what do you find? The minds of the people in those places are not as developed as yours. No, don't mock dem de way de AC politicians used to mock you! It's not their fault. They live in isolated places where their minds are influenced by landlords and backward preachers. If dey don't see the light yet it because nobody *show* dem that light!"

He held up a warning finger. "But listen mi nuh! In this situation ignorance can be a dangerous thing. If somebody come along and give dem a pretty message—the *wrong* message! — dem could swallow it and go from neighbour to enemy. An' somebody *has* come along, sistren and bredren. You see this singer from America performin' here tonight? If I'm right, his message will be different from Sister Davinia's. Sister Davinia say you muss work and struggle hard to build dis country and you accept dat because you understand, because you enlightened. But dis Billy Joe Harrison will tell you no, you muss relax an' leave it all to God! My bet is he will sing and preach against the government you elected. Why? Because that what him paid fe do. Who pays him? Washington, of course.

"Sistren and bredren, I don't know if you plannin' to attend dis concert, but my advice would be to turn up an' give Billy Joe Harrison hell if he attack your government. But no violence, especially not against the poor people them bussin' in from Manchester an' Plymouth way. No, jus reason wid the people-dem, but give Billy Joe an' him band hell!"

As the crowd began to disperse, Wilfred Elkins had the appearance of a worried man. "If I had known this, Brother Lemay, I would never have granted these people a permit to perform." Close to despair, he shook his head. "But how can I cancel the concert at this stage?"

Lemay placed a hand on his shoulder. "You can't, Brother Elkins, of course you can't." He grinned. "But don't worry: it may turn out for the best: if your people chase Harrison out of town it will be a great victory for progress—and a big boost for their self-confidence."

Unconvinced, Brother Elkins shook his head. "Brother Lemay, my people may have a certain level of understanding, but I don't honestly think they will be a match for a professional preacher."

"In that regard, Brother Elkins, I think the people of Palmerston may have assistance."

31

The Palmerston Guest House, its ochre-painted walls facing onto the square, was, although basic, clean and comfortable. Having checked in, Davinia Lee, Drummond and Lemay went to their rooms to change and freshen up. Their rooms were all on the second floor, the two men's next to each other, and Davinia Lee's at the other end of the corridor, on the opposite side. The wooden floor up here was stained red, and Drummond noted with a sinking heart the eighteen-inch gap between the tops of the walls and the ceiling; while this aided the circulation of air, it did little for privacy.

By the time Davinia Lee joined the two men at the small bar on the ground floor, they were each into their second Red Stripe. Drummond barely recognized Davinia Lee: she had removed all her makeup, combed her hair straight back and held it with a band, and had discarded her trouser suit for a simple light blue skirt and white blouse. She wore no jewelry. While Lemay ordered her a drink, she turned to Drummond to demand, "Well, how do I look?"

Drummond could see that this was a test, that she was making a statement: like it or not, this is how I really look. "You look very pretty, Davinia," he murmured. "And desirable."

She swallowed hard and he knew he had passed the test.

Lemay handed Davinia Lee her 7-Up and looked at the change in his hand. "Shall we have some music?"

"They have a jukebox?" Drummond sounded as if he thought this was good news.

Lemay jerked his thumb over his shoulder and there it was, tucked away against the far wall. He walked over and inserted two coins; as he made the return journey, Aretha began to demand respect.

Drummond stepped back from the bar and peered out of the front door. "Pretty dark now. Can't hear the band tuning up, though."

"I guess they're waiting for their audience to arrive," said Lemay.

"Talking of which," said Davinia Lee, "how will they get here? The people out that way are too poor to own vehicles, and the buses won't be running for much longer."

Lemay smiled. "With its very deep pockets, Billy Joe Harrison's organisation will bus them in on hired vehicles. They'll also pay the people to come. Because, as you say, the people out there are dirt poor, there will be plenty of takers. Once here, of course, the idea will be to give the impression that this is sizeable audience of Palmerston people, eager to hear the anti-communist, anti-Robinson message of the squeaky-clean Billy Joe."

"Well, I..." Davinia Lee struggled for words. "I've a good mind to..."

"No, don't do that, Minister," said Lemay. "And it might be an idea if you told our police inspector not to get involved, either. I suggested to Brother Elkins that he tell the local police to exercise maximum tolerance."

"Garry, you and Roger fly back to London the day after tomorrow, right?"

"Right."

"Then call me Davinia, dammit! I'm tired of all this Minister this, Minister that. And while you're about it, as you seem to be in the know, you can tell me what's going to happen later."

Lemay sighed. "You don't need me to tell you, Davinia. When it happens, you'll ask yourself why you didn't work it out yourself." He tightened his lips and gave her a frown. "You're not going to instruct me, are you? Davinia? Minister?"

She laughed. "No, I'll wait. But understand that if this turns out bad, it will be your arse rather than mine."

He nodded. "Understood. By the way, where are our police escorts staying?"

"Here."

Drummond groaned inwardly. First the walls that didn't quite meet the ceiling, now this.

Davinia Lee, sensing his disappointment, turned to him. "The police and the drivers are on the first floor. Doesn't that make you feel secure?"

Lemay looked at his watch. "If we're quick about it, we can have dinner before the fun starts."

The others nodded and drained their glasses. Just then, Davinia's driver, in conversation with one of the police constables, walked into the bar.

"So what yuh know about this Harrison?" asked the constable.

"Im was mi favourite Beatle," came the reply.

*

After dinner, the trio returned to the bar, now occupied by their police inspector and his sergeant, who sat at a table by the jukebox, which was playing "Twilight Time," an old Nat King Cole number.

"Appropriate choice," said Lemay. He lifted his chin in the direction of the hotel entrance; darkness had fallen, and the weak streetlights bathed the square in a dull yellow glow. "Any excitement yet?"

The inspector shook his head. "Plenty bus and truck come, but nothin' start yet."

It was 7.30 when a single chord was struck on a guitar and an emcee stepped up to the microphone. "Christians of Arawak," announced an American voice, "we greet you and offer you our sincere support. We know that times are hard for you and that some of your leaders have turned against God. But He has not forgotten you. Lay your hearts before Him and He will protect you and save you from the flames. But I am not here to deliver His message, my fellow Christians, as He has given that job to the poet and songwriter you've all come to hear. This man's songs praise the glory of the Lord. His poems are dedicated not to any earthly beauty but to the everlasting beauty of the Lord Jesus Christ! It is my very great pleasure and honour to present to you, the Christian people of Arawak, the singing bishop—Billy! Joe! *Harrison!* Praise the Lord!"

Drummond raised an eyebrow at Lemay. "Shall we take a look?"

"Might as well." Lemay picked up his Red Stripe bottle and carried it with him.

Davinia Lee placed a hand on Drummond's arm. "Am I invited?"

"The inspector may not allow you, Davinia. Could be a spot of bother."

"Well, I may join you later. You're not going onto the square, are you?" She looked worried.

"No, we'll watch from just outside."

She took the strap of his shoulder bag in her hand. "Better leave this with me."

He thought for a moment before, having weighed the alternative scenarios, slipping off the strap and handing her the bag. "You're probably right."

He and Lemay stood on the steps outside the guest house and saw that the roadies had rigged up a spot that bathed the podium in a harsh white light. Billy Joe wore a white suit and strummed a sequined acoustic guitar. Tossing his mane of corn-coloured hair each time he belted out a chorus, he was the cleanest-looking person Roger Drummond had ever seen. He was accompanied by a country and western group and a black girl chorus. All were dressed in white. The steel guitar whined, and the girls did their heavenly chorus thing. Billy Joe began with "Troublesome Waters," a gospel song Drummond had first heard on Johnny Cash's *I Walk the Line* album over a decade earlier. His favourite track on that album had been the regrettably misogynistic "Understand Your Man," about a man who, leaving his wife/lover, tells her that she can give his other suit to the Salvation Army. Cash had written that song himself, whereas "Troublesome Waters" had been co-written by Mother Maybelle Carter, soon to be his mother-in-law, and Drummond now found himself wondering whether "Understand Your Man" had been directed at Cash's first wife.

"He's trying to win them over with the music before he starts to deliver his message," Lemay commented. "Pretty clever."

It did seem to be working, as the audience, including many of those from Palmerston, seemed appreciative. After the Cash song, Billy Joe launched into another well-known gospel song, Hank Williams' "I Saw the Light."

When Drummond began to tap his foot, Lemay looked at him askance. "What the…?"

"Sorry. I had an instrumental version of this on a Floyd Cramer album. Always liked it."

Drummond assumed that country music was not a part of the normal diet for the few hundred people in the square, but that the evangelistic content of Billy Joe's first two offerings undoubtedly was. Some of the women in the audience were beginning to clap, while one or two of the older men sometimes injected a "Praise the Lord!" at the end of a line, although during "I Saw the Light," of course, they could sing it. The heavy air was made piquant with the scent of perspiring humanity. Casting his eye over the square, Drummond saw that only a minority of the people here were under fifty. He noticed one old woman, hands clasped at her breast, eyes screwed shut as she concentrated her energy on seeking that light which would ease the burden of her day-to-day existence, and he realised that for people such as her the words "communism" and "socialism" had to be anathema, as they appeared to threaten this form or consolation. Then, at the edges of the crowd, he saw a young man pressed against a girl. She had dropped her eyes in modesty, but a tiny grin was tugging at the corners of her mouth as the young man sweet-talked her. Drummond's faith in humanity was somewhat restored.

At the foot of the podium stood a white man, what remained of his hair combed straight back to end in a single rat's tail hanging over his collar. His shirt was unbuttoned to reveal a heavy gold crucifix nestling in the small forest on his chest. Drummond would later learn that this was a man called Edwards—"Honest Joe" Edwards to some—who acted as Billy Joe Harrison's "promoter." The verandas of the single-story wooden houses bounding the square were filled and a handful of youths had climbed onto the roofs for a better view, and as Billy Joe and his band worked towards a crescendo, these young men drew some curses in rural dialect as they hammered on the roofs with their feet.

The number ended and the volume of applause and the number of "Praise the Lords" seemed to indicate that the audience had been won over to the music. The square had become a pulsating mass of excitement.

"Billy looks surprised at the reception he's getting," said Lemay. "You would think that this was the last thing he expected."

"Well," Drummond chuckled, "he's probably not taken in by the stuff he's singing, so he's possibly wondering why an Arawakian audience should be."

"Oh, I suspect he's taken in by it, alright. These guys tend to be believers."

Drummond noticed a slim black wrist appear in front of Joe Edwards' shirt and snatch the gold crucifix. Edwards jumped as the chain was pulled from his neck and, turning to the group of people nearest to him, began shouting something, his face contorted with rage. But the crowd was still praising the Lord and Edwards' words were inaudible. One of the men at whom he had shouted them, however, was obviously offended, for he had taken a knife from his pocket and was waving it in Edwards' face. Edwards' face reacted accordingly, producing an insincere smile and sweating even more profusely than it had been.

"I have to say, Garry," said Drummond, "that I'm disappointed."

"With?"

"There doesn't seem to be any reasoning going on."

Lemay grinned. "True. But that's due to Harrison's choice of material. When he starts peddling his own stuff, you should see a change."

There was certainly a change of material.

> Don't spend your lifetime wishing
> For what you can't afford;
> Can't you see what you're missing
> Is the love of our Lord?
>
> Don't follow communism,
> It'll lead you straight to sin;
> Don't fall for socialism,
> If eternity you'd win.

Billy Joe sang this with minimal accompaniment, just the drummer stroking his kit with the brushes and the girls adding the odd "oohh" and "aahh." There were, Drummond noticed, several frowns in the audience, and some people were turning to each other to shrug in incomprehension. And, yes, the reasoning began, with a few Palmerston men threading their way through the crowd, haranguing those who had been bused in.

As Billy Joe gave them more of the same, the audience's confusion increased and the reasoning became more urgent. The crowd began to murmur rebelliously and Billy Joe, his self-confidence on the wane, whispered urgently to the band, whereupon the rhythm guitarist struck a chord, heralding a new number. Actually, it was an old number, as Billy Joe had decided to reprise "I Saw the Light" in an obvious attempt to recreate the audience enthusiasm it had generated earlier.

It was at this point that someone pulled the plug on the generator van and the spotlight shut off, leaving only the weak street-lighting to cast a dim glow on the square. If any of the five-hundred-and-forty-nine people in the square had ever wondered what a singer with a high-powered band and all the voice-enhancing equipment that the modern audio-electronics industry had made available would sound like if someone were mischievous enough to flip the switch, they were now given a brief demonstration as Billy Joe, who had his eyes closed when the spotlight was extinguished, carried on singing and strumming his guitar. To the discerning ear this would have proven beyond a doubt that the electronics, and not Billy Joe, had been the star of the show. But no one noticed. Everyone, apart from the old woman Drummond had noticed earlier, had their eyes open at the moment of malfunction and were too busy screaming hysterically and stampeding out of the range of pickpockets to notice the thin wail coming from Billy Joe's throat.

Billy Joe, on the other hand, heard all the screaming and took it to be nothing less than the sound of adulation which had once greeted performers such as Elvis (with whom, Billy Joe had claimed in a recent interview, he was in constant touch since the King's death the previous year) and Flip Jackson (unknown to the wider world but very big in Billy Joe's home town of Pilger's Crossing, Kentucky). His surprise must have been considerable when, upon opening his eyes, he was confronted with a complete void. Had he been blinded for his hypocrisy? The thin nasal whine became a scream. But, again, no one noticed.

A crackle of semi-automatic fire issued from the direction in which the people had run, whereupon they turned and ran back again, knocking Honest Joe Edwards to the ground.

"Calm yourselves, brethren!" a voice, very loud, commanded.

"Aaaaaahhh! Is God a-talk to we!" wailed a woman's voice. "Him come fe punish we for we sin!"

But Drummond recognised the voice to be that of the Reverend Mr Bassfield Thomas, enhanced by a battery-operated hailer.

"Calm yourselves, brethren," the voice repeated. "No one will harm you. It is not God's Will that you be harmed, merely that you are not misled by this pretty boy who pretends to bring you His word. Are you so foolish as to believe that because someone tells you that he is with the Lord that it must be so?"

"Lord God, have mercy pon we!" cried the woman. "We never did know we was doin wrong."

"Shet up, yuh fool-fool woman," someone hissed. "Yuh don't know Bassie Thomas when yuh hear him? Bassie don't mean we no harm."

"If dem bad, how come dem play fe free?" enquired a rebellious spirit, doubtless emboldened by the semi-darkness enveloping him.

"Because, fool, they are paid by someone else. What message did they bring? Was not their message that socialism is bad? That a Christian way of life in which each has his opportunity and in which no man exploits another is bad? Was that not their message? And because it was wrapped up with hypocritical words about praising God, you believed it. No, my friends, their wages are paid by the Central Intelligence Agency in America, by the Pharaohs' secret police. And why? Because the Pharaohs, both those in America and the little Pharaohs in Arawak, want to continue exploiting you, sucking your blood, forcing you to continue living in squalor and misery."

Billy Joe now learned that, despite the enthusiasm with which he had been greeted throughout the island, the people of Arawak had been less than thoroughly converted. More, it was demonstrated that they could, once they suspected that they had been fooled, turn quite nasty. Under the direction of the Reverend Mr Bassfield Thomas they were now smashing the guitars and amplifiers. Someone commandeered a paraffin lamp that had just been lighted on the veranda of one of the houses and hurled it onto the wreckage. Soon, a ten-foot column of flame was licking the night sky.

It was by the light of this flame that Drummond made out the figure of Thomas across the square. He stood, legs apart, in a black combat suit and beret. The Reverend Mr. Bassfield Thomas also saw Drummond and Lemay. His face cracked in a smile as he raised his loud hailer in the air in greeting.

"How did you know that this was going to happen, Garry?" asked Lemay.

"I knew that something *like* this would happen, but not precisely *this*."

"But how?"

"When I heard that Washington intended to send a bunch of born-again Christians to Arawak, I had a word with Bassie Thomas in London and suggested that he might make himself useful."

"Does the government know about this?"

"Oh, of course not. This was purely a personal initiative." He frowned across at the bonfire on the podium. "Seems to have got out of control, though."

"You mention a *bunch* of born-agains..."

"Oh, yes, Billy Joe would have been just the first." He grinned. "Hopefully the others, or whoever controls them, will have second thoughts now."

Out on the square, the Reverend Mr Bassfield Thomas had by this time rounded up his followers—some twenty young men in similar attire--and issued appropriate instructions; as a result, the people from Plymouth and Manchester were being herded back onto the vehicles that had brought them here. Arms folded across his capacious chest, the leader of the Wrath of God Gospel Mission monitored the progress of this operation and, finding it satisfactory, turned and walked towards the Palmerston Guest House.

"Well, well," he boomed as he arrived at the entrance, "Bredda Lemay and Bredda Drummond. Good evening to you both. I do believe we have routed the messengers of the Pharaohs." He turned to look across at the podium, which was now empty apart from the burning equipment. "But I see you're not entirely happy, Bredda Lemay." He frowned sympathetically. "What concerns you, Bredda?"

Lemay leaned forward, hissing. "Bassie, I heard *gunfire*!"

The religious leader laughed, drawing something from a side pocket. "You mean this?" He pressed the play button on the cassette recorder and, yes, there was indeed the sound of gunfire, albeit faint.

"No, that's not what we heard!"

"Oh, excuse me." The Reverend Mister Bassfield Thomas pressed the play button once more, this time bringing the cassette recorder into proximity with his megaphone. The result was sufficient to provoke sounds of alarm from inside the guest house and to bring the police inspector, pistol in hand, to the door, Davinia Lee at his shoulder.

"Drop the gun, Bassie." The inspector and the Reverend Mr Bassfield Thomas were old friends.

"Gussie Fredericks! So dem meck you inspector!" He gave the policeman a small bow. "Good evening to you, Inspector." He nodded first to his cassette player, then to the megaphone. "Dis is all de guns mi have, Gussie."

"An what about de guns yuh teck from de officers in John Crow Bay, Bassie?" Inspector Fredericks had lowered his pistol and was almost smiling.

"Left outside a police station in AC, Gussie, on the banana truck we commandeered."

The inspector lifted his chin in the direction of the square. "An you give your word nobody was shot or wounded out here?"

"Ohhh, some cuts and bruises, but that's all."

"You seem to know most of the police in Arawak, Reverend," Drummond said almost respectfully.

"Oh," chuckled Inspector Fredericks, "better say most of *us* know *him*. Mebbe not de younger ones, but most veterans like me have had dealins wid Bassie Thomas in our time."

The Reverend Mr Bassfield Thomas spread his arms. "So, why yuh not arrestin me, Gussie?"

"Two reasons, Bassie. Number one, this is not my jurisdiction: my only job is to provide protection for Miss Lee an your shipmates here. Number two, Miss Lee tells me that all you have to do to become a free man is report to the govament." He looked at Davinia Lee, who had stepped around him and stood before the religious leader. "Mebbe you can come back with us to AC."

"That sound like arrest to me, Gussie."

"No, no," intervened Davinia Lee, "I can assure you that you will not be under arrest, Mr Thomas. We have business in Port Santiago tomorrow, and the following morning we'll be travelling back to AC. The only role of Inspector Fredericks and his men will be to provide me with an escort. You can ride in my car, with just me and my driver."

"Then I'll see you in Port Santiago tomorrow, Miss Lee."

"In fact, Mr Thomas," said Drummond, "tomorrow afternoon you may be able to witness the arrest of the man who stole your money."

The Reverend Mr Bassfield Thomas raised a finger. "That's a date!"

*

There was no air-conditioning, just a fan, although the gaps between the walls and the ceiling provided some additional relief.

"I thought this would be our last night," he whispered.

"You heard what I said downstairs, my darling."

"Yes, but I didn't know whether you had firmly decided. I still don't, Davinia."

"Keep your voice down." Davinia Lee's room was at the far end of the corridor, but anyone with a keen ear could pick up what was being said.

"So you will stay with me tomorrow night in Port Santiago?"

"Yes, my love. Now hurry up or you'll miss the music."

Drummond laughed. "The music?"

"Shhh. Yes, you'll see. Or hear, rather."

He deposited his clothes on the floor at the foot of her bed before lying down next to her. Naked, she folded her arms around him, pressing her body to his. Drummond recalled having read, years ago, a novel by the Cuban writer Alejo Carpentier (was it *The Lost Steps*?) in which the protagonist assures his lover that their third coupling will be more wonderful than the first two, as by now their bodies will have adjusted to each other, will know each other. And so it was now. Davinia Lee's former reticence was gone, and she welcomed his body into hers, smiling up at him as, magically, from downstairs drifted the sound of The Flamingos singing "I Only Have Eyes for You."

Oh, this was perfect! Drummond thought that Alejo Carpentier certainly knew what he was talking about. He felt not only love but an intense form of gratitude, for Davinia, in somehow arranging this, was surely telling him something.

She came on top of him and, when she leaned forward to rub her breasts over the stubble on his face, he tasted her salt as The Platters sang "Only You."

"This is so nice," she whispered. "Do you like it?"

"I'm not complaining."

Next came the Stylistics with "You Make Me Feel Brand New."

"Davinia," he whispered in blissful amazement, "how did you...?"

"I left a list. And a supply of coins. Behind the bar. No more questions now. Just. Give in. To it."

He gave in to it, and The Shirelles came in with "Will You Still Love Me Tomorrow?"

"Will you, Roger?"

"Yes, Davinia. Oh yes!"

32

The following day was cloudless and, with no mountain to cross, the journey to Port Santiago took only two hours. This time, the police Land Rover led the way, followed by the ministerial car and then the two trucks, one having been sent back to AC, empty. Drummond began by paying close attention to the countryside through which they passed—a banana plantation here, a ricefield there, and small hamlets flashing by—but soon he began to nod off until, as yesterday, he and Davinia Lee, her head on his shoulder, snoozed together. It occurred to Lemay, sitting in on the front seat, to make some jocular comment to the driver, but he resisted; the man was, after all, in the employ of Davinia Lee, and respect must be maintained.

For years afterward, Drummond would think back to this journey, when he and Davinia Lee felt the warmth of each other's slumbering bodies and, blinking awake for a few seconds, bathing in the memory of the previous night's lovemaking, both blissfully unaware of what lay ahead.

He came awake just a few miles outside Port Santiago.

"Tres Lagos," he murmured.

"Mm?"

"Signpost back there pointed to a place called Tres Lagos."

"Mm, Three Lakes: a tourist resort."

"From the Spanish period?"

"Yes. The name, not the resort."

As soon as they cleared the outskirts, where the poor resided in the inevitable shanties, it became obvious that Port Santiago, far from being a sleepy seaside town, was a relatively prosperous, bustling city, with well-maintained streets and brightly painted buildings. To get to their destination, they had first to reach the coastal road and travel eastwards for half a mile. Tourists were much in evidence—mostly Americans by the look of them, the paunchy men in garish attire. The docks lay further to the east, but Drummond was unable to see whether the *Burgos* was tied up at the pier, and before he could get a closer look the Land Rover turned right and led them up a gradient to where, overlooking the bay, the hospital stood, gleaming whitely and fronted by a row of evenly spaced palms.

Having alighted from the Marina, Drummond stood and gazed up at hospital frontage. "Looks more like a hotel, Garry."

"Port Santiago is a tourist centre, so I suppose they can't have it looking too shabby."

Drummond turned to Davinia Lee. "Are you sure they need the largesse of the UK government?"

"Believe me," she said sourly, "it's not so smart inside."

And there on the steps to meet them was the grey man.

"Thurprithed to thee me, Mr Drummond?"

Drummond barely looked at him. "You could say that." He pushed past him, and waved Davinia Lee ahead of him, intent on reaching the officials waiting in the entrance.

"I'll have my thay thith time, Mr Drummond."

Drummond turned. "Oh?"

Hesketh-Brown spread his arms. "Who'th to sthtop me? Bethideth, I've cleared it with the mayor and the hospital adminithtrator."

To seek guidance, Drummond raised his eyebrows at Davinia Lee.

"Best not to make a scene," she murmured. "Anyway, hardly anyone will hear what he has to say."

Having overheard, Hesketh-Brown smiled. "Oh, you're wrong there, Mith Lee. I've taken the liberty of inviting a few media people along."

Drummond looked at Lemay and mimed the word "Fuck!"

After the introductions, the chief administrator led the way into a large meeting room where the ceremony was to be held. There, the administrator had assembled the senior staff and those in the lower ranks who could be spared. The "few media people" were few indeed: a radio reporter who acted as a stringer for the BBC and a freelancer with access to the Miami press. The mayor of Port Santiago, a light-skinned man in his fifties with wiry grey hair who dressed in a dark blue suit with an equally conservative tie with diagonal stripes, acted as emcee and made the first speech, ponderous and predictable.

After the administrator had made the expected speech of thanks, the mayor turned to Davinia Lee, but she shook her head and pointed firmly and sternly in the direction of the grey man.

The warm smile that Hesketh-Brown gave his audience said "I am your friend. I will always be here when you need me," and his speech said much the same thing: we are all part of the same family, the Commonwealth; yes, the senior members of the family made mistakes, sometimes dreadful mistakes, in the past, but we are anxious to make amends. And so on. All was fairly predictable and harmless until, with a tight grin to Drummond, Lemay and Davinia Lee, knowing that no one would stop him, he said, "At the rithk of being controverthial..."

Quite audibly, Drummond, Lemay and Davinia Lee groaned.

"At the rithk of being controverthial, I would like to offer a little advithe to the people of Arawak, and to the thitizens of Port Thantiago in particular: be very careful how you choothe your friendth. Arawak hath in recent timeth moved clother to Cuba, and while thith might bring thome benefitth, like the training of doctorth that Cuba hath agreed, there are very real dangerth.

"Shortly after the revolution in Cuba, the United Thtateth imposed an embargo on that country. Among other thingth, thith meanth that American tourithtth can no longer vithit Cuba." He paused and regarded his audience. "Think about that, ladieth and gentlemen. Port Thantiago is a touritht thentre! What would thith thity be without American tourithtth?" Hesketh-Brown turned to the city mayor who, a member of the opposition party, found himself desperately wanting to agree with the Englishman and yet fearful off calling down the wrath of Davinia Jones upon his head. "It would be a tragedy, ladieth and gentlemen, if Arawak threw away the opportunity of a brilliant future to purthue what can only be dethcribed ath an ideological fantathy. I trutht that you will not let that happen."

To a certain extent, Hesketh-Brown's address had, of course, been compromised by his lisp, but while he received only scattered applause, the pensive frowns among the audience indicated that he had scored with his last point.

Drummond started by delivering his by now well-practiced remarks about Merritt & Thwaite's desire to help Arawak to the best of the company's ability, but ended with a rebuttal of Hesketh-Brown's claims.

"Mr Hesketh-Brown sought to frighten you with the prospect of US-imposed sanctions if Arawak moved closer still to Cuba. And, yes, the USA might well pose a threat to the genuine independence of Arawak. But, far from seeking to redress the so-called 'mistakes' of the past, Mr Hesketh-Brown's own government initially *denied* the grant which has made this gift of medical equipment possible. Would this not have been a form of sanctions? And why is Mr Hesketh-Brown here? Is it to try to demonstrate that the United Kingdom is now a friend of the Third World, or is it to threaten you with dire consequences if the government which you have elected seeks an independence with more substance than that granted in 1966? I leave you to decide."

The grey man had turned scarlet, for a good half of the audience, somewhat to the dismay of the city mayor, clearly sided with Drummond.

Davinia Lee, conscious that she was here as Minister of Health, paid much attention to the improvements in the wellbeing of the people of Port Santiago and its environs which the new equipment would make possible. And then she looked around at the hospital staff, assembled in white, before lapsing into dialect.

"There's one thing mi sure of, sistren an bredren: you don't want to be treatin no gunshot wound in this hospital! On your behalf, mi ask Mr Hesketh-Brown fe tell im friend-dem in CIA not fe send any more gun to Arawak. An mi ask Mr Mayor fe tell im party leader-dem to get rid of de gun dem receive aready. Yuh see de terrorist act in recent weeks? De attack on the Workers' Party office? De shooting of our Assemblyman? Praise God our Defence Force ketch de last plane dat come in wid gun! Why more guns? So dat before the election supporter will kill supporter and de whole country will be terrorise!" She turned to the mayor and Hesketh-Brown. "You think tourist-dem will come to Port Santiago if dat happen? Of course not!"

This got her steady applause. She nodded, moderated her speech, and lowered her voice.

"And, Mr Mayor, let me say this about tourists. This government wants tourists to come to Arawak; we welcome them. But Mr Mayor, we need to build our country so that the income from tourism is a *bonus*, so that we feed, house and educate our people by what we *produce*!"

It ended well.

As the guests made their way to the boardroom for a late lunch, Hesketh-Brown, recovered from his rebuffs at the hands of Drummond and Davinia Lee, took Drummond to one side.

"As a matter of interetht, Mr Drummond, what will you do now?"

"Well, after I check into the hotel, I have some business down on the docks…"

"No, no, I mean for a job."

Drummond gave him a blank look. "A job?"

Hesketh-Brown looked genuinely appalled. "They haven't told you, have they?"

Drummond had a premonition of shock. "Told me what, Mr Hesketh-Brown?"

"Merritt & Thwaite hath been thold."

*

After lunch, which Drummond could not very well escape without embarrassing Davinia Lee and Lemay, he told them his news.

"Sold to whom?" Lemay asked.

"Guess."

"No!"

"Yep. Merritt & Thwaite is now owned by International Enterprises, Inc."

"So you're now working for a CIA proprietary company." This from Davinia Lee.

"I doubt that, Davinia."

After they had checked in at the Starlight Hotel, which seemed to be worth at least four stars, Drummond went straight to his room, threw his luggage on the floor, and sat on the bed next to the telephone. He looked at his watch: 3 p.m. here, so 10 a.m. in London. He lifted the receiver, dialed 9 for an outside line and then called his home number. It rang. And rang, and rang. He tried the office number.

"Merritt & Thwaite. How may we help you?"

"Hello, Susie, it's Roger Drummond. Put me through to Mister Ronald, please."

"I'm sorry, Mr Drummond, but Mister Ronald is on holiday."

"Then let me speak to Mrs Sharma."

"Roger."

"Shirley? Listen, I'm still in Arawak. I've bumped into that berk Hesketh-Brown, who tells me that the company has been sold to International Enterprises. Is this true?"

"I'm afraid so, Roger."

Although he had expected no other answer, he found himself forced to pause in order to regain his equanimity.

"Are you still there, Roger?"

"Sorry, Shirley, I was regaining my equanimity."

"You are a card, Roger."

"And what has happened to Uncle Joseph?"

"Mr Thornton has decided to retire."

"And so who is the new exports manager?"

A long, embarrassed pause.

"It's Lal, isn't it?"

"Yes, it's Lal...They said they thought a brown face would be a good idea."

"And has Ronald been retained by the new owners?"

"Oh, yes. He's told us that he will be the public face of the company."

"Now tell me, Shirley: what is my current employment status?"

"Unemployed, Roger."

"Just like that?"

"Well, no, not just like that. A severance cheque has been sent to your home address."

"Oh. Enough to tide me over, is it?"

"I should say so, Roger."

"I don't suppose you know where Hilary is, do you? She doesn't seem to be at home."

The slightest hesitation. *"She went on holiday with Mister Ronald, Roger."*

"Was this before or after the severance cheque landed on my doormat?"

"Oh, before."

"And when are they expected back?"

"Towards the end of next week."

"So I'm out of a job, and my wife has left me. Would that be an accurate summary of my situation, Shirley?"

"Well, yes. But you should look on the bright side. Roger."

"Oh, I do, Shirley, I do."

*

Ronald had duped him on both fronts. On the home front, the religious niece had been used to fool Drummond into thinking that she, and not he, had driven Hilary home in the early hours. On the office front, Ronald had used first the possibility, and then the reality, of closer ties with Libya to simply drive up the price that Streeter and his people were willing to pay for the company. But how would Streeter & Co deal with the fact that their new proprietary had commercial relations with Libya? On second thoughts, this would not be a problem, as the CIA would now seek to use Merritt & Thwaite to funnel its operatives into Libya. What Colonel Qadhafi might feel about this was, of course, another question entirely.

Presently, there was a knock on the door, and he got up to let Davinia Lee in. She had showered and changed and was now wearing a plain skirt and blouse.

"So what will you do?" she asked after he had told her the news as they sat together on the bed.

He smiled and shrugged. "I don't have a clue, Davinia."

She touched his cheek. "You don't seem very upset, darling."

"Why would I be upset, sweetheart? I'm free."

"But you don't seem very happy, either."

"I guess I'm disoriented. I'll need a while to get my bearings."

"You could always stay here, Roger."

He looked at her steadily. "Could I, Davinia?"

She nodded, almost smiling. "Yes."

"Do you realise what you're saying, Davinia?"

"I think so, yes."

He sighed, his gathering elation ambushed by practical concerns. "But I have things to sort out in London, my love: a house, a car, not to mention a severance cheque."

"Then sort them out and hurry back. I'll be here, Roger."

My goodness, she means it! When he leaned over to kiss her, the telephone rang. The receptionist told him that the police were waiting to see him downstairs.

PART THREE

33

A sombre-looking Lester Robinson attended the funeral dressed in a black safari suit. Drummond himself was wearing a dark suit—far too heavy for this climate—which he had packed but had never expected to wear. Robinson introduced Drummond to Davinia Lee's father, a short man, half Chinese, who looked up at him in some confusion, as if wondering where this tall white man fitted in, and wept continuously but silently throughout the ceremony. After shaking Mr Lee's hand, Drummond took a step backwards, intending to hide himself amid the large gathering of Assembly members, Arawak National Party members, health service officials and trade union leaders at the graveside; there was even a token presence from the Arawak Democratic Party, and earlier Lemay had introduced him to Daniel Morgan, general secretary of the Arawak Workers' Party. But Robinson placed a hand on his sleeve, detaining him. "You belong here, Roger," he murmured. "You were close to her." So he knew.

There were speeches, most of them obviously sincere, from Lester Robinson, Dr Ransome of the General Hospital and several others unknown to Drummond, and he earnestly hoped that he would not be asked to speak. What would he say? He had only known Davinia Lee for a matter of weeks, and their relations had been largely carnal. And yet he had loved her. More than that, just days earlier he had looked into the future and, at her urging, had seen a life with her in Arawak. And now it was all gone, swept away by a policeman's gun. He would never look upon her again, never hold her in his arms, never be irritated by her moods, never kiss her face. There was within him a dark void in which his grief howled and echoed, constricting his heart and rendering his face a mask of desolate, desolate loss. Without a doubt, this was the most powerful emotional experience of his life; but there was not a speech in it.

After Davinia Lee's body had been lowered into the grave and people began to drift away, Lester Robinson touched Drummond's arm again. "Time for another little chat, I think, Roger. We'll go to my office, if that's alright with you."

They sat at the same table as before, each with a cold Red Stripe in front of him.

"I'm not sure this is a good idea, Prime Minister." Drummond tapped his bottle with a finger-tip.

"Why is that, Roger? And call me Lester."

"Because if I drink too much of it, I'm not sure I'll be able to control my thoughts, Lester. And if I start thinking of Davinia, I may become lachrymose."

Robinson nodded. "This has really devastated you, hasn't it?" He seemed both surprised and impressed by the genuineness of Drummond's grief.

Drummond's eyes misted up. "That about sums it up, yes."

Robinson squared his shoulders, as if he were pulling himself together. "Well, let's see if I can cheer you up."

"You can try."

"Let's see if I can make you laugh."

A shrug. "Impossible."

Robinson took the beer bottle from his mouth and pointed the neck at Drummond. "What do you think attracted Davinia to you?"

No need to think. "It was because I wasn't afraid of her."

It was Robinson who laughed. "Yes, I can understand that."

Drummond almost grinned. "Why do you say that?"

"Because she struck terror into people—men especially. Roger, I've seen grown men—*important* men—try to hide themselves when that frown would crease her brow and her eyes would sweep the room."

Some images of Davinia Lee may well have made Drummond shed a tear, but this one made him laugh.

Once more, Robinson gestured with his beer bottle. "Told you!"

And the despair which had gripped Drummond's heart for the past few days did, in fact, seem to relax its grasp. "That was partly an act, you know; beneath all of that, she was quite vulnerable."

Robinson was not entirely convinced. "It may have started out as an act, Roger, but over time I think it became part of her personality: the body-count attests to that!" He laughed again but then softened, giving Drummond a sympathetic glance. "But you know what you saw, and that's something that not many other men can claim. She must have trusted you."

"I think she did."

"That didn't happen very often, you know."

"No, maybe not." He sighed. "It seemed to me that her adoption of that frightening demeanour had backfired: she had nobody really close to her, and so she was never able to gain the confidence to drop the mask."

"That's very perceptive, Roger." Robinson held up his empty bottle. "Join me in another?"

Drummond saw that he only had an inch left. "Why not?"

As Robinson pressed a buzzer and ordered two more beers from the head that peered around the door, Drummond decided the time had come to change the subject.

"Garry flies back to London tomorrow."

Robinson raised his eyebrows. "You're not going with him?"

"Surely I'll be needed here, as a witness."

Robinson heaved a sigh. "But that might take a while. The legal position is quite complicated. The murder was committed on Arawak soil—or, rather, while the ship was tied up at Port Santiago—and so the accused will obviously be tried in Arawak. But the same man is also accused of robbing passengers on the same ship while it was at sea, out of our jurisdiction. Similarly, the woman who assisted him did so while the ship was in international waters. Those cases, therefore, should be tried in London. No problem as far as the woman is concerned, but what about the man? Should he face theft or burglary charges in London first, or should he first be tried for murder here?"

"The latter, I think," said Drummond.

"I agree, and our Attorney General has told London that he intends to go ahead with the murder trial. That won't take place immediately, though, and so I would suggest you return with Garry. Is your ticket still good?"

"Yes, in view of the circumstances, both Arawak Air and Laker Airways agreed that I can simply rebook." He frowned. "That means, of course, that I'll probably be a witness at the London trial as well."

"Our Attorney General will let you know when our own trial is due to take place. We can give you free passage on Arawak Air when you return. Will you be okay for the London to Miami leg?"

Drummond nodded. "That should be okay: Laker is cheap."

Robinson looked at him thoughtfully. "You know, Roger, if you ever felt like returning to Arawak for good, I'm sure we could find something for you."

"That's very kind of you, Lester, and I'll keep it in mind, but I need to get my bearings." He had thought of this possibility before, but had found himself wondering what would happen to him if Robinson's party lost the next election.

"Of course you do. But I'm not saying it to be kind, Roger: you could be a great help to us."

"Whatever help I've been so far, Lester, has been in London."

Robinson acknowledged the point with an open hand. "True, but you're no longer with Merritt & Thwaite."

"And neither is Arawak, I suppose," said Drummond, deftly changing the subject.

Robinson grimaced. "We can hardly maintain a relationship with a company owned by a CIA proprietary." He narrowed his eyes at Drummond. "Maybe you could scout around for us, and recommend an appropriate alternative." He glanced at his left wrist.

"I could do that." He placed his empty bottle on the table. "But I've taken up too much of your time."

Robinson got to his feet. "No you haven't, Roger, but there *are* a couple of things I have to do." He extended his hand.

34

Upon his early-afternoon arrival in Acton, later than anticipated due to the tragedy in Port Santiago, he dumped his luggage in the hallway and gathered up the mail from the floor, sifting through it until he identified the letter from Merritt & Thwaite. The cheque was, indeed, generous. Leaving his luggage where it lay, he went to the garage and, surprised that the car started after just two turns of the key (Hilary had obviously driven it while he was away), he drove to the Midland Bank and first opened a new account with the cheque and then, having checked the balance of his joint account (Hilary had withdrawn just a few hundred pounds), transferred most of it to the new account.

Back home, he checked the bedrooms and confirmed that Hilary had indeed gone for good, leaving only clothes that should have been thrown out ages ago. He got a black bag from under the kitchen sink and stuffed the clothes into it, placing the bulging bag next to the front door, ready for the dustman on Tuesday. Then he unpacked his luggage, hanging what was fit to be hung and making two piles of the rest, one for the dry cleaner and one for the laundry.

These tasks completed, he kicked off his shoes and lay down on the bed he had until recently shared with Hilary and started to plan.

Divorce seemed a priority. Presumably, Hilary would want to marry Ronald as soon as possible in order to inherit his wealth when (surely not too far in the future) he popped his clogs, so she would be amenable to a divorce. Best to go for an uncontested divorce, which could be done by post, although it would mean waiting for two years. But would she agree to go the uncontested route? Wouldn't she demand half of the house? That was hardly likely, as there were still twenty years left on the mortgage, and Ronald would surely provide for her. He decided to write suggesting this the next day. But where to find her? Presumably, she was staying at Ronald's house in Colchester, although he neither knew the address nor felt like asking for it; he would therefore write to her care of Merritt & Thwaite.

Where to live? He had a hankering to return to the Ladbroke Grove area, and maybe buy a two-bedroomed flat. Given the size of his severance cheque, he would be able to pay off his current mortgage, buy a smaller place and still have money in the bank. No, hang on a minute: now is not the time, because if Hilary were to turn nasty and demand half of the house, he would be in trouble. Best to stay here until after the *decree absolute*.

He knew that he would soon need to devote some time to the forthcoming court cases and the evidence he would give, but that would entail thinking about what had happened to Davinia Lee, and he realized now that he had kept busy since arriving home to avoid that. He was hungry but had not looked in the refrigerator and was not in the mood to go out to a restaurant. He closed his eyes and was soon snoozing.

When he awoke, it was 9.50 in the evening. He went downstairs, switched on the television, and went to inspect the contents of the fridge before *News at Ten* came on. There was nothing immediately edible: two frozen chicken legs in the freezer part; some mouldy cheese and a wilting lettuce down below. In the cupboard, he found cans of baked beans and soup and a packet of salted peanuts. He emptied the peanuts into a cereal bowl and returned to the living room. It looked as if dinner was going to be tomato soup and baked beans.

Reginald Bosanquet had little to offer in the way of interesting news, although Drummond's attention perked up when he heard that 200,000 people had attended a concert at Blackbushe Aerodrome at which Bob Dylan, Joan Armatrading and Eric Clapton had performed. Wouldn't have minded being there. And on the subject of music...He left the sofa and walked over to the record collection and could see, running his eye along the spines that, as a further confirmation that her current status was permanent, Hilary had taken her albums. No longer would this house endure the bland warbling of Des O'Connor and Vince Hill. In a mildly celebratory mood, he returned to the sofa and his salted peanuts.

At halftime, there was an advertisement for the new Ford Capri, but when the news returned Drummond's thoughts were elsewhere. If he wasn't going to sell the house immediately. he would need to meet the monthly mortgage payments, and unless he dipped into his savings he would need to find employment. As what? He recalled his exchange with the bus crew in the café a few months ago, and his chat with Lester Robinson about working at an "ordinary and useful job" alongside ordinary people. Would he? Would he really? Yes, he might.

*

"Of course," said the instructor, addressing himself to the assembled new class, "we've had 'em all here, some on the way up, others on the way down. There was one bloke who spoke very posh, a grammar-school boy by the name of John Major. Tory, he was. Wanted to be a conductor but didn't make it. I live in South London and blimey, a few years later I'm reading the local paper and what do I see? John Major elected to Lambeth Council. I suppose you could say that he was on his way up when he passed through here, although to be honest I can't see that he'll make a go of it in politics."

This instructor (although his duties appeared to be purely administrative) was a fearsome-looking fellow, bearded like the character actor James Robertson Justice, and yet amiable enough. Here he was, giving the Monday-morning intake the introductory lecture, relaxing the lads and lasses with these reminiscences.

"Then there was Cyril Henty-Dodd, another posh geezer." He paused, considering the proliferation of frowns. "What, you've never heard of Cyril Henty-Dodd?" He paused. "Oh, yes you have!"

His audience played along, giving him a chorus of "Oh no, we *haven't!*"

"When he was on Radio Caroline, the BBC and ITV, he called himself Simon Dee."

This called forth a prolonged "Aaaaahhhhh" of recognition.

"Yes, you remember him: had a programme called *Dee Time* that always ended with him driving away in an E-type Jag. Well, he was definitely on his way down, because he went from an E-type to a London bus. But, to give him credit, he did pass out as a driver."

He rubbed his hands. "Now, who's next? Rocky Marciano, heavyweight champion of the world. Was he ever in this room? No, of course he wasn't, but the man who fought him in 1955—Don Cockell—was. Don was never the same after he lost against Marciano, and at one point he came here to train as a conductor. He worked for a time at Sutton garage. Poor Don—a lovely man, by the way—was obviously on his way down.

"And, finally, our biggest success story: Terry Parsons, known to the world—wait for it!—as Matt Monro. Yes, gentlemen, Matt Monro drove a number 27 bus out of Turnham Green garage, so there's hope for you all!"

Drummond wondered whether the instructor was aware of his own history and, if so, if he would weave it into monologue. Imagine what that would be like:

"And now, gentlemen, allow me to introduce you to Mr Roger Drummond. He passed through this training centre some years ago, qualifying as a conductor, and now he's back to train as a driver. Sounds like he's on the way up, doesn't it? Ah, no, because after a year on the back Mr Drummond left us to join a medical supplies company, where he ascended to the position of assistant exports manager. But you must have heard of him recently, gentlemen: played a role in the arrest of two thieves aboard a British ship and witnessed the murder of the Health Minister of a small Caribbean country. With whom, most people assume, he was on intimate terms."

There was, of course, none of this.

The first recruitment officer who had interviewed him had asked him to stand up (he had been sitting at the man's desk).

"Bit tall for a conductor, aren't you?"

"It wasn't too much of a problem last time."

"Ah, but you're getting on in years now. Don't want to be forever bending when you're forty, do you?"

"So are you turning me down?"

"Not at all, not at all. I'm suggesting you train as a driver." He leaned across the desk, lowering his voice. "Besides, a few years from now there won't *be* any conductors." He tapped his nose. "OMO."

"OMO?" For a moment, Drummond suspected a subtle homosexual approach.

"One-Man Operation. They're getting rid of conductors to save money."

He agreed, therefore, to train as a driver.

35

"Welcome back to Middle Row, Roger."

The garage manager, a friendly Irishman called Jim O'Bryan, hands folded on his desk, smiled across at Drummond. He had been a garage inspector during the time that Drummond had been a conductor.

"Thank you, Jim. It's good to be back."

O'Bryan cocked an eyebrow. "Really? How long will you be with us this time, Roger?"

"Oh, a bit longer this time, I think, Jim."

"Well, glad to hear that, Roger." He pursed his lips. "Now, what can I do for you?"

"I have a couple of court appearances coming up, and..."

"What?" Both eyebrows this time.

"No, no, Jim, you're getting the wrong idea. I'm a witness. The first case will be in London, and shouldn't take more than a day, but the other one's in Arawak and..."

"Of course!" O'Bryan gave his desktop a thump. "The murder of the health minister a month or so ago! I saw the television report, but I didn't realise that you were the chap involved. God, that must have been a terrible experience."

Drummond nodded. "It's taking a while, but I'm getting over it."

"So you'll be needing some time off. Well, look, if the London case won't take more than a day, we'll do a rest-day exchange for you. If it goes into a second day, just let us know. But how long do you think you'll need for the Arawak case? That'll be the murder trial, I suppose."

"That's right. Well, with travel there and back, I suppose a week to be on the safe side."

"Okay, we'll bring forward a week's annual leave. No problem." He grinned. "There are half a dozen Arawakians at the garage now. Do they know about this?"

"If they don't, I suppose soon will."

"Oh, they'll make a fuss of you, Roger."

*

And they did.

There were, of course, questions put to him in the output after he had signed on for his duty, but there was little time for discussion, and so the Arawakians—and the Jamaicans, come to that—paid him the most attention when they encountered him in the canteens at Kensal Rise and Westbourne Park station. At Westbourne Park, which was actually an Underground canteen, he would sometimes be approached by Caribbean rail workers, and at Kensal Rise, Willesden crews, who worked route 52 with Middle Row, would often ply him with questions. The women who worked in the canteens, all Caribbean except for one Nigerian, tended to treat him like royalty, heaping his plate, especially when curried chicken, rice and peas was served; this, they assumed, was his favourite dish—and they were right.

Not all of the questions concerned the forthcoming trials.

"Hey, Roger, yuh know the place them call Partway Stone?"

"Not sure that I do, Clem. Where is it?"

"A few mile outside AC. It stan at a crossroad, so when de people come from nearby parish, it mean dem partway to AC. A big ting, yuh cyan miss it."

"Oh, yeah, I passed it on the way to Palmerston."

"Yuh go to Palmerston? Bway, dat deep country!"

"That was where the Reverend Mr Bassfield Thomas turned out the lights on the American religious singers."

"You meet Bassie Thomas?"

"Close friend of mine, George. Even closer since I found out where his money had disappeared."

"Bway, Bassie is one hot preacher! You did hear him preach?"

"Only in John Crow Bay, when he spoke to the banana loaders about the Pharaohs. That was when his supporters came and disarmed the police so he could get off the ship."

"What a life yuh live, Roger! Bway, mi never know white man stay like you."

During these sessions, a crowd of black faces, male and female, would gather around Drummond's table, and by the door there might be a white inspector looking totally bemused.

The questions about the forthcoming trials tended to be direct.

"So the man who shot Davinia Lee—what you plan fe him, Roger?"

"If I have my way, Petrine, he'll go straight to hell—or spend the rest of his life in an Arawak prison, which is probably just as bad."

This would trigger a chorus of approval and a small forest of raised fists.

*

He began to attend union branch meetings, held upstairs in a local pub. Here, the talk was of Bus Plan 78, the first of a series of planned cuts by which the staff establishment would be reduced from 23,500 to 20,800. The workers had initially resolved to oppose the plan, announcing a series of one-hour strikes, district by district, although in practice this had been less than impressive, with some branches not taking part at all, leading to the resignation of two members of the union's Central Bus Committee. Nevertheless, London Transport agreed to defer some of the cuts until March 1979. Around the time that Drummond was returning from Arawak, the monthly conference of bus reps had, by a one-vote margin, agreed to accept the programme.

After Charlie Wilson, the branch rep, had given his report, Drummond raised his hand.

"I'm confused, Charlie. You say that the plan is to reduce staff by 2,700 or so, but they're still recruiting at Chiswick: I'm the living proof of that."

Charlie, who had known Drummond when he was a conductor, smiled. "What they want to reduce is the staff *establishment*, Roger. The fact of the matter is that at the moment we're 3,600 short."

"So no one is going to lose their job through this?"

"That's right, and that's why the response to the call for one-hour strikes was less than a hundred percent."

"So how is this going to save London Transport money?"

"They're reducing the scheduled mileage."

"But they don't have the staff to cover it anyway."

"That's right, but part of the shortage is covered by overtime and rest-day working, so they'll be less of that."

"Ah. And we'll all be working a bit harder."

"How do you mean, Roger?"

"Well, if they're reducing the mileage, they'll have to cut out a few buses here and there, so the time between buses..."

"The headway."

"Yeah, so if there's a bus every ten minutes on a particular route and that goes to twelve minutes, we'll all be picking up more passengers."

"That's the idea, Roger, yeah."

"But that also means that more people will be pissed off with the lousy service and will look for other ways to travel, so that won't solve London Transport's financial problems."

"So they'll increase the fares again."

"And lose yet more passengers…"

"Roger, do you fancy coming onto the branch committee?"

"I haven't been a member long enough, Charlie. Besides, there's not an election due."

"No problem: we can coopt you, if the rest of the committee agrees."

"Okay, count me in."

*

Hilary agreed to the two-year wait for a consensual divorce, announcing that she had no plans to claim half of the mortgaged house.

The trial of Ellen Listor was, as predicted, a one-day affair, albeit with an unpredictable outcome.

Now for the big one.

36

"And how, Mr Drummond, did you come to suspect that the accused was the thief?"

"A member of the crew advised me that some time earlier he had sailed with Mr Listoff on a Mediterranean cruise, and that there had been a number of robberies on that ship also."

"I'm sure, however, Mr Drummond, that the defence will argue that this could have been mere coincidence."

"I agree: all I had at that time was a suspicion. That suspicion became a conviction when the same crew-member further recalled that Ellen Listor had been a passenger on that same cruise."

"And what did you do then, Mr Drummond?"

"With the help of the purser, I contacted Scotland Yard from the ship…"

"This was while you were in John Crow Bay?"

"Yes. I suggested that they investigate the couple…"

"Whom we now know to be brother and sister."

"That's correct. That they investigate them and, if the results justified it, ask the police in Arawak to detain them when the ship arrived in Port Santiago."

"I see. Now, Mr Drummond, I'm sure that counsel for the defence will ask why you did not simply suggest that they be detained when the ship arrived in Southampton."

"Tilbury, actually. That did occur to me, but the ship would be stopping in Bermuda on the way home, which would have provided them with an opportunity to escape if they thought they were under suspicion. Alternatively, they would have had over a week in which to commit further robberies."

"Quite so, Mr Drummond, quite so. Now we come to the tragic events of 23 June…"

The trial was being held in the High Court, across the street from the new Assembly. Before the proceedings began it was obvious that the building would be inadequate, and it was not long before people were being barred from entering the courtroom; with a man on trial for the murder of a popular government minister, this should have been expected. The ceiling fans spun at full speed, but still the heat was almost unbearable. The jurors, nine men and three women, either mopped their brows or fanned themselves. One might have expected that the lawyers present, in the wigs and gowns bequeathed by British colonialism, might be the greatest sufferers, but they appeared to be coping: the prosecuting counsel, a young barrister out to make a name for himself with a case impossible to lose, remained cool, sipping from a glass of water at regular intervals; the defence counsel, who if he had a lighter complexion would resemble the US character actor Jack Elam, seemed not to be bothered by the heat, giving the impression of a man patiently biding his time; the judge sat expressionless, his hands folded before him. The behaviour of these leading legal characters appeared to be influenced by British television dramas such as "Boyd QC" and "Rumpole of the Bailey" (then in its infancy but already available on Arawak television). Niklaus Listoff, the accused, understandably looked nervous, but may have found the temperature less oppressive than that in the cell in which he was being held. He had been led to his place by a guard who, Niklaus having shown himself to be a violent man, had then taken his walking stick away.

"And so, Mr Drummond, on 23 June, after lunch at the hospital, you checked into the Starlight Hotel. What did you do there?"

"I made two telephone calls to London, and shortly after that reception called to say that the police were downstairs."

"These were Detective Sergeant Price and Detective Constable Marshal? And what did they have to say to you?"

"Yes, Price and Marshal. They said that they had been asked to accompany me to the *Burgos*, where they would interview Mr Listoff and Ms Listor."

"And did you leave immediately for the ship?"

"We did."

"How was it that Ms Lee accompanied you, Mr Drummond?"

"She had also checked into the Starlight and was present when I spoke to the two detectives. Inspector Fredericks was also present."

"And who is Inspector Fredericks, Mr Drummond?"

"He was the head of the security detail assigned to Ms Lee."

"And did he give Ms Lee any advice regarding her intention to accompany you?"

"He advised her against it; so did I."

"But she disregarded your advice?"

"She was a strongminded woman."

"Yes, quite."

"But Inspector Fredericks insisted that one of his men also accompany us, and eventually she agreed."

"And what happened when you arrived at the ship, Mr Drummond?"

"The crew were just finishing a boat-drill exercise..."

"Is this relevant, your honour?"

"If Mr Joynson will bear with me for just a moment, your honour, its relevance will be quite apparent."

"Very well, proceed, Mr Louison."

"So the crew were just finishing boat drill, Mr Drummond..."

"And at the rail on the second deck I saw the crew-member who had passed me the information about Listoff and Ellen Listor; upon recognizing me, he beckoned discreetly, meaning that he wanted to talk to me.

"Will we ever know the name of this person, Mr Drummond?"

"He wishes to remain anonymous, your honour. Apparently, life aboard ship can become difficult for someone who has informed on a shipmate, regardless of the circumstances."

"I see. Well, the informant's identity is not essential to this case, is it, Mr Louison? Do you agree, Mr Joynson? Very well, Mr Drummond, carry on."

"As we entered the ship from the gangway, we were met by the purser. Having made the introductions, I explained the purpose of our visit to the purser, who then suggested that, given the lack of space in his office, we meet in the messroom used by the deck crew, which would be empty at this time of the day. I then told the purser that I needed to use a toilet. Instead, I located my informant, who was waiting in the alleyway leading to the galley. He passed me further information, and then I returned to the messroom."

"Are we going to learn the nature of this further information, Mr Louison?"

"Very shortly, your honour, very shortly."

"Very well, Mr Louison. Please continue, Mr Drummond."

"Detective Sergeant Price asked that Ellen Listor be brought to the messroom, and the purser sent a steward to fetch her."

"Now, Mr Drummond, just pause there for a moment, if you will.

"Your honour, this modestly-sized messroom was beginning to get rather crowded at this point, and so to avoid confusing the jury I seek your permission to submit a diagram showing the positions of everyone involved."

"Do you have a sufficient number of copies of this diagram, Mr Louison?"

"There is, your honour, a blackboard and easel in the corridor. With your permission..."

"Of course. Usher, allow the blackboard and easel to enter the courtroom."

*

"Now, ladies and gentlemen of the jury, your honor, you see that on the far side of the table, with their backs to the porthole, from left to right, are Mr Drummond, Detective Sergeant Price and Detective Constable Marshal. Seated opposite them, with their backs to the door, are Sergeant Corliss and Ms Listor, and at the ends of the table are Ms Lee on the left and the purser on the right."

"And who is Sergeant Corliss, Mr Louison?"

"Sergeant Corliss, your honor, is the member of Ms Lee's security detail assigned to accompany her to the ship."

"Ah, of course."

"Now, Mr Drummond, what happened upon the arrival of Ms Listor?"

"She looked rather bewildered to find us sitting there, and asked the purser what was happening. He told her that the police wished to question her and that she should sit next to Sergeant Corliss, which she did. Detective Sergeant Price then asked if she had any knowledge of the robberies that had taken place aboard the *Burgos*. She replied that, yes, she knew that Mr Garner had lost a large amount of cash, a camera, and possibly some other items, and that the Reverend Mr Thomas, according to him, had $25,000 stolen from his cabin. When Sergeant Price asked her if she knew the current whereabouts of these items, she asked angrily how she could possibly know such a thing. She would probably know, said Sergeant Price, if she had been an accessory to the robberies. Ms Listor stood up and said that she was not prepared to listen to such an outrageous allegation. Sergeant Price, however, was very firm with her, explaining that she could, if she wished, continue the interview at the police station. She then calmed down and resumed her seat.

"Sergeant Price then paused, consulting his notebook, before asking Ms Listor if she was familiar with a steward called Nicholas. She asked the purser if this was the blond one, and he nodded."

"Apart from this, what was her reaction? How did she look when asked this question?"

"A little nervous, I think."

"Your honour, Mr Louison seems to be asking Mr Drummond if he was able to read Ms Listor's mind."

"I agree, Mr Joynson, but you have missed the main point: we now know that she and the accused are siblings, so this line of questioning is quite pointless. Confine yourself to what she did and said, Mr Louison, not how she looked."

"Certainly, your honour. Please continue, Mr Drummond."

"She said that he had served her in the dining saloon once or twice, and that was the extent of her knowledge of him. Sergeant Price then suggested that by entertaining Mr Garner in her cabin she had ensured that the coast was clear for Nicholas to enter his cabin and steal his belongings. Was it not the case that Nicholas was the thief and she was his accomplice? She again became angry, asking Sergeant Price how he dared to make such a suggestion. He said he dared to suggest it because it was most probably true. As he said this, he was looking across the table at her with a poker face. She fell silent.

"The sergeant then consulted his notebook again and asked Ms Listor if she had been on a Mediterranean cruise in 1977. She did not reply; her thoughts seemed to be elsewhere. When the sergeant prompted her, she asked if he would repeat the question. When he did so, she replied that, yes, she thought she had been on that cruise; she was very fond of cruises. Did she recall any of the stewards on that cruise? Oh, of course not! She said he might as well ask if she remembered the guard on the train on which she travelled to Tilbury. Oh, wait! There *was* one steward she recalled, because by a remarkable coincidence he was now working on the *Burgos*. A short young man called Jimmy.

"Sergeant Price asked her if she did not recall that Nicholas was also on that 1977 cruise. *Was* he? She seemed amazed that this could have been possible. The sergeant asked her plainly if she was saying that she did not recall seeing him on that cruise. No, she had no recollection of him. Sergeant Price now told her to stop playing games, as it was known that both she and Nicholas were on that cruise: Scotland Yard had confirmed this with the company. Ms Listor simply shrugged. Well, if that was what the company said, it must be true, but she had no recollection of having seen him; it was, after all, a large ship.

"The sergeant then asked if she recalled that there had been a series of robberies during the 1977 cruise. She said that she had a vague recollection, but was unaware of the details. When Sergeant Price put it to her that Nicholas was the thief and she the accomplice, just as they had worked together on the *Burgos*, she vehemently denied this.

"Ms Listor had come into the messroom carrying a handbag. The sergeant now asked if it contained her passport; if so, he wanted to see it. Apparently unconcerned, she took her passport from the handbag and slid it across the table. Sergeant Price picked it up and, instead of looking for visas and entry and departure stamps, turned immediately to the last page. When he asked her if she recalled what she had written there, she bowed her head, realising that the game was up."

"On the last page of the United Kingdom passport, your honour and members of the jury, the bearer is asked to give details of the next of kin or the person who should be contacted in the event of an emergency. And what had she written there, Mr Drummond?"

"She had entered the name of Niklaus Listoff."

"And this was the steward known as Nicholas."

"Yes, the purser confirmed that his actual name was, indeed, Niklaus Listoff, and later provided the police with his discharge book to confirm this."

"Now, Mr Drummond, when you say that Ms Listor realised that the game was up, are you saying that she then confessed to being the accused's accomplice?"

"No, not at all. She admitted that the man was her brother. As children, they had been brought to England from Eastern Europe at the end of the war. Her original name was Elena Listova, but she had changed this by deed poll. She said that she and her brother were very close, and that, as often as she could afford to, she travelled as a passenger on the ships on which he was employed. The purser found this impossible to believe, saying that as far as he could see they barely spoke to each other and he had never seen them together when Nicholas was off-duty."

"And how did Ms Listor respond to this?"

"She simply shrugged, as if to say that was her story and she was sticking to it, virtually challenging the police to prove otherwise. The police were unable to budge her from this."

"And that was the end of her interview?"

"Yes, the purser told her that he would accompany her back to her cabin, and that she was not to leave the ship; a deckhand would be posted outside her door."

*

On his way back to the messroom, the purser had collected Nicholas from the dining saloon, where the stewards were preparing to serve dinner. Upon seeing the occupants of the messroom, the accused had remained perfectly calm; probably having observed the party approaching the ship while he, like Jimmy, was at boat drill, he would have expected this. Without being asked, he sat at the table, with Sergeant Corliss to his left. Detective Sergeant Price made the introductions and then told Nicholas that they had just interviewed his sister.

*

"And how did Mr Listoff respond to that, Mr Drummond?"
"He asked what the interview had been about."
"He was not surprised at the mention of his sister?
"No. In fact, Sergeant Price asked him about that."
"And what was his reply?"
"He shrugged and asked why he should be surprised; the fact that Ellen Listor was his sister was not a secret, he said. The purser then intervened, asking why, if that was the case, no one knew of it. Mr Listoff said that while it was true that they had told no one of their relationship, that was not the same as a secret. Why, then, asked the purser, had his sister initially denied the relationship? Best to ask her, Listoff replied.

"In an attempt to trick him, Sergeant Price then claimed that his sister had confessed that she had acted as his accessory in the robberies on board the *Burgos*, and that the same had been the case during a Mediterranean cruise in 1977. Mr Listoff laughed at this, saying that she could have made no such confession because it simply was not true. He was then asked how he could explain the presence of his sister on two ships—and maybe several more—on which he worked. After some delay (he appeared to be a little upset), he said that he had had a troubled childhood and sometimes got in trouble after drinking. His sister insisted on travelling as a passenger on his ships as often as she could afford it.

"The sergeant then became quite heated, insisting that he *knew* that Listoff and his sister were guilty of the robberies on the *Burgos*. Mr Listoff said that he understood that Sergeant Price might believe this, but there was no proof. Where were the stolen goods? If there was nothing else to discuss, he said, he would return to the saloon in order to serve dinner.

"At this point, I asked the purser whether, on the previous trip of the *Burgos*, there had been an attempt to smuggle a quantity of ganja into Britain. He said that it appeared to have been a successful attempt, because although the rumour had been circulating all over the ship, a thorough search had revealed nothing. The Customs officials in Hamilton had come aboard but found nothing. Ditto Customs in Tilbury.

"I then asked the purser if there was a walk-in freezer on the deck below the galley. He confirmed that there was, saying that it was used by the chief butcher and the chief baker for the storage of meat and certain confectionary items. When I asked him whether this had been included in the various searches, he said that he doubted it. I then suggested that it be searched now, as there was a good chance that the stolen goods had been hidden there."

"And what led you to this belief, Mr Drummond?"

"The informant I contacted just after I came aboard told me that rumour had it that the ganja had been hidden in the freezer and taken off the ship after it had been in Tilbury for a few days. If ganja could be hidden there, he thought, why not the Reverend Mr Thomas's small fortune and the belongings of Mr Garner?"

"And was the freezer then searched, Mr Drummond?"

"The purser stood up and announced that this was his intention. Detective Sergeant Price instructed Detective Constable Marshal to accompany him."

"Was there any particular reason why Sergeant Corliss was not instructed to accompany the purser?"

"Well, you would really have to put that question to Detective Sergeant Price, but I imagine it was because Sergeant Corliss was there to guard Ms Lee, whereas Constable Marshal was under Sergeant Price's command."

"Of course. Now, Mr Drummond, what was Mr Listoff's demeanour during this latest development? Did he remain calm?"

"Far from it: he became very agitated, and demanded to know how, even if the stolen goods were found, they could be connected to him. Detective Sergeant Price then told him that the temperature in the freezer would ensure that any fingerprints were well-preserved..."

"Does a freezing temperature preserve fingerprints, Mr Drummond?"

"I have no idea, your honour. Neither, I suspect, did Detective Sergeant Price."

"We'll have no laughter in this court. This is a serious case and laughter is entirely inappropriate. Continue, Mr Drummond."

"Mr Listoff looked from Sergeant Price to me, from me to Sergeant Corliss, from Sergeant Corliss to Ms Lee and back again, his whole body moving, not just his eyes. He was like a man demented. Then he stopped moving, and clenched his brow, as if he had just arrived at a decision. Suddenly, with his left hand he reached for Sergeant Corliss's pistol and snatched it from its holster. He stood up and pointed the pistol at Sergeant Price, telling him to place his own weapon on the table and push it across to him. Sergeant Price—he had a shoulder holster—did as he was told. Listoff reached over and took it, placing it in his trouser pocket and transferring the pistol he had taken from Sergeant Corliss to his right hand.

"I should explain at this point, that when I first arrived in Arawak, as the security situation was very tense, Ms Lee gave me a pistol for my protection. For many days, I had carried that pistol in my shoulder bag. That same bag was now at my feet. As I reached down for it, however, I could tell from its weight that it was almost empty. I had overlooked the fact that, in Palmerston the previous evening, Ms Lee had taken the pistol back from me. There was a movement to my right, and I turned to see that Ms Lee was drawing the pistol from her own bag. Obviously Listoff, who was on the point of running from the messroom, also noticed this..."

"Take your time, Mr Drummond. We all realise that this must be very distressing for you."

"When I had been reaching for my bag, Listoff had turned his pistol on me; now, he pointed it at Ms Lee, who had almost removed her own pistol from her bag, and he...he pulled the trigger and Ms Lee fell backwards from her chair onto the deck. There was a visible wound on the left side of her body and...and she was clearly dead. Listoff then ran from the messroom."

"Once again, Mr Drummond, take all the time you need. We understand."

"Sergeant Price told Sergeant Corliss to call for an ambulance from the purser's office while he went in search of Detective Constable Marshal in order to borrow his pistol. By the time Sergeant Price reached the gangway...."

"Mr Louison, surely Mr Drummond's testimony should terminate at this point. He has told us, very clearly and in great detail, what he saw and heard; surely the evidence regarding the apprehension of the accused will be given by Detective Sergeant Price and the Reverend Mr Thomas."

"Very well, your honour. In that case, I have no further questions for Mr Drummond."

*

In the brief recess before the cross examination, Drummond wandered out to the witness room, hoping to renew his acquaintance with the Reverend Mr Bassfield Thomas. He found him, in a sober dark suit befitting his ecclesiastical status and the solemnity of the occasion, seated with the police witnesses, laughing and swapping stories. As his visitor entered the room, he got to his feet, beaming with pleasure and opening his arms for an embrace.

"Well, Bredda Drummond, you certainly are a sight for these sore old eyes! Come here and let me hug you."

"Good day, gentlemen," Drummond nodded to the police officers as he moved into the Reverend Thomas's energetic embrace. "And, Reverend Thomas, how are you doing? I'm surprised to see you enjoying yourself with the forces of law and order."

Drawing back, his hands still on Drummond's shoulders, the Reverend Mr Thomas laughed. "I'm rehabilitated, Roger! Partially, anyway. And call me Bassie."

Bassie Thomas had, indeed, been the hero of 23 June. By the time Detective Sergeant Price had secured a pistol and reached the rail, Listoff was running along the quayside in his steward's attire, a pistol in each hand. Sergeant Price had fired one shot in the air and shouted "Stop that man! Stop that man!" The Reverend Thomas, having arranged the previous evening to meet Drummond and Davinia Lee in Port Santiago, was at this time strolling towards the *Burgos*. Seeing Listoff, and hearing Price's exhortation, as everyone else in the vicinity was running for cover he had calmly drawn his pistol and put a bullet in Listoff's leg. A few minutes later, Price had disarmed and handcuffed the screaming fugitive, turning to call to Detective Constable Marshal, "Better make that two ambulances!"

"Nothing hanging over you?"

"Not a thing. Thanks to you, the *Burgos* got its money back and so the company decided not to prefer charges. And the authorities have decided that the incident in John Crow Bay was, while regrettable, hardly worth the time and expense of a prosecution."

"What about Billy Joe Harrison's people? Any charge from them?"

"No, they borrowed instruments and tried to hold a concert in Port Santiago, but we put a stop to that. They ended up leaving the island with their tails between their legs." He gestured to the chairs lining the walls. "But Roger, sit down for a while; we have a thing or two to talk about."

As they took two seats opposite the two police officers, Bassie Thomas tapped Drummond on the knee. "Is it true what I heard?" he asked in a low voice, frowning in disbelief. "The Listor woman got off?"

Drummond nodded grimly. "Almost: suspended sentence. One problem was that all the evidence was circumstantial. Yes, she and her brother had been on a number of ships together, and there had been robberies on all of them. When he had sailed alone: no robberies. It was obvious to the jury that she must have been his accessory, but there was just this glimmer of doubt.

"Then again, her lawyer gave the court a sob story about her background. She and her brother apparently came from minor nobility in Eastern Europe. In the closing stages of the war, at the age of eighteen months, she had been taken, along with Niklaus, who was a year younger, in the direction of the setting sun."

"They were kidnapped?"

"No, their parents had them whisked away by a loyal retainer called Vasily. He had been with the family for years, having in some way commended himself and escaped a life of drudgery down among the peasantry. He took them to the West."

"Running from the Red Army."

"Just as fast as he could. In July 1945, they ended up in Earl's Court."

"What happened to the parents?"

"When the children were old enough to understand, Vasily told them that their parents had elected to stay and fight the Soviet barbarians. The truth died with him a few years later, when he was run over by a number 49 bus in Kensington High Street. In fact, their parents had been killed by peasants on their estate, and if they could have found Vasily they would have killed him too."

"Because he had joined the Pharaohs."

"Exactly."

"How do you know all this, Roger?"

"The British press, Bassie. As the case was coming up for trial, a couple of broadsheets did a fair amount of research. Also, Ellen Listor sold her story to one of the tabloids—for the second time, in fact. There were quite a few inaccuracies in her account, but the research done by the broadsheets unearthed the truth.

"For some time, Ellen and Niklaus dreamed of returning home to reclaim their estate..."

"Ha! They thought they would be welcome?" Bassie Thomas may have been wondering what would have happened if a former slave-owning family had returned, expecting a tumultuous welcome, to their plantation in Arawak.

"Maybe, because they're not very bright. In reality, they would probably have received some very discourteous treatment from those who remembered the Listoff family—and the new rulers made sure that everyone did. Anyway, Ellen eventually came to the conclusion hat there would be no going back—at least not to an estate.

"By now, she was 32 and unmarried, and she realised that unless she did something about it that tiny flat in Earl's Court would be her home until she died (or at least until the government of a communist Britain cut off her small allowance)."

Bassie Thomas laughed. "You're making this up!"

"No, that was the way she thought. First of all, she tried to find a man with money. Ten or twelve years earlier this would have been no problem. Men, with money and without, even minor members of the British nobility, had fawned on her when she was twenty. But she always stopped short of marriage, thinking that once reinstalled on their estate the eligible bachelors of Europe would be hers to choose from. Now it was too late."

"But she told us she was divorced."

"A lie, Bassie."

"So what did she do?"

"She began by trying something legal. She wrote the story of their escape from Soviet-occupied Europe for a Sunday newspaper, putting Niklaus's name to it and adding seven years to his age so that he might have *just* been able to remember the details contained in the three-part story. While it brought in a nice sum of money, however, and gained Niklaus appearances on a few chat-shows (where he told stories which conflicted not only with each other but also with the newspaper series), it was not the start of a career. Ellen and Niklaus were used during one of the booms which the anti-Soviet industry enjoys about every six months in Fleet Street and they were then dropped, having been milked dry.

"The turn to illegality began with shoplifting in Harrods and Fortnum & Mason (with both she and Niklaus concealing their swag beneath ponchos) and progressed to an ingenious variant of the accident insurance racket. This consisted of Niklaus allowing himself to be knocked down by cars driving from the House of Commons carpark. As the principal witness Ellen would, if the Member were driving himself, insist that she could smell alcohol on his breath. In most cases, of course, this was true."

Bassie Thomas laughed uproariously at this, joined by the two policemen.

"They would then accept a bribe (or "out of court settlement" as it was called). Eventually, they were recognised, and the last time they tried the scam the Member, a brash young left-winger representing a mining constituency, told them to 'piss off back where you come from' before he completed the job the Russians had started."

"They were never arrested for any of this?"

"Never, Bassie. Anyway, they then turned their attention to the high seas, and the rest you know. The jury found Ellen Listor guilty of having been an accessory in the *Burgos* robberies but the judge, taking into consideration her background, the circumstantial nature of the evidence, and the fact that she had spent some time behind bars, both here and in London before the trial, gave her a suspended sentence. Obviously, if she commits another crime in the next two years, she'll be put away."

The Reverend Mr Bassfield Thomas shook his head. "Bway, that woman had me fooled!"

Detective Sergeant Price now cleared his throat. "Do you think the trial will be over today, Mr Drummond?"

"Well, I've finished giving my evidence, and next comes the cross examination. Maybe all three of you will be seen this afternoon. But I think there may be some adjournments along the way. Listoff has pleaded not guilty to murder but has said he would have pleaded guilty to a manslaughter charge. I think his lawyer may well take some time trying to persuade the judge and the prosecution that the charge should be reduced."

"Mr Drummond! Mr Roger Drummond!" The usher's call came from the corridor.

Drummond rose and shook hands all round before making his way back to the courtroom.

*

"Mr Drummond, when Mr Listoff entered the messroom, according to Mr Louison's very helpful diagram, you would have been looking right at him. Is that right?"

"Yes, that's correct."

"And did he look like a man intent on killing someone?"

"Well, no, of course not."

"Why do you say of course not, Mr Drummond?"

"Because he came into the messroom, fully expecting what was to come, and thinking that he could talk his way out of it."

"Why would he have expected what was to come, Mr Drummond? He had had no contact with his sister, and so how could he have known?"

"He, along with the rest of the crew, had been at boat drill and he would have seen us approaching the ship. He knew me, and one of the other people I was with was a uniformed police officer. He would therefore have expected to be interviewed about the robberies."

"So it was a fairly confident-looking Mr Listoff who entered that messroom."

"I would say so, yes."

"But that self-confidence evaporated when you mentioned the freezer?"

"Yes, that's right."

"And when Sergeant Price made his point about the fingerprints Mr Listoff became, I think you said, like a man demented."

"I did say that, yes."

"And do you stand by that?"

"He was angry and frightened."

"Not in his own mind?"

"You might put it that way."

"Do you think Mr Listoff intended to kill Ms Lee?"

"How could I possibly know that, Mr Joynson?"

"Do you not think it possible, Mr Drummond, that the accused, in his agitated state, pointed the gun at Ms Lee with the intention of warning her to leave her pistol where it was, and his own weapon was discharged accidentally?"

"I would think it possible..."

A stir in the courtroom at this unexpected development.

"...but for one thing."

"And that was?"

"He had disengaged the safety catch."

An audible sigh in the courtroom, Jack Elam blinking and thoughtfully passing his tongue over his upper lip.

"At what point did Mr Listoff disengage the safety catch? Was it when he pointed the pistol at Detective Sergeant Price, at you, or at Ms Lee?"

"It was when he pointed it at Sergeant Price and told him to put his pistol on the table."

A smile of satisfaction from Mr Joynson. "Thank you, Mr Drummond." A licking of the lips. "Now, you say that you detected movement to your right, and turned to see Ms Lee withdrawing a pistol from her bag."

"That's right."

"By the way, Mr Drummond, you have said that this same pistol was in your possession for several days. Did you have a licence to carry a firearm?"

Louison on his feet. "This is entirely irrelevant, your honour!"

"I agree, Mr Louison. Mr Joynson, Mr Drummond is not on trial here."

"I beg your pardon, your honour." Joynson puts this setback behind him and frowns down at his clipboard before turning that frown on Drummond. "How did Ms Lee look as she withdrew the pistol from her bag? What was her expression?"

Drummond has long been trying to avoid picturing Davinia Lee's face, for while the grief has eased, he still finds himself short of breath when her face appears. And now this Jack Elam type is asking him to remember what she looked like seconds before she died. He shakes his head. "I can't remember. My attention was really on her hands rather than her face."

"Just relax and try, Mr Drummond." Joynson sounds like a hypnotist or a psychiatrist, his voice low and soothing. "Close your eyes and let your mind go back to that afternoon of 23 June in the crew messroom on the *Burgos*. Mr Listoff has just seized Sergeant Corliss's pistol; the room is full of tension; you turn to your right..."

Drummond tries to disregard Joynson's words, but still the image comes: Davinia Lee, eyes narrowed, lips held tight as she draws the pistol from her bag and, determined to plug Listoff, prepares to lift it and fire. "No, I can't see it. I'm sorry. I was concentrating on her hands."

"I put it to you, Mr Drummond, that you remember very well the expression on Ms Lee's face as she took that pistol from her bag."

"I have told you that I do not."

As he walks towards the witness box, Mr Joynson looks more like Jack Elam than ever, licking his lips, glancing now to the jury and now at the witness, and giving the impression that he might at any moment surprise Drummond with a quick-draw demonstration. He stands silently before the witness box, studying the clipboard he holds before him; then comes the quick draw: "Have you ever thought, Mr Drummond, that if you had suggested to Scotland Yard that Mr Listoff and his sister be detained in Tilbury, Ms Lee would still be alive today?"

Amid the uproar, and despite it, Roger Drummond's face dissolves into a mask of pain, as he cries: "Have I *ever* thought of it? Dammit, I've thought of nothing else for weeks, man!"

Finally, Mr Louison is able to make himself heard. "Irrelevant, your honour!"

It would seem so, Mr Louison. Mr Joynson?"

"Not really, your honour: Mr Drummond's reaction to the question surely demonstrates that he was emotionally involved with Ms Lee."

"And?"

"This would explain why he pretends not to remember how Ms Lee looked when she withdrew her pistol from her bag. He is protecting her—or her memory—and in doing so he is putting an interpretation on the action of Mr Listoff which I will contest."

His honour screws up his face. "Yes, I think I can see where you're going with this, Mr Joynson, but"—a warning finger—"be very careful."

"Were you having an affair with Davinia Lee, Mr Drummond?"

Gasps from the jury and members of the public. Drummond at a loss, mouth agape, turning to Mr Louison, who attempts a rescue. "This is entirely irrelevant, your honour, and I must ask that the question be withdrawn!"

His honour, who has neither gasped nor batted an eyelid, looks calmly at the defence counsel. "Well, Mr Joynson, is this you being very careful?" He sighs. "Are you able to demonstrate the relevance of this question?"

"Simply by reference to my previous remark, your honour: if Mr Drummond had such a relationship with Ms Lee, it would explain why he has avoided my question regarding the demeanour of Ms Lee as she removed the pistol from her bag."

"Could you not be a little more diplomatic, Mr Joynson?"

"I will try, your honour." He turns to the witness box, confident that his point will be made. "Were you, Mr Drummond, in love with Davinia Lee?"

Sighs from the jury and members of the public. Drummond looks across at the jury and sees that their sympathy is with him. If he answers in the affirmative, they may even be fond of him, but this will strengthen Jack Elam's argument. He sighs, looks gunslinger Elam in the eye, and says "We were very close."

"Are you saying that you were *not* in love with Davinia Lee, Mr Drummond."

His honour clears his throat. "I think, Mr Joynson, that Mr Drummond's reply is perfectly adequate for your intended purpose."

"Quite right, your honour, quite right." Yes, agreeing with the judge, because he thinks he now has Drummond where he wants him. He looks down at his clipboard, then shoots one glance to the jury before launching into his final assertion. "So I put it to you, Mr Drummond, that Ms Lee's expression, as she withdrew that pistol from her bag, was one of grim determination, and that she had the *obvious* intention of shooting Mr Listoff. And Mr Listoff, for his part, already agitated and afraid, saw that look upon her face and, fearing now for his very life, fired the pistol in the hope that this would at least cause her to drop her weapon. He fired, in fact, in self-defence! Is that not what you observed, Mr Drummond? And I remind you that you are under oath."

Finally, Drummond relaxes. Jack Elam is just a man doing his job, doing the best he can with not very promising material. His show of aggression just now was not so much directed at Drummond as a show to impress the jury. Drummond almost smiles sympathetically at the man. "I'm sorry, Mr Joynson, but I have already said that Listoff was angry and afraid and that I do not recall seeing the expression on Ms Lee's face. Not being a mind-reader, I'm unable to say whether Listoff was afraid for his life or whether Ms Lee intended, come what may, to shoot him."

"I repeat, Mr Drummond: you are under oath!"

"I do believe, your honour, that Mr Joynson has had his answer."

"Yes, I agree, Mr Louison. Will that be all, Mr Joynson?"

Apart from a wry grimace, Jack Elam takes it well. "No more questions, your honour."

*

After lunch, Elam had a last throw of the dice, asking the judge if he and Mr Louison could come to see him in his chambers. When he reemerged thirty minutes later, he looked thoroughly disappointed that the good guy had come out best again, given Listoff a subtle shake of the head as he approached the defence table.

"As predicted," Mr Louison told Drummond before the judge returned, "it was Mr Joynson's view that the charge should be reduced to manslaughter. He argued that there was obviously no premeditation, and that on the balance of probabilities Listoff was in fear of his life when Ms Lee drew her pistol."

"But that cut no ice with the judge?"

"Not at all. He said that, on the evidence so far, no one could say whether Listoff's life was in danger. He pointed out that Listoff was the criminal here, and that he had stolen a policeman's pistol. It could be argued that the lives of everyone else in that messroom were at risk. He also reminded Mr Joynson—who, by the way, is a very good lawyer—that there was such a thing as statutory murder."

"What's that?"

"If someone kills another person, whether intentionally or not, during the commission of another crime, that is murder. The judge said that he would point this out to the jury at the conclusion of the trial."

"Which will be when, do you think?"

"Oh, this afternoon. There are three more witnesses for the prosecution, but their evidence should not take long at all, although I assume that Mr Joynson will tackle the policemen on the same grounds as he did you: was Listoff in fear of his life?; did Ms Lee look as if she intended to shoot him?" He tapped Drummond on the forearm. "You did very well, by the way. Well done!"

It went as Mr Louison had predicted: Sergeants Price and Corliss gave much the same account as Drummond, denying that Davinia Lee had appeared intent upon shooting Listoff, and the Reverend Mr Bassfield Thomas described his encounter with Listoff on the quayside.

"Was it your intention to shoot the accused in the leg?" asked Mr Louison.

"It was," boomed Bassie Thomas, "but if I had known that he had just killed Davinia Lee I would have aimed higher."

The fact that this response drew a smattering of applause from members of the public, and even a few members of the jury, did not bode well for Niklaus Listoff.

Mr Joynson put Listoff on the stand and, no longer in Jack Elam mode, gently asked him to describe his state of mind as he had pointed the pistol and fired at Davinia Lee. Trembling, Listoff told the court that he had been terrified, convinced that she intended to shoot him, perhaps fatally.

After the closing speeches and the judge's summing up, at 4.30 the jury withdrew and forty minutes later returned to announce that they had found Niklaus Listoff guilty of statutory murder. When the judge sentenced him to death by hanging, Listoff collapsed.

"The sentence will probably never be carried out," Mr Louison told Drummond as the courtroom emptied. "Men spend years and years on Death Row, and in this case, it's almost certain that the British government will intervene and have him transferred to one of their prisons."

*

Drummond returned to his hotel and changed from his suit into a pair of lightweight trousers and short-sleeved shirt. Outside again, he hailed a taxi and told the driver to drop him on West Princes Street. He wanted a beer—several beers, although not in the hotel bar where he would be either pestered or avoided by middle-class types who knew he had been in court. No, he wanted to rejoin the friendly folk he had met during his visit to the Antonio Bar with Garry. Was he hoping to see Tina? Might as well admit it.

The truth of the matter, he thought as he rode through the darkening streets, was that his grief over Davinia Lee had eased during the weeks since her death. Yes, he had become emotional in the courtroom, but he had been goaded by that Jack Elam character. Besides, it wasn't as if he had lost all feeling for Davinia, just that the grief has lessened. Driving a bus around London, and everything that went with it, had obviously played a part in that: the union branch meetings, socialising with his workmates in the pub; one Sunday a month attending meetings of the Arawak Support Group. But was he really ready to reach out to another woman? Maybe.

Dusk was falling and, as he walked down the lane towards the Antonio Bar, cooking and woodsmoke smells came from some of the crumbling houses. The evening was alive with reggae music. This part of the city was studded with bars and every one had a jukebox which served both as a means of separating customers from their ten-cent pieces and, hopefully, a magnet to further trade. Somewhere, a woman let out an anguished cry: "Lord God, im spen out de money!" An old man in crumpled white cricket slacks stopped to urinate against a fence and from the manner in which he did it, glancing at Drummond with such studied unconcern, it was difficult to tell whether he was doing it from necessity or merely to demonstrate his right to do it. On a balcony, two men with Rasta locks played dominoes, looking down as he passed below. One raised a domino high and brought it down with a crash, oathing "Babylon!" as he did so.

It was early, and in the Antonio there were only a couple of seamen, Scandinavians by the sound of them, and a few prostitutes. Lurleen gave him a nice welcome, telling him that the beer she placed before him was on the house. Not wanting to be overheard, as she let her hand fall from the bottle she asked him in hushed tones how things had gone in court. He gave her a one-word answer: "Guilty." She nodded her approval. He changed a small note to get some ten-cent pieces and walked over to the jukebox, taking care to avoid the songs that had been played in Palmerston.

He sat at a small table against the wall and for a while watched the seamen as they hurried along the path to drunken oblivion. Their attitude to the girls had something of the conqueror's air about it. They pinched, slapped and fondled as if by right, as if the whores were of some inferior species which existed solely for the purpose of satisfying their appetites; and Drummond realised that, the ways things were, this was all they *did* exist for. In vain, he scanned the face of each girl for a sign of rebellion, but all he found was dull acceptance. Of course, once the seamen returned to their ship the girls might curse them and the conditions which forced them to submit to this treatment, but that was not the same: that was rather like letting down the tyres in the directors' car park.

He wondered why Tina was not here. Had she turned her back on this life and returned to the countryside? If she had, he would be glad, although sorry that he would not be seeing her this evening; and he knew now that she was the reason he had come here.

After a little while, workers began to drift in, ordering their overproof white rum. Two of them, who had been here when he had visited the bar with Garry Lemay, turned and, recognising him, came over to congratulate him on the result of the court case, which they had heard reported on the radio. Word spread and his small table was soon surrounded, reminding him of the Kensal Rise canteen. He had told himself that it was these men he had been hoping to meet here, perhaps to rekindle the warmth of the previous encounter, but he now found that he was irritated, as they completely blocked his view of the bar and the entrance. No doubt about it now: he was here for Tina.

Drummond called to Lurleen, asking her to bring a round, and told the guys to pull up a few chairs, thus unblocking his view. For the next twenty minutes or so, they took him through the court case, and in doing that they also had him replay the events of 23 June, and he found that he could do it without choking up or becoming tearful.

"So what yuh a guh do nuh?" asked the man with the patchy beard.

"You mean right now?"

"Naw, mi mean inna Henglan."

"I'm a bus driver."

"Yunnerstan what mi a-seh?"

"Obviously."

"How comes?"

"I listen to guys like you every day—in the canteen and at the garage."

The man with the patchy beard slapped the table. "Well, kiss mi neck!"

There was a chorus of affectionate laughter, and then he saw her walk in.

She was with a big man, also Scandinavian. Somewhere in his thirties, sporting a little goatee on his powerful chin and wearing a T-shirt he had outgrown, as he approached his shipmates he raised both thumbs to indicate that the sexual encounter from which he was returning had been entirely satisfactory. When his shipmates turned to the girl for confirmation, she, no longer the modest, diffident Tina Drummond remembered, raised her own thumb and, smiling, patted the man's crotch. She glanced at the table where the five or six working men were having a good time with a white man, but she gave no sign of having recognised Drummond.

Checking his watch, Drummond saw that if he left now he would still be in time for dinner at his hotel.

37

Upon his return to Middle Row garage Drummond was, of course, something of a hero—to his black workmates in particular. Here was a white man who had testified in order to send another white man to the gallows for killing a black woman. You didn't come across that every day. Fortunately, he was hardly every asked to give chapter and verse about the trial because the press coverage—not just in the overseas edition of the *Chronicle*, but also in the Fleet Street papers—had been extensive. He sometimes got the impression that some of the guys wanted to ask him just *how* close he had been to Davinia Lee but, possibly out of respect for his feelings, they never went that far.

The women, even Mrs Denham, looked at him differently. Mrs Denham was a slender, dark Arawakian woman a year or two older than Drummond. Very pretty in an understated way, she was also extremely quiet. Whenever Drummond worked with her on the 7s, if they had a few minutes' stand time in the yard at Acton, they would sit opposite each other on the rear seats, he reading a paperback and she frowning down at a pocket-edition of the New Testament. But even she, if she thought he wouldn't notice, would sometimes surreptitiously shift her gaze to get a good look at him. On one such occasion, he tried to engage her in conversation.

"Could I ask you a question, Mrs Denham?"

"What is it, Mr Drummond?"

"What's your first name?"

She frowned, apparently angry. "Why you aks me that?"

"Because I've never heard anyone call you anything but Mrs Denham."

"That's because I don't tell people my first name, Mr Drummond."

"Oh. I'm Roger, by the way."

"Yes, I know, Mr Drummond."

He laughed at that, and even she was unable to suppress a grin.

He thought at first that she refused to divulge her forename because she didn't want anyone getting too close to her. But he wasn't interested in her sexually. Well, he found her attractive, and if she had not been married and religious… But, no, he just wanted to be friends with her. Anyway, he eventually discovered the reason for her reticence.

He was in the office of Jim O'Bryan, who had just given him advice, rather than asking him to sign his record for a caution, for running early.

"Alright, Roger, off you go."

"One more thing, Jim. What's Mrs Denham's first name?"

O'Bryan leaned forward and whispered, "Requiem."

"Requiem?"

"Requiem."

Drummond gave the name some thought and then shrugged. "Well, that's not so bad."

"I know, but she's embarrassed by it, so you didn't get it from me."

"No, of course not."

"And watch your step, because she's married."

"Oh, I'm not interested in her in that way."

"No?" O'Bryan was sceptical, grinning.

One evening, as he was leaving the garage, he passed Mrs Denham on her way to pay in.

"Good night, Requiem," he said softly.

She turned and glared at him. "Oh, *you!*"

"It's a nice name. Anyway, goodnight."

With a sigh, she relented. "Goodnight...Roger."

After that, whenever he saw her she would tighten her lips and pretend to be angry, although her eyes were smiling. They were now friends—or, at least, friendly.

While at Merritt & Thwaite, Garry Lemay had been his only real friend. Now he had several, black and white, and was never short of a drinking partner. True, a few of the black guys had looked disappointed when he confessed to a lack of interest in cricket, but that wasn't an immediate problem as the cricket season was now chilly months away.

As he recalled the Merritt & Thwaite job, it had been, while in a way a more "responsible" occupation, hardly enough to fill his days and nights. He was now keeping himself busy, no longer to avoid thinking about Davinia Lee, who had become a beautiful memory, but because it was his new life: a socially useful job, plenty of union activity and the occasional public meeting or rally, and the growing feeling that one day he might make a difference.

One frosty morning, driving up Earl's Court Road on his second rounder on route 31, he had what might be called an epiphany, as the sun suddenly emerged from behind a cloud and he realised that he was happy. And then just ahead, coming his way, he saw Garry Lemay driving to work. He threw open the door, sounding his horn and waving as Garry drew near.

Roger Drummond, celebrating his new life, one hand on the steering wheel and one hand waving free.

About the Author

Having left school at the age of fifteen, Ken Fuller has been an office boy, a baker and confectioner, a merchant seaman, a bus driver and a trade union official.

Over the years, he has contributed many articles regarding events in the Caribbean and the Philippines to the *Morning Star, Tribune*, and the Caribbean press in London. His first book (a labour history of London busworkers) was published in London in 1985.

He emigrated to the Philippines in 2003, since when he has published a further twelve books, both fiction and non-fiction. He has also contributed columns to the Manila-based newspapers *BusinessWorld* and the *Daily Tribune*.

Printed in Great Britain
by Amazon